THERE GOES THE GALAXY

by JENN THORSON

Jenn Thorson

Waterhouse Press

PITTSBURGH, PENNSYLVANIA

Published by Waterhouse Press. Pittsburgh, Pennsylvania, U.S.A.

ISBN: 978-0-9838045-0-5

Cover Art by Dave White

Printed in the United States of America

I don't pretend to understand the Universe—it's a great deal bigger than I am... People ought to be modester.
—THOMAS CARLYSLE (1795-1881)

Outer space is no place for a person of breeding.
—LADY VIOLET BONHAM CARTER (1887-1969)

Yeah, it's a real chance you take coming to an unevolved system. Some places just everyone's curious to meet your vital organs.
—CAPT. ROLLIAM TSMORLOOD

ACKNOWLEDGMENTS

There were many fine folks who helped make *There Goes the Galaxy* become the quirky space fantasy and/or creative beverage coaster it is today. Many thanks to Scarlett Townsend, for lending her Super Copyeditor Powers to Bertram and the gang. Thank yous also go to Dave White for all his great advice and for sharing his mad artistic skillz on the cover. Cheers to Claire Pitt for the long-distance brainstorming and all the kind encouragement on days I felt a little lost in space myself. Thanks to Jessica Enos and Lynette Guerino for back-checking my brain. Much gratitude to all the terrific online folks who've offered both support and wisdom throughout the process. And special thanks to my cat, Alice, for examining the work and deciding an entire page of "Gs" was just what the story needed. Sorry, Alice, I couldn't use it for this particular book, as it didn't quite fit the tone. But maybe next time.

1

Bertram Ludlow's head felt twice-baked, his skull scooped out and restuffed. He tried to sit up, but his body wasn't his. It was three sizes too big and filled with sand.

He moved to look around, but the sand rushed to his right ear. It buried his equilibrium, sinking him back onto the cold, tile floor.

What the hell happened?

Oh, that's right...

That guy happened, taking the day from coffee to kidnapping in record time.

The morning had started out well enough, Bertram thought, still groggy from both The Incident and general *Caffeinatus Interruptus*. He had jarred himself awake three minutes before his alarm, as routine, because spotty apartment wiring meant he couldn't trust a timely beep.

He grabbed a cold shower, like most days, because Mrs. 1B had to be running either a Roman Bath or Chinese Laundry in the creaking morning hours before daylight. He liked imagining it was a Roman Bath, a wry contrast to her cardigan sweaters and polyester pantsuits. Either way, hot water was a rare commodity for those who rose past dawn.

Bertram nuked himself a bowl of ramen noodles—the Breakfast of Frugal Aspirations—per the usual, too, and put on the Jumpin' Jimmy Jive swing album he'd found last week, poking from a trash bin outside his building. Probably part of the dramatic domestic

JENN THORSON

fluctuations in 3A, he guessed. But he'd played it a dozen times now, and he liked it—liked it almost as much for its retro hipness as the fact it was free. It wasn't even scratched.

He enjoyed the ramen and was just waiting for the coffeemaker to finish perking the strong, black java that brought each morning to life. He looked over his class notes then shrugged into a t-shirt, plaid flannel over-shirt, and a pair of jeans—the working uniform for a great day of student teaching.

Pouring a mug of the eye-opener, Bertram noticed Mr. 1C's Rottweiler anointing the azaleas outside his basement apartment window. He was right on schedule, too.

The pounding that followed, however... that was entirely new.

The sound was heavy and insistent, like a man kicking his way out of a cask of Amontillado or the Ghost of Christmas Past trying to make a big entrance. At first, Bertram wondered if the water heater pipe had finally broken. Or if Mrs. 1C was driving the Bonneville with a flat again.

But then he realized the sound was coming from the other side of his door. Bertram turned down ol' Jimmy right in the middle of "Swingin' on Saturn's Ring" as the door banged open, and it looked like Death himself had gotten into the building.

This man filled the doorway, dressed shoulder-to-boot in black, hands thrust into the folds of a long, shiny coat. The only colors surrounding him were his ruddy complexion, the pale jaundice-yellow of his wild, cropped hair, and the whisky-tint to his aviator glasses. In a quiet, urgent voice, he asked, "You Ludlow?"

"Ludlow." Bertram blinked up at him nervously. "Yes... Ludlow. I'm Ludlow."

"*Bertram* Ludlow?" A serrated smile cut across the man's face.

"Yeah, but who—?"

"Stellar," said the man, pulling a weapon. It was a gun, a pearlescent silver with no hammer, chamber or visible safety. He aimed it at Bertram, peering over his shades with eyes a disconcerting amber orange and, so simply, pulled the trigger. It was a quick sting and then nothing—nothing at all.

Bertram was there. And now Bertram was *here*.

Here was a tiny, narrow room with bright ceiling lights and dull metal walls. As his vision slowly sharpened, Bertram noticed the trunks, enclosed shelves, piles of books, strange flags, record albums, single socks, cases, and questionable containers littering the floor.

—2—

Some appeared to host hopeful ecosystems.

It was storage and Bertram stored. But why had anyone stored Bertram Ludlow? The question was long-contemplated but fast-forgotten once the door slid away again. Death was back, clomping in on black, buckled boots. The man crouched beside Bertram in one surprisingly lithe movement and frowned over him exhaling an irritable booze-laced sigh. The kidnapper's sunglasses were off now and his eyes were, yes, a bright, eerie orange. (*Contact lenses, of course, contact lenses,* Bertram told himself.) But the depth of color looked all too real, and eye contact between them caused a pang of unsettling foreignness to shiver down Bertram's nerves. His eyelashes and eyebrows were such a pale yellow they almost weren't there, while the man's bone structure seemed to come in excess—an effect that turned his expressions striking, though not comfortably handsome.

The stranger scrutinized him, dispassionately pinching Bertram's arm, a knee, a wrist, a toe, and gauging reaction.

Finally in his odd, clipped accent, the man asked, "Your fingers. You can feel your fingers, then?"

Bertram's tongue was rubber. "Yyyuh," he managed.

"Hindered motor and verbal response." The foreigner gave a curt nod and rose. "It'll likely wear off."

Likely? Bertram's stomach spasmed because of this guy and his "likely." His eyes fell on the belt system at the man's waist, visible now his coat had been set aside. There were at least ten different cases strapped to it, not counting the gun holster. "Hhhwwwhoo—?"

"Introductions aren't productive, what with our time together so brief." The man was rolling up his shirt sleeves to reveal lean, corded forearms that were a battlefield of burns and jagged scars. Similar marks, Bertram now noticed, crossed his hands, his temple, and lurked at the open throat of his shirt—old wounds that stood out white on ruddy skin. The man's right thumb was a mess. It looked like it had been severed off and sewed back on again by a sixth grade home ec student sporting a C+ average. It jutted at an unnatural angle.

Bertram felt panic welling up inside him and the words just wouldn't come. "Yuh…you…gonna…kuh-kill…muh…m—"

The man offered the razorblade smile by way of comfort. "Could've done days ago."

"D-days?"

But the stranger just grabbed Bertram's feet, dragging him through the threshold and into another room. He thumped them back to the floor, then stepped away to a counter.

Bertram struggled to sit, but the sand in his bag of a body shifted his arms out from under him, settling him again to the icy floor. As he stared up at the riveted ceiling beams, he heard a snap, then the sounds of heavy liquid slopping against crackling ice.

Like the too-orange eyes, this kidnapping was hard to even wrap the brain around. Obviously, the foreigner had meant to target some other, more fortunate Bertram Ludlow—one with global influence, money, prestige, intrigue. One who didn't owe over 100 thousand dollars in student loans at 29% interest. "Misss..." began Bertram, "misss..."

"Mister," corrected the man.

"Mistake," finished Bertram.

"Oh, is it?" The voice sounded coolly amused. "Let's see: Bertram Ludlow, graduate student, Plus-D'Argent University, cognitive psychology. Your acute knowledge of the human mind helps you understand why you don't like people. You subsist entirely on ramen noodles. You stare for hours at a game where men slide about with sticks. You secretly wish you were taller. You sing. In the shower. Badly. Mistake?" said the kidnapper. "Doubtful."

Bertram Ludlow's jaw was too slack to drop. He was a target—and that just proved what a shoddy kidnapping outfit this was.

It must be his research They wanted. (The idea that the amber-eyed foreigner soldiered for a secret "They" agency did hold some guilty James Bond appeal. It also went pretty far toward explaining the advanced stun-gun technology.)

The thing was, sure, Bertram's thesis had its merits. But was it so cutting-edge as to be useful to dangerous self-interest groups? He doubted international intelligence cared much about how humans prioritize and procrastinate tasks; and even if they did, no reason they couldn't put it off until his dissertation published.

Now the foreigner returned, clutching a glass of murky pink-gray liquid, a light scum swirling ominously on top. He crouched down, clamped onto Bertram's jaw with long, thin, bruising fingers and poured the drink down his throat. It was a chunky primordial soup that smothered Bertram's senses, enveloping them in a fetid pool and sucking them under. Bertram struggled back to the surface, gagging and choking. "Whaaa'ss—?"

"High concentration of carbs, electrolytes and proteins. I highly suggest," the foreigner said firmly, "you keep it down."

Since Bertram had no taste for threats or seconds, he fought his gag reflex for control. His captor was still crouched, elbows on knees and watching silently over the tapered steeple of his hands.

Watching, contemplating, waiting. The piercing appraisal seemed to last entirely too long. Something must have gone as planned, though, because as Bertram's waves of nausea ebbed, the man gave a nod, set the empty glass aside and hoisted Bertram into one of the chairs that lined the wall. He propped Bertram up like some crash test dummy and pushed a button on the side of the chair. This released a padded metal harness that flipped over Bertram's head, clamping to his ribs and across his knees like an amusement park ride. "Wwwh...?"

"For touch-down," said the man. He yanked the harness and, satisfied it was secure, turned his attention to a control panel embedded in the wall. With a punch of a button, a door slid away and the kidnapper stalked through it, disappearing. Bertram wobbled a little in his wake.

Touch-down? Was Bertram actually on some kind of renegade plane headed out of the country? He took the leash off his research/kidnapping theory and let it stretch its legs again. After all, Bertram Ludlow was not an otherwise productive kidnap. How long before anyone even noticed he was gone? A few hours? A day? A week? After that, how slim was a chance of rescue and how anorexically thin the chance of escape?

Bertram turned to the dingy white walls and the sparse gray furniture for answers, but the most striking thing about the room was the absence of things striking. It was as if all frivolity had been locked in the storeroom to keep this functional exterior uncorrupted. Just a series of smudged wall panels, a scuffed floor, four harnessed chairs lining the outer edge, a console on the side, an empty counter, and a few angular couches bolted to the room's core. Did four harnesses indicate a four-man operation? Three other (South African? Nordic?) mercenaries lurking behind that sliding door, equally armed and efficient? Then those were unevenable odds.

So when Bertram Ludlow actually noticed the window, he'd expected it to overlook some snow-capped European mountain or jungle rebel retreat. He might have concocted hazy plans of breaking free and slipping down narrow cobblestone streets to the U.S.

Consulate, or begging local authorities for help using a friendly smile and persuasive bits of first-year languages.

Instead, beyond that window lay a black endlessness, unfettered by countries or borders. Embedded there in that unfathomed dark was a planet of deep rust, a planet baking under the fury of three small flaming suns. Bertram looked twice and a third time for good measure, the scene as obvious and yet as innately wrong as a Philadelphia Flyers jersey in a Pittsburgh sports bar.

Bertram Ludlow had not been kidnapped and hidden in an abandoned warehouse, a plane, or a secret government hideout. He hadn't been spirited off by some free-lancing Dutch operative.

Bertram Ludlow was the victim of alien abduction. And it wasn't even a Monday.

Bertram came-to lying at the bottom of a ramp, and any embarrassment at having fainted was nicely smoothed by terror as the ramp rattled to life and grinded its way back inside the spacecraft.

He leapt to his feet, fear of abandonment tossing aside his nausea, prickling limbs, worries about breathable atmosphere and any other more practical concerns. Being abducted by aliens was bad enough. But being abducted and then dumped off on a planet that wasn't even yours? He found himself waving his arms at the craft, a lumpy, graceless ship that bore more resemblance to a brachiosaurus in need of a diet than Earthen concepts of alien transport. "Wait! Wait!" he shrieked. "Don't go!"

He sprinted to the slowly retracting ramp, getting a foot up onto it, then another, before the ramp slipped out from under him, burying itself into several thousand tons of metal. Leaping to his feet, Bertram pounded on the ship's hull with bruising fervor, before realizing that all had gone silent. No rumble of rockets. No whine of turbine.

Bertram stood. He paused.

"We don't have big skulls you know," a voice said from behind him. And Bertram Ludlow turned, squinting up in the burning sunlight to see his extra-terrestrial kidnapper. Under the blazing suns, the stranger's short, untamed hair looked precisely as full of white light as his clothes didn't. And in a single spidery hand, he clutched some sort of remote control.

Bertram's knees wobbled. "Uh…?"

"Big skulls," repeated the alien conversationally. "We don't have them. And very few of us are actually green. That," he continued, "should be made abundantly clear." He dropped the gadget into a pocket at his thigh.

"My God," Bertram breathed. Because now it *was* clear. Now he understood that this was never about alien abduction. It was never about stun rays and parallel evolution, worm-holes and other too-slim probabilities. It was about only one thing…

Bertram Ludlow had cracked under the pressure of getting his Ph.D. It had been known to happen. He'd just expected to pick up on some warning signs first.

"It's what you Tryflings are always flapping on about, aren't you?" persisted the figment of Bertram's imagination, wiping his brow. He patted his pockets and, after one trial-and-error, withdrew a pair of sophisticated-looking binoculars. "Aliens: the hairless little slaggards with big heads and eyes, dialing home and giving everyone enemas? I mean, you people, you've got the universe just dripping with rampaging acid-spitters, half-breed progeny, and lizard babies, don't you?" He peered through the binoculars, scanning the vast empty horizon. "In my experience, only one species bears lizard babies. And you wouldn't want to *call* them that. Unless you were up for one fragging huge fight…Ah! Hello, there we are!" The man tucked the binoculars back in a pocket and motioned. "Come on, then."

"Why? Where?" Bertram shielded his eyes. The rust-colored landscape was bone-dry, exhaustively rocky straight to the horizon and completely devoid of life. It didn't even have a smell. There were no wafting blossoms or the territorial musk of skulking beasts. If there were a smell at all, it was the scent of hot. The only sounds? The crunch of gravel underfoot.

But his abductor just pointed to an area every bit as flat and rocky as the rest, differing only by the long, mysterious shadow that fell beyond it.

And as they approached, Bertram glimpsed two figures—rather big-skulled, he thought—until closer inspection proved them to be their own distorted reflections in the wall of a tower.

The tower was rendered virtually invisible by mirrored glass. Its walls were built on an outward angle, reflecting the earth below. And its roof was angled to catch the sky. From a different position now, the structure was almost blinding.

A tower. Bertram had expected more from his subconscious than such blatant Freudianism. An age-old symbol, representing any of a variety of control issues, he supposed, though none sprung to mind for him personally. At twenty-eight, single, and with his own key to the psych lab, Bertram Ludlow had all the freedom necessary for academic excellence. He'd wrap up his thesis this semester, defend and then, barring some unforeseen setback—like, say, a severe psychotic breakdown—graduate to a prime research position in the university of his choice.

Maura and Larry Ludlow might even journey the miles from New Jersey to watch their youngest be granted the title "Doctor." But chances were, this would coincide with one of the endless baptisms or germ infestations of his brother's brood. (Who could ever have predicted that a retired dentist and a former computer engineer would, in their twilight years, view every grandchild's sneeze, babble and spit-up as such Nobel prize-winning material?) Of course, they'd send Bertram a card and, maybe a stethoscope. (He was never quite convinced they knew what it was he was becoming a doctor *of.*) And yes, they'd congratulate his voice mail. But for as strong a case of middle-child syndrome as Bertram had developed in this two-child family, brother A.J. was the one wrapped and trapped in the ties that bound and gagged; Bertram was 300 miles away and completely unfettered.

And that was especially odd, since you didn't need a Ph.D. in psychology to know that imagining yourself getting stunned, yanked around and strapped to a chair by Boba Fett was a manifestation of at least *some* underlying sense of impotence.

As if to demonstrate, the kidnapper shoved Bertram through an opening hatch in the tower, which snapped shut behind them, leaving them in the middle of what was, startlingly, a completely packed reception area. In the room was an array of vaguely human creatures waiting in shackles and wearing fluorescent polka-dotted jumpsuits with symbols printed on them. Others were dressed in subdued shades and talking to themselves. *No*, into small silver chips implanted next to their mouths. Some were frozen stock-still in their seats and covered with dust and cobwebs. There were monitors on three of the four walls, all playing different, painfully loud programs, over equally loud alien Muzak. No one seemed to notice.

At the end of the room was a desk fronted by a frosted glass panel, behind which, the large outline of some creature could just be seen moving. Bertram's kidnapper pushed past everyone as he swept to this desk, dragging Bertram along by the fabric of his shirt sleeve. The alien rapped on the glass and a little door slid away. A large, lime-green eye filled the door. "Yes?" the voice shouted over the waiting room din.

"We're here to see your employers," the kidnapper shouted back. The eye blinked. "Do you have an appointment?"

"What?" The kidnapper cupped a hand to his ear.

"Appointment. Do you have an appointment?"

"You're not serious? I—"

"They're very busy right now. But if you'd like to make an appointment, they'll be delighted to meet with you then. Let's see..." The eye retracted from the window and the voice sounded muffled. The mountainous shadow behind the frosted glass shifted. "The next appointment I have available is...um...457 Universal days from now. How does your schedule look?" The eye reappeared at the window and blinked again with interest.

The kidnapper grinned fiercely. "See here, you giant mass of ocular tissue: they asked for us. We have business, understand? So you just get on that comm of yours and you tell 'em Rolliam Tsmorlood is back. And quickly, unless you're looking for some heavily-discounted opti-laser surgery." He pulled back his coat to reveal enough of the gun holster to make a statement.

The figure behind the glass sniffed, though what part did the sniffing was impossible to say. "That should have been picked up by our sensors and checked here at the desk," the receptionist said snippishly.

"And?" the kidnapper asked, offering a small, slow smile. His fingers twitched over the gun, like a hungry waiting tarantula.

The eye darted from the gun, to the kidnapper's expression, to the gun again. "Mmpf." The tone was unimpressed but compliant. "One moment." The receptionist retreated back behind the foggy glass.

Rolliam Tsmorlood shook his head, muttering, "Flaming Altair, I never imagined getting into this place was going to be even harder than getting out of it."

The eye appeared at the window once more. "Thank you for your...er...patience, Captain Tsmorlood. They said they will see you now. Just through that door, please."

Between a pair of guards to the side of reception, a hatch swung open. Based on the crowded waiting area, Bertram had expected a conference room, a courtroom or a cell. But instead, when the door clanged closed behind them, they found themselves in the grave-like coolness of a pitch black tomb.

Out of that darkness came a smoky white light. And as Bertram's eyes adjusted to the light, he saw it was caused by three ancient life-forms—breathing skeletons inside white painter's overalls. White sightless eyes, white waxy skin, white tangles of hair, they gave off a soft white phosphorescent glow as they rested in luminescent, upholstered recliners.

Hard to say what they were symbolic of.

"Welcome to Rhobux-7," resonated a voice as old as the beginning of time and as young as last Tuesday. "Rolliam Tsmorlooood," it announced, "we knew you would returnnnnn."

"We kneeeeeeewwwwww," echoed the other old people.

"Yeah, brilliant," said the kidnapper flatly. "So I'm clear, then? You'll blank my archive?"

"Ohhhh," lilted the breeze of a voice, "sooooo anxiousssssss."

"Anxioussssssss," agreed the others. It sounded like a room full of punctured car tires.

"Confinement does that," Rolliam Tsmorlood said with a scowl. "Look, I kept my blasted end of it. I expect you'll keep yours."

"And where is our Bertram Ludlooowwww?" asked one of the elders, peering sightlessly into the dim room. "If you would bring him herrrrrrre…"

"Heeerrrrrre," agreed the others.

With a low grumble, the kidnapper seized the smaller man's shoulder and shoved him up to the platform steps. Bertram stumbled and landed unceremoniously at the feet of the life-form in the center. This being leaned toward Bertram, oozing forward, breath stinking of moldy basements and stagnant wells. Bertram stared into the gooey blank eyes and flinched, as squeaky, clammy talons crept across his face and grasped at his hair. They were the kind of hands a firm handshake might splinter like wet, rotting wood, and Bertram was equally amazed and repulsed at the sensory detail his mind conjured; usually his dreams were more vague than vivid.

"Bertram Ludlow is torn within himsellllf," the being announced. "He questions realllityyyy. He questions his sannnity. Yet, in spite of his rational mind, deep down he finds he cannot help but wonder why he's herrrre."

"Why he's heeeeerrrre…heeeeerrrre…" echoed the voices.

Bertram *was* kind of wondering.

"We are the Seerssss, Bertram Ludlow. I am Kaenmoor. And this is Glyddon, and that is Kravsmin." The Seers to the right and left each gave a slow, hypnotic nod. "And we are the guardians of the Master Floorplan for the Cosmossss."

"Cosmossssss..." agreed the Seers.

Kravsmin spoke up, this second glow in the darkness. "Think of the universe as a vast home-unit, Bertram Ludlow. A domicile containing all living thingsssss. Within that structure you will find the systems that run it. Limitless levels of mechanisms that allow it to function...that hold it uuuuup...that keep it from collapsing in on itssselfffff...We Seers keep that building. We note where the structure is sound and predict which points will weakennnnn."

"We maintain it, Bertram Ludlowww," added Glyddon, "maintain the systems of the universe. We detect the weak points and we try, at those times, to reinforce themmmm."

"So you're caretakers for time and space," Bertram said.

The Seer waved an all-encompassing, skeletal hand. "Time... Space...Destinyyyyyy..."

"The penal colony," muttered the kidnapper.

His words were met with uneasy silence.

"They're wardens for the blasted Rhobux-7 penal colony, Ludlow," Rolliam Tsmorlood repeated. "The only thing they 'maintain' is that reeking cesspit of a confinement area that's under this tower."

"Insolent Hyphizite!" Kravsmin screamed, the Seer almost shaking apart with rage and certainly losing a lot of its ethereal delivery. "You well know that's a day job! You try living for a thousand years without health benefits."

"Or stock options," sneered the second Seer.

"Or retirement plans," snapped a third, then remembering itself. "Er...plannnsssssssss."

"Plannssssssss," the other Seers chorused quickly.

Bertram had never perceived the extent of his mental illness.

Then, in a flash, a broad dimensional schematic lit up the room. Layers upon layers of neon lines formed its body, twining and intertwining like a great ball of strung lights, or the Pink Floyd laser light show down at the Science Center. Bertram almost toppled off the platform. The kidnapper stumbled back against the wall. What was it?

"It's Faaaaate, Bertram Ludlow," Glyddon said. "Do you hear it? Do you hear the hummmm of Fate's paths before you? Hear the ssssubtle chorus of possibilitiessss converging? Lissssten to the tones of great channnnnge? The cackle of pure triumphhhhhh and the shriek of final undoingggggg?"

"Also, traffic's snarled on the Mig Verlig Expressway," input Kravsmin.

"I *see* it," Bertram said. Because in spite of all logic to the contrary, Bertram Ludlow was dizzy with Fate, surrounded by the lines that crisscrossed the tower's core. Some of the trails were crisp and firm, almost tangible. While others faded off into illuminated mist. Approaching it slowly, cautiously, he dragged a finger through the haze of light. "Fate's blurry."

"The universe isn't ssssstatic, Bertram Ludlow," reminded Kaenmoor. "These are projected pathssss, not absolutesssss. And even weeee cannot always followwww the paths during times of great fluxxxxx."

Having found his legs, Bertram skirted the circumference of the schematic, pausing beside a very dense knot of light. "So what about here? Where all the lines are colliding?"

The Seers exchanged unseeing glances and smiled. "That, Bertram Ludlowwwwwww," Glyddon said, "is why we need youuuuuu."

"Youuuuuuu," agreed the others.

"What?" Bertram asked, a pang of fear running through him. "To untangle all the existential wiring? People, you don't need me. You need a good electrician."

"If those paths remain as they are, the results will be cataclysmiccccccc."

(*Catatonic*, thought Bertram. *I am definitely headed toward catatonia.*)

"Those lines indicate the complete end to Life As You Know It on the planet Tryfffffe," said Kaenmoor. "The planet youuuuu call Earth."

"Eartttthhhhhh."

"I see." Bertram stroked his chin. "So what you're saying is that I've been singled out from the billions of other life-forms on my planet—maybe even the universe—as the sole individual capable of saving the planet?"

"At this juncture," said the Seer, "yesssss."

"Indeeeeeed," agreed Kravsmin.

"Yepperssssssss," said Glyddon.

"Ah." Bertram nodded gravely. "Megalomania."

"Um," the Seers blinked, "pardon?"

"I said I must be suffering from megalomania," he explained. "I mean, sure, 'Bertram Ludlow: Savior of the Earth' does have a certain ring." He savored the words as they rolled off his tongue. For a brief, wistful moment, he could even picture the business card, all silver lettering and understated design. That would certainly be something to pass around at Thanksgiving dinner. "But it's kinda on the overmuch side, isn't it? I mean, couldn't we go with something a little less God Complex for this hallucination today?"

The Seers looked at each other with those egg-white eyes. One shrugged.

"Okay," said Bertram, realizing this wasn't going anywhere. "So let's say the Earth really is in danger, and out of billions of other people—astrophysicists, and presidents, and spiritual leaders, and the dude down at the comic book shop—I somehow happen to be the only guy for the job. What do you need me to do?" Bertram persisted. "You guys are omnipotent, right? And you went to all the trouble to have your Terminator snag and drag me here." He shot a glare that direction. "You must know something. A starting point. Some sort of advice. Helpful hints. A handbook. *Doom Prevention for Dimwits* maybe?"

The Terminator cackled.

The Seers just shifted nervously. "It…it's not that sssssimple, Bertram Ludlowwww." Glyddon's hands kneaded each other.

"Human minds are incapable offfff…" Kaenmoor seemed to be sweating.

"It's too difficult tooo…The lines of Fate arrrrre…" Kravsmin's eye twitched just slightly.

"You don't know, do you?" Bertram said. "I'm supposed to save Life As We Know It and you have no clue how." He pushed on his temples and paced a little. It always helped to pace. "But I know why."

Kaenmoor smiled thinly, "Because we're in your mindddd, are we, Bertram Ludlow?"

"An elaborate psychotic episode, granted, but a self-generated representation of my problems that can never go beyond what I myself can create." Bertram glanced around quickly, on chance that this great revelation would knock down the facades in his mind, transporting him back to his apartment.

It didn't.

"Bertram Ludlowwww," Kaenmoor began in weary tones, "The Seers of Rhobux know only what can be pulled from the Linesssss. Were we 'omnipotent' as you say, we would have anticipated this adverse reaction of yours and not wasted vital time on petty rationalizationnnnn."

"Of course, if we were in his mindddd," piped up Glyddon, "wouldn't we say the same thinggggggg?"

Kravsmin sneered. "Can it, Glyddon!"

"Cannnnnn itttttt," the Seers sang.

"Now you mention it," Bertram considered, "Glyddon's right." And Glyddon looked delighted at the affirmation. "How do I prove that I didn't break under the pressure of getting my degree? How can I be sure that right now, I'm not in Western Psychiatric Hospital, sitting in striped pajamas, staring glazedly out the window while my mind goes where it's never gone before? Simple: I can't."

After a moment, Kravsmin propped a pointy chin on bony hands. "Then the real question, Bertram Ludlow, becomes: what do you have to lossssse?"

It was a good question, really. It wasn't like extricating himself from a psychotic episode was exactly something he'd learned about in class. Cognitive psychology was focused on thought processes, problem solving, memory, behavior and decision making. A clean sort of science of the mind, in some ways—particularly if you were in the research end of things. Nothing like the heavy-duty pain and suffering stuff that abnormal psych counselors had to deal with every day, anyway. In fact, the difference between cognitive research and abnormal psych counseling was pretty much the difference between being an eye doctor versus, say…a proctologist. Bertram was totally unprepared for the path he was on.

He might as well take a deep breath and go with it.

"Gooood," said the Seers, sensing his resignation.

"So you will need thisssss." Kravsmin leaned forward, extending to Bertram a strange object. It was about five inches long, bright yellow, and looked roughly like a starfruit on a cord.

"Soap on a rope?" Bertram frowned, dangling it on its string. He held it up to the kidnapper, who shrugged.

"You will know what it is when you neeeeeed to knowwwwww," said Kravsmin with a sightless wink.

"When you neeeeed to knowwwww," chorused the Seers merrily.

Rolliam Tsmorlood gritted his teeth. "Classic."

"Just rememberrrr," warned Kaenmoor, "you must keep it with you during your journey alwayssss. To lose it? Would be perillllll!"

"Dooomm!" added Kravsmin.

"Bad, tooooo," agreed Glyddon.

"Er, 'kay," said Bertram, giving it another once over, then hanging the cord around his neck. "Cool. Thanks for...er...for my yellow thing."

"Well, at least that's settled," Rolliam Tsmorlood cut in, dusting off his hands. "And since it looks like your little 'Life for Tryfe' club really has got all the members it needs, what say we go ahead, disengage security, and I give this place the launch while I'm still in my eighties?"

The Seers mouths twisted into narrow little smiles.

Warily, the kidnapper said, "What?"

"We find your thin attempt at persuasion amusing, Rolliam Tsmorlood," said Kravsmin. "And unnecessary. You see, today is the day we left the door unbarredddd. Todayyyy, the only confinement you faced was your ownnnn."

"The only punishment you endured was self-imposedddd," said Kaenmoor.

"The only torment—"

"Yes, it's irony, I get it," the captain said. "What of the charges?"

"Soon you will rejoin Universal societyyy, once again partaking of freedom and all its manyyy—"

"I could've partaken of Freedom and All Its Many without picking up your Tryfling Takeaway for you," he interrupted. "The charges. What of the charges?"

Kaenmoor laughed, high, hearty and fully-entertained.

"You think I'm joking?" the kidnapper asked, his voice cracking with rage and desperation. "I could have vanished, conveniently forgetting all about Seers, and confinement cells, and crawlies in the Rhobux-7 personal facilities the size of well-fed progeny. But then I remembered: my infraction archive is still wide open. And so, on good faith, I did your little A to B. Now I expect you to hold up your end of our deal."

"Your archive will be blanked of all charges, Rolliam Tsmorlood," assured Kaenmoor.

He nodded. "That's more like it. Stellar."

"Just as soon as you complete..."

"Oh, here it comes."

"...An errandddd for us!"

"An erranddd!" said Kravsmin and Glyddon joyously.

"An errand," Rolliam Tsmorlood said darkly. "You want me to run another errand for you." Bertram was a little concerned about the tone of the man's voice. It had become entirely too quiet and smooth to be reassuring. It sounded like a frozen lake just before it cracks, dumping half the Currier and Ives landscape into the drink. "You do remember, I just did from A to B?"

"The errand," the Seers tittered. "The errandddd."

"That's it." By now he'd visibly tensed, hands clenched, back straight. "I am not running a fragging transport service here. I gave you the Tryfling, held up my half. Now you."

"After the errand," whispered the Seers, like little kids on Christmas morning. "The errannnndd."

"Think of it as a final gesture of goodwill between friendssss," said Kravsmin.

Bertram took a step back as the captain's eyes narrowed, his fingers twitching, hovering over the laser grip at his side. "Funny, then, me having another gesture in mind."

"We don't need to blank your archive, Rolliam Tsmorlood," Kaenmoor reminded him. "We don't need to suspend your sentence. Quite franklyyyy, your departure from the colony will inconvenience us even more than your presencccce has. With your absence in KP, the prisoners will no longer enjoy cleverly dressed-up rationssss. It doesn't take a Seer to predict some serious backlashhhhh."

"Protestsss," agreed Kravsmin.

"Beans on toastttttt," sighed Glyddon.

"In the interest of colonial harmony, we could quite easily ensure you stay indefinitelyyyyy."

"Indeffff—"

Glyddon interrupted, "Um, but since right now you're thinking of shooting us and making a run for the doorrrrr—"

The kidnapper gave a slow nod.

"—In that case, we might remind you that we haven't blanked your charges yet. So if anything unfortunate happens to us between now and the completion of our little errandddd, you'll be carrying that hefty archive of yours along wherever you goooo."

"As we understand it," Kravsmin continued, "given the charges against you, if you so much as litter, the Hyphiz Deltan RegForce will have no choice but to send you for a brief but exciting stay at a certain placccce I know we need not mentionnnnn?"

"Altair-5," said Kaenmoor, mentioning.

"Funnnnnn," wheezed all the Seers.

The prisoner winced.

"Of course, it is your choicccce," said Glyddon.

"Choicccccccce."

After a moment, the captain's hand moved slowly from the weapon. "Choice," he grumbled. "To think it sounded so much like blackmail, I almost didn't recognize it."

And Bertram asked, "What's the errand?"

Kaenmoor pointed to a pale blue line tangled in the blueprint of lights before them. "See this line? This is youuuu, Bertram Ludlow. And the lines of Fate say the journey to save your world begins herrrreeee." The Seer pointed to a place on the grid. "Podunk-17."

"Podunk-17? Seriously?" The captain laughed. Yet at the solemn faces around him, the laughter fell away. He shook his head in bewildered acquiescence. "Even great journeys begin with small steps, I guess."

"What's Podunk-17?" Bertram asked.

"Rolliam Tsmorlood," said Kravsmin, "you will take Bertram Ludlow to the capital city of Podunk-17."

"Well, I'd have to, wouldn't I? That's all there is, really, the one city. Unless you're keen on flatlands and Podunkian livestock." He shook his head again. "And what of it once we get there?"

"You will go," said the Seer, "for a drink."

"For a drinkkkkk," they cheered.

2

"A drink," muttered the kidnapper. "Take him for a fragging drink,' they say. 'On Podunk-17,' they say. 'Establishment of your choice,' they say. 'Then you're clear." In the captain's seat of the spacecraft, Rolliam Tsmorlood yanked down on a lever like it was somebody's neck. "'Give me a reason to believe you,' *I* say, and what's the Seer answer? 'Truth lies always with the one unchained.' Classic example, standard issue, first-class Seer excrement."

Watching from the co-pilot's seat as Rhobux-7 grew distant, Bertram Ludlow reflected on the possibilities of his situation. If he could claw his way back from insanity, with the market these days, he'd be right in line to whip out a major self-help book. The analysis of his own hallucination's logic patterns, perhaps in combination with the co-writing of an expert in abnormal psychology, would offer all the potential for an NYT best-seller. *Around the Bend and Back: One Man's Journey from Madness.*

It was only a working title.

Granted, he could expect a certain amount of stigma involved in baring his current psychological challenges to the world. But that was small sacrifice for becoming a forerunner in the field. Only a handful of cognitive psychology researchers could expect to make the big bucks, anyway.

Frankly, Bertram hadn't felt this energized about something since he began the doctoral program.

The pilot however, Bertram noticed, was still grumbling. "Backspace life-forms: so extraordinary on their own jerkwater little worlds, but got to be shuttled round space like half-wit progeny. Just my luck, I get to play the fragging ambassador to the Greater Communicating Universe." The captain scanned the controls before him and turned a dial, shaking his head in disgust.

Fumbling open one of the many cases on his belt, the kidnapper fished out a small, metal cylinder printed in bright colors and covered in unfamiliar symbols. "Here."

Bertram dubiously eyed both cylinder and pilot. "What is it?"

"Gum."

"Thanks, I'll pass," Bertram said. What about *Stress: The Final Frontier?* Too pop culture, maybe. Or how about *Lift-Off of the Mind: The Bertram Ludlow Story?* Bertram jumped as the gum cylinder cuffed him off a rib. "Hey!"

"They won't know your language, Ludlow," Rolliam Tsmorlood said.

"What? Who won't?"

The alien gave the slightest shrug of a shoulder. "Anyone. I'd be very surprised if anyone did."

Bertram scowled. "The Seers did. That receptionist did. *You* do."

"Yes." He tapped a gauge. "*I* do."

"Well, how do you, then?" Bertram had been under the impression that everyone spoke English in his mind.

But the alien figment just flashed an unpleasant smile and continued to evaluate the control board.

Bertram pushed at a temple. Yep, with every conversation, it seemed he was falling, drifting down deeper into madness. "What does gum have to do with any of this?"

The captain checked an overhead monitor. "It's Translachew®. That's what it does, translate."

"Translates what into what?"

"Most into others." He rose from the chair. "If you'd stop flapping your gums and started, er, flapping your gums, you'd see."

"But the receptionist," said Bertram.

"Vocal translational interpretative projection device."

"The Seers?" Bertram queried.

"Relative omniscience and a lot of blasted time on their hands." His amber eyes narrowed in a scowl, as he vanished into another room. "Look, just chew the gum, Ludlow."

So Bertram cracked open the cylinder and a ball of gum tumbled into his palm. It was so smooth, round, and compellingly blue, Bertram instantly mistrusted it. It was a Grimm reminder of a hundred childhood fables with candy and curiosity at the sour center. Unmerciful tales where no one ever made it out of the woods quite the same. It would change him somehow, wouldn't it? This tiny violet bomb, this crazed Wonkafied wonder, that rolled and Roald in Bertram's hand as his mind went from Dahl to Dali?

From the doorway, the captain cleared his throat. "You do know it's not osmotic?"

Bertram nodded, eyes still on the confection that silently seemed to threaten more than tooth decay. He gathered his bearings and looked up hopefully. "It won't taste anything like that gunk I drank earlier, will it?"

"Doesn't compare," said the captain, waving it away. "This is a prototype. This stuff is nasty."

Excerpt from:

How To Gain Pals and Sway Life-forms in Cosmic Commerce
Chapter Two

With permission from the
Eddisun Center for Ideas, Interceptive Marketing and Cliché Prevention

How To Talk to Anyone, Anywhere, in the Greater Communicating Universe

Overview

Want to discover new forms of life at a party on Zarquon-9? Need to make anti-matter matter at your next big meeting on Marglenia? Hoping to charm the astro-togs off that hottie at the Vos Laegos bar? The key to these and other successful intergalactic relations is good communication.

Yet anyone who's been around the Greater Communicating Universe (GCU) a time or two recalls the awkward moments and unexpected challenges of inter-species chit-chat. Experts predict that "within the next five Universal Years, there will be over 200 billion different discourse communities in the GCU market; and of those, only 3% are expected to have the slightest clue what their neighbors have been yammering about," (Eddisun Center, "The New Uni-Market," Reference Point: 2312).

Add to this, the hundreds of cultures, and thousands of unique customs for every world, star system, and Quadrant across the CGU, and things get really sticky. The only thing you can truly count on is that what's simple courtesy to one group will offend the gravity boots off another. So how do you understand and be understood without looking down the business end of one of the more popular hand-lasers?

Simple: you either connect with an **organic or non-organic translator**, or you select an **oral translational product**. Let's talk about these exciting options!

Organic Translators: Your Discourse Manager On-the-Go
Organic translators are paid specialists in certain languages and customs, hired to initiate smooth inter-cultural relations. These life-forms will translate your communications, make recommendations for polite conduct, and help you avoid those embarrassing social blunders that historians sometimes preface with "Battle of."

Organic translators can be hired for as little as an hour, and as long as you keep paying them. During the T'Pow/Teedle merger, for example, holding partners, the T'Pow Royal Family and Parr Teedle, CEO of Teedle ICV Manufacturing, used the same organic translators over a ten U-year period to successfully negotiate their choice of the right corporate-branded mug cozy. Experts estimate the transaction would have taken more than 30 U-years, if not for the tireless efforts of translators on both sides. (Eddisun Center. "The New Uninet." RPs: 1529-1640.)

Yet organic translators do have their disadvantages. One is their capacity for error. Even the most well-trained organic translator's knowledge is limited by personal experience, temperament, biases, and the ability to stay awake in negotiations that can last upwards of ten Universal-years.

Also, organic translators aren't always practical for simple pan-galactic tourism. Their presence raises travel, food and lodging costs, and they tend to order quite a lot from the mini-bar. (Eddisun Center. "Stress and the Organic Translator." RP: 140.)

Non-Organic Translators: Your Plugged-in Pal for Palaver
Non-organic translators come in two types: **Non-Organic Simulants** and **vocal projection devices**. Both are electronic options with scripted programming. And each offers a level of consistency not guaranteed with their organic counterparts.

For corporate translational needs, a **Non-Organic Simulant** can be a wise selection. Combining translational skills with other support functions, these stylized, life-like robots function much like in-house staff, while remaining a comfort barrier between organic executives and any actual responsibility for failed negotiations (Eddisun Center. "Today's Non-Organic Translator Sales, Cumulative.")

But for the GCU tourist on a budget, a **vocal projection device** may be a better fit. Here, the user speaks into the compact technology, and the sound that projects is a digitized version of the user's own voice, instantly translated into an array of pre-programmed languages. The patented audio-wave technology process filters the right translation for the right listener, so multi-language discussions feel virtually seamless. **Murminn Corp.** and **Kinesynn Ltd.** both offer lines of affordable vocal projection devices in a wide range of models and fashion colors.

Note that both Non-Organic Simulants and vocal projection devices are limited by the quality and thoroughness of their programming. Also keep in mind, better-made Non-Organic translators may not be the most expensive models. For example, **Neo-Natelle Manufacturing** offers the CR-29, a low-cost, adaptable Simulant with proven reliability. (*SimmiWorld* e-mag rates it four out of five golden gears!)

Oral Translational Products: Fast, Friendly and Fun!

Oral translational products offer some of the fastest and most economic ways to communicate with life-forms around the GCU. Among the most popular is Translachew® gum, a candy that helps the consumer participate in free, comprehensive conversation with virtually any sentient species.

The gum, like oral translational wafers or soft drinks, works by releasing strings of language-oriented chemical coding into the bloodstream and on to the brain. Chewing discharges pre-programmed information for practical everyday inter-galactic expressions such as, "Where is the nearest vis-u console?" and "No, I can't spare a couple of yoonies, get a job," in over fourteen billion of the most prevalent cosmic languages. Less necessary communicative terms follow, until the gum loses its flavor and all of the coding has been released.

Refresher chews are necessary every two to six U-months, varying by species. Though there are other translational gums, soft drinks and wafers on the market, **Translachew®** is the brand we recommend, because of its strong track record and wider base of phraseology.

Note: all oral translational products can have difficulty deciphering tone, some local slang and certain humor, such as sarcasm. If you operate a product like Translachew gum, remember anything you say will be translated literally, so choose those words carefully!

Translachew gum and other translational products can be found in most convenience stores and intergalactic transit ports.

While currently there is only one major type of Translachew gum available on the market, DiversiDine Entertainment Systems and Aeroponics is expanding the product line to target more specialized needs. A new novelty form of the gum, in trials now, offers all the capabilities of regular Translachew, but adds the phraseology of three billion archaic, obscure or "backspace" languages. The gum is expected to reduce the time it takes to analyze ancient historical documents and understand less-evolved public transit systems, by eliminating the painful chore of learning new languages.

DiversiDine executives predict this version will be popular at top universities, major research labs or anywhere users might need a unique pick-up line.

Though the gum has been well-received for its functionality and convenience, test groups have complained about the taste, which is commonly described as having "a metallic tang, if that metal stewed for months at the bottom of a barrel of well-fed, tri-bladder hamsters from the planet Erk."

DiversiDine flavor engineers are now working to create a more universally-palatable taste. The product should be available to the public in the next U-year.

3

It was like biting deep into a nine-volt battery that had spent years in the bottom of a gerbil tank. Gagging, Bertram Ludlow spit out the half-chewed gum, wondering how to get rid of it without being caught. In haste, he tacked it under the co-pilot's chair and dropped the cylinder into his shirt pocket.

Sensory detail. He would have to discuss sensory detail in his book, with a special section dedicated toward flavor as represented within the confines of his hallucinatory state and, specifically, how it sucked. He thought it would be interesting to attack the topic in light of positive and negative reinforcement, self-reward and self-punishment. He'd worry what the Freudians would choose to misinterpret later.

With the ship stabilized, Rolliam Tsmorlood had left the pilot's station for the inner cabin, tossing both his attention and himself toward a modest computer console that jutted from the wall. The click of a single switch sent the systems grinding to life, shrieking and groaning a mechanized tirade that extended from the terminal to roll along the very innards of the craft. Walls shook. A panel popped open and rained alien clutter. The overhead lights winked and threatened to go out. All the while, the screeching grew louder... louder...rattling like a runaway locomotive. Bertram cradled his head in his arms and prayed for a merciful end.

Rolliam Tsmorlood slammed a fist into the terminal and the whole ship dropped into subservient acquiescence. The walls stilled.

From the floor, a screeching turbine wound down to a whimper. Bertram peered from under the protective shelter of his own elbow, his right ear ringing.

The captain answered it. "Protostar model 340-K," he explained. "Very rare. Only two others still operational cross-galaxy."

"The computer system?" Bertram asked.

"The ship," the man said, tapping something into the terminal. Bertram sighed. His mind, he was learning, was riddled with muddy recesses. And he supposed he'd need to produce some solid theories about the origin of this one, if he ever planned to write that book.

Maybe the black-clad alien was symbolic of Bertram's fear of the unknown. Or of mortality. Or a lifetime of repressed, pent-up hostility. Maybe even resentment, he considered, of the very same high-powered educational system that had driven him to madness in the first place.

Of course, if Bertram were a Freudian, he'd have theorized that the captain was the Id, the personification of the dark, untamed part of the mind responsible for basic human drives. Only Bertram wasn't a Freudian. And, anyway, he'd never pictured the Id quite so brisk and sarcastic.

Bertram made a mental note to include a Freudian among his book's support staff.

"So, it's pronounced... 'Tssssmore-lood,' huh?" Bertram said, attempting that slight click of the "T" he'd heard the man do. A "T" that was there, but not there, sliding into the "S" like it depended on it for survival. The result sounded a lot like somebody had just cracked open a new bottle of soda-pop. "Rolliam."

The alien raised a suspicious, almost translucent eyebrow. "Rollie, if you must," he mumbled. He gave Bertram barely a glance before returning to the computer.

Rollie. Didn't sound quite like the kind of nickname you'd readily associate with a six-foot-four, weapon-wielding, alien ex-con. Also not very Iddish... Idly... Idesque. Bertram shrugged and offered his most affable smile. "So, Rollie. I was wondering: what exactly were you in for?"

Silence. Stillness. Only Rolliam Tsmorlood's weird gold-orange eyes moved as they flicked across the data on the screen.

Bertram hesitated. Should he repeat the question? What if he hadn't heard? Then again, if he had, what if Bertram accidentally ticked off the most volatile part of his own mind? What then?

After a moment, Bertram cleared his throat and tucked the smile back on. "Um, on Rhobux-7, I mean. What...what were you—"

"Forced entry into private property. Illegal seizure and removal of goods. Use of unlicensed armament with criminal intent. Three points of assault..." Rollie Tsmorlood glared at the screen and scrolled the images down.

Bertram nodded, wishing he hadn't asked.

Rollie tapped the screen, selecting something from the page, which began to load. "Um, unauthorized combustion of a Non-Organic Simulant," he continued. "Failure to extinguish said Non-Organic in a 'No Combustion' zone. Failure to surrender on command of RegForce Officer. Seizure of official armaments. Attempted fragmentation of a RegForce Officer. Inadvertent detonation of livestock. And willful destruction of a Regimental Enforcement vehicle."

"Ah," said Bertram.

"Kidnapping a member of the Wykanian royal party," Rollie went on absently. "Removal of said royal personage outside Realm of Regality in violation of Farquotch Treaty of 35,272. Irreparable damage to third-party flora vending establishment. Leaving planetary atmosphere without proper clearance. Abandonment of Royal Personage outside regal no-fly zone. Piloting interplanetary cruise vessel with lapsed inspection. Piloting ICV with lapsed registration. Piloting ICV that no longer meets GCU ICV Travel Bureau Safety Standards Regulations. And Navigating While Inebriated." He leaned back in the chair, still contemplating the screen.

"Let me guess," said Bertram, "you pled innocent."

The captain's eyes flicked up distractedly. "What? Oh. No. The NWI was complete rubbish but..." Something whirred from the computer unit and he sat up to face the monitor. "Right, well, Tryfling, looks like this is it."

A new screen had formed, one of flashing oranges and lime greens. The writing was just out of focus, characters that seemed beyond Bertram's mental grasp by only the breadth of a cognitive fingertip. It was close, so close. There was too much animation. There were photos of well-lit food and drink Bertram couldn't make sense of. A video played, featuring life-forms he couldn't understand. It was too much at one time. The whole thing made him flinch, twitch and squint.

"Like I said before, we're dealing with Podunk-17," Rollie explained. "Not much to work with, really, in terms of options. In fact, this is the only boozer I could find on the Podunk Uninet. So, what say you, Ludlow?"

One meaningless symbol after another covered the screen. And still the flashing greens and orange and a swirl of garble. Bertram tried to unfocus his eyes like he'd done for those 3-D books that had been so popular in the 90s. Maybe that would help.

"Ludlow?" The voice was concerned.

The gum, Bertram thought suddenly. The gum would have made the difference.

And it was amazing, he considered, how this dream state was such a sucker for detail! Most dreams would have let the fact that Bertram had never really chewed the gum just blow on by—one insignificant moment in a string of nonsensical, ever-shifting scenes. But not this one. He'd experienced nothing like it before. He genuinely began to believe he should have chewed the gum.

He subtly touched his shirt pocket and felt the cylinder's smooth form through the plaid flannel. It was still there: remarkable! And more surprising, it hadn't changed into a garden slug, a toothbrush, a copy of his fourth grade report card or a million other non-sequiturs that any other dream would have effortlessly tossed into the mix.

All he needed now was the right moment to get the gum, without tipping his hand. He just hoped he could recall enough of these details for a later, more thorough examination.

If he ever came out of it, that was.

"Imagine: only one canteen on the whole planet, and in this day and age, too," Rollie was still marveling. He had pulled up what looked like a navigational program and was shuffling through virtual star charts. "That's why it seems zonked to me—them sending you to Podunk to start your World-Saving and all. I mean a place like that, so new to the GCU and suspicious of everybody; they're not exactly going to greet a Tryfling with osculation and open upper limbs."

Given the creatures he'd seen so far, Bertram viewed that as a plus.

But amusement had overtaken Rollie's angular features. "Fact, more I think on it," he said, "almost sounds like the Seers sent you somewhere knowing full-well you'd get into trouble."

Still chuckling, he clicked on the coordinates and the terminal began to rev itself up again. The walls wobbled. The floor joggled. Another compartment opened up and spewed.

Then with a second click, all of the ship's dials neatly reset themselves.

"We're off, Ludlow," Rollie announced.

Oh, I'm off, all right, Bertram thought. In fact, it was the first sensible thing Rollie had said to Bertram since they'd met.

Bertram peered out the portal window and watched the stars whiz past. It reminded him of the starfield screensaver he'd had back in the day. The one where pixilated celestial bodies soared out of the blackness of space, while the customized words, "Cognitive psychologists do it from memory" regularly jogged into view. *A little bit of psych major humor there,* he recalled, smiling to himself.

His friends had found it *hilarious.*

Bertram turned from the twinkling cosmic vista before him, feeling wistful about this lack of reality. "Ah, to be the first person from my planet with real answers to the mysteries of intergalactic space travel. Now that would be cool. I mean, we've been theorizing about it for decades. Imagine being able to say once and for all, 'Yes, wormholes exist.'"

Rollie had spread his gunbelt and all its cases across a table, along with a number of small tools. With a fine brush, he was intent on removing particles from the workings of one of the guns. "Well, you *could* say it." He looked up and blinked. "'Course, why would you?"

This wasn't quite the response Bertram had expected. "What, are you saying there's nothing to String Theory?"

The pilot didn't bother to look up this time. He blew away some dust. "I suppose it keeps a lot of your people busy. And life-forms need employment."

"But they're working with Superstring Theory now."

Rollie gave a sharp laugh. "That's what I've always liked about you Tryflings. Just enough knowledge to make a really good mess of things."

"But—"

"Just leave it, Ludlow. I don't have that kind of fragging time, and it's a lot to ask of your Tryfling brain right off the launch." He rested the gun and brush on the table, and motioned at Bertram with a twitch of long, bony fingers. "That thing the Seers gave you. Let me see it?"

Bertram found himself clutching the item around his neck in paternal hesitation. "They said to keep it with me always. They said to lose it would be 'peril.'"

"You don't know peril, mate. Hand it over," Rollie said. The expression on Bertram's face must have been one of reflexive horror because the alien gave a tired sigh. "I just want to look at it, Ludlow. I'm not going to do anything to it."

Slowly, Bertram pulled the cord up over his neck and handed the yellow thing to him.

As Rollie set it on a table and frowned, Bertram edged over to get a better look. "You really don't have any idea what it is?"

The kidnapper removed a thick-lensed object from one of the belt cases in front of him, and hooked the device over an ear. He squinted in the light, rolling the grooved, vaguely dirigible-shaped item in his hands. "Dunno. But it's organic, that's for sure."

"It is?"

"It's not molded. It's got individual cells. Looks vegetative. But that doesn't quite look like a cell wall to me. I can't really be sure." After a moment, Rollie handed Bertram the yellow thing and peered at him through the microscopic lens. One golden-orange eye, rimmed in pallid lashes, was magnified many times from its match and to startling effect. "It's alive, anyway."

"Alive?" The idea that all along he'd been wearing an unwieldy accessory that was alive was somehow unsettling. He suddenly didn't like the feel of the Yellow Thing in his hand; it seemed greasy and a little like it might be trying to breathe. "Alive..."

"Alive as you or me." Rollie removed the eyepiece and popped it back into a case. "Well, *you*. Not an overtly evolved life-form, and..."

Bertram ignored the comment. "Could we scan it?" he suggested, looking around the ship's cabin. "You don't happen to have an x-ray machine or an ultra-sound or something?"

"On a Protostar 340-K?" Rollie clapped him hard on the shoulder, nearly jarring the Yellow Thing from his hands. "Ludlow, the joy of owning this finely-tuned example of classic, high-tech design is in not being burdened by all that fancy, unnecessary equipment. It flies the way it does because it's so spare. It's got none of those extras to weigh it down that so many fools insist on these days." He began to slide the items into the gunbelt one by one. "Frankly, I was probably overdoing it by installing the bucket seats, the hot plate, and the Uninet system. Still," he said, "it makes the place home."

"It's alive," Bertram murmured again, just to hear it aloud.

"Great." This was the trouble with this dream. He never knew what direction things were going to turn. Try as he would to clinically-distance himself, he kept finding himself involved, curious, or—as he replaced the Yellow Thing around his neck—disconcerted.

Like right now, he didn't particularly like the way the Yellow Thing thumped against his chest. It sounded a little hollow inside, like it was a husk. Or a pod. Or a cocoon. Some outer shell designed to protect something vulnerable inside. As it grew, and changed... and waited...

Perhaps for the single right moment?

Bertram winced, wishing he hadn't gone to that sci-fi marathon down at the SuperSaver theater last week.

"So it's alive." Rollie shrugged. "That's all right, though, innit? Least you've got yourself a friend, more or less. And you'll be needing the company soon, anyway. We're almost to Podunk."

"We are?"

"Yup. And there, young Tryfling, me and you will be parting ways."

If they had simply disembarked from the ship onto a terrain that looked like, say, downtown Pittsburgh, Bertram Ludlow might never have questioned it. He might have surrendered to the illusion, strode into the bar, ordered the $2 draft and settled in to watch the game.

But when they landed, the meager space-port was a cluster of rounded buildings laced together with thick, strange shrubbery, crossed by a still, alien street and rimmed with a small array of silvery wheel-free vehicles. Three steps down the ship's ramp, Bertram was greeted by a breath of the most pure oxygen that had ever filled his lungs. He had never breathed so well, so deeply, bringing a clarity of mind and a lightness of spirit like none since his last intra-mural tennis match.

He could almost taste this air, like sweet mountain water to a thirsty man. Crackpot celebs paid the big bucks for oxygen therapy in

Hollyweird, yet here Bertram Ludlow was getting the good stuff for one ticket to a mind melt.

Then the wind shifted and the smell went barnyard. Not so inspiring, Bertram admitted. But still very sensory-oriented. He made a mental note of it.

Bertram's alien companion, however, didn't seem to notice the air or anything else, instead pressing onward into the domed little town. He paused only to target a brightly-lit structure, and in a moment, he threw open its door like he was a regular.

A few steps behind, Bertram jarred to a halt in its threshold.

It was the Murray Avenue Tavern.

Simulated dark wood paneling wore water-damaged, curling veneer, as genuine replica antiques fought to cling tight. Neon logos blinked and bubbled in familiar fermented revelry. In the half-light, it was all there: the bar on the left, tables on the right, a game room tucked in back and the jukebox in the corner belting out 80s hits. Even now, as the door swung shut behind him, the machine cranked out J. Geils' "Centerfold" and Bertram Ludlow was overcome by a brief, inexplicable homesickness for the world he'd never left.

"The Murray Avenue Tavern. I came here every semester, right after finals," Bertram told Rollie's back. "I watched that big screen during the Stanley Cup playoffs. For God's sake, I met a terrific girl here once."

Rollie sniffed. "Not fragging likely."

"You're just not seeing me at my best," assured Bertram.

And it was only as Bertram began to drone along with the jukebox that he realized: he and Rollie really *weren't* talking about the same thing. Something, he began to sense, was deeply wrong with this place. Something almost as off as his own singing.

First of all, the music's key didn't fit. The melody turned around in it just fine, but it never quite clicked—a note shy here, a beat off there. Just enough to draw attention to the fact the lead singer crooned from that jukebox in some deceptive, alternate tongue. It was the simple case of a Peter Wolf in cheap clothing, and Bertram's blood ran cold.

Bertram's eyes now flew to the tavern walls and he saw the items hanging there in organized chaos weren't the croquet mallets, elixir ads and antiquated garden implements he'd grown to expect. This was a different clutter: metal pointies, wooden swirlies, and reverently-framed stills of beings, the likes of which made a carnival freak show look like Ward Cleaver's annual Christmas photo. Even the neon signs, he realized, were impostors of the beer logos he'd come to know. But every time he just about got a handle on their meaning, it broke off.

His hand flew to his shirt pocket, half-expecting its contents to have vanished now that he wanted them most. But the cylinder was still there. So he rolled out two of the three remaining pieces of Translachew gum, and crammed both into his mouth, bracing himself for the chew. As his taste buds passed out and his uvula trembled, he diverted his attention to the big screen, where players of a six-legged variety were either wearing terrific protective equipment, or bearing exoskeletons. They swung giant metal ladles and some of them surfboarded on air.

"It *seemed* like the Murray Avenue Tavern," Bertram mumbled through the gum.

Having commandeered a table in a far corner, Rollie dropped down in a chair, back to the wall. "Guess it's not totally surprising," the man in black said contemplatively. "Backspace cultures do tend to have commonalities. Things that hold 'em back from joining the GCU."

"The what?"

"Greater Communicating Universe." Rollie pushed a chair out for Bertram with the toe of his boot. "Least this place is in transition. You know: using the Uninet, no one shrieking at the sight of us."

"You get that reaction a lot?" Bertram glanced around the room at the other patrons. They were largely humanoid, but hardly human. Mental demons and disturbed nightmares with twisted faces and extra limbs that made Rollie Tsmorlood, with his angular features and jack-o-lantern eyes, look like Mr. Rogers. Yep, if there were any shrieking to be done, it should start here. He just wished he'd picked up on it sooner.

"Yeah, it's a real chance you take coming to an unevolved system," Rollie went on. "Some places just everyone's curious to meet your vital organs." The captain's gaze had latched firmly onto a drink server who seemed to be buzzing around every table but theirs.

"She is *buzzing*, right?" Bertram whispered.

"She's Mathekite." Rollie glared a hole through her antennaed, inattentive skull. "Place must really be hurting for servers. Mathekites aren't exactly known for hygiene." He turned the same sharp gaze on Bertram. "So, what'll you have?"

"Have?"

"I want to make this quick, Ludlow. My first night free in a Universal Year, and if it's all the same, I won't be spending it with you." Rollie pitched him the menu, which was on strange pulpy paper and coated in spilled goo. "What'll it be?"

Bertram looked at the card before him, a thick sprawl of illegible symbols. Still, the text seemed close, closer...His jaws worked the gum with new fervor.

Now there was a faint scent of overripe vegetables and Bertram turned. The waitress fluttered at his shoulder. She rubbed her hands together and uttered something that sounded a lot like static.

Nodding, Rollie spoke in a second language, this one with hissing, guttural tones that, together, sounded like the unfortunate genetic product of a snake and a Scotsman. "*Tsaargh-tsoo Zlorgon tchkaagk?*"

And the waitress said: "*Bzzzzshzzzzuzzzshzzjjzzz...*"

He held up the menu. "*Feegar-tsoo, na tseenee. Sha? Tsargh-tsoo Feegar?*"

And again the waitress responded, two of her six arms pointing to the menu. "*Bzzzzzzhzzzz.*"

Rollie sighed and shook his head at Bertram. "No Zlorgon Subatomic HB, no Feegar bourbon... 'Course, I might have guessed this lot wouldn't know a Feegar from a Klimfal if it ate 'em alive, but..." He readdressed the waitress, slipping off another series of strange syllables. He then indicated Bertram and the waitress let out a horrible, wheezy noise.

Rollie laughed warmly. And the Mathekite waitress continued laughing, because that's what the horrible noise was. In fact, Rollie and the waitress were both still laughing as she buzzed away.

It was hard to know just how ticked off to be without understanding what they'd said. "I think I was supposed to order," Bertram said.

"And if you'd started the Translachew when I'd told you," there was a glint in Rollie's eye, "you'd have heard me give your order, wouldn't you?"

Bertram felt a reflexive pang, like a willful child caught in a lie. He recognized it for what it was, though—a prime symptom of how complex things had grown. Perspective was slipping away. Bertram's critical thinking was shutting down. The unease felt very real.

"So." Bertram cleared his throat and forced himself to sound conversational. "Er, where are you from, exactly?"

Rollie didn't answer right away. He seemed to debate further verbal flogging, but then just settled on making a short derisive sound. "Okay, Ludlow, we'll play it your way. I'm from Hyphiz Delta. Fourth planet in the Hyphiz system." At Bertram's blank expression, he added, "If you're coming from Tryfe, you hang a bit of a left off of Alpha Centauri and then just—" He broke off, attention shifting to the front doors as someone new entered the establishment. Bertram noticed him tense, survey the situation, then relax again.

"See something?"

"No. And that bothers me." He took another careful glance around, and then turned back to Bertram. "I can't figure it. Why'd those sightless slaggards send us here? I highly doubt it's for the stellar service, the fine scenery and the great drinks value. So what then?" His eyes flicked to the Yellow Thing at Bertram's neck and he frowned, adding, "And why am I the only one asking these questions? Aren't you at all concerned?"

"About more things than I can name," Bertram told him.

"Well, then?"

He cleared his throat again. "So, um, hey—now that you've been released from your unfortunate incarceration, what are your plans for the future?"

Grumbling, Rollie helped himself to a handful of round, green snacks from a bowl in the center of the table. Over their crunch, he said, "Launch yourself, Ludlow."

"Hey, I'm not trying to condescend," Bertram insisted. "It's interesting. I mean, it's not like we really got to chat much before you, you know, shot me or anything."

Rollie considered this while clunking his booted feet onto an empty chair seat, one by one. "Vos Laegos," he said finally.

"Pardon?"

"I'll probably go to Vos Laegos. It's a planet. Y'know, hit the Simmiparlors, make up for everything I couldn't do in my luxurious ten-by-ten confinement cube…Then come to, rinse and repeat. Do that six or seven times, then sink into a hot *tchutsaaree* steak with cold *kaargoogk* dressing." He closed his eyes, savoring the image of alien dinners past. "I can almost see it melting."

Bertram feared they'd lose the thread in extra-terrestrial cuisine. "How about long-term?" he pressed. He wished he could take notes. They'd be helpful for future analysis.

"How about, why do you care?" The man's eyes opened and seemed to flicker. "You're still thinking you're in your head, aren't you, Ludlow? Or, rather, that I'm in your head, and you're completely out of it." He leaned across the table and poked Bertram in the chest. "Listen to me, Ludlow, if those Seers aren't dishing dung, mate—if they actually know what they're talking about—then I do pity your little planet."

Bertram scowled. "And why's that?"

"Because its great Tryfling savior's too fragging weak to face an uncomfortable truth. Too unevolved to even try and stretch his tiny mind around a concept so disturbingly vast. Instead, he's stalling for time and playing duck-and-cover." He dusted the snack crystals off his hands and settled back into his chair. "Might as well wave good-bye to it now, Ludlow. Bid Tryfe *paar too* and save yourself the pain later. Because you'll never get through the GCU like this." He shook his head. "I just hope most of your people are reconciled with their favorite deities, is all."

"And I'm sure they'd appreciate your concern," Bertram grumbled. He pushed at the pain hovering between his eyes. Savior or madman, he'd never felt more wearied and lost than he did now.

"Look," Rollie said finally, "it's nothing personal against your planet, Ludlow. In fact, I rather liked its unenlightened charm. Was as ego-centric as most backspace worlds, I s'pose, but certainly as good as any. Better, maybe."

"Is," Bertram said, "is."

"Is, then." He shrugged. "'Course, I'm not exactly a rep for popular opinion, am I? Most life-forms round the GCU wouldn't be able to pick your solar system from space salvage. I happen to appreciate the obscure, me." He offered Bertram the bowl of snacks, but Bertram wasn't really in the mood to imagine eating. "Anyway, I guess it's possible they're just pulling your trigger."

"Who?"

"The Seers. Making up all this 'Tryfe in Peril.' Having us on."

"Why would they do that?"

"Do I know? I'm just the A-to-B man. Or, rather, the A-to-B-to-C man. Hard to say if they're even half as powerful as everyone says they think they are." Rollie looked up over Bertram's head. "Ah, about time."

The Mathekite waitress hovered with a tray of drinks. She placed a tall, thin glass in front of Rollie. Then she began to heave the foot-wide, globe shaped, sherbet-colored creation of Bertram's. With half of a giant squash floating in it, there was still somehow room for a dozen tiny drink decorations, which danced and sang every time anyone touched the drink. Bertram peered around it to see Rollie's white crocodile grin glinting in the light of the bar.

Bertram felt oddly relieved his hallucination seemed to have a sense of humor. "Does it come with a diving board, or do I order that separately?"

"It's a nectricium bowl. Lowest booze content this side of Daglann-Da. Didn't know how your system'd react to anything stronger."

"Or smaller?"

"Enjoy." Chuckling, the alien raised his glass and took a long swig from it.

Bertram weeded through the chorusing drink decorations to locate a straw. He was just about to exchange the Translachew gum for it when, from somewhere in the bar, a single voice caught his attention.

Bertram froze, the straw dangling from his lower lip. "Did you hear that?"

Rollie clunked his already-empty glass to the table. "Hear what?"

Bertram waved him off and listened.

"...And so I told him..." continued the voice from somewhere in the bar.

"That," said Bertram. "I can't believe it—English!"

"No English there, mate," Rollie said. "I told you, you're lucky that I even know it. And I doubt anyone here could afford a projection translator. Must be the beckoning call of a refill you hear." He motioned to the waitress for a second round.

"I'm *sure* I heard something." And again, Bertram tuned into the rumble of alien gibberish trying to filter out that one familiar sound. It seemed like a long, long moment before it reached his ears again, and he leapt up from the table, almost overturning his chair. He stretched to scan the crowd.

"Um, Ludlow, what are you doing?"

"Thank God! Finally, some good news!" The elation Bertram felt now was greater than any he'd experienced in a long time. More than passing finals. More than getting his T.A. position. More than even getting that phone number of Rozz Mercer in the Murray Avenue Tavern.

But Rollie's pale blond brows drew sharply together in what, oddly enough, looked like genuine concern. As Bertram's host for the hallucination, obviously the man couldn't understand that some reality was seeping in, couldn't see that maybe the outside world had found a chink in the glass and sounds from home were actually, finally, beginning to get back through.

"Ludlow, it's the gum," said the captain. "The gum's kicking in, right? All of the languages can't synch at once. Sit down."

But Bertram was already dodging through a sea of oddities, following the sound like a shot, straight to the speaker in question.

He was surprised to discover the voice belonged to a lean humanoid male, with fair hair in thin wisps that gave the impression he was crowned with a low-flying cloud. From face to neck to arms, his skin looked thick, grooved and browned, like burled wood, or an ancient canyon wall. He spoke with an authoritative resonance that made Bertram wonder whether the man's companions were stone, stone-deaf or just stoned, as they sat unmoved and unmoving before the game board on their table.

"Excuse me," began Bertram. But the man carried on with animation and a deaf ear.

"It's a blasted shame what's happened to the industry," the man was insisting to his companions. "See, you got your Simulant pilots. Then you got your hired Organics. Not to mention, all sorts of newfangled security devices. Such that, nowadays, how can a fellah even know what to expect when he overtakes a freighter? I *ask* you. I mean, obviously, it's easy enough to dismantle a Simmi freighterman—I don't need to tell *you* mates the tricks. But it's only easy when you know that's what'll be behind the blasted hatch when you latch target and bust in, that's *my* point. You think you're dealing with a Simmi crew, but then find out the Organics called off the strike and it's back to work for the natural life-forms…Well, one minute you're trying standard Simmi disarm. And the next you're looking down the fragmenting end of an XJ-35." He fired off an imaginary shot from one knobby, tan finger. "Why, in my day—"

"And which millennium was that?" a voice asked, and Bertram made a quick step out of Rollie Tsmorlood's path.

The life-form at the table stopped in mid-sentence as he focused on the captain through the haze. His eyes sprang into sight from under its heavy creases. "Son of a Keeltsar! Rollie Tsmorlood, I cannot blasted believe it!"

He rose quickly, clapping Rollie on the back. Even the other two beings at the table came to life with words of greeting and surprise.

Rollie beamed at the man. "Backs, you old prib, no one's killed you yet?"

"Too fast for 'em, mate, too fast," laughed Backs.

"And just what in the name of Karnax are you boys doing in this system?" Rollie asked.

"We're a bit too popular in Quad Four right now, so we're killing time between jobs." Backs swung back into his seat. "Question is, where have you been hiding yourself? Don't tell me all those rumors were right and you'd actually got yourself life-merged again? Why, I'd been telling the fellahs here, after the last time, there was no way our boy Tsmorlood'd launch his freedom just to cohab with some jab. You make me a liar?"

"Never need me for that," Rollie said, moving an extra chair to the table. "It was confinement."

One of the life-forms groaned. The other nodded sympathetically as they made room in their circle.

"Where?" asked Backs.

"Rhobux-7."

"The penal colony? You poor slaggard."

"Rough one," agreed another gravely.

Rollie just offered the one-shouldered shrug. "Well, it was hardly lounging in the purple sands of Blumdec, but the place did have its benefits. Ended up heading KP. Decent supplies, chose my own menu, a nice kitchen unit. A little primitive, but then it is a blasted confinement center, isn't it?"

"And what's this?" one of them asked. He was a short, slim being with bluish-black, slicked-back hair. His eyes were hidden behind navy-tinted glasses, and his stark white face was hidden in a neatly-trimmed, navy-tinted beard.

He had indicated Bertram, and Bertram gave a start.

Rollie said, "This, Wilbree, is a Tryfling."

Wilbree's mouth dropped open. "I believe I've never seen one of those before," he breathed. With a small, trembling finger, he poked Bertram in the arm. "And I hardly believe I'm seeing one now."

The second life-form looked up from the gameboard with electric blue eyes behind thick, crystal-faceted lenses. The color reflected and flitted in the glass like tropical fish in a bowl. He took a draught of his drink. "A Tryfling? Hey wow, where'd ya get it?"

"Where do you think I got it, Fess? Snatched it up from one of the many Tryfling tour groups roaming the cosmos?" Rollie snapped. "I got it on Tryfe."

Fess pushed up his glasses with two of at least twenty fingers. Bertram almost couldn't look away, as the being simply sprawled with appendages of different shapes and sizes. It was to the point that Bertram wasn't sure where Fess left off and the chair began. "Whatcha gonna do with it?"

"Nothing, I got no use for it," said Rollie. "Anyway, it's not mine, is it?"

Wilbree's expression grew grave. "Better put it back then, before someone misses it." He turned to the game before him.

"I am not fragging putting it back, Wilbree," Rollie said in strained tones. "It's…it's got stuff to do, I don't know, I'm not involved anymore. Ask it yourself."

"Do you have stuff to do?" Wilbree asked Bertram gently.

Bertram blinked. Did he? He wasn't sure now. Somewhere along the way, Bertram began understanding languages other than the only tongue he'd ever thoroughly learned. He had a vague awareness that there were three different languages, and possibly two dialects, being bandied about at this table alone. And yet, it was as if they all somehow were one. It was very confusing.

"I…I think," he said, "I'm supposed to save Life As I Know It."

"Ohh," cooed Wilbree. "That's *lovely*. How do you plan to do it?"

Bertram opened his mouth to answer, then closed it again. This was seriously beginning to be a problem.

"Oh no, I've frightened it," Wilbree observed, concern creasing his brow. "I'm sorry, Rollie. I didn't know it was skittish."

"It—" Rollie exhaled and raked a hand through his choppy yellow hair. "*He. He* isn't. Look, mates," he said, "this is Bertram Ludlow. Ludlow, this is a group of beings I loosely refer to as friends. At my right is 'Backspace' Bungee, self-proclaimed scourge of the outer sectors. Backs, here, fancied himself my mentor half-a-century ago, when I was young and deluded and he was still an old slaggard. Taught me everything he knew about the intricate cosmic network of underground dealings. Then I met Fess and Wilbree here, and actually learned something useful."

"Unappreciative," Backs told Bertram. "He was always unappreciative. And not one molecule of respect. But you ask him. You just ask him where he'd be this minute if it hadn't been for me."

"'Still rotting in a third-galaxy confinement,'" chanted Fess and Wilbree.

"That's right," said Backs. "And you want to know why?"

Fess moved one of his playing pieces. "'Cause bail's kinda pricey these days?"

Backs threw a handful of snacks at him. "Because he's got no vision, that's why."

"I disagree," Rollie said, helping himself to Fess's drink. He flicked out a couple of errant snack-food pellets. "I can see through you."

"Ah, now, I'd be careful what I say here, boy," cautioned Backs with a grin. "You are, after all, talking to the future Official Leader of the Intergalactic Underworld."

At this, Rollie didn't even bother to hide his amusement. "Oh, is that so, now? The OLIU? I'm afraid I must have missed that Uninet flash in my confinement cell."

"What'd I tell you?" Backs appealed to the group with a wave of his arms. "Totally lacking in imagination." Over the beings' laughter, Backs explained, "It'll take a certain amount of effort to get there, of course. And I don't expect it to happen overnight. I predict it'll be a U-year or two down the road. But the merchandising rights, sponsorships, and endorsements alone make it a very tempting campaign on my part."

"If I didn't know better, I'd say you sound like a man who's serious." Rollie leaned back and thumped Fess's now-empty glass to the table. "Or off his orbit. Tell me this man isn't actually serious?" he asked Fess and Wilbree.

The pair snickered and bobbed their heads in affirmation.

"Running for OL-fraggin'-IU?"

Backs didn't answer, just folded his arms under a smug smile.

"Well, you *are* ancient; your brain was bound to go free-space at some point. But flamin' Altair, Backs. You really think you've got what it takes to sway public opinion, pull some major Underworld scores, and scrap that self-important slaggard, Zenith Skytreg?" Rollie asked. "Because, you know, I was rather hoping to do that last bit myself someday."

"Who's Zenith Skytreg?" asked Bertram quietly.

Fess cringed. "Aw, here we go..."

Backs was already gathering in a chair for Bertram, and motioning him into it. "Zenith Skytreg is the current Official Underworld

Leader for the whole GCU. Big into overblown PR and fundraising, but offering absolutely no substantial reform for our group interests."

"You make it sound like you're organized," Bertram observed. "Like a union."

"Union? Hardly. Smart Underworld dealing, son, is a craft. An *art.*"

"Formally, we're a Society," Rollie explained.

"And Skytreg has made a mockery of that art," continued Backs. "Publicly, he takes credit for all the key Underworld deals, the biggest unifications, the greatest in illegal acquisitions, and the most important uprisings..."

Nodding, Rollie input, "Last time I saw him, Skytreg was all over the Uninet, claiming to have personally led the Feegar Rebellion. The *Feegar Rebellion*, if you can believe that!" The other beings exclaimed with shock and outrage.

Bertram had never heard of the thing.

"Well, three of us fought in the fragging Feegar Rebellion," Rollie went on, "and I know firsthand that Skytreg wasn't out tending to the fallen Klimfals or rallying our troops to victory. Zenith Skytreg is a liar and a coward. All celebrity and no *tsarangees*. And he has sullied the good name of the Underworld by his example."

"He's very popular, though, isn't he?" said Wilbree. He moved one of his playing pieces on the board.

Backs grinned. "Not for long. That's what I've been saying. So shall we show him, fellahs?"

"Errr," Wilbree choked and coughed. "Show him? Show *Rollie?*" He tossed a quick, terrified expression to Fess. "Um, you all go ahead. I've got to...um...got to...Fess?"

"Gonna finish up here," Fess said, twirling a playing piece between his digits. "Wilbree's gonna owe me a serious pile of yoonie cards by the time I destroy him in this game. I'm not missing out."

"That's right," said Wilbree with a relieved grin. "Fess is going to destroy me. We'll catch you gentlemen later."

"Suit yourselves." Backs turned to go.

"But, say, Backs!" Fess called, putting up a thoughtful digit. "Ya sure you guys don't want to just hang around with us instead, and watch Wilbree's painful defeat?"

"It's certain to be dramatic," encouraged Wilbree.

"No, Fess," Backs said pointedly. "You know how I hate reruns."
He motioned to Rollie. "C'mere, Tsmorlood. Got something you'll
want to see."

✧

Bertram might as well have been invisible, and this total shift in
attention intrigued him. Out in back of the little domed bar, he tried
to tug the tail of his flannel shirt out of the now-closed hatch of
Backs' spacecraft.

His admittance had been close—almost painfully so—and he
could still hear the metallic ring of the door clanging shut just behind
him. What would it have sounded like with just a fraction more
Bertram in its path?

Cursing quietly under his breath, he unbuttoned the shirt and
slipped his arms from the sleeves, feeling chilly and strangely
vulnerable now in the underlying t-shirt of his prestigious Plus-
D'Argent University.

He'd assumed he'd been invited—and why not, really? It was *his*
hallucination. But now Bertram found himself hanging back in the
dark entryway, silent and unsure. Beyond him, Backs pressed a
button revealing a room, empty except for a few supply crates, crates
that sat like a small island in the room's center.

Backs grinned up at Rollie. "Ready, mate? You ready to see the
score that'll put me on the Underworld star charts?"

Arms folded, Rollie gave the crates a critical glance. "Plan to
impress me with your non-perishables, do you?"

But at Backs' voice command, the entire back wall dropped into
the floor, opening up a second storage area behind. Stacked straight
to the ceiling were rows of pressurized shipping boxes, all of them
emblazoned with the logo of a robotic hand holding what looked to
be a snack cake. They were marked with various sets of numbers.

Bertram was just trying to make sense of them, when Rolliam
Tsmorlood already had. He flew toward those boxes like a large,
wrathful raven. "DiversiDine Quad Four shipments? Sector Nine?"
he spat. He spun on Backs, eyes narrowed and jaw set. "Oh, 'It's a
craft. It's an art.' Very nice, you hypocrite! Might as well have just
fragged me permanent, you two-faced Deltan slaggard."

"Now, son, surely—"

He clenched and unclenched his hands, then turned to the cases once more, shaking his head. "Not enough companies in the blasted GCU for you, you have to go after *my* target group, in my assigned Quadrant, my Sector? Were you working it all along, or just when you thought I'd gone soft and left the game?"

"I—Well, it wasn't the first time you fell off the back of the GCU, kid, so—"

"And you dragged Fess and Wilbree in, too, didn't you?... No, don't even bother lying, it was written all over Wilbree's pasty face. Tell me—" Rollie seized Backs by the throat and shoved him up against the wall. He had pushed him to the rafters, removed Backs' gun and tossed it out of reach in one fleet move. "—What's to keep me from killing you as you stand?"

Backs' feet *were* well off the floor.

"You were out of circ, kid," Backs croaked, trying to strike a casual pose, despite his place on the wall. "Vanished. You could have been living large on Blumdec, life-merged to another young lady who didn't appreciate your career path, or sucked into a black hole clear across Quad Two, for all we knew." He gasped for another breath. "Way I see it, I was helping you out," he wheezed. "Picking up the slack."

"The slack," Rollie growled. "The slack." He dropped Backs and turned away, closing and unclosing his fists. "RegForce'll be picking you up, you flash this stuff around. You've just proven the Underworld's gone to rot. There's no solidarity, no honor anymore; someone'll spill. Then when DiversiDine learns their pretty packages took a detour... They aren't hesitant to haul in fellahs who cross them. Believe me, they're not as charitable as I am."

Bertram sighed quietly in the shadows. Backs sighed against the crates and massaged his purpling throat.

"In fact," Bertram caught an orange spark in Rollie's eye, "*I'm* not that charitable." He pulled the ergonomic gun from its holster and waved it generally at Backs and the crates. "Let's have a look and see if it's something I want."

At first Backs acted like it was a joke. Then Rollie aimed more precisely and Backs realized the wind had changed direction. "Now, come on, Rollie... Rollie... this was my big break. As you so often point out, I am not exactly young anymore. I may not get many more opportunities for OLIU."

"You can work on becoming OLIU with your next big score. I won't challenge you; you know I hate titles. Now open it," he said.

Frowning, grumbling, Backs pressed a panel on the side of a crate and the crate opened. From his vantage point, Bertram couldn't make out what the box contained, but Rollie stepped forward and peered right inside.

A smile spread across his face, slow and amazed.

And then he started to laugh.

"What?" asked Backs. "What's so funny?"

Now laughter rang out off of the metal ship walls. It was like it was the best joke anybody had ever heard, but Bertram hadn't caught the punchline.

Backs' face had drained of color under its indelible tan. "You've really lost it, Tsmorlood, you know that? You're zonked. You always were a little not right. But now you need to see somebody. Rhobux-7 fragged your mind."

"Soft drinks? A load of DiversiDine Entertainment Systems and Aeroponics *soft drinks?*" Rollie clapped Backs on the shoulder and holstered his gun. "Holy Karnax, Backs, you had me all worked up for nothing! You rip off the single biggest manufacturer of prime piratable goods…And is it holowatches? Or vis-us? Or the latest implantable phone seeds? No! You loot a freighter full of fizzy kiddie drinks. You were gypped, mate. What a scab kind of score. If I was you, I'd be blasted embarrassed to show my ugly face round the Underworld while toting this."

"Your ugly face, and I'd be embarrassed anywhere," Backs said, but without his previous ease. Realizing he'd lived to utter it, he nudged Rollie. "Really, Tsmorlood, how can you not love this? It's a brand new product, not even hit the shelves. I should be able to grab a pretty yoonie for something that's not yet been released. Not to mention the publicity it'll bring on Uninet news when DiversiDine reports the theft."

Rollie raised a doubtful eyebrow and picked up one of the bottles. "DrinkThis? They named it DrinkThis? Well, I'll say one thing for it: it's direct. You try it?"

"You know I leave the soda-pop to the little ones. You feel free, though. At least take one and save it. For posterity." Backs winked. "Be able to say you knew me when."

"Like I won't remember you long after you can't anymore, you old zonker." Rollie examined the bottle amusedly and, shaking his head, dropped it into the pocket of his coat. He looked up, only to spot Bertram's shirt dangling from the hatchway.

Backs zeroed in on it a moment after. "Where'd that come from?"

"It seems we have a guest." Rollie scanned the room, and it was no time before he'd settled his gaze on the shadows in the corner.

Bertram could only hold his breath and try to be very, very small.

"Ludlow, I see you," Rollie said. "And you can stop scrunching. You'll pull a muscle."

Bertram exhaled, straightened, and took a half-step into the light.

"Son of a Keeltsar," said Backs, hand to his forehead, "how long's he been?"

"Whole time, it looks like."

Bertram said, "Uh, well, the hatch was…" He hooked a thumb toward the hatch and how it was…

"Closed," observed Rollie.

"Um, yeah," said Bertram.

Backs grimaced. "What is the deal with this Tryfling, Tsmorlood? Did you get him on a bet or something?"

"Were it that simple," Rollie acknowledged. "And you're right, mate. This has gone way too far. Looks like I'm going to have to take care of it." Rollie stalked toward Bertram and twirled a dial on the wall, opening the hatch in the door. The plaid shirt tumbled to the floor and, as Bertram snatched it up, Rollie grabbed hold of his other arm and started ushering Bertram Ludlow down the ramp.

"Look, Rollie, don't. Don't 'take care of it,' um… It- it's already 'taken care of.' It's great, it's fine, it's practically fixed itself."

"We've a miscommunication," said Rollie quietly, "me and you."

"Oh, I don't think so."

"Real or delusion, you're under the misapprehension that just because the Seers bribed me to pluck you from the comfort of your primitive Tryfling home-unit and drop you into the cold, black expanse of the GCU, that I am in some small way responsible for you." Rollie's low, firm tone was actually more chilling than if he had been shouting.

"No, no, never," Bertram insisted.

"But I'm not the answer man, am I? I'm the A-to-B-to-C man. So this saving your planet gig? It's out of my range. Will it be natural disaster? Or war? Ten to one, it's just some fragged-up fantasy from three spaced-up wardens. So what I suggest you do is, raise a few yoonies, find an understanding cosmic tour guide, and just hire yourself a—" A large shadow fell over the ramp and they gaped up at a sleek, low-hovering space vehicle. "—Interplanetary Cruise Vessel," Rollie breathed.

"OOGON BUNGEE," buzzed the voice from the audio projection system. "HALT IN THE NAME OF THE PODUNK PEACE GUARDS." The pulse from the sound rattled Bertram's vital organs.

"Strange," Rollie whispered. "Local boys."

"And looks like they have a new toy, too," said Bertram, squinting at the gleaming, flawless ship surface. Flawless, except for the price tag still stuck to the side.

"OOGON BUNGEE, YOU ARE BEING PLACED IN OUR CUSTODY UNTIL YOU CAN BE EXPEDITED TO QUAD FOUR FOR A HEARING ON COUNTS OF PIRACY. DO YOU SUBMIT?"

Rollie called up to them, "I submit that if you'd learned to do a voice print or, perhaps, proper sneeze identification in that fancy contraption of yours, you'd see you've got the wrong fragging men."

"WE HAVE CORRECTLY IDENTIFIED THIS AS OOGON BUNGEE'S ICV. YOU HAVE NO CHOICE BUT TO SURRENDER."

"And what if we just bought this ICV from some guy out in Quad Four before we came here, eh?" asked Rollie. "That all the same to you, too?"

There was static for a moment, then transmission cut off abruptly.

The portals of Backs' ship were dark and still. Bertram wondered if Backs were in there, securing himself into storage with his stolen soda-pop.

There was some whirring from the Peace Guards' vehicle overhead. Bertram tried not to look nervous. Rollie gnawed at a fingernail in a bored way.

Then: "OUR COMPUTER-MATCHING SYSTEM CONFIRMS THAT WE HAVE MADE A MINOR MISIDENTIFICATION, AND THAT NEITHER OF YOU ARE POSITIVE VOICE PRINTS FOR OOGON BUNGEE."

"There you go," said Rollie.

"WE DO, HOWEVER, HAVE A POSITIVE A-LEVEL MATCH FOR ONE ROLLIAM TSMORLOOD, WHO WE SEE SHOULD

PRESENTLY BE SERVING A 300 U-YEAR SENTENCE FOR
FORCED ENTRY INTO PRIVATE PROPERTY, ILLEGAL
SEIZURE AND REMOVAL OF GOODS, USE OF AN
UNLICENSED ARMAMENT WITH CRIMINAL INTENT,
THREE POINTS OF ASSAULT, AND … OH, A *LOT* OF OTHER
STUFF." The voice sounded thrilled.

That happy, elated voice was the last thing Rollie and Bertram
heard before the Peace Guards figured out how to work the ship's
exterior stun ray. Bertram imagined vaguely, before his brain numbed
over, that they'd probably started working that one out the first day
they got the thing.

4

"Okay, 'Lock up'... Lock-up... Lock-up..." Bertram heard a sigh from somewhere beyond. "Hey, Zlotni, I don't see no 'Lock-up' listed."

"Try looking under 'Containment,' then," suggested someone, presumably Zlotni.

There was a pause. "Nothing. Why didn't this manual come on infopill?"

"Because I asked for print. I don't trust those infopills. I don't like putting foreign contaminants in my body."

All of Bertram's effort went toward turning his head, and the world did a 180 swivel with him. His stomach tried to turn itself inside out and expel the nothing Bertram still had left inside it.

A third voice piped up, sounding nervous. "Ohh, he's twitching! Hurry, Wezzag, one of 'em's twitching!"

"You want hurry, Nak? Here: you look for it, then." This was followed by a loud thump. "I miss our old cells, Zlotni. What was wrong with our old cells? And our guns, our old guns? And our old—"

"I've found it!" said Nak. "'For Arming the System.' Page 63!"

"Great, let's hear it."

Peace Guard Nak cleared her throat. "'Now that you finish install of Klinko LK-31 Prisoner Confinement System, kindly ready yourself to enter a very exiting new realm of inbreakable security. Please to welcome to the knowledge that, in proper use, the Klinko LK-31 will be always having for you a highest level of safety comfort with even your most dangerful apprehensions. It has specials super sensor to detect movement in confinement cell area. Also, it measure heart rate of cell occupant (if occupant is containing heart organ), as heart rate rise may indicate suspicious activity and nervousness in many life-form. Klinko LK-31 Prisoner Confinement System is unharmable to hand-laser shooting, flame, and extreme weather condition if outside in its placement…'"

Zlotni grunted. "Are you using Translachew on that at all?"

"Look," said Nak, "that's what it says."

"Skip a little," Zlotni told her.

Bertram opened an eye and could make out some blurry uniformed beings standing in the narrow hall on the other side of the bars. One was leaning over a technical manual roughly the size of a mini-fridge.

"'To begin good use of Klinko LK-31 Prisoner Confinement System, you are first to be finding the Klinko Prisoner Confinement System keypad.'" Nak looked up as one of her fellow Peace Guards motioned toward the shiny new keypad.

"Good," she continued. "'Once it is to be in your eyeball-looking, find yourself pushing the green Start button.'"

Wezzag reached over and depressed a button on a keypad mounted on the wall. A bulb embedded in the hallway ceiling went green, bathing the cell block in a weird, slimy glow. "Next?"

"'… But only after you to push the blue Clear button for clearing system…'"

Grumbling, Wezzag presumably pushed "Clear" and then the green button, which re-lit the hall light. "What now?"

"'Now enter sixteen-digit number code which you choose.'" Nak looked up. "Anybody got a number in mind?"

Zlotni handed Wezzag a slip of paper, and he keyed the numbers into the system.

"Okay. 'Now you are to be pressing the red Arm button.'"

Wezzag pressed the red button. The light in the hall shifted from the bright green to a warm, deep red.

"'And congratulations are to be had for your arming the system with good happy success,'" finished Nak.

Wezzag peered over her shoulder at the manual. "That's it? We've done it?"

Nak reread the passage, apparently determined that nothing was missed and, throwing her entire weight against the tome, managed to snap the giant book shut.

"Very nice, P.G.s," said Zlotni. "This here is a momentous day for us, and we should be real proud. Through the installation of this advanced prisoner confinement system, we've just taken another big step into the Greater Communicating Universe." He moved towards the cells and peered through the bars at Bertram, shiny black eyes in a determined scaly face. "All locked up and comfy? Don't worry, we won't forget about ya in here. When Tsmorlood wakes up, you can just let him know that we've called some old buddies of his to come and see him."

With a final satisfied glance at the bright red light, Zlotni turned and motioned the Peace Guards out of view. Down the corridor, the door clanged shut.

"Bleedin' Karnax, I thought they'd never leave," came Rollie's voice from somewhere inside the cell. A cot creaked. "Stunning sure is blasted hard on you Tryflings, innit? Wasn't even much of a hit they gave us, and you look chewed up and processed."

"You're..." Bertram forced his mouth to form words. It was easier now than the first time he'd been stunned, but it still sounded as if he were talking through paste. "I thought you were still out cold," said Bertram.

"Good," Rollie responded. He was standing by the bars now, trying to peer down the hall. "So how many? How many, do you s'pose? I heard three. Figure three Guards, and possibly more out front. Think this is the only passage in?"

Bertram began the struggle to prop himself up against the wall.

Rollie waved a hand absently at him. "No, no, don't strain yourself, we've time."

"For what? What do we have time for?"

Arms folded, Rollie gave a critical survey of the concrete ceiling. "Before the Deltan RegForce get here, of course."

Bertram sagged back against the pillow. "Refresh my memory?"

"Law enforcement. From Hyphiz Delta. My home planet."

Bertram rubbed half-numb fingers across his half-numb face. A trickle of drool curled from the corner of his mouth. "The 'old buddies.'"

"Sounds like they're being notified, if they haven't been already. All depends on if these local boys have learned to work the vis-u yet." Rollie glanced at the red light in the corridor and sniffed. "If they've *got* a vis-u."

Bertram peered through the mental fog. "So you're saying, you're still wanted back home, and I'm imprisoned here for, what, color commentary?"

"'Course not," Rollie said, examining the door's hinges, "you're an accessory."

"An accessory! To what? How am I accessorizing when *you* kidnapped *me*?"

"Well, that's hardly common knowledge, is it?" Rollie told him. "Ludlow, don't you understand? When we left Rhobux-7, the Seers didn't blank my archive. They didn't tell anyone they'd let me off. In the eyes of every law enforcement outfit in the fragging GCU, I am an escapee and you are an accomplice."

Bertram swallowed, feeling flushed, his stomach rolling from the heavy pulse that drummed behind his eyes. "But why would the Seers do that? It's a little extreme just because they can't get anyone else for kitchen detail, don't you think?"

"Better," Rollie corrected. "They can't get anyone better for kitchen detail." He peered at the heavy iron lock in the cell door. "But it doesn't matter. I won't be sent to Rhobux-7 for this one."

"That's right, the Seers said Altair," Bertram recalled. "Isn't that a star?"

"Altair-5, and it's a planet off that star." Rollie paced in front of the bars with nervous energy.

"Not exactly a day spa, I gathered."

Rollie stopped in mid-stride and faced Bertram, his expression drawn and tense. "Hyphiz Deltan parents tell their progeny if they misbehave, they'll be sent to Altair-5 to work the tarpits. It's blisteringly hot, shelterless, completely uninhabited, and infested with 4,000 of the most dangerous, ravenous, and eye-poppingly hideous examples of flora and fauna in the entire cosmos. Consider it my culture's equivalent of your Hell. Only this place has coordinates."

Bertram Ludlow grimaced and closed his eyes. His head felt better without the light, actually. It was easier to concentrate. "Do you think the Seers might've just made a mistake? An oversight, about the charges? I mean, maybe they didn't get around to it in time. Didn't realize it'd come to this."

"If they're to be believed, they maintain the lines of Fate, Ludlow. I'd say that's pretty tapped in to current events, wouldn't you?"

"Valid point," said Bertram. He swung the cot's pillow over his face as an added barrier to light. It smelled like sweat and some alien hair treatment, but he was past caring now. The blackness was soothing. He wondered if there were any GCU analgesics tailored to stun-gun migraines.

"You know," Bertram reflected, "just this week I was thinking how with my Ph.D. almost wrapped up, a research position ahead of me, and an amazing girl who actually seemed to like me, things were really looking good. Soon I could afford to expand my culinary horizons outside of the ramen genre. I was even planning to get an apartment above basement level; someplace where the holes in the walls, and around the windows, weren't spackled in with toothpaste. I was really looking forward to that. The windows bubble when it rains." He recalled too vividly the thin rivulets of minty water, trickling down the wall onto the green shag carpet. At least it smelled good.

"Yep, the Good Life was just about to kick in for ol' Bertram Ludlow," he went on wistfully. "I'd worked hard, made sacrifices, and the payoff was coming. But then that knock came at my door. Was it Opportunity knocking? Opportunity *pounding*, and I was lucky enough to be home? Nope. It was Delusion, dressed like a steampunk funeral guest." The stink of the pillow was getting to be too powerful. He tossed it off, coughing, and looked at the socked feet that lay splayed out before him. He'd never even gotten to grab his sneakers. The socks were dirty and worn through at the heel and toe. Bits of sand from Rhobux-7 had gotten crusted in, along with spilled drinks from the Podunk bar and a hundred other residues. "Now there are more holes than ever."

Rollie, he noticed, was stepping back into the cell, sliding the barred door behind him. "Should look into a pair of decent boots, then, if you aim to save your planet, yeah?" the alien suggested pleasantly.

Bertram looked at the bars. He looked at Rollie. "Where did you just come from?"

Rollie hooked his oddly-bent thumb toward the hallway. "Just the three of them out there, far as I can tell. And I located the vis-u." His face lit with amusement. "Bought some cheap do-it-yourself job and they've parts of it spread across the room. Best of all, they were sent the assembly instructions on video chip, which they can't read because they haven't got a video decryption device except for the vis-u. Stellar stuff."

"But the light." Bertram pointed at the red light in the ceiling. "The alarm, the Klinko Whatsis Confinement System…"

"Not on," Rollie said.

Bertram blinked. "Seriously?"

"Never was. The directions were wrong. Red is green. Green is red."

Bertram's mind glazed over. Green was red, red was green…

Rollie exhaled impatiently. "Red can't mean the thing is armed, Ludlow. In the Klinko star system, red is a color symbolizing welcome, contentment, emotional warmth, a new beginning. Never a color of warning."

"And green?"

"Shade of their entrails," Rollie answered. "Also panic, pain and, understandably, a pretty grisly death. Our Peace Guards seem to have overlooked that rather obvious point."

"Geez, the oversight," Bertram muttered.

Rollie sat down on one of the cots and turned his attention to the sole of his boot. "Should've got more intelligence on the species they buy from, is all. Common mistake in the GCU. We all rely too much on Translachew to do our work for us." Rollie slid something on the side of the boot's sole, and then began to twist off the heavy-treaded heel. "Life-forms blindly assume that intergalactic communication is just the same as intergalactic understanding. It's easier that way. Then we end up going to war over some grave cultural insult that we're all just so very surprised about." He slid back a panel and removed what looked to be a black polymer cylinder of about three inches long from a hollowed-out space in the bottom of his boot. He also retrieved a narrow L-shaped tube with a rubber stopper on its end and then two small disks—one a mirrored black and one of red glass. All of this, he set on the cot.

He flipped back the panel, screwed the heel back on, set the lock and went to work on the other boot. He did the same thing as with the first one: release, twist off and lift. From there he removed a second black piece of plastic—this one rectangular—along with a thimble-sized bag of some kind of dark blue sand. There was also a tiny capped bottle and what looked to be a crystalline marble. Bertram stared at the collection of objects on the cot.

"Prime example is when the Moegak military invaded right after the Jarendi Premier used a QR-260C vocal projection translator to greet their Empress," Rollie continued. "What the Jarendi Premier had planned to say was: 'O Great and Beneficent Empress, your fine reputation precedes you.' But with direct translation, what everyone heard live on the Uninet broadcast was: 'O Empress of Generous Size, you used to be a high-priced whore.'"

Rollie went on reassembling the second boot. "Runny mess that was. The interplanetary incident, the attack, the retaliation... Thousands dead on both sides and more product injury lawsuits against the translator manufacturer than you can shake an XJ-37 at." He shook his head as he rolled the crystal into the tube and capped it with the red glass disk. Pouring the sand into the other end of it, he closed it off with the black cap. He slid the flat piece into a notch in the tube until it clicked. In a matter of seconds, he'd hooked the L-shaped piece until it snapped in place, and sprung back on a hinge mechanism located in the cylinder. Bertram noticed that from the inside, the rubber knob was now stopping up a hole that went through the side of the chamber.

Rollie moved to the cell's sink and filled the tiny bottle with water. "Could have all been avoided with a little insight. And that's what you'll need if you plan to spend any time in the GCU, Ludlow: insight. Insight and preparation. Assume the worst because you'll get the worst. Get the best, and the worst just hasn't arrived yet. Prepare for 'em both and you've no regrets. But prepare for nothing, and you won't be able to hang the blame on Destiny." He closed up the bottle with a small, foil-like stopper and affixed it, upside down, into the hole on top of the cylinder. He delivered a chilling smile over the top of what now appeared to be some sort of gun. "Feel like a walk?"

Bertram first saw the Peace Guards' faces with any degree of clarity as he wavered in the doorway, his knees still uncertain. Their expressions were those of wide-eyed shock at the unexpected appearance of their former prisoners...

Or perhaps their lack of eyelids gave that impression.

Either way, Rollie had brandished his homemade hand-laser long before the Guards knew to draw theirs.

"This," he explained, "is a ZT-112G polymer-casing hydro-reactive collapsible hand-laser. It can frag the tail off a skaggett at 30 kroms. Imagine what it could do at this range." He motioned for them to toss their holsters to the floor, and three weapons clattered onto the ground instantly. Rollie surveyed the room. "My personals. Where are they?"

"Oh!" piped up Bertram, patting his chest where the missing item wasn't, "and my Yellow Thing!"

"And the Yellow Thing," Rollie added. In the right mood, Rollie could even make the phrase "Yellow Thing" sound menacing.

"Your RegForce is on their way, you know," one of the lawmen said. "We've contacted them."

"Oh, have you?" said the captain, flicking his gaze to the pile of vis-u parts on the floor. "What with? Two tin cans and a very long line to Hyphiz Delta?" But by now, Rollie's attention had drifted to a nearby cabinet. Wordlessly pressing the collapsible hand-laser into Bertram's palm, he stepped over to investigate the cabinet's drawers.

Bertram was bewildered to find the gun in his grasp. It was light, with a surprisingly good, solid grip. Not that Bertram knew from grips. His gun-savvy was pretty limited to video game assaults and the local amusement park shooting gallery.

The Peace Guards seemed to pick up on a certain hesitation of his, too, and their black eyes bored through him, eking out his inexperience with every second. He looked to Rollie's back, wondering how long he'd have to hold the fort. But the captain was still busy digging through the cabinet, treating paperwork and information chips to brief moments of flight.

Bertram turned back to the Guards, greeting them brightly. "Um, hey there!" He offered his biggest, most congenial smile. "Wow, I bet you guys are damned curious to learn how we got out."

But they were silent. There were just the dark eyes, eyes like black holes themselves, staring, drawing him in, pulling at his resolve and stretching it thin.

"Er, red was green," Bertram explained over the barrel of the laser. His palms were sweating.

He wrenched his gaze from the Peace Guards and gave another status check on Rollie, who was now booting the bottom drawer shut and attacking a second set of cabinets. "Green was red," Bertram went on.

The Guards exchanged glances, their lid-less eyes staring onward. One of them made a move as if to step forward, but Bertram found himself waving the gun.

"Okay, don't push me, Sleestak," he warned, his smile shaking away. "My head's killing me and I have a case of spacelag like you wouldn't believe."

From across the room, Rollie held aloft two sealed and labeled bags, one carrying a single item and the other stuffed to the seams. "Got 'em!" He tossed the bag with the Yellow Thing to Bertram, then withdrew a hand-laser from his own extensive bag of stuff. Bertram watched in fascination as the man from Hyphiz Delta swiftly directed the laser on each of the Peace Guards' weapons. And one by one, the weapons collapsed into puddles of liquid metal on the floor.

Then he flipped a switch in the handle and repeated the task, this time targeting the Peace Guards. Now *they* appeared to melt, transforming into scaly skin-sacks of organs and rubber bones, gelatinous piles left to dry out on the tile flooring.

Bertram had never seen vertebrates look more inverted. It was all so real. So vividly real. He found himself just pointing and stammering. "Oh God! Oh God, oh Lordy, oh God, Jesus, holy shit, Lord…" He knew the Deltan was a little volatile. But he had never imagined this.

"Time to haul, Ludlow," Rollie said, and after what he'd just witnessed, Bertram wasn't about to argue. Gagging and retching, he let himself be directed out through the front door.

They were only outside for a moment before the alien went to work fusing the door shut with that same laser. "Jesus, Rollie, holy shit, man…" He forced himself to catch his breath. His heart was doing the Pogo. "Look, I don't want to get on your bad side here, bro, but you dissolved them into Jell-O. Isn't that *enough*?"

Rollie just gave an unreassuring smile and headed for the Intergalactic Cruise Vessel impound.

"You made me into a fugitive," Bertram said.

With the spacecraft in-flight and stabilized, the alien was busy spilling the last of his personal possessions from the bag onto the table. He did it just as calmly as if he were sifting through a box of puzzle pieces.

"*Before... before* we might have just gotten off on explaining your early release from prison as an oversight—some confusion—a little mistake, you know? But now, *now...*" Bertram shook his head. "Jail break? Totally liquefying the local police? Entombing their remains in the station?" Bertram felt like he couldn't breathe again. Was it possible to hyperventilate during a hallucination? He didn't know. He was so out of his league with this.

Rollie was buckling on a holster.

"Damn it, you *liquefied* them, Rollie. Sealed the evidence in the jailhouse and—" Bertram gasped, "—sweet Jesus, I covered them!" Bertram sunk into a seat. "What was I thinking? I covered them while you ransacked their file drawers."

The captain busied himself reseating lasers into various housings, gadgets to various pockets.

"And now I'm a fugitive," Bertram said, tossing up his hands in defeat. "Maybe it's symbolic of running away from something, some fear. The pressure to succeed, the working world, or getting older and finally having to, I don't know, get a mortgage and stop watching so much hockey."

"How about life in confinement?" Rollie suggested, adding a dagger to a sheath.

Bertram frowned. How many weapons did he have, anyway? He shook his head. "The question is, what am I running away *from*? Until we figure that out and address it, well...I...I just don't see this coming to a satisfactory conclusion." Bertram looked out the hatch window. "Where are we headed?"

"To get some real questions answered," Rollie said. "Questions for three back-stabbing Seers."

"Rhobux-7?"

"We should be just about there," Rollie said. "You look out that portal and you'll see it in a minute."

Bertram moved to the window and peered out at the fabric of space. Waited, waited, waited...

"I'm not seeing it."

"It'll be coming up there on the port side."

"Sure, port." Bertram tried to remember.

Rollie rolled his eyes. "Your left."

Waiting, waiting...Bertram chewed absently on a thumb-nail. "What does Rhobux-7 look like again?"

Rollie growled. "Blast it, Ludlow, it's the great big rustish planet out there plain as…" He stopped, gazing out of the portal with his eyes brightly orange and wide, an expression of total unguarded surprise that Bertram had never imagined he'd witness. The man stammered something in a language even Translachew couldn't grasp, and darted to the cockpit.

Bertram followed, watching, as the Hyphiz Deltan moved from meter to meter, tapping this one and that—the taps gaining more force as he proceeded down the line. Bertram dodged as Rollie reached around him to get into a metal box on the right, pulling out what looked to be some kind of flexible chart.

Rollie spread the thin digital grid out across the control panel, smoothing it out with a hand and looking from it to the sight before him. He stood there comparing the chart to the universe outside for a long, long time.

Finally, Rollie whispered, "Well, I'll be fragged."

Bertram waited.

"It's gone, Ludlow," Rollie said. "It's just…" He held out empty hands before him. The grid rolled itself back into a tube and toppled to the floor. "Gone."

"Rhobux-7 is gone," Bertram said.

Rollie opened his mouth as if to say something, closed it, ran a shaky hand through his hair, and nodded.

"The *planet* of Rhobux-7 is gone," Bertram clarified.

"Well, what would you say, Ludlow?" Rollie pointed. "There's Rhobux-6 and if you look beyond, you can make out Rhobux-5." He shook his head. "I don't know. I'm as shocked as you are."

Bertram found it a little unnerving to hear anyone was as shocked as he was. Especially not a guy who had just unhesitatingly melted several innocent officers into pudding. And when Bertram spoke, it was more to console himself than anything else. "Could it have been… blown up, or something?"

"Yes," Rollie said quietly, "blown up, yes, absolutely could be blown up. But even so, it wouldn't just vanish, would it? There would be fragments." His voice was beginning to show signs of strain. "Bits of matter floating all round the system. Bleedin' Karnax, how come there aren't any fragments?"

Bertram looked. No, no fragments. And then his eyes zeroed in on something. "Well, what's that?"

Rollie leaned in. Bertram leaned in. Yes, there was definitely something small out there. One smallish thing where Rhobux-7 used to be.

So Rollie tossed himself into the pilot's chair and moved the ship in closer. He directed the ship's scopes to focus in. A magnified area formed in the window-screen. "It appears to be..."

"Yes?"

"...A sign."

And the sign read:

**You have reached the former location of Rhobux-7.
Sorry our planet's not able to come to these coordinates right now, but leave us a message at our Uninet site—
uninet.seersofrhobux.rbx.7.q1.gcu—
and we'll be sure to get back to you.**

**For metaphysical emergencies,
visit our fellow prophets in the Nett star system.**

Thanks for stopping by!

"Nett?!" Rollie snarled. "The Nett system is all the blasted way in Quad Three. We'll be trekking half way across the fragging GCU to get there. And even then, who's to say their colleagues on Nett won't have vanished only to greet us with a sign that reads, 'Sorry, we're not in. Go see the fragging Seers of Rhobux-blasted-7'?"

"You could leave them a message."

"Oh, sure, and say what? 'This is Rollie Tsmorlood, did you by chance forget something on your To-Do list?'"

Bertram acknowledged that wasn't completely practical. "Guess it's Nett or it's nothing, then," he said.

Rollie gave some low sound from the back of his throat. "We're going to need some supplies."

5

Mimsi Grabbitz guided the interplanetary cruise vessel closer to the swirly blue-and-white planet, making sure to sweep in on an angle that used the light of the system's central star to display the orb to its best advantage. "It really is a cosmic opportunity, you know," she confided. "I can't emphasize enough how rarely properties like this come along."

Her passenger gave the kind of "hmm" that held only polite interest; it offered no real feedback.

Inwardly, she sighed. These days, clients all acted like she should have intra-cranial cognitive downloading abilities for their secret needs and desires. Like even though they might *say* they wanted a sky-tower rental situation with a two-moon view, she should just know what they *really* wanted was a dome-encapsuled bubble in Ragul-Sfera's rural district.

And, though she simply hated to stereotype, these indigenous Ottoframans were the *worst*. They all *claimed* they wanted to leave Ottofram and plant themselves in new territory. But the moment she'd try to show them anything beyond some simple glass walls in a plain patch on their old turf, there they were: digging their heels in and insisting they only wanted a nice quiet sunroom on their home planet.

She wasn't sure the same could be said of Eudicot T'murp, of course. After all, he was a Name. He was an Innovator. He was DiversiDine Entertainment Systems and Aeroponics.

But seeing him sit there in her passenger seat, he really did look like the average middle-aged Cardoon you might pass in the street. The soft gray-green complexion. The dark green hair starting to flower a little purple at the temples. The nice but modest suit. You'd never know the man had more yoonies to his credit than some small galaxies.

She would just have to wait and see how the day went. Anyway, no one could ever say that Mimsi Grabbitz discriminated; she was willing to make money off of positively *anybody*.

They swooped in closer to the planet's surface, the swirls of white steadily being replaced by the browns and vivid greens of the land. "Note the planet's fine color. It's a nice look just to have in your portfolio, really, even if you weren't planning to do anything specific with it just yet. And it is virtually guaranteed that as the GCU expands, this will be prime property."

"Virtually" was one of those delightfully vague words Mimsi Grabbitz loved to use. Words that helped avoid a universe of lawsuits. Ah, if only to have more of them. Non-committal, positive, non-binding…

She glanced sidelong at Eudicot T'murp. He seemed more entranced by the planet's single sun, a smallish star as suns went, than the actual property. Still, she wouldn't lose hope. That's what made her a trillion-yoonie agent. That's what made her Alternate Realty's Employee of the Month.

"It is, of course, a unique fixer-upper," she explained. "Perfect in the hands of someone like yourself, who can see its innate merit. It does need to be stripped of some pollutants and have a little time to replenish its natural resources. Also, there are some native life-forms—some Tryfe-humans—who have, as of yet, to become a part of the Greater Communicating Universe. I think, however, you'll find that they can quite easily be disposed of. If the seller accepts your bid for Tryfe, I'll gladly put you in touch with a good extermination service who can do either a part of the planet, or the whole world, depending on your needs. Also, they do tenting, so it's friendly to the other planets in the solar system."

"Actually," said Eudicot T'murp, "my interest in this world lies mainly *in* the Tryfe-humans."

"*Really!*" chirped Mimsi. This was an unexpected turn of events. She'd been sure T'murp was looking to expand the manufacturing facilities of DiversiDine Entertainment Systems and Aeroponics.

Possibly, to place the factories somewhere well-away from anyone that actually mattered, or where they'd spoil the view. She had misjudged. "Well, I'm sure you'll find the Tryflings to be high-quality life-forms that will only help the planet appreciate as the GCU becomes—"

But T'murp was laughing now, a warm rustling sound. "Crumblin' craters, Mimsi," he exclaimed, "you put any more spin on that patter of yours, it'll go clear off its axis!" Still chuckling in a way she did not currently share, he wiped merry moisture from his eyes, and nudged her in a congenial way. "Aw, I'm sorry, Mimsi. It's just I already know quite a bit about the Tryfe-humans. I've done my research and I've spent a little time observing. They're highly-suggestible, optimistic, largely unaware, and perfectly suitable for a pet project of mine."

"Oh, and that is?"

"No offense, but I like to keep things pretty zipped tight to the ol' astro-togs." He patted the breast of that modest suit. "I *can* tell you, I'm mainly interested in their herd instinct. Their need for group validation is one of the strongest I've seen. They become very erratic over perceived threat to their status quo. And they go to great lengths to set comfortable, nurturing boundaries for themselves that each Tryfling is strongly pressured to follow." His face had flushed a darker green in his enthusiasm for the subject.

"*Really!*" Mimsi said again.

"Most interesting—to me, anyway—is how this relates to the way they prefer to retro-fit truths based on preconceived notions, even in the face of facts. Yes, I've had my teams run the numbers on this, and all data suggests a large chunk of their population will provide a nearly perfect test case for the marketing of one of my enterprises."

Mimsi gave him her Intrigued Face. It was harder to do since the 259th aesthetic facial reconstruction. In fact, after the last 23 surgeries, mostly she just managed somewhere between Dazed and Jabbed-by-a-Sharp-Object. But if she could close one eye just slightly, and jut out her lower lip, it seemed to work almost as well as actual emotive expression. At the moment, her face looked a lot like an introspective beachball.

"I have another backspace group—very resistant, very self-determined—that's evolved an entirely different set of reactions to new information, ideas and, of course, product advertising," continued T'murp. "That's why the Tryfe people appeal to me. It's for contrast purposes. Double-blind tests. If I can get the attention of both groups through user testing, think of the marketshare!

"Also, y'know," he continued with a confidential grin, "the Tryfe people are just so gosh-darned *funny*. Sweaters on small fur-bearing animals? Rushing down mountains on planks for fun, just to return to the top again?" He gave another jovial laugh, one that seemed to come straight from inside the belly. "You can't make up stuff like that—Backspace Reality at its finest!"

"Programming potential, hmm?" probed the realtor.

"Zipped tight to the astro-togs, Mimsi," he said, winking. "Zipped tight to the astro-togs."

The Interested Face that Mimsi had been wearing inadvertently triggered some thinking of her own. She would have frowned introspectively, if those muscles hadn't been aesthetically cut 20 years ago. "So, if you don't mind my asking, dear: since you already know all about Tryfe and its humans, why did you want me to show you the planet?"

"Well, I feel ashamed to admit it, Mimsi. It was sort of a pretext," said T'murp, his fronds curling a little at the edges. "I was actually hoping you'd be able tell me something about the planet's current owner."

"Oh, I simply c—"

"Mimsi, now, you know all the bidders have been asked to make presentations on our plans for the place. And presumably the one with the most appeal gets to buy the planet. It's a zonky process, to my thinking. After all, I could pay whatever the seller asked. What's the point behind it?"

"Mr. T'murp now, I'm not at liberty to say and—"

"It would help me and my marketing team," continued T'murp, "to know who, exactly, we were dealing with."

Here, Mimsi put on her Wide-Eyed and Sincere Face. This allowed her to relax from the strain of all that lip-extending and eye-closing. "Oh, now, Mr. T'murp, I would *love* to help you with that. Really, I would. But I'm afraid in this particular case, Alternate Realty is just not allowed to reveal the identity of our client."

He started to speak, but she put up a halting hand. "I know. Believe me, I do. It *is* highly unusual in the industry. And I'm sympathetic to your frustrations. But we've had to assure our client the utmost in privacy for this," she said. She pulled the ICV over a nice mountain range. The sun was just rising over them, purple mountains majesties and all that. "To be honest with you, even I don't know who it is. This assignment goes farther up the chain of command than I do."

"Then I hope you won't mind if I take it up with your management," said T'murp.

"Be my guest," Mimsi told him, minding just a little. "I agree with you completely. And I do wish I could help." She pulled in low over an area of flat, golden fields. "Now. Since we have come all this way, would you like to just pop by one of the Tryfling sites I'd scouted out for you?"

Eudicot T'murp offered that mild, homegrown boy smile that easily made her forget he was one of the most powerful business minds in the GCU. "Well, as long as we're here, and it's not going to cause a problem. I know how important it is to be subtle about these things. Tryflings are very susceptible to outside stimulii."

"Oh, don't you worry about that. Alternate Realty is all about subtlety," said Mimsi, coming in for landing.

Robert Randall Rodell, better known to friends and family as "Triple-R," liked to watch the bats flap around at night. He'd sit out on that back porch of his with a cold mojito (mojitos had just become all the rage in Whipplefork, Iowa) while the bats flapped over the cornfield, their fleshy wings beating the sky.

He often thought about them, those bats. Whether they ever tried to get up to those stars that seemed to hang so high over their furry backs. He wondered how far they could get up to the heavens and what they sensed from up there.

Oh, they probably didn't appreciate it, them being bats and blind and all. Not taking advantage of their advantage, not seeing the freedom in their flight. He often wondered what else was up there in the great, big blackness. What was looking down on those bats, and on him, and what it was thinking. If anything.

"Triple-R?" called his wife. "You coming in?" He could hear her over the sounds of the TV, which suddenly stopped with a click. Bonnie's slippers scuffed and creaked around the house.

"Not just yet, hon. You go ahead." Such a big sky, he thought, as he thought every night. A big sky and those bats, they didn't appreciate it. And Bonnie, God bless her, she hardly looked at it either, anymore. The last time she'd sat out there with him, was when he'd asked what she'd thought was out there. Out there in the big sky. And Bonnie had bit that lower lip of hers like she did when she was thinking of something real hard. And she'd taken a sip of her mojito, and she was quiet for a long while, head on his shoulder.

Finally she said, "Well, Farmers Flats, I guess, Triple-R." And she pointed at the skyline. "Right past Jim Willoughby's and Marlon Sample's." And she'd nodded, satisfied with her answer. Then she'd handed him her mojito glass, stood up, and kissed his cheek. She went inside to watch one of those reality programs that had gotten so big. And Triple-R figured she was probably right, it was Farmers Flats.

He sighed because, practically, that's all there needed to be.

But when the light got brighter in the September night sky, and one of the stars seemed to be coming down to pay a visit, Triple-R was pretty sure this wasn't a crop-duster on its way from Jim Willoughby's, Marlon Sample's or Farmers Flats at all. It swooped in looking every bit like some airborne luxury car, all chromey and shiny black, and probably with all the options.

And as it got closer, Triple-R saw how big it was, so big, why nearly ten times the size of the crop-duster and looking pretty determined to settle in the cornfield. It didn't have any wings, any propeller, and had that finely-designed sleek look that Ben Nebley had to his Viper. And even though Ben Nebley had been the talk of Farmers Flats for buying something so damned impractical while not a person for miles wasn't salivating at the sight of it, Ben Nebley's Viper was a beater by comparison.

Sure enough, this flying object, this Viper from the heavens, it settled smack in the cornfield and Triple-R stood there a minute, fixed on its gleaming exterior. He started to croak out Bonnie's name to come and see, but she was probably in putting cold cream on her face, and would only be fussing about the stalks crushed under the weight of the thing.

With a hiss, the ship seemed to settle and a hatch began to open. A sliver of light cracked into a wide open door. Alien space craft: the kind of thing that only ends up in the middle of nowhere. Or Whipplefork, Iowa.

Triple-R wasn't afraid, though. It seemed he'd been leading up to this for a while. He stepped off the porch and started across the yard toward the field, finding himself buttoning the top couple of buttons on his shirt, tucking his tail into his jeans and smoothing out his hair a little. This was the monumentous occasion for him personally, for Whipplefork and—heck, for the whole darned planet Earth. Triple-R wanted to at least make a good first impression.

Two extra-terrestrials were standing by the ship now. They looked to be a male and female respectively—at least by Whipplefork conventions—though they sure didn't seem too Earthly by other standards.

The woman had this face that reminded him of a balloon, oblong, stretched smooth and so shiny, it'd squeak if you kissed her. Her lips were pulled into this rubber-pink unyielding smile, and her hair seemed to perch on this head as if it weren't quite attached.

The man was funny, too, though not for the same reasons; he had a gray-green look to his face and hands, and his face extended straight into layers of some leafy-like points that rose up almost like a crown. Around the rim of this was a soft violet haze. On his personage was a fine woven suit of green and gray.

Triple-R stood a few paces away, considering a minute what he wanted to say. He hadn't been much of a talker in his 37 years, and now that he was going to be the first guy to communicate with aliens, he wished he'd been more of a conversationalist. Earth needed someone who could say something profound, something that would represent the locals as they deserved to be represented to the Universe. Like maybe Jeff Nesbitt who worked at the mayor's office and wrote the speeches. Or Annie Oleson down at the Gazette.

But without Jeff or Annie, Triple-R had to shoulder the responsibility himself. And he imagined somebody had better say something pretty soon. He briefly considered all those *X-Files* episodes, but there was nothing good in that. Finally, he just settled on being himself.

"Hi," he said, with a tenuous wave. "Welcome to my cornfield." It wasn't fancy, but it was honest and sincere. And Triple-R hoped that would be enough to at least start things off on the right foot.

The aliens stood there a moment more. Triple-R pretty much had imagined they wouldn't say, "We come in peace," or "Take us to your leader," or some such thing, since aliens would have to be a little more clever than your standard B-movie writer.

But he wasn't really prepared for what they did say.

"So they really all will come with the planet, at no extra charge?" the man asked, looking straight at him.

"Pardon?" said Triple-R. He'd understood it. It sure wasn't in English—and it seemed to be emanating from some sort of mechanical device on the alien—but Triple-R had understood it. He just didn't know how to answer.

"That's right," said the woman, her rubber smile pulled just a bit wider. "It's one deal: the property and all its resources and inhabitants. All a part of its atmospheric charm."

"Um, hi," the Earth man tried again. "I'm Rob Rodell, and this is Whipplefork, Iowa. United States. Earth." He didn't want to extend his hand in case that was a sign of insult where they came from. Better to err on the side of caution. "So where are you all from? Pretty far from the looks of things." He laughed nervously. "Can I, um, get you a mojito?"

"Carbon-based, too," said the alien man, approvingly. "Carbon-based life-forms with a basic humanoid structure. That adds some versatility."

"Stellar," said the woman, her head bobbing. "So you're still planning on making the bid, then?"

"Who should I speak with at your agency regarding the current owner?" asked the alien man.

The woman's smile faltered for a moment, and Triple-R wondered if her head would pop. "That would be Ms. Magglestig, Mr. T'murp. She's our branch manager."

"I'd just feel better knowing who I was dealing with," said the alien called T'murp.

"You know," the woman continued, "if you're truly uncomfortable about the arrangement, my agency would be more than happy to find some alternate investment property. One more fully suited to your tastes?"

"It just has so much potential," T'murp admitted.

"It's virtually *screaming* with potential," agreed the woman.

Triple-R tugged at his collar, not overly comfortable with the sound of that screaming part. He wasn't sure why.

"Well," said T'murp, "thanks a heckuva lot, Mimsi, for your time and for the tour."

"It was my pleasure," and the woman turned and headed toward the ship. The man smiled to himself a moment, then followed.

"Wait!" said Triple-R. "You're going? Don't you want to have a cultural exchange? Impart ideas for intergalactic peace or something?"

"No, no," said the man, through the translator, "that won't be necessary."

"Well…" Triple-R looked back at his home and then to the ship, feeling an emptiness in his chest that seemed almost the size of space itself. "Don't you want to abduct me?"

"Blazing stars, no!" exclaimed the woman, "I just had the upholstery cleaned."

"What about a hair sample? A tissue sample?"

The woman was heading up the ramp, quickly. The man said, "Thank you, no; we're good for now," and vanished into the craft.

"Probes?" asked Triple-R weakly. His disappointment was manifest now. It wasn't that he was so very jazzed about probing, but it was an alien encounter. There just had to be more somehow.

The woman waved, "Okay, take care." The ramp disappeared, the hatch closed and the spaceship silently began to rise off of the crushed cornstalks. Triple-R watched it rise up into the sky, all black and silver and shiny, like some big lit bat. He watched it until it was nothing but a vague flicker, and then it was gone.

He sighed and slowly headed back toward the house. The night sky would never be the same.

Excerpt from:

How to Gain Pals and Sway Life-forms in Cosmic Commerce
Chapter Seven

With permission from the
Eddisun Center for Ideas, Interceptive Marketing and Cliché Prevention

DiversiDine Entertainment Systems and Aeroponics: The Captivating Case for Invasive, Cross-Pollination Marketing

Overview

They're the delights we devour while watching holovision and the holovisions we buy. It's the Uninet programming that binds us to our seats and the product promos scripted right into our favorite shows.

It has a choke-hold on our daily lives from Alpuck-2 to Zerplix-37Q and we savor each second as we gasp for air.

What is it? It's the clever cross-pollination marketing of **Eudicot T'murp**, founder and CEO of **DiversiDine Entertainment Systems and Aeroponics**.

Newsmillenium voted T'murp "Life-form of the Year" eleven times to-date. *Universal News and Worlds Reports* named him one of the "Top Ten Inter-Galactic Visionaries Ever, Even of Those Who Died Tragically." *Rational GeoGalactic* called his business "The greatest addition to modern universal society since the ICV gravity field." And the *Dogstar* teen Uninet channel voted him "Most Snarggable Ear Lobes" two U-years running. (Eddisun Center, Data on File.)

Yet how has Eudicot T'murp, this daring darling of DiversiDine, raked in these accolades? How has he taken the smallest seed of an idea and nurtured it into flowering good fortune? In this chapter, we'll examine how T'murp began with one simple innovation and turned it into a vast network that's quietly wrapped around consumers and won't let go. And we'll even shovel up some techniques *you* can use to spread over your own marketing strategies!

Deep Roots in Ottoframan Frugality

Eudicot T'murp broke pod to Cardoon parents, Harb and Fissel, in a simple one-story greenhouse in South Klorofil on the semi-arid planet of Ottofram. There, the indigenous Cardoon people worked to cultivate the soil, and make the most of the produce they grew. Stems, leaves, seeds, roots: the farmers wasted nothing. And it was this background that led young Eudicot T'murp to take a fresh look at Cardoon cuisine. (*Eudicot T'murp: Leaf and Let Leaf.* Eudicot T'murp. RP: 11.)

Fertile Imagination Spreads Spores for Snackin'

A favorite delicacy of Cardoon children was the "smorg," a mottled brown spherical fungus with a sweet and flavorful spore-filled center. The fungus was filling, cheap, easy to grow, and portable.

Why, wondered the teenaged T'murp, couldn't they export this myecological munchy and share it with other hungry life-forms across the GCU? Its sales could do wonders for their people. It could fund bigger greenhouses, expanded roads, and planet-wide Uninet access. "Back in those days, we only had one local station: *Germination Live*," recalled T'murp. "All germination, all day. You ever tune in to watch a seedling grow hour after hour? Nah, me neither. I knew we needed more contact with the GCU. And I had this feeling it needed us, too." (*Eudicot T'murp: Leaf and Let Leaf.* Eudicot T'murp. RP: 21.)

But when T'murp and his family pitched the smorg to the people on neighboring planets, the response was surprisingly cold. "Turns out, the smorg looked too much like the speckled poisonous plants they had on their own worlds," said T'murp. "And the idea of fungus for dessert... They just couldn't get past it."

Yet T'murp had some other tricks up his fronds. "I figured if looks were the main sticking point, we could work on that. So that's when I got a new hobby: smorg bio-reengineering." (*Eudicot T'murp: Leaf and Let Leaf.* Eudicot T'murp. RP: 27.)

It took nearly a U-decade of development, 400 failed attempts, and several months of market positioning, but Eudicot T'murp transformed the dangerous-looking fungus into the creamy-white Smorg® "cake" that's beloved today. Suddenly, the Smorg won the Ottofram City Agricultural Days' "Food of the Year" award. It teased taste buds as a favorite at the Aeroponic Gastronomy Club Annual Meeting. And it ultimately exploded into the Quad Four Comestibles Show and Expo when it was voted "Most Likely to be Stashed Away

JENN THORSON

Selfishly and Eaten at Two a.m." (*Eudicot T'murp: Leaf and Let Leaf.* Eudicot T'murp. RP: 39.)

Branching Out with New Product Lines

Soon South Klorofil became a bustling aeroponic agriculture town. Yet Eudicot T'murp felt he could do more. He examined other traditional Cardoon delicacies for their own unique marketing potential and soon Sleemy Snaps®, Flinky Rolls® and Frallip Squash® joined the Smorg snack family. (*Eudicot T'murp: Leaf and Let Leaf.* Eudicot T'murp. RP: 75.)

By this time, T'murp had moved from the family's tidy little greenhouse into an elegant five-story glass domicile. T'murp's family was happy and comfortable, and his city thrived. Yet T'murp worried that the GCU's enthusiasm for Smorgs was just another passing fancy. "Through our new Uninet access, I saw the rise and demolecularization of trends on an hourly basis," said T'murp. "The market was fickle. I knew my products could only stay on-top if consumers couldn't get away from them." (*Eudicot T'murp: Leaf and Let Leaf.* Eudicot T'murp. RP: 84.)

So T'murp made two purchases: the GCUnivision Holotheaters, a company with entertainment megaplexes across most GCU worlds; and StarLite Productions, a unimedia development and marketing company responsible for blockbusters like *Epochageddon Eclipse* and hit Uninet programs like *Qeeping Up with the Qeegles.* (*Eudicot T'murp: Leaf and Let Leaf.* Eudicot T'murp. RP: 93.)

Drawing everything under a canopy now called "DiversiDine Entertainment Systems and Aeroponics," T'murp's holotheaters offered entertainment otherwise unavailable on the Uninet—the first information of its kind intentionally disconnected from Uninet access since the second GCU Boundary Expansion. There, holotheater-goers enjoyed a wide selection of tasty treats, and all of them DiversiDine brand.

T'murp's production company followed by creating quality entertainment options for both the holotheaters and Uninet, featuring DiversiDine products liberally as both background scenery, script talking points, and major plot items. (*Eudicot T'murp: Leaf and Let Leaf.* Eudicot T'murp. RP: 140.) Who can forget the scene in *Epochageddon Eclipse* when action great Rix Manglutes faces the Altair-5 tarpit monster? He pulls a Smorg from his pocket, devours it in seconds and rasps, "That delicious, fresh-grown Smorg from

DiversiDine lasted longer than you will, you slimy slaggard!" Such is T'murp's subtle marketing at work. Today, DiversiDine's reach has extended to the production of holovisions, pocket vis-us, and other technologies. Purchase of the Translachew company has also added a line of well-known translational products to DiversiDine's holdings. (*Eudicot T'murp: Leaf and Let Leaf.* Eudicot T'murp. RP: 152.)

Overall, the Translachew transition has been successful, though recent independent research suggests there may now be a weighted DiversiDine-related bias over competing brands in the gum's vocabulary. Eudicot T'murp denies the claims. "If consumers are reporting uncontrolled outbursts of words like 'Smorg' and 'Frallip Squash,' I can only suggest it's user error, influenced by the great flavor and high quality of those products." (*Heavy Meddler News.* Data on file.)

Turning Over a New Leaf with T'murp's Techniques

GCU entrepreneurs looking to fertilize their success The T'murp Way might want to branch out with the following strategies:

- **Market like an invasive weed.** Make sure your products spread wildly, are hard to dig out, and impossible to spot-kill. Strengthen connections between products by cross-pollinating. Develop tangled root systems of marketability that leave customers firmly entwined.

- **Inspiration blossoms from what you already know.** In T'murp's world, success comes from cultivating what you know well and love best—then branching out and wrapping tightly around every aspect of everyday life until consumers get a head-rush.

- **Remember, your first crop might not yield the juiciest results.** Eudicot T'murp knows it can take a less-than-fragrant public response to help define market need. So tend your idea, do spadework on what the market will handle, and use *lots* of fertilizer. You'll grow fresh ideas that really produce—or, at least, make half-decent compost.

6

"What do you think of *this?*" Rollie asked. In the airy, domed marketplace on Golgi Beta, he held up something dark green and oblong that looked a little like a small, weirdly-shaped melon. He tossed it to Bertram and Bertram was surprised how soft it was, how velvety the outside.

"Pretty cool," Bertram said, turning the casing in his hands. "Some kind of vegetable?"

"Kidney, actually," said Rollie. "From an Alganitan mathgar."

Bertram dropped it back into the bin like a hot potato. Rollie nodded knowingly. "Yeah, never cared much for mathgar kidney myself."

Harvested organs might have explained just one of the aromas in the market—smells that overwhelmed in wondrous and conflicting ways with every new stall. Some were as unfamiliar as they were enticing. Others, Bertram would forgo the familiarity. Bertram sniffed his hands and grimaced...

He was *never* going to get that mathgar kidney off.

"Now I want to do this quickly," Rollie told him, "hear me? In and out. Keep a low profile."

"A low profile, understood," Bertram agreed.

Bertram followed Rollie through the stalls of hot foods, cold foods, freeze-dried foods, underwear, outerwear, beasts of burden, burdened shoppers, infopills, herbs, kachunkettball memorabilia, jewelry, holographic images of celebrities, Non-Organic Simulants, hand-lasers, stunguns, flat pack assemble-it-yourself interplanetary cruise vessels, star maps, maps to the stars' homes, vis-us off the back of a hovercraft, knock-off designer levitating boots, towels able to suck up an entire planet's water supply, portable communicator implant seeds, firewater, rocket fuel, fuel for thought, 60 kinds of soup, and plaster yard statuary. (Even in the Greater Communicating Universe, consumers aren't immune to the lure of one-of-a-kind hand-painted lawn art.)

They stopped at a long counter with a sign above it that read, "Shop-O-Drome Customer Service Station #12."

A robot wheeled up to them. "Good afternoon, dear life-forms, and welcome to the Golgi Beta Shop-O-Drome. I'm Erl, your personal merchandise conveyance expeditor for this visit. How may I enhance your shopping experience?"

Robots were so polite. Bertram glanced to Rollie as Rollie pulled a small machine from his pocket. From it he read, "We need *looktas*, say, five toks of them. And four *tchutsaree* steaks—good cuts, none of that stuff your thief boss tried to pass off on me the last time. Seven cases of Zlorgon Sub-Atomic Headbanger, two cases of zaffney, a new hydro-bratometer, four hyper-rotostation J's and...here." He pushed a button. "Just sent you the list. Oh, and did Marlok happen to hold that special package for me? I know it's been some time..."

"Captain Tsmorlood!" exclaimed the robot with tinny recognition rippling through its speech diodes. "Forgive me that I did not initially register your voice print; these sensors aren't what they used to be, you know. I will process your order and check with my employer for your package."

Rollie nodded. "Stellar."

The robot rolled off and Rollie leaned against one of the shelves, juggling a couple of kidneys as he waited.

Bertram stilled the man's arm. "What's that about? The package?"

Rollie tossed the kidneys over his shoulder, back into the crates. "Just this little thing I was working on the side."

"Legal or illegal?"

"Depends on what part of the GCU you're in," Rollie said with a grin.

"I thought we were going low profile."

"No harm in tying up a loose end or two along the way, is there?"

Bertram was about to say it would depend on how many armed and angry law enforcement agents got tangled up in the threads, when out of the corner of his eye, he noticed a strange movement to his left.

It was something slinking toward them with an eerie, sideways step, its eye-stalks bent in their direction with keen interest. It edged closer, tilting this way and that in slow, careful appraisal. Finally, the being nudged Rollie, and in a gruff, clacking voice said, "Hey. How much you want for the zakari?"

Rollie peered disinterestedly at the creature. "Eh?"

"The zakari," said the being, giving another nudge, and yet another. "How much?"

"Him?" Rollie stopped the thing at the approach of Nudge Four. He hooked a thumb at Bertram, an amused smile spreading across his features. "A zakari?"

"What's a zakari?" asked Bertram warily.

Rollie beamed. "He thinks you're a prize show animal."

"A prize show—" But the thing was trying to open his mouth and examine his teeth. Bertram slapped away the creature's hand, which was actually a large purplish claw. "Hey, pal, do you *mind?*"

"Zakaris are known for their small stature, curly fur and high-pitched whine," Rollie informed him.

"Oh yeah? Well—" Bertram blocked the being, who was now trying to test the firmness of Bertram's tennis arm. "Dude, don't make me get the drawn butter."

"Thirty-thousand yoonies," Rollie said.

Bertram shot him a furious glare. "Jesus, Rollie."

Rollie struggled to keep a straight face. "Thirty-thousand yoonies and I'll consider letting you have him."

"Son of a bitch," exclaimed Bertram, "this isn't funny."

Rollie whispered, "Thirty thousand yoonies is an insane amount, Ludlow. He'll never, ever go for it. Not in a trillion U-years."

"Deal!" said the being.

"Deal?" said Bertram, eyes wide. "Deal?!"

"Wow, that's high," breathed Rollie, mopping his brow. "Bleedin' Karnax, I never thought he'd agree that high."

The being was sorting out some kind of money cards.

Bertram hissed. "You are *not* going to take this thing's money, are you?"

Rollie blinked. "Well, frag it, Ludlow, it *is* awfully high."

"Okay, and just how are you going to get in to the seers on Nett?"

"10,000," counted the being, "12,000…17,000…"

Rollie frowned. "Explain."

"Don't you think," said Bertram, "that they might just want to *see* the guy from Tryfe who's supposed to save the planet and help with the lines of Fate and blah, blah, blah? For all we know, to these Nett people, you're just some alien hood. Do you really believe they know about the arrangement you had with the Seers of Rhobux? And if the Seers of Rhobux used you and skipped town, who's to say you'll get any better reception with their branch office? Hm?"

"25,000...27,000..."

"You need me for this," Bertram proclaimed.

"30,000." The being looked up and held out the money cards with its largest claw-like hand. "This is right. Now, zakari, come. We go to many shows and win prizes, yes?" It motioned to Bertram.

"*Rollie*," snarled Bertram through gritted teeth.

"Er, my exoskeletoned friend?" Rollie called. "Been having a rethink; and I just can't let the zakari go."

At this, the being turned abruptly. "What is this you say?" it queried.

"It's a favorite lower life-form of mine. Inherited it from my Second Level Maternal Archetype...y'know: Gran. It's not that it's so valuable. I mean, it's total rubbish on the show circuit. Arthritic and terrible for breeding. Impotent and chock-full of parasites—"

"Rollie," Bertram growled, "I should—"

"—But it's got sentimental value, you see," Rollie concluded, his expression placid and sincere.

"I do not understand 'value of sentiment'," the alien replied. The eyes perched on its stalks narrowed with suspicion.

"Okay, then, I'll make it simple: not selling, mate," said Rollie. "Sorry."

"Not sell? You *must* sell. There was a deal." The being gave a loud crack of its claw.

"And you, mate, are not using your listening antennae. As I already said, what with the zakari being in the family for so long..."

At this moment, the robot returned on squeaky wheels. "Captain Tsmorlood," Erl began, "I believe you'll be pleased with the news. My employer did indeed hold onto the package you had requested some time ago, and my assistants are ready to load this and the rest of your order into the ICV."

"Stellar," said Rollie, handing Erl a wad of paper currency from his pocket without counting it. He then turned to the zakari-enthusiast. "Sorry, mate," he told it, "it's just not going to work out." He and Bertram followed the robot to the exit.

But the life-form wasn't so easily deterred. It trailed them, raising its voice as marketgoers turned to watch. "On my planet, he who retreats on his word is the lowest form of vileness, the scum at the bottom of the Well of a Thousand Screams." It reached out and gripped Rollie's arm with one of those knobbled claws.

Rollie whirled swiftly around, eyes narrowed. He wrenched his arm away, an answering gash crossing his coat sleeve. "Look, mate, I never actually *said*—" he began, but the creature wasn't much interested in what Rollie had never actually said.

"Do you know what we do with those who lie in my culture?" the being hissed.

"I'm fragged if I know what your culture is," Rollie admitted.

"Liars must stand up and recite the Verse of Regret."

"A'right then, if gets us out of here any quicker."

"And then throw themselves on a pit of spikes."

Rollie rolled his eyes to the heavens. "Couldn't have mentioned the blasted pit of spikes first?"

"He's right," advised Bertram. "Next time: pit, then poetry."

"Come. The pit is in my ship," the life-form told them with an energetic snap.

Bertram let out an exasperated huff. "Dude, you get lied to so often you need a portable pit of spikes?"

"Should make you want to reflect on why no one's ever straight-up with you," Rollie said.

"You will come," sneered the life-form, "or I will—"

But they never found out what the being *would*, either. Because Bertram Ludlow was suddenly very tired of having his subconscious take lead. He was tired of being pushed around, and stunned, and jailed, and given impromptu dental examinations and—and sold!—to pushy aliens with irrational best-in-show fixations.

Most of all, he was tired of running around the universe of his mind in holey friggin' socks.

So before he even realized what he was doing, he heard his own voice saying: "Hey Crustacean Boy!—How do you feel about... mathgar kidney?" And with one great swoop, he was pushing over a nearby stand.

Hundreds of roundish, bluish things tumbled out one of the crates and rolled around the life-form's feet. Moving sideways as it did, the zakari-enthusiast was slipping and sliding, uneasy on its strange jointed legs.

And that was all they needed. By the time the aspiring zakari-trainer gained its footing once more, Bertram and Rollie were bursting from the doors of the Shop-O-Drome and racing to the ICV park.

"Calderic moon polyps," Rollie called, as they sprinted the last length to the ship.

"Pardon?"

"Moon polyps, that was back there. Not mathgar kidney."

"Potato potahto," shouted Bertram, running up the ramp into the ship. "Where's that robot with the supplies?"

"'How do you feel about…mathgar kidney?'" Rollie laughed appreciatively, shaking his head. Having set course for Nett, now he was unpacking some sort of raw meat and tossing it in a metal pot. "I mean, I was just gonna frag-up the fellah, but then you went all Keeltsar on him and saved me the trouble."

"You were going to *sell* me to that thing," Bertram said. The memory of it was still too fresh with the stench of his mathgar kidney-coated hands.

"Aw, I was not really," said Rollie. "Probably." He dumped something else into the pot. "Almost certainly probably not really. Anyway, what an exit strategy! Didn't know you had it in you."

"Oh, it's in me, all right," Bertram replied. "You just haven't been seeing me at my best."

Rollie admitted he'd heard that somewhere before, and tossed three more things into the pot. Then he drew his laser. Bertram flinched, but the captain directed the gun potward. "ZOT!"

"FFOOF!" Up shot a blazing flame and a cloud of smoke licked the ceiling. It spread across, thick and blackish-blue, until it dispersed into stray, lingering feathers. Soon an enthusiastic sizzle popped and fizzed, followed by a hearty, smoky-rich smell.

Bertram crawled out from under a table, watchful for more laserfire.

Rollie said, "Smell that? Hyphiz Deltan Flash Stew. Just like home." He considered it a moment, adding, "Not my home, o' course. But someone's I'm sure."

Bertram's stomach was already rumbling about a Five on the Richter Scale, and whatever had been lasered into medium-well smelled unexpectedly good. He didn't recall being ravenous in his dreams before.

He wondered how long he'd been operating on that one cup of breakfast ramen and just where he really was. In a fetal position on his apartment floor? Tucked into bed in the mental ward of the local hospital? It depended on how time translated from the real world to his mind. It was likely his students had already missed him from class. The department head would be contacted. And she'd have called his apartment, maybe even gotten someone to check on him.

His semi-girlfriend Rozz, perhaps? Though, he imagined, one jointly-run psych experiment and three actual dates didn't really solidify her role much for any Checking-to-See-if-He's-Dead-and-then-Admitting-Him-to-Western-Psych kind of activities. Not a great way to advance their fledgling relationship either, Bertram considered, him going all Syd Barrett on her and skipping out to Orangeville.

A girl might have second thoughts about Date Four over a thing like that.

Rollie flipped on the hotplate and put a lid over what he'd just seared. "Supposedly there's been these huge advancements in food preparation units," Rollie mused, "but you can't tell me that pre-programmed stuff is ever as good as what you can laser up yourself."

He dropped into a seat as Bertram's gaze fell on the last of the supplies. The package sat on the table next to him, the unopened rectangle in yellow paper that someone named Marlok had held onto for so long. Bertram pointed, "So, what is it? Drugs? Counterfeit money?...Spice?"

Rollie smirked, his eyes seeming to shine very orange in the light. He folded his long fingers into that thoughtful steeple again before him. "Open it."

Bertram picked up the package and blew off a thickness of dust. He looked up, hesitant.

"Go on."

He then began to unwrap it from its container, carefully from each end. Finally, he peeled back the paper to find...

A book. A musty, tattered old book.

Bertram could barely make out the faded title on its leather-bound spine. "*Belief Systems of the Kegnis Karb?*"

"That's right, Ludlow," said Rollie, the glint still flickering, "print." Taking the book from him, he inhaled the musty pages with relish. "Ah, that smell's history, that is. Can't get that any better way, to my thinking. And still so portable, so tactile, so easy on the eyes. Doesn't require any power. Nothing to swallow. Extraordinary!"

"You collect old books," Bertram said after a sneeze. Somehow, it didn't fit with the jail breaking/police pureéing image he had going.

"Old, new." Rollie shrugged and leafed eagerly through its pages. "Not easy to get a hold of now, though. Not since Spectra Pollux and those Forwardist slaggards have had their way."

"So print is finally dead." At the thought, Bertram felt a dry, weighty disappointment fill his chest.

Rollie rose and moved to the hotplate. "I still hear 'er wheezing in backspace corners like your Tryfe. But that's all the breath left in 'er, I'm afraid."

"And it's all gone digital?"

Rollie stirred absently. "Oral."

"Oral? Like…" He conjured up images of aliens sitting around rustic campfires telling epic space tales about the evening news, "Beowulf?"

Rollie blinked, a stranger to Beowulf, and he settled the lid back on the pot. Funny, Bertram expected there'd be a lot more shared knowledge with his hallucinations.

"Like Translachew gum does for languages," Rollie clarified. "They've coded print into pills. Want to read the Calderian classics? Have a pill. Want to check out the Ottoframan news? Subscribe to today's pill. Want to discuss the latest Fensteev Gnik bestseller? Buy the pill."

"So, digest the latest digest, and devour the book of the month?" Bertram offered.

"That's the idea." The Hyphiz Deltan sat back down again, sprawling comfortably in the chair. "It's about retention. Most everyone you'll meet knows core mathematics, science, literature, local etiquette, solar system history, whathaveyou, right off the top of their heads. Coded capsules freed 'em up. Schools do hands-on training now. Stuff you can't get in a safety seal packet."

"I never did get through the *Last of the Mohicans*," admitted Bertram.

"Well, first, last, and every Mohican in the series, you'd be set," he said.

Bertram managed to turn his laugh into a little cough. "Er, so who are these Forwardists?"

Rollie's face clouded over and his knee twitched spasmodically. "When infopill technology came along, most everyone was very launched about it. But some were still afraid to take the pills—worried about long-term effects, you see. Or they just preferred the print experience. So the Forwardists decided the only way to ensure the GCU advanced properly was to fragging-well see to it there wasn't any print left to muck things up. Their answer was the LibLounges."

"LibLounge." Bertram chuckled. "Sounds like somewhere you'd go to discuss Gloria Steinem."

Rollie looked intrigued. "One of your Tryfe religious songs?"

"Not so much."

Rollie shrugged and leapt from his chair. "Clever idea the LibLounges were, I s'pose." He pushed a button, opening a cabinet, withdrawing a chipped tumbler and examining it with a critical eye. He scraped a bit of gunk from it with a fingernail and set it prominently on the counter.

He opened a second cabinet. "The Forwardists knew something dramatic like forced banning or burning would only make everyone more resistant to giving up print. So best way to purge it? Make purging trendy." He was now echoing, crouched somewhere half-in the cabinet. "Forwardists raised big yoonies and built these Print Liberation Lounges."

Bertram saw a hand rise up and clomp a large green glowing mug next to the glass, only to submerge again. "The idea being, 'why weigh yourself down with heavy boring print when you can be free and all-knowing? Be Your Best You.' That's their motto. Got everyone real excited about eradicating their print, too. So these Lounges are—Ah, here we are!"

He rose with two mismatched bowls and a couple of smudgy translucent spoons in his hands. He put them with the tumbler and mug. He blinked. "Er... What was I saying?"

"'The Lounges are...'?" Bertram prompted. He was getting the vague idea that Rollie had some kind of alien ADHD.

"Oh, right. Well, the Lounges are designed so you can bring your print to demolecularize, then sit round and chat about the latest works you've digested. They have comfy chairs, sell copies of the latest book pills and exotic beverages to wash 'em down. You get

1/100th of a yoonie for each book you recycle. But I imagine most of it goes back to the café."

He brought out a bottle and poured a clear liquid into the two glasses. He handed one to Bertram. "I try not to think how much print gets fragged. And how much never makes it to capsule first."

Bertram envisioned the last copy of something big being wiped from the universe. Theories from the next Einstein or Hawking, stories from the next Twain, eradicated unknowingly over coffee and overpriced Martian danish. He took a bracing sip of the drink in his hand. It had a strange, fruity-woody-spicy flavor to it. Like iced orange pekoe strained through a 70s spice rack. He was pretty sure he didn't like it. He also thought he could get used to it quickly. "Don't they keep track? Isn't there a system?"

Rollie tipped the stew into the bowls. "Oh yeah, and systems are always just so flawless, aren't they?" He handed Bertram a bowl. "That's why we're blasting halfway across the fragging GCU to see these slaggard prophets bunkered down all the way on Ne—"

A buzzer rang out over the ship. Momentarily, an upper cabinet panel flashed to life with what appeared to be a display. Its screen featured a two-faced woman.

That wasn't a judge of character, either. She—or they, as the case may have been—had two faces, and both on the very same head. One face beamed with warmth. The other held a bored air. Bertram caught himself in mid-gape, so busied himself with his dinner. It seemed wrong to stare.

"My, my, my. So Fess and Wilbree told no lie!" said the smiling face in a musical, genteel tone. One set of large violet eyes shone with good humor. "Rollie Tsmorlood, as I live and respire! I was convinced you'd fallen out the back of the Universe."

"Xylith," Rollie said coolly. "Been a while. What is it you want?"

"Always so direct, you Deltans. You never waste a minute on the little pleasantries." She waved his question away like a fruit fly buzzing around her mint julep. "Aren't I right, dear? Have you ever heard him waste time on pleasantries?"

Bertram realized he was being addressed now. But he was right in the middle of a big mouthful of surprisingly good Flash Stew. "Well," he mumbled through the food, trying to savor every bite and still speak, "he pretty much just showed up and shot me."

"Ohhh," cooed Face One sympathetically. "You poor, poor thing. Shot by way of introduction...Yes, yes, well...That's just his way, I suppose. One of his many, many idiosyncrasies. Something we all must find within ourselves the forgiving strength to overlook." She nodded with empathy at Bertram.

Bertram nodded affably with another spoonful of stew.

Rollie frowned from Bertram to the woman on the screen. "I assume you didn't buzz to chat-up my bad habits and your forgiving nature. What is it you want?"

"Ah," Face Two exclaimed with a mischievous smile, "But, my star, the question is what *you* want."

Rollie perched on the edge of the counter. "What do *I* want?" He folded his arms.

"Why, I do believe you want to be at the next Underworld Society meeting." She let the words sink in, slow and patient, like syrup to pancakes.

Rollie's expression went from perturbed to puzzled.

"You want to be there to make your historic mark on the shining inner-society governmental system that provides our fine organization representation, leadership, justice and the brotherhood found in skirting around GCU trade regulations." She smiled like the Rose Queen in the Tournament of Roses parade.

"Official Leader of the Intergalactic Underworld," breathed Rollie, recollection filling his voice. "Holy Karnax, the OLIU elections! We could finally vote Zenith Skytreg outta there!" He hooted and cheered like his team had just scored in overtime.

"See?" smirked Face Two, "I knew he'd forgotten."

"He's been in confinement," persisted Face One. "Priorities shift."

"Xylith," Rollie interrupted, "pull yourself together. When and where? The meeting?"

"Vos Laegos, my star," said Face One. "Two Universal days. Crater Club, The Core. Fess and Wilbree were saying they forgot to mention it when Backs was regaling you with his future career plans, and so *I* said I hadn't spoken to you in simply a *Klimfal's* age, and so then *they* said they would give you a buzz, but then *I* said I'd be happy to—"

"Two U-days," muttered Rollie thoughtfully. "All right, count me in."

Bertram looked up sharply from his stew. "Wait, no. Absolutely not. What about Nett? Talking to the prophets? Blanking your archive? ... *Saving my planet?*"

"S'kay, Ludlow," said Rollie, unruffled. "Vos Laegos is right on the way to Nett."

"Yeah, so?"

"So, how do you know you can't save your planet by going to Vos Laegos?" Rollie leaned in and whispered, "Has the Yellow Thing told you?" His smile was diabolical.

Bertram drew back and glared. By now, he had more than a few thoughts on aliens and their lofty attitudes. But rather than say something he'd regret—and maybe get himself lasered into oblivion—he took out his annoyance on the last few stew molecules.

Rollie sensed a win. "We'll be there," he told Xylith.

"Stellar." She nodded. "Oh, and one more thing before you go…" It was Face Two doing the talking now, her violet eyes narrowed. "Was it really confinement, Tsmorlood? Or did you get yourself life-merged again?"

"You're the second one to ask that."

"And I know how it happens," she said. "The pearly moons… The out of the way spot… the music… the laughs… the Zlorgon Sub-Atomic Headbanger flowing like dihydrogen monoxide. Just the setting for romance, poor decision-making and life-shattering disast—"

"*Paar too,* Xylith." Grinning, Rollie touched a knob and the screen went blank. A tiny blip of light clung to the its center and faded away. The cabinet panels returned to their simple cabinetry duties.

Bertram set his empty bowl aside. There was a vague stew residue in the bottom, but Bertram thought licking the bowl probably wasn't the right image for the guy who was supposed to save Life As He Knew It. "Your ex, huh? She seems…" He searched for a safe adjective. "…Nice."

Rollie shrugged a shoulder and made a non-committal noise. "Could've worked out. Just there was one too many of us in the fragging relationship. Now then—" He gave an hearty clap of his hands and moved to the cockpit doorway. "—Coordinates for Vos Laegos?"

Bertram had already resigned himself to the brain's storyline. He felt vaguely manipulated by stew. "Give 'er all she's got, Kiptin."

But as soon as he said it, he wished he hadn't. Alien hallucinations these days were sorely behind on their Tryfan pop culture references. And as far as the reaction went, Bertram Ludlow might as well have licked the bowl.

7

"Okay, whose is this?" On Podunk, the female Peace Guard held up a third arm—a thick male one—currently attached to the center of her chest.

She peered around its twiddling fingers, which interrupted her line of vision. With a sigh, she steadied the hand in a less obtrusive spot. "An arm? Anyone?"

"Mine!" One male Guard raised the stump of his shoulder in response, then switched to his remaining arm for better effect. With that hand, he rolled up his pants leg and pointed out the body part currently jutting from his knee. "Anyone need an ear?"

"What?" asked a second male Guard, his lidless eyes unfocused.

"I said, anyone need an—Oh." The officer noticed his colleague's missing ear and nodded. "I'll tell you later."

"I'm dizzy," said that officer loudly.

"It's your equilibrium."

"Ickle what?"

"Later, we'll talk later."

It was to this scene that the Hyphiz Deltan Regimental Enforcement Squad finally broke down the fused front door of the Podunk confinement center. W.I. Mook was the first to enter. He took one look at the mixed-up mess before him, clasped his hands in front of him in a tidy parade rest position, and said, "So would I be completely off-mark by asserting there've been some...challenges... with the prisoner?"

The Podunk Peace Guards froze and eyed him in stunned silence, this blond, middle-aged tower of a man, a bit on the heavy side, with an intelligent, poetically-sensitive face and rigid posture. Then the room exploded with dialog.

"I'm going to need my arm, and she's got it!"

"Red was green... Green was red."

"We should sue the manufacturer!"

"The weapon you're looking for is a ZT-112G polymer-casing hydro-reactive collapsible hand-laser."

"Everyone knows Podunk regeneration gets tricky in proximity to other unregenerated Podunks! This was clearly a diversion designed with malicious intent."

"Hey, my ear is gone!"

W.I. Mook allowed this flood of discussion to surge around a moment, let them purge it from their systems, and then gave a slight bowing motion to his colleague, W.I. Tstyko. Igglestik Tstyko had been Mook's partner for almost half of a Hyphiz Deltan century. He was equally tall and fair-haired, but wiry and with large, protuberant eyes that always made him look faintly unstable. Which he was.

Fortunately, Mook found it a pleasant, heady sort of professional balance between them. Mook's higher ups had always rated him personally as efficient but his tactics somewhat on the low-key side. In contrast, Tstyko lacked consistency but was fiercely devoted to nabbing anyone stepping remotely outside of Deltan regimentation schedules and regulatory procedures. Particularly if it involved lengthy intergalactic chases and weaponry in excess.

They both enjoyed cheese.

These were the reasons their partnership had flourished.

At Mook's gesture, Tstyko whistled sharply. Even the Peace Guard missing the ear jumped at the sound.

"Thank you," said Mook with a tight little smile.

"My pleasure," grinned Tstyko, scanning the group for signs of further unruliness.

"Now," began Mook, "I'm W.I. Mook. And this is W.I. Tstyko. The prisoner is gone, I take it?"

As the Podunks opened their mouths to rain a torrent of response, Mook waved them to silence, "No, no." He pointed at the female Guard with the three arms. "You. Peace Guard...?"

"Nak, Sir," she said, slapping the third arm out of her view. Cowed, it rested its hand on her shoulder.

"P.G. Nak, proceed."

"Yes, sir, the prisoners are gone. You see, we just got this new Prisoner Confinement System, sir. The day we contacted your department from the ICV, we hadn't used it before, sir. It's a Klinko system, sir. And the instructions were, well, they were—"

"Prisoner*s*, P.G. Nak?" interrupted Mook mildly. "More than one prisoner? You sent us the I.D. on Rolliam Tsmorlood. Who else is missing?"

"That's just it," said Nak. "We're not sure. The life-form's voice print didn't come up with a match for priors. But the life-form was traveling with Tsmorlood and was located in Oogon Bungee's ICV."

"Describe him, please?"

"Male humanoid, sir," she responded. "Not Hyphiz Deltan, but pink and void of scales. I'm unsure of his species. We have images if you'd like. It should have been recorded through the Klinko LK-31 Prisoner Confinement System surveillance component." She looked uncertainly at her colleagues. "Anyone know how to check the recording of the Klinko LK-31 Prisoner Confinement System surveillance component?"

(Forty-five Podunk minutes later...)

The Podunk Peace Guards and Hyphiz Deltan W.I.s gathered around the display and all but Mook took a horrified step back. The image of the life-form on the confinement cot was stunned cold, hair askew, facial muscles over-loose for the stunning, and he appeared to be drooling lightly on the covers in a long, damp string.

Tstyko laughed. "Well! I think we can safely rule out last year's Miss Big Dippers."

"Can I get a digital copy of this sent to my ICV?" asked Mook.

"Uhhh...sure..." considered P.G. Nak.

(One hour and fifteen Podunk minutes later...)

"Stellar," said Mook, feeling a little like he'd been left stunned and drooling himself. "We have what we need. You write up the report on the incident and send us a copy. And we'll place an alert on the Uninet. If your escapees are anywhere in the Greater Communicating Universe, we'll hear of it soon enough."

"Thank you."

After all of this space travel and technological sorting, Mook's mind now turned to the journey home. From there, it was a short leap to a nice mootaab cheese on toast. The food preparation unit on board their ship could do just wonders with a nice mootaab cheese toastie. He'd always considered it one of the simple pleasures in life. "*Paar too*, friends. Thank you for your assistance. We'll be off."

He reached out and shook hand after hand, yet one hand—the one in the center of P.G. Nak's chest—wouldn't let go.

"But V.I. Mook, what about us?" P.G. Nak said, black eyes shining with unshed tears.

"*W*.I.," Mook corrected gently with a smile.

"Excuse me?"

"*W*.I. It stands for '*Waassall Issen*.' It's Hyphiz Deltan. A title for senior-level crime investigators." His years of service came flooding back to him in a warm wave of fond reminiscence. "It took me ten Deltan years to work up to *Waassall Issen*. Sadly, Translachew gum's rubbish making sense of any of it." He shrugged it away, one minor disappointment in a lifetime of job satisfaction.

"*W*.I. Mook," P.G. Nak corrected in pleading tones, "I have three arms." She pointed to a colleague. "P.G. Zlotni has an ear on his knee. P.G. Wezzag is dizzy and half-deaf."

"Oh!" W.I. Mook evaluated this information with some surprise. "Are you saying you don't *want* them then?"

"*Yes*," she exclaimed, releasing his hand like it was diseased, "of *course* we don't want them! They're not *ours*."

"What?" shouted P.G. Wezzag. "My hours are the same this week as they always are, why do you ask?"

"Hm," Mook considered this interesting new perspective and stroked his chin. "Funny. Time and again, I've wanted an added hand or an extra ear-to-the-ground, so to speak. But perhaps detective-work is done differently here on Podunk."

He turned to his partner and W.I. Tstyko nodded. "To each his own and all that, eh?" Tstyko agreed.

"So what can be done about it?" Nak persisted.

"Well, to be quite honest, I don't really know, P.G. Nak," Mook said. "I'm regrettably unfamiliar with the finer points of Podunk anatomy. Perhaps a talented surgeon might do the trick? Or a really good lasering, centripetal DNA sorting, and a follow-up regeneration?"

"A strong astringent," suggested W.I. Tstyko.

P.G. Nak's head bowed in disappointment, a simple gesture yet deeply moving.

"Surely, your people have dealt with this before," Mook said, finding himself patting her shoulder like a kindly uncle. "What do you do in cases of natural disasters? Mass transit accidents?"

"We're not a very populated planet," said Nak. "There's one city. One store. One bar. One doctor, whose patients are mostly livestock and they keep to themselves. We've only joined the GCU because the GCU found us and they liked the view."

"It *is* a rather lovely view, isn't it?" agreed Mook heartily, wishing to cheer her. "The colorful sunsets are from the...the livestock methane, is that right?"

"Yes," she mumbled. "It's fine unless you're downwind."

"Hey, I heard of a rancher who got struck by lightning and merged with one of his livestock," piped up P.G. Zlotni.

"Oh, very good," said Mook hopefully. "And what happened to him?"

"He won the first prize trophy at the Podunk Northern Hemisphere Fair and gets all the grass he can eat."

Mook exhaled. "Ah." He turned to Nak. "Include the physical damages in your report. I'll confer with my supervisors and see whether they don't have any ideas. At the very least, we can tack on a few years to Tsmorlood's sentence for assault and, er..." He looked at her extra arm. "...Shuffling things about a bit."

She thanked him.

"Take heart, P.G. Nak. We'll do what we can."

"Refusing to adhere to the Deltan Regimentation Schedule... Escaping from confinement twice...And now scrambling up a bunch of Podunk Peace Guards. I tell you, Mook, when we find Rolliam Tsmorlood, I am making sure Altair-5 is the very next—and last—planet he sees." Tstyko bit fiercely into his mootaab cheese toastie.

They were back at the ship and Mook examined the image of the unknown escapee on their screen as he enjoyed his favorite sandwich. A robust flavor, just the right level of stretchiness. Perfect.

Tstyko continued, "I don't understand why some of these Deltans just won't hold with the planet's Regimentation Schedule. It always starts with that, you know—the criminal element does."

This was a speech Mook had heard many times. He chewed his sandwich meditatively.

"I mean, Hours One to Three: sleep. Hours Four to 15: pre-determined productivity. Hours 16 to 27: mandatory recreation. Is it so difficult to support?"

"I've found it a very pleasant existence," Mook agreed.

"Precisely! It assures everyone is busy, happy, prosperous, balanced...It's good for society. It reduces crime significantly. And yet there are a handful of pribs like this Tsmorlood that simply won't come to. I think it's a genetic defect."

"Well, he does have systemic hypermotocerebrostasia." Mook had noticed it in Tsmorlood's case file once. It was a condition that hit about 1% of the Hyphiz Deltan population, represented by excess energy, bursts of movement, rapid, non-linear thought, manic episodes and, if uncontrolled, even madness.

"That's no excuse," said Tstyko. "There's medication for that sort of thing. To slow down...er...energy whosis in the blood...or..." he twiddled his fingers wildly, "nerve sensory thingies or...brain whatnot." He shook his head. "No, I won't have that kind of half-hearted pretext."

"I wonder if he might not be from Tryfe," Mook said thoughtfully. He dabbed at his lips with a napkin and popped it in the waste incinerator.

"Tsmorlood? Oh, he's Deltan, all right..." But then he noticed Mook looking at the unknown escapee on the screen. "Oh, him." Tstyko crammed in the last of the toastie. Through the food he said, "Tryfe. Isn't that that little wishy-washy blue swirly planet outside of Quad One?"

"It is," Mook said. The coloring, the facial features, the response to stunning...They reminded him of a documentary he'd seen once on backspace life-forms.

"Well, I don't see how he could be from Tryfe. That lot isn't a part of the GCU. They don't do space travel as we know it. And the only ones who go there are cheeky teenagers for fly-by pranks looking to impress their girls at their brave determination to go somewhere so terribly remote and dead boring."

Mook turned his mild gaze on Tstyko with curiosity. "And was the future Mrs. Tstyko impressed?"

"Not so as you'd notice," Tstyko said, clearing his throat. "But it's her icy stoicism that still gets me moony. Another toastie?"

8

If only she'd installed a new fragrance in the air recycling system before they'd left, Mimsi Grabbitz thought. And maybe put down some plastic. The overripe vegetable scent that seemed to radiate from her current client was one she'd figured she'd get used to over the course of their journey. But so far, it only left her thinking about the time her on-board refuse incinerator glitched, just as the vegetarian take-out went whiffy.

Still, a sale was a sale. And never let it be said that Mimsi Grabbitz let her sense of smell override her sense of better business. "I think you're really going to like this property, Mr. Mij," she said with a beaming smile, as she moved the craft in swiftly over the planet's surface. "Tryfe is a unique fixer-upper opportunity if ever there was one, virtually ideal for someone of your creative thinking."

"You know my work, do ya, Mimsi?" Musca Mij asked, his multi-lensed eyes shimmering with green-violet iridescence. His voice, even through the projection translators, buzzed with a vibration that rattled her eardrums.

"Why, indeed, I do! The Blumdec timeshare ads...the Galacti-Gorgefest Cruises...and—oh!—the *Heavy Meddler* newscapsule and Uninet channel—both of which I am simply addicted to, dear!" It was true, she enjoyed her *Heavy Meddler* with breakfast and dinner each day. Lately she'd been riveted to the *Meddler*'s coverage of the romantic get-together, break-up, reunion, split, life-merger, attempted murder, criminal investigation, trial, merge-fragging, reunion, joint adoption of 437 Biblucian orphans, nasal congestion, orphan PR shots, public drunkenness and the Coalition of Planets annual awards ceremony dinner of celebrity darlings, Stella Cygnus and Jet Antlia. But who wasn't?

Mij rubbed a pair of hands together merrily at this. "Glad to have a fan."

"Your biggest! And that's why, knowing your work as I do, I was thinking that if you'd care to share your potential plans for Tryfe, that would really help me help you better." She gave him the Interested face. The Interested face, she noticed, was getting easier to do; meaning, it was time for her Facial Tightening Touch-up again. She'd have to book an appointment quickly before full-deflation.

But Mij waved her interest away with two sets of arms. "Sorry, Mimsi. Love to dish, but no-can-do. Preliminary stages. Hush-hush. That sorta thing."

"I understand completely. Forget I even mentioned it," she said, donning her Wide-Eyed Sincere face, and pressing on, directing his gaze to the ground below. "So, as you can see, the planet is located in a quiet neighborhood. It has its own sun. There's a breathable atmosphere for oxygen-dependant life-forms. And it comes complete with some absolutely charming Tryfe humans."

At the last point, Musca Mij's wings twitched. "Yeah," he said reflectively, "about that. I'm probably gonna have to wipe them all out."

"Oh," Mimsi said, trying to disguise her surprise. Eudicot T'murp's earlier enthusiasm for the Tryfe people had put her somewhat off her game. "Of course, absolutely! Easily done. Then, I suppose you won't need to see any of the inhabitants...? That's fine. We can head back, if you feel you've seen enough."

"Look, do whatever you had planned," said Musca Mij cheerfully, "I'm game. You arranged a little pitstop or something?"

"Just a brief one."

"No problem," he said. "It'll give me a chance to stretch my legs and wings."

"It's equity, Stephanie, *equity*," insisted Justin Van deKampf as he directed the Lexus along the golf course, toward the Mapletop Gardens Apartment Complex on the other side of town.

"I just don't see owning an apartment building as Us, Justin," she said, tucking a lock of raven hair behind her ear. "Do you realize those people have no homes of their own?"

"Yes, Stephanie, that's why they rent."

Stephanie didn't care for Justin's condescending tone and gave him a sour expression. "You know what I meant, Justin. Renting? It's one step away from being...*gypsies*, really." Justin opened his mouth to speak but she wasn't finished. "They have nowhere to go. They can't afford their own places. And that either demonstrates—One: a complete lack of ambition or Two: poor fiscal planning." She removed a small tube of sea-sponge-infused cream from her purse and began to apply it to her hands. "So how can we be assured their inadequate financial situations and personal underachievement won't, in time, directly affect us?"

"There are contracts. We'd check references. We'd require first and last month's rent up-front. It's done all the time, Bun-Bun."

She popped the lotion back in her purse gingerly, careful not to smear her bag. "And you do realize this would make us... *landlords*." She didn't even like the way that word rolled around in her mouth. It had a gritty feel to it. It made her wish she had hand-cream for her tongue.

"*Property management*, Bun-Bun," Justin corrected. "That's the terminology now. Property management. It's very entrepreneurial."

"Hm," said Stephanie, doubtfully. She didn't think anything could be too entrepreneurial if it involved roaches and background checks and toilet plungers. But typical Justin, once he became enthused about something, they would simply have to agree to disagree.

It was just as they were going past the ninth green, that the car started making a strange whumm-whumm-whumping noise that actually wasn't anything to do with the critically-acclaimed industrial experimental artist on the stereo system. "Justin, didn't you have your guy look at the car just last week? What are we paying him for, anyway?"

"I did, Bun-Bun," Justin responded, pulling the Lexus to the side of the road. "But it sounds like we have a flat."

"I see." Stephanie drew her phone from her purse. "Calling AAA."

"Oh, don't bother. I'll change the tire," said Justin.

Stephanie gave him a good hard look. Justin, change a tire himself? Justin wasn't mechanical. He'd had so many problems with the espresso maker that eventually they'd resigned themselves to spending eight dollars apiece daily for pressed coffee shots from the Little Box of Beans on Oakside.

"Sometimes I think I don't even know you anymore," she said.

"I'm a man of layers, Stephanie," Justin responded.

Stephanie got out of the car and leaned against the door, arms folded, while Justin began fooling around in the trunk, trying to figure out where the spare tire was without looking like he hadn't a clue. The man of layers, she determined, would be there all day. But perhaps they'd miss their appointment to see the apartment complex.

One could only hope.

Mimsi Grabbitz found just what she was looking for along an area of rolling green fields and settled the ICV down in a level spot along a road. "You can see, the land here is very lush," she told Musca Mij, releasing her safety harness. "Not to say that all of Tryfe is this way, but there are a surprising number of areas just like this all over the planet. Unfortunately, there seems to be some sort of white spherical creatures indigenous to these places. They make holes in the earth and can really mess up the terrain." She chuckled. "The few times I've passed by here, I've seen the Tryfe-humans swatting at the things with sticks, chasing after them in small land vehicles and cursing. Such a brutal, primitive way to dispatch them, but it seems to keep them under control. Have you ever seen such thick grass?"

"Maybe a good pesticide'll take care of 'em," Mij suggested.

"I'm sure you're right," Mimsi said.

They both filed out onto the green lawns of Tryfe.

"Ahhh! After a long flight, it's always so good to get out and stretch the ol' wings," Musca Mij proclaimed, elongating and fluttering his shimmering appendages, and surveying the area through those opalescent eyes of his.

There before them were the Tryfe humans Mimsi had spotted from the air.

"Well, look here!" exclaimed Mimsi, trying to sound spontaneous. "Just what I'd hoped for! Here we have a male and female Tryfe human."

The female Tryfe human was eyeing them suspiciously, arms folded before her. "You can't park that there. The helipad for the club? It's that way." She pointed across the rolling field to a large white building, then resumed her folded-armed stance.

"Who are you talking to, Bun-Bun?" came the male's voice from inside the back of his vehicle.

"These people who've completely missed the helipad." She addressed them again. "I'm telling you, you're going to want to lift off and get closer to the club. You're not allowed to walk across the greens unless you're playing. And, anyway, it's a hike. You'll ruin your costumes."

"Costumes?" echoed the man's voice from under a panel and carpeting.

"Someone at the club must be hosting a benefit," she explained to him. "Remember that one last year, when Judge Stanford went as a restraining order?"

"Ha, yes. I never saw a court-issued document with a toupée before." Lifting a wheel from the back of the vehicle, and laughing to himself, he glanced at Mimsi and her client. "Oh, yes—*very* nice! Let me guess. Gregor?"

"Does he think he knows you?" Mimsi asked.

Musca Mij shook his head. "I'll say this for the Tryflings: they're friendly."

"That's why I was thinking you might want to see them in person," Mimsi told him. "I mean, I hear they're very high-quality. It occurred to me you could export them and use them for entertainment on one of your cruises. Or as labor for your newscapsule factories. Or perhaps they could just assist you with your project here?"

Mij considered it a moment, two hands stroking his mandibles introspectively. "Yeah, but ya know… I leave 'em here and then— what—all of a sudden I'd be their permanent *landlord?*" He shuddered at the thought of it. "Not my style. I enjoy the in-and-out turnover we get with hotels and timeshares. I don't do residential. Anyway, look around you. The place is gorgeous! The Tryflings would completely ruin the view."

"I suppose you're right," Mimsi agreed. "Ready to go then?"

"Ready when you are, Mimsi!"

And with that, they got back in her ICV and lifted off.

"Out-of-towners," sighed Stephanie, rolling her eyes.

Excerpt from:

How To Gain Pals and Sway Life-forms in Cosmic Commerce
Chapter Twelve

With permission from the
Eddisun Center for Ideas, Interceptive Marketing and Cliché Prevention

MetamorfaSys Inc. and the Buzz on Musca Mij:
Mathekite Marketer to the Masses

Overview
Infomercials, timeshares, hotels, all-you-can-digest intergalactic cruises, and sizzling, up-to-the-nanosecond celebrity gossip: **Musca Mij**, lead creative mind behind the mighty **MetamorfaSys Inc.**, digs up the deepest, darkest emotions of the masses. Desire, jealousy, hunger, insecurity, fear, avarice, and nausea are each his special domain. And within their crevasses, he injects them with the marketing messages that wriggle deep under consumers' skins, itching them to action.

Critics have described Mij's work as: "pandering to the lowest common denominator if that denominator were in the negative numbers and also in the basement of subterranean cavern" (*NewsMillenium*); "The products you watch from the corner of your eye, then order when you're alone" (*Rational GeoGalactic*); and "excess served with overindulgence, slathered in glut" (*The Quad Two Epicurean*). But while MetamorfaSys Inc. may not always earn noticable intergalactic applause, eight of ten life-forms surveyed indicate they have purchased or used at least one MetamorfaSys product or service in the last Universal year. The other two of ten being consumer advocacy representatives who have *also* bought MetamorfaSys products and services, but just really don't want to talk about it.

So what is it about Musca Mij's entrancing strategy that encourages the masses to succumb to their yearnings, ignoring their better judgment in favor of the items he markets? How does Musca

Mij pinpoint the soul's most unspeakable longings, cravings, and needs, package them, and then charge for shipping and handling? In this chapter, we'll take a look at the Mathekite behind MetamorfaSys Inc. and see how his products and services have slipped under the barriers of critical good taste to infect the hearts and minds of the masses.

Hatching into a Household Name

Musca Mij grew up as one of 536 larvae in a small, 80-chamber flat in Mathek's capital city, Bintopia. Yet even with so many siblings vying for attention, it was not long before the young Musca stood out from the crowd. "The other progeny would see a pile of used fruit peels and say, 'Look: dinner,' but Musca, he could always find the art in them," said Dipterra Mij, Musca's mother. "That's what Musca brings to everything he touches. Art. And I think it's wonderful the way he shares his visions with the Greater Communicating Universe." (*Musca Mij: Trash to Treasure*. Musca Mij. RP: 29.)

"It's about hunger," Mij explained. "It's recognizing that life-forms in the universe are hungry for so many things they never talk about. My work has always been about taking the empty stomach of Consumerism and filling it up with just as much as it'll hold, and then adding a little more, and a little more, right until it yaks. Then I know my work is done." ("More is Never Enough: An Interview with Musca Mij." *Heavy Meddler*. Zaph Chantseree. Newscapsule vol. 39,045,149.)

Mij started his career trying to fill that hunger by making a series of independent films. Crafted on an atom-thin budget and relying on friends, siblings and puppets made of refuse for his acting talent, Mij created strange, fascinating, yet repellant worlds, showcasing the greasy, deranged underbelly of universal desires and fears. *Sole* is about the detailed fantasy life of a limbless, wingless Mathekite with a sock fetish. *Go-Go Gooligans of Uvula-9*—the tale of exotic dancing, adrenaline junkies, and unnecessary dentistry—is what Mij now calls an "exercise in an experimental medium." And *Backspace Hermaphroditic Food Service Employees Do the Daegon System*, Mij indicates, was designed to test his characters' emotional range. The films were sold by Mij's equally home-grown infomercials during late night Uninet broadcasts, targeting as many markets as Mij could afford on the wages of his daytime food service job. (*Musca Mij: Trash to Treasure*. Musca Mij. RP: 86.)

Upon release, B-movie critics panned the films, one calling them "the most singularly dreadful examples of filmmaking, acting and cinematography since single-celled organisms slunk from the ooze and decided to make a documentary about it." (*MovieMeteor* entertainment newscapsule vol. 15,296.)

Naturally, Mij's pictures have developed a strong cult following.

But Mij left his indy film days behind, without so much as a backward glance. He explains, "While high visual art in the film medium had its rewards, I discovered I could reach a lot more people through mainstream advertising and journalism." So using his film background, and forging a partnership with inventors from the Popeelie religious sect, Mij went on to create the string of highly popular infomercial ads for the group's products. Favorites like Cloak-in-a-Can®, Pocket Pulpit® and the latest offering, Jerky Divine®, the GCU's first non-perishable food product created from the regenerated and cloned cells of deceased Popeelie prophet, Chawtu Champs. "You can't get any closer to your religion than this," stated Mij. "Plus, it's got a great smoked taste!" (*Musca Mij: Trash to Treasure*. Musca Mij. RP: 187.)

With new capital from his Popeelie product marketing rolling in, Mij next tapped into the cult of personality with the *Heavy Meddler* newscapsule. Today, the *Heavy Meddler* has innumerable subscribers across the GCU, with trillions of delivery stations across various solar systems. "Life-forms want to know that celebrities are just regular folks like them—only richer, better looking and available for more embarrassing photos if you stalk them long enough. The *Meddler* has managed to turn something as simple as an unexpected expression of nasal mucus into the headline story everyone's talking about. I'm proud of that." (*Musca Mij: Trash to Treasure*. Musca Mij. RP: 217.)

And time-shares on MetamorfaSys-owned planets are also increasing in demand. Mij is quick to mention his company not only redevelops the resort planets but does the time-share advertising.

"Who'd even heard of Blumdec, until we gave it a facelift and started buying up ad time on the Uninet? But with our ads running every 37 universal seconds on at least 600,000 channels, repeated in eight-time loops, now Blumdec's one of the hottest vacation destinations in Quad Three. Tourists don't even have time to pack for home before we've got the next set of 'em peering in the windows of the beach house, steaming up the glass with their breath.

We've finally gotten the exposure we needed." (*Musca Mij: Trash to Treasure*. Musca Mij. RP: 243.)

Now corporations pound on Mij's door, begging for the MetamorfaSys branding treatment. Most-recently, Musca Mij was buzzed by the Galactic Festival Cruises, looking to aid flagging guest numbers. Mij recounted their initial talks. "I told them, I said, 'What's the incentive for people to go here? What do you have for them to do once they get on your giant ICV that they can't already do at home?' 'Up the buffet count,' I told 'em, 'Tailor it specifically to your nervous eaters, bored eaters, picky eaters, overeaters, maneaters and bulimics. You advertise it to life-forms who want to eat every minute of the Universal day, and market it. You won't be sorry.'" And so, the Galati-Gorgefest® cruiseline was reborn. (*Musca Mij: Trash to Treasure*. Musca Mij. RP: 310.)

So what does the future hold for Mij and MetamorfaSys Inc.? Today, it looks like as much as possible, then a *little* more.

Messages from Mij's Marketing Mastery
Want to discover *your* finess through marketing excess? Try some of these proven Mij tactics:

- **Anything worth selling is worth selling loud.** Mij turns up the volume on each of his timeshare ads to 300 decibels louder than the programming around it. "Being hearing impaired is no excuse for not buying my products. Plus shouting shows you really believe in what you're selling. It promotes trust."

- **Repetition gets sales repetition gets sales repetition gets sales.** Mij shows each infomercial no less than five times in succession and up to a record 65 times, depending on airtime availability. While some critics call the looped messaging "overkill," "obnoxious," and "seizure-inducing," studies show that with so much audio and visual stimuli coming at consumers every moment, it takes *at least* five sequential runs for messaging to receive conscious recognition. Additionally, surveys show that many life-forms have actually purchased products in MetamorfaSys ads just to make the ads stop.

- **Lies shouldn't hold back a snappy commercial.** Musca Mij is master of finding the hidden benefits in any product and richly magnifying the challenges they solve. Who doesn't remember the commercial where Popeelie worshippers risked spontaneous combustion from the sun's harmful rays, until they got Cloak-in-a-Can? Interestingly, current research shows that only one Popeelie in the religion's long history has ever died due to spontaneous combustion—and that case has not directly been linked to sun exposure. But the Spontaneous Combustion Scare of Glat-b5 increased Cloak-in-a-Can® sales by 500% in under a week. Mij knows how to create need.

9

"It's not an Vernjoolsian mollusk!" Bertram shouted, leaping back from the violently swinging tentacles of the 3-D creature on the screen and comparing it unfavorably in an instant to the Yellow Thing around his neck.

The mollusks were yellow, yes, and their shells a general star-ish shape. But adult mollusks grew to twice the size of small ICVs and were known to overtake spacecrafts, crack them open and slurp out the insides. This included the fuel tanks, fluids and any unlucky passengers. The hyper-realistic projection imagery here showed the creature not to scale, but in more vivid detail than Bertram's nervous system expected. "*Not* a Vernjoolsian mollusk," Bertram repeated, hand to his pounding heart.

From across the room, Rollie put down his book. "I coulda told you that. Hear tell, a Vernjoolsian mollusk once got hold of Backs' ship. Never knew what hit 'im, he said." The alien's features took on a reflective expression. "Come to think of it, I don't recall hearing how Backs survived that." He pondered it a bit longer and shrugged. "Thing probably just didn't like the flavor."

"Maybe a little dry," Bertram suggested.

Heart rate now returning to a more normal pace, Bertram drew a few deep breaths and turned back to the Uninet version of *P.K. Flutterbitt's Virtual Encyclopedia of Verified Fauna Across the Greater Communicating Universe and Its Habitats.* 536th Edition.

With their course officially set for Vos Laegos, Bertram had focused his energies on answering two important questions: why was Earth in trouble?; and what the hell was the Yellow Thing the Seers gave him?

Bertram found research and analysis a comfort in these confusing times. They gave him a sense of normalcy, power, strength. Also something to do since there was no in-flight movie. Rollie set Bertram up on the shipboard Uninet, and away he went.

But efforts revealed that Uninet gab barely touched on Bertram's little blue planet, unless you counted a listing in *Galaktipaedia* and a *Heavy Meddler* mention of teens buzzing backspace planets as pranks.

So Bertram turned his efforts to the Yellow Thing, and that's when he found P.K. Flutterbitt's informative online work with fauna. What Bertram *hadn't* been prepared for was such an…interactive… Uninet experience. The mollusk was the most memorable one so far, but all the videos were up-close-and-personal. Then there were the sounds, the *smells*. Various cheeps, roars, rumbles and caws pierced his ears as if their originators were roaming free overhead or twining around his feet. And musks, briny mists and general zoological stenches of the intestinal kind steamed from the system with every keystroke.

He couldn't navigate away fast enough from the Vernjoolsian mollusk. And it gave him second thoughts about clicking the next item on his search list: "Ratuk Flappameria." He made the selection with nervous fingers and then jettisoned backwards in the levitating desk chair, just in case.

A small, yellow, burst-shaped leafy creature took wing out of the computer, soaring and spinning like a miniature kite. Its movements were gentle, free, as if filled with an inner joy expressed solely through the dance of flight. It sang a light squeaking song, melodic and faint. Like someone slowly adjusting the air escaping from a teeny-tiny balloon.

Up, down and around, it twirled and swirled, like a petal on the wind. It wasn't what he was searching for, but the Ratuk Flappameria was entrancing in its own right. Bertram found himself gliding back in toward the computer console to get a closer look. Catching his eye from across the room, Rollie, too, rose and drew closer for a better examination.

"What is it?" Rollie murmured, crouching nimbly, amber eyes riveted on the delicate creature.

"Ratuk Flappameria," Bertram said.

Now they could see fine, almost opalescent hairs or feathers on its rich leathery surface.

"Cosmic," breathed Rollie.

"Truly," said Bertram.

Now they could see the stem was not a stem at all, but a shimmering sprout-like antennae, waving sinuously, iridescent before their eyes.

"The colors," observed Bertram.

"Stellar," agreed Rollie.

Now they could see the eyelash-like fuzz on the antennae, undulating like a belly-dancer to and fro with sultry rhythm and grace.

"Hypnotic," whispered Rollie.

"Amazing," Bertram nodded.

Now they could see it suddenly expand to four times its previous size, open a mouth just about the size of that, and bare two tiered sets of razor sharp teeth, which gnawed with the brutal force of an uncontrolled jackhammer.

"G-ahh!"

"Bleedin' Karnax!"

Bertram raced Rollie for the Cancel button. Rollie dove and got to it first.

As pixels of light vanished in the air like sparks, Bertram sunk back into the desk chair and exhaled. "Jesus, Rollie, isn't there *anything* beautiful in your universe that doesn't crush, explode, slash or bite?"

Rising, the alien captain looked unexpectedly pale and rattled himself. "Well, er…Vos Laegos showgirls," he suggested, a twitch of a smile, a strained attempt at levity. "Ah—no. Scratch that, what *they* do is—"

"Later," Bertram told him. Bertram was about done with acts of nature for the day. "Save it for later."

"So no luck yet with the yellow thingummy?" Rollie asked.

"Hard to say. There are tons more search matches in my list, but I may have a coronary before I finish it."

"Mm," Rollie agreed. Then sudden inspiration filled his eyes. "Wait, how about—?"

"PING!" said the computer.

"How about you—?"

"PING! PING!"

"You might be able to—"

"PING! PING! PINGPING!"

"What *is* that?" Bertram noticed a happy icon in the corner of the screen was hopping up and down like it had to use the restroom.

"Must've bumped the fragging—"

"PINGPINGPINGPINGPING"

It was growing louder, and faster, like submarine sonar with a stuttering problem. The icon in the corner was now bigger on the screen, too, and performing a more desperate dance for attention.

Rollie raised his voice over it, "—Bumped the fragging Uninet News Update. It defaults—"

"PINGPINGPINGPINGPINGPINGPINGPING"

"—To ping every time a new bit of news comes in."

"PINGPINGPINGPINGPINGPINGPING"

"All of those are new news items?" Bertram shouted, but Rollie couldn't hear him over the rapid-fire sound.

Rollie motioned Bertram from the desk chair and commandeered it himself. He attended to the icon, which was, at this point, contorted into an elaborate and painful-looking mosh, taking up the whole screen.

It responded by popping up four different squares onto the display. Four different videos played, all of them talking at once. In the blink of an eye, this doubled, then tripled, quadrupled, and on and on. Soon there were hundreds of little squares on the screen, and hundreds of different languages clashing and vibrating from the sound system. Bertram's Translachew gum was having a hard time processing it all, so intelligible snippets only came to him in bursts. Frowning, Rollie surveyed the newscasts and selected a small section from their ranks, collapsing them back down to four.

"—Foobaz Frabblagundger, leader of the hit band Dumbbell Nebula, had a hangnail today," one newscaster droned. "Close friends speculate on his ability to perform in the band's current tour, or whether he can brave through this bleak personal crisis. Fans reacted to the shocking news with a flood of get well wishes for the Calderian heartthrob, and the development of the GCU Foobaz Frabblagundger Hangnail Prevention Awareness program…"

Rollie closed that window.

"—Forwardists welcomed 450 new fiction pills into the CapClub library today. The new infopills will be available no later than ten Universal minutes from now in more popular LibLounge locat—"

With a click, that window vanished.

"—Celebrating Stella Cygnus' and Jet Antlia's successful adoption of their 438th Biblucian orphan. Census experts for the planet Bibluciat indicate that there are now more progeny under ten residing with the famous poet and dancer than there are on the planet of Bibluciat itsel—"

"Zap," went that window.

"—Podunk Peace Guards are in stable condition with experts currently determining the best way to restore the victims' physical forms to their original arrangements. Hyphiz Deltan RegForce officer, W.I. Tsmarmak Mook is cited as saying, 'Not since our brethren in law enforcement broke up that orgy on Caligula-19 have I seen such a startling discombobulation of body parts.'

"The suspects are described as one Rolliam Tsmorlood—" Here Rollie's likeness projected from the screen in perfect 3-D realism, if looking wild-eyed and a bit hung-over. "—An exiled Hyphiz Deltan mercenary well-known within GCU Underworld circles for his erratic behavior, cutthroat leadership and quick work with an XJ-37. With him was *this* life-form…"

Here the image of Rollie was swapped for one of Bertram, an unflattering shot of him stunned and snoring on the cot in the Podunk jail cell.

Bertram groaned. Rollie cackled.

"The being is believed to be a humanoid male from Tryfe, a backspace planet not previously thought to have had off-planet contact with GCU inhabitants. This suspect's identity remains unknown, while Tsmorlood is already wanted in conjunction with his escape from the historically-inescapable penal colony planet, Rhobux-7. The Seers of Rhobux-7, wardens for the planet, are currently unavailable for comment as Rhobux-7 is, remarkably, no longer located at its expected coordinates.

"In an exclusive *Heavy Meddler Live* interview, renowned astrophysicist Krut Tangin examines this never-before-seen phenomenon."

A silvery-haired, humanoid female projected into the room. She had a bald spot at the top of her head comprised of a giant protuberance of lumpy skull matter like a fleshy peak from the higher Alps. She stared at a live image of the coordinates of Rhobux-7.

"So hey, you peoples," she greeted cheerfully, "you want to know of Rhobux-7, yes? Well, in expert opinion of mine, me, I say is completely gone. Missing. Not for being there no more. So too freaky! Wowee, baby! It just not should do that thing. Why?—Well, I get back to you, yes? Maybe next Universal year. More maybe."

"Thank you, Krut Tangin, for that enlightening analysis," said the newscaster. "In the meantime, the Hyphiz Deltan RegForce is on the lookout for both Tsmorlood and the unidentified Tryfling. They urge anyone spotting Tsmorlood or the Tryfling suspect to contact Hyphiz Deltan authorities immediately. Consider them armed and extremely dangerous."

Bertram moaned and closed the screen. "See? This is exactly what I was worried about. And—" Bertram cursed at the latest interruption, "What now?"

The vis-u buzzer had just sounded, giving Bertram's heart another stutter-step. Surely the RegForce hadn't found them *already*. Surely, they wouldn't *call* first.

In a flash, the screen panel on the cabinet revealed a cloud of gray smoke, and within it, a figure moved like a shadow. "Tsmorlood, ya there?" The figure leaned toward the camera, and Bertram could almost discern a ruddy-skinned blond man, eyes glittering a keen peridot green through the haze. In his hand was some kind of pipe. It poured forth charcoal clouds.

"Tseethe! Long time, mate," Rollie exclaimed, dropping into a seat in front of the vis-u. "What goes?"

"You're all over the Uninet, man," Tseethe told him with a toast of his pipe.

"So we learned," Rollie said. They both looked a little too pleased with this news to suit Bertram.

"Yeah, well, you're coming here to Vos Laegos, right? For the vote? Xylith said she talked to ya, and you said ya were." Tseethe had a way of speaking that transformed each sentence into short, urgent bursts of words collapsing in on each other, like a verbal avalanche.

"Xylith was right," Rollie said. "I'll be there."

"Okay, then I'm telling ya right now, rethink it. Word on the street is, the RegForce knows about the meeting, and they're coming here. You're here, they'll be here, understand? And while you're at it, you'd better cloak up, pal. Or you won't know what hit you when those RegForce tractor beams lock on, knowwhatI'msayin'?"

"I was just getting to that." Rollie turned to Bertram. "Ludlow, push that button there." He indicated the shipboard computer wall panel just to Bertram's left.

Bertram moved to the panel, his finger hovering over a big red button. "That one?"

"Down."

"This one?" He indicated a large black button.

"Left."

"Here?" He pointed to a square yellow button.

"Lower still. There!" directed Rollie. "That there."

That area was completely empty. "Excuse me?"

"Just that button there. Press it. Now."

Bertram pushed at the painful space between his eyes instead. "I don't see a button there."

"Of course you don't," Rollie snapped. "It's a cloaking button. Why would you want to *see* it? Just press it without all the fragging backchat, would you?"

Bertram pressed the button he couldn't see. To the touch, there did seem to be something there.

"Boy," Tseethe shook his head slowly, pipe between his teeth in a grin, "you got a winner there, Rollie. That's the Tryfling?"

"Yeah," Rollie snickered.

"Why's he even here? Did ya get him on a bet, or something?"

"More like progeny-minding," Rollie told him. "Look, Tseethe, thanks for the heads-up, but I got some things to do before I hit Vos Laegos airspace. See you at the meeting?"

"You're not still comin'?" Bertram could see Tseethe tense even through the smoke. "Aw, come on, did ya even hear what I said, or was I just wasting a lotta fraggin' time telling myself a story? The Regimental Enforcement Squad knows about the meeting. They'll be waiting."

"I got it covered," Rollie assured him.

"Well, I hope ya do. Otherwise, I hope you willed me your..." Tseethe seemed to search his recollections for just the right thing, "Nah, you don't have anything I want. Nevermind." He gave some sort of military salute in the fog. "Captain..." And he reached for a button.

"One thing," said Rollie, and Tseethe paused. Rollie indicated the pipe. "I thought you'd quit that."

Tseethe eyed the pipe in his hand with a grimace. "Yeah, for like, two Universal hours. Turns out I've evolved to actually feed off the stuff. It's weird, I'm drawing nutrients from it. I stop smoking, I'll lose vital stuff my body's depending on now and I'll die."

"Seriously?"

"I'm a fraggin' marvel of Deltan medicine, if ya can believe that," said Tseethe. He gave a last resigning look at the pipe and tucked it back between his teeth. "Well, I won't keep ya. *Paar too*, man."

"*Paar too*," Rollie responded. He turned away from the vis-u.

Bertram was shaking his head in disbelief. "There's a manhunt on for us, we're going to Vos Laegos, the cops know we're coming, and half the Underworld's expecting us. Your own friend is begging you not to attend. Can't we just go on to Nett?"

"Look, I said I had it covered, didn't I? The question is…" Rollie stood in the center of the room and surveyed all the cabinets, "…where on flaming Altair did I put it?"

"Put what?"

Rollie strode over to a wall, pushed a button and disappeared into the storeroom.

"Hey, put what?" Bertram asked the door. "Rollie?"

Inside the private Vos Laegos office, W.I. Tsmarmak Mook offered the manager of the Crater Club a warm, beneficent smile.

"Please do pardon the intrusion," he said, after introducing himself, "I know you must be extraordinarily busy, managing a bustling business such as this. But I can only assume that someone who has his digits on the very pulse of intergalactic life, as you do, has already heard about the two fugitives we're seeking?"

He paused just long enough to let the compliment soak in through the pores. "Shortly," he leapt in as the manager opened his mouth to speak, "we expect these fugitives to turn up here for the Intergalactic Underworld Society meeting. And we'd like to ensure that while they may come here with nefarious plans, they will leave safely within our custody. I was hoping you might allow us access to that meeting."

"Ahhhh," responded the manager, one Mr. Otar Eeday. "I would *love* to help you, W.I. Mook. In fact, nothing would give me greater pleasure than to provide assistance to your solar system's illustrious keepers of justice. But it appears there has been some mistake. I'm afraid we *have no* Underworld Society meeting scheduled here at this time." The manager was a long, lean life-form, with an expensive suit, a pointed face, soulful eyes, and a pale blue complexion that caused him to look perpetually chilled. Hairs jutted from beneath his nose in a handful of stiff long bristles. It could be less called a mustache than whiskers. It gave him a somewhat prickly, unyielding appearance, particularly when he smiled tautly. As he did now.

"Why, you can see our schedule here." Mr. Eeday motioned to the wall at his left, bearing a large screen showcasing all the events on the Crater Club's calendar in the coming days. "No Underworld Society meeting. I am so sorry to say, you've been misinformed."

W.I. Mook nodded. He'd been prepared for this sort of protective behavior from Crater Club staff. It wasn't that the Intergalactic Underworld Society wasn't *legal*, per se. Actually, the GCU's organized criminal element was looked upon quite favorably by the public as a good way of getting stuff done. The thinking was, the Underworld was only slightly more corrupt than legitimate corporate business, anyway. And the Underworld was a lot more fun at parties.

So the need for secrecy really was more a question of image than necessity. As Underworld pickpocket, Retty Fingfowcher, once famously said, "What's the point in being a part of the deep, dark, skulking underbelly of the Universe, if everyone can talk to you about it over a sandwich?" The Underworld enjoyed its mystery. And if retaining that sense of mystery meant the Society members would be happy repeat guests who spent lots of money on food and drinks and the gaming tables?... Well, the Crater Club was clearly willing to play along.

"Ah, yes," W.I. Mook agreed heartily, peering now at the event schedule with exaggerated interest. "Why, look at that; you're quite right! I see *no* Underworld Society meeting listed here. There's clearly *no* Underworld Society meeting about to begin. And, well, color me just so embarrassed!"

W.I. Tstyko was staring at Mook with those bulbous eyes of his, like his friend and colleague was suffering from bends of the brain. His mouth hung open on its hinges. His brow furrowed. It was true, the blushing apologist before him *was* laying it on a bit thick even for Mook's personal style, but Mook felt sure Tstyko knew better than to comment. Mook supposed they'd be having an interesting discussion about it later over mootaab toasties.

The Crater Club manager, on the other hand, was acting like the issue was resolved and Mook should be about to make his grand exit. "Well, we all make mistakes," Mr. Eeday told him, offering another tight smile that made his whiskers stand out straight, like quills. He stepped toward the door in a final gracious gesture.

But Mook just stood rooted to the spot, an introspective expression washing over his poetic face. "And even if there *were* an Underworld meeting being held here—"

"Though there isn't," input the manager.

"No, there *most certainly* isn't," Mook exclaimed, as if horrified at the very accusation. "But if there *were*. Your organization offers its utmost privacy to all of its clients, assuring them the highest quality of service throughout their stay. Certainly, if you *were* hosting such a meeting where privacy was in order—"

"As a hypothetical concept only," emphasized Mr. Eeday.

"And then you had parties such as myself and W.I. Tstyko here *violating* said privacy... Well, what would that say for the reputation of your establishment?"

Mr. Eeday blinked the soulful eyes. Mook imagined he'd expected cajoling and then some serious leaning—possibly with weapons and personal injury. Agreement and empathy were not the most trendy RegForce approaches to problem solving. "Um, yes, well," began Mr. Eeday primly, "customer privacy is, of course, always very important to us. It's been stellar chatting with you. Thank you for stopping by, W.I. Mook." He remained at the door with a now-hopeful gaze.

Mook pressed on. "Now, if you *were* hosting the Universal Underworld Society meeting, and yet you *did* care to help the Hyphiz Delta RegForce bring two intergalactic fugitives to justice— something sure to get quite a bit of positive PR for the Crater Club, too, I'd wager— well, you'd simply need to strike a careful balance."

"Oh, yes?" murmured Eeday. His tone held the mild curiosity of a man who's seen something on his dinner plate he can't quite recognize but might want to pursue its identity.

"Certainly. You'd simply fulfill your obligation to your client, the Underworld Society, while simultaneously making it easy for us to get our men." He offered another engaging smile. "Hypothetically speaking, of course."

"Of course," said Mr. Eeday. Mook could almost see him lingering on that idea of positive PR for the Crater Club. *Heavy Meddler* headlines, Vos Laegos commendations, the eye of new investors, and so much more. It was all practically written along Eeday's whiskered face. "And how would one go about doing that?"

"Well," began Mook, looking ceilingward in thought, "not knowing where a super-secret event like that would be held, if it were being held here…"

"We have no facilities of that kind," Mr. Eeday said.

"…I would suggest allowing us undercover access to any entrances to the festivities. Permission to scan the guests before they enter. All very subtle. Very tasteful. That way, the little matter would be taken care of prior to reaching the Society meeting. Or it could be shifted outside the building altogether. The Underworld need never be bothered." Mainly, Mook didn't want to take on half the Underworld just to root out Tsmorlood and the Tryfling. After so many years on the RegForce, he knew: sometimes the simplest way was best.

Otar Eeday drummed his fingers together thoughtfully, his long clawlike nails clicking with a gentle rat-a-tat. He pursed his lips, causing the whiskers to spring out again. "If that sort of situation ever came up," he began, "I can see the Crater Club being amenable to a procedure along those lines."

W.I. Mook gave a bow of his head.

"I would ask that there be absolutely no uniforms."

"Certainly."

"And that any apprehension would be done keeping the complete safety of our guests in mind."

"Stunning can very easily be made to look like sudden illness, if it came to that. But ultimately our goal would be to identify the targets and extract them from the Crater Club altogether. The Hyphiz Delta Regimental Enforcement Squad is nothing if not the very epitome of discretion." Mook could feel Tstyko's buggy gaze beating into him at this one. He didn't dare look, or he would laugh. Instead, he settled on clearing his throat. "If we *were* to implement something like this, Mr. Eeday, where would we need to position ourselves?" queried Mook.

"I would give you a facilities map. Like this one," he pulled a floorplan of the Club from a drawer. "And I would mark it, like so." He handed Mook the map with a key location circled.

"Where," Mook said, frowning at the map, "would the meeting room itself be? Hypothetically?"

"For this hypothetical situation, that really isn't pertinent to our discussions, W.I. Mook," said Eeday. He gave another ice blue smile. "You know, the Crater Club is a lot like one of our charming Vos

Laegos showbeings. They must retain a few secrets for themselves. It's part of their allure. I hope you and your men will respect that."

It was not the answer he was hoping for, but it was the answer Mook expected. "Understood," he said. "And respected. And one last thing, Mr. Eeday..."

"Yes?"

"When won't the meeting begin?"

"The meeting won't start later today."

"So, there's no hurry then." Mook moved to the door himself now. Tstyko looked startled at the sudden conclusion of their discussion and rose from his chair.

"Discretion," Mr. Eeday called after them. "We never spoke of this."

"And it was absolutely stellar not talking to you," Mook said with a parting wave.

Rolliam Tsmorlood had it covered. Bertram knew this, because the Hyphiz Deltan just kept saying it. So when the man unveiled the box from the storeroom like it contained nothing less than the Crown Jewels, Bertram was braced for extra-terrestrial wonders.

Then the box opened and...

"Wristwatches." Bertram unbraced. "That's useful. We'll know down to the second what time we're arrested and being deloused."

"Holowatches," Rollie corrected. "Here. Put this on and I'll show you."

Bertram took the slim black device and snapped it around his wrist. It was somewhat heavier than a standard watch, but the weight felt solid and reassuring. "Okay?"

"Press the silver button and scan yourself head to toe."

"Er... Scan... how do I—?"

Rollie grumbled impatiently. "Watch me, then." He'd grabbed the second watch, strapped it to his wrist, pushed the silver button and then waved his arm in a vertical motion from the top of his head to the metal tips of his boots. He then repeated the process from the feet up again. "There. Now go to it."

Bertram did so.

"Excellent!" Rollie flashed a wicked grin. "Now, the fun part." The Deltan pushed a blue button on his timepiece, and in an instant there stood a dark-skinned, humanoid male with three shining black eyes. The figure wore a long, brown hooded cloak that fell in waves over his short, stocky frame. His hands were thick and wide. His feet were thick and flat. And they were clad in heavy, rough-hewn sandals. He was anything but Deltan. "Your turn."

After this, Bertram couldn't wait to see his own transformation. He pressed the blue button and then patted his arms, his face. It all felt exactly the same. He looked down at his legs, his filthy socked feet, but nothing seemed to be any different. The same toes poking through the fabric. The same old jaw in bad need of a shave. He felt a pang of disappointment. "It didn't work."

"Are you so sure?" Rollie snatched up the crusty stew pot from the hotplate and held its shiny base before Bertram's face.

The face of a dark-skinned, three-eyed, cloaked, corpulent old woman reflected back. "Aw, hell." There was a large mole on the side of the old woman's nose. A sprig of fine black hair sprouted from it like hopeful flowers. Bertram touched the spot alongside his own nose expecting to feel its tickle.

"Was a lady friend of mine's who also had a spot of tricky business with the RegForce," the dark figure explained with Rollie's voice. "Keep meaning to return it to her with her other effects, but just haven't got round to it." The dark man beamed. "Lucky break for us, eh?"

"Oh, yes, absolutely. Swap me?" Bertram suggested.

Rollie laughed in a "not-fragging-likely" way.

"I'm going into the dragon's den, looking like Grandma Ludlow forgot her waterpills. Not much of a confidence-booster," Bertram told him.

"Sorry." Rollie pressed his holowatch's blue button a second time, and ZAP! The optical illusion slipped away.

Bertram sighed, picked up the pot and took a last look at his new reflection. "I'm tapping into my inner fugitive from intergalactic justice, as a century-old granny with a weight problem."

Rollie tossed him an unconcerned glance. "No one ever said saving the world would be glamorous, Ludlow.

10

They came in low over Vos Laegos City, capital of the planet Vos Laegos, giving Bertram an astounding view of the world below. Never had he seen such crazed combinations of architecture and color springing up in such a tangle of ideas. It made St. Peter's Basilica look like Amish workmanship.

One of the buildings below appeared to undulate and pulse, like some strange living tissue. Another looked almost transparent, the inhabitants inside seeming to stand on air alone. Yet another was shaped like the head of a giant creature, partially buried in the sand, life-forms entering and exiting through its nostrils. There was a building that appeared as a swirl of light and color, enveloping all who stepped into it. One construction looked like a giant nest of opalescent green hornets, burrowing into the land. Another appeared edible, like a great castle of some mad alien confectioner. There were colors so bright they teased and taunted the eyes with their glare, and colors so dark they didn't even exist. There were metallic sheens in shades Bertram would have been hard-pressed to describe, and ethereal glows that radiated with an almost unnerving lifeforce. Things shone, glittered, flashed, and transformed before the eyes. They were hyper-realistic and gone in a wink.

The Interplanetary Cruise Vessel passed over all of this and landed some distance away, at the edge of the city. Here was desolation, gray sand, and small scuttling animals that appeared with a pop, and disappeared the same way. It was like Vos Laegos had put all its energy into giving birth to the unhinged brilliance of its capital, and there was nothing left for the land itself.

Vos Laegos City was the planet's most glorious ungrateful child.

"Why are we so far out?" Bertram asked, peering out the portal for another glimpse of those strange city spires.

"Can't very well park a cloaked ICV in the middle of a lot, can you? One poor slaggard thinks the space is free and tries to land, we'd be done for. It'll be a hike, but believe me, we're safer leaving it here."

"What if we have to make a quick escape?"

Rollie fired up the holowatch. "We'll just put faith in our three-eyed friends it won't come to that, eh? Ready?"

"Say hello to Grandma Ludlow."

They lowered the ship's ramp and stepped out onto the surface. And soon, Bertram and Rollie wound through the narrow alleys, the broad boardwalks, and the teetering skywalks of the planet's capital.

Nothing was where it seemed it should be. The size of the buildings was misleading, so a structure that looked only a block away still took forever to reach. The path led them up moving staircases, across flying discs, through dim hotel lobbies, and on and off tiny bullet-trains. Life-forms of every size, color and type passed by—some singing or staggering, some bustling on through, some wrapped in the company of new companions, and some wandering without a care in the world.

Vendors lined the way offering Bertram cocktails, genetic makeovers, all-you-could-digest buffets, and dealers' tricks to win at games called "piggelties" and "Emperor's G'napps." There were do-it-yourself massage techniques which claimed to be illegal in 12 solar systems. And life-forms willing to share the ancient alchemists' secret of transforming plain old rocks into fully-loaded yoonie cards.

The tricky part, with all this buzz, was to keep pace with Rollie. The path was maze-like. The Hyphiz Deltan knew where he was going, and he walked quickly, with a long, purposeful stride. Even in decent shape, Bertram still found himself working to keep up.

"You wanna slow it down a little?" Bertram asked.

"You want to get something for that throat, old lady?" Rollie asked, giving him a warning look.

Bertram forgot he was Grandma Ludlow. Of course, the real Grandma Ludlow had also been fond of cigarettes and Sidecars, so it wasn't like she was that far from a tenor. "Terrible way to speak to your honored elders," Bertram snapped, raising the Gran-o-meter a little.

Rollie might have chuckled, but his tone was still firm. "Just remember who you're supposed to be. No slip ups. We're almost there. And there's where it counts," he said. And in a moment, Bertram saw he was right. They had arrived at the Crater Club.

✧

"This place is an absolute pit!" exclaimed Bertram. He peered into the gaping black abyss before them in wide-eyed marvel. The only part of their destination on surface-level was an ample flashing sign that, in regular increments, exploded with heat and color as a careening, holographic meteor struck it. The sign read:

The Crater Club.
Vos Laegos' #1 Hole in the Ground

"How do we even get in?" Bertram asked.

But at that moment, a being with lavender skin and backwards knees brushed past him with a gruff, "Sorry, lady," and jumped straight down into the cavern.

The three-eyed man in the brown hood turned to Bertram and grinned in answer.

"Oh, that can't be right," Bertram found himself saying as he peered into the void before them. "This is a business establishment, a tourist spot. We can't be expected to just jump into—"

But, still grinning, the three-eyed man gave a snappy salute and sprung neatly into the blackness below.

"Of course," Bertram muttered to himself, as Rollie vanished from view. "Well, I never was big on extreme sports. But—" And Bertram made the leap himself.

The drop was like a lazy elevator, gently sinking into the Vos Laegos sands. A drinks server on a balcony to the side tucked some glowing alien beverage in Bertram's hand. "Welcome to the Crater Club," she said with an engaging alien smile.

Another handed him a map of the facilities and winked. "Welcome to the Crater Club!"

And a third put a cheap novelty spelunker hat, complete with light, on his head. "Welcome to the Crater Club!" she said warmly.

It was like Alice down the rabbit hole, but the service was a whole lot better.

When he finally came to the bottom of the passage, his feet touched down so gently, not a drop of his beverage was spilled. Bertram took a sip. "Mm. Weird!" It *was* weird, too—somehow wet and dry at the same time, yet cold, sweet and refreshing. He noticed his three-eyed companion was already there, stalking back and forth like a hungry tiger. Bertram held up his drink. "Hey, did you get one of these? I think those waitresses were flirting with me."

"*Grandma*," Rollie began firmly. He relieved Bertram of first the hat and then the drink, tossing them into a passing disposal robot.

"Aw." Bertram was surprised at his own sinking disappointment. Also the fact that Rollie threw away a drink. "Right."

"This way, if you will?" Through reception and to the right of miles of roaring, plinking gaming tables was an area marked "Conference Center and Expo." There the crowds were already thick.

A dozen conferences were going on, each with large electronic registration kiosks. There was the Aeroponic Smorg Growers of Quad Four Conference; The Association for the Fraternal Order of Fraternia-12 Fraternities' Assembly of Brotherhood; there was the Calderian Moon Polyp Education and Edibility League, PR Branch annual meeting; and the Forwardist LibLounge Future Bestseller Best Guesstimation Summit. There were professional meetings for professions Bertram had never heard of. And unprofessional meetings that were being really unprofessional right there in the conference hall.

Some attendees carried armfuls of equipment, some handed out brochure pills, and many trundled along drawing levitating carts behind them—carts overflowing with informational gadgets and giveaway items as diverse as the life-forms in attendance. Bertram spied everything from strange hats, electronics and clothing to something that looked a lot like a green camel. It chewed placidly as it floated along in its cart, being led from the exhibits to the next conference room.

There were no signs anywhere mentioning an Intergalactic Underworld conference going on at this time, and Bertram thought that was odd. He wondered if the Society lacked the funds, or if a particularly zealous member, swept up in the spirit of the gathering, had simply walked off with the kiosk and kidnapped the staff.

Bertram was about to ask Rollie about it but noticed how the Deltan's borrowed eyes had been scanning the crowds, black, keen and constant.

"You seem worried," said Bertram conversationally, trying to keep pace.

"Not worried, watchful," said Rollie. "There's a difference."

"I'm not worried, either," volunteered Bertram. "I feel great." And on further consideration and against all logic, Bertram realized this was true. He did feel great. Pretty much from the moment they'd left the ship, really, it was like he was a new man. Unafraid, unconcerned and even unfettered by his own obvious madness. He should have been concerned about his lack of concern. But he just couldn't be bothered.

"It's the jubies," Rollie explained.

"The what?"

"They call it the Vos Laegos jubies. A sort of euphoria. It's the air here. Has an effect on those not used to it. This way."

Rollie led them down the hallway marked "Ballrooms."

"Jubies," Bertram murmured to himself, liking the way the word felt on his lips. "Juuuu-beeeees."

Rollie's glare cut through euphoria like an XJ-37.

Bertram cleared his throat. "Xylith said the meeting was in The Core. Which way?"

"Leave it to me."

They passed by the Impact Room. There, life-forms were heading into a session surrounding a giant 3-D pie chart in berry flavor. Next, they came to the Echo Room and the Cavern Room, both of which were empty. In the Collision Room, two speakers were involved in violent debate. In both the Meteorite Room and Volcano Rooms, it looked like the audiences were having a blast. And in the Quake Room, some being with large floppy ears was leading a session looking pale and wan, like he'd never spoken in public in his life.

It was outside the Shockwave Room, in the very center of the long corridor, a cluster of people loaded down with tacky conference souvenirs stood, waiting for the next session. Among them, Bertram noticed the same Hyphiz Deltan RegForce officer who he'd seen on the Uninet, talking about the attack and reassembly of the Podunk Peace Guards.

Bertram couldn't remember his name, but he was a tall, hefty wall of a man, with a placid oval face and uncharacteristically doughy middle for a Deltan. He munched from a plate of hors d'oeuvres in a deceptively casual way, Bertram thought, as a closer look indicated he was giving equal attention to the guests in the corridor as the snacks at hand. Next to him, Bertram guessed, was his partner, hands clasped behind his back in a military stance, rocking back and forth on his heels with the nervous energy of a Hyphizite who would rather be leading a foot chase than standing in a hallway scanning the tourists. That one looked taut as an overstretched piano wire and ready to snap at a second. He wore a t-shirt that read, "Aeroponic Farmers Have Higher Standards" and showed a cartoon cluster of Smorgs growing six feet off the ground.

As disguises went, it needed something.

Bertram didn't dare let his eyes linger. He wondered whether Rollie had spied the Deltan officers, too, though they'd have to discuss that later. Right now Rollie was busy having quiet word with the door marked "The Rim Room." It opened with a hiss and he motioned Bertram inside.

Inside was not a conference room, but a dim passageway. On the wall was a lit arrow. It pointed down the long hall.

At the end of the hall was an elevator, and as they approached it, the doors opened automatically with a rush. They stepped inside, the doors closed—and the contraption dropped so quickly, Bertram was almost sure the cable had snapped. His feet lifted lightly off the floor. The elevator careened, down, down, down. And then, with a jar, the elevator stopped. Bertram and Rollie's feet dropped with a clatter. As the doors shooshed open, Bertram half-expected them to reveal a circle of Hyphiz Deltan RegForce officers waiting for them, their weapons drawn and glinting in the light.

It opened onto a busy, working kitchen.

They stepped into the room and strode down the hallway. Down a kitchen passageway, past robot chefs and humanoid chefs, and steaming foods and freezing foods, things on fire, and things on ice.

Further and further through the bustling room they went, no one questioning who they were, and what they were doing there. Bertram considered how he would have been really worried about that, worried they were headed for a clever trap—if he were actually worried about anything these days, which he wasn't.

He also would have been worried when Rollie opened the giant refrigerator door at the end of the hallway and walked through it.

A worry-free Bertram walked into the refrigerator, too.

Bertram rubbed his goose-pimply arms as they moved past the shelves of alien cuisine to finally—*finally*—stop at a small white door at the back. "If we're going into the freezer, I could use shoes."

Rollie grinned and disappeared through the door...

Into a conference hall. This was The Core, and the place was packed.

"Welcome to the Intergalactic Underworld Annual Society Meeting and Marketplace" glittered an electronic banner spanning the room. The ballroom itself was a great cavern, with stalactites dropping down from the ceiling and stalagmites jutting up from the floor. There was an auditorium off one end and an exposition hall off the other. But right now it was the ballroom that was abuzz with activity, and not for any excess of Mathekites. This was the place a thousand forbidden ideas were born. Where criminal minds collided in brainstorms. Where lunch meetings nourished illicit plans. And where goods slipped quietly from one life-form to the other like well-choreographed dance.

Rollie scanned the crowd carefully, then approached a booth marked "Registration."

"Dax Q. Phlyjollee," Rollie said, adding, "and guest." He passed the agent a Society card.

The life-form manning the booth entered the info into the system and nodded. "One moment, Mr. Phlyjollee. We're printing up your entry badges."

Rollie was still giving a wary eye or three to the beings around them. As far as Bertram could tell, no one else looked like Deltan RegForce, and Deltans, he was discovering, were easy enough to spot. Half a head taller than everyone else, and typically so fair they seemed to have no eyebrows or eyelashes at all, the look was distinctive. Of course, that didn't mean some of them hadn't gotten a hold of a couple of holowatches themselves.

"Here you go, Mr. Phlyjollee," said the attendant, using a delicate suction-cupped tentacle to hand them each a badge. "The Welcome Remarks start in the auditorium there, and the Marketplace in the Expo Hall is open for any fencing or buying you'd care to do during your visit."

Rollie offered a twitch of a smile. "Stellar, thanks."

"Dax Q. Phlyjollee?" Bertram asked as they headed toward the auditorium.

But Rollie just shrugged as they entered the room.

Like the ballroom, the auditorium ceiling erupted with stalactites, its floor covered in rows of stadium seats carved right into the rock. To the front of the room was an immense stage, a backdrop of shining crystals sparkling in the light.

Around the perimeter of the room, friends greeted each other. Standoffs were bubbling up over old vendettas. And laser fire whizzed invisibly past Bertram's ear over one such altercation. He had become all too familiar with the tingle of its energy.

Rollie must have spied someone he knew in the far corner, because soon Bertram was rushing to follow. In a moment, he spotted the faces of Xylith, Fess, Wilbree, and...

"Tseethe Tsardonee," Rollie said, addressing a figure in a smoke-filled bubble-like helmet. He gave that strange, light clicking hiss to the "T's" that so many Deltan words seemed to have.

Inside the helmet, Tseethe's eyes glowed a bright catlike green through the smoke, then narrowed to slits. Bertram discerned what was probably a pipe slide from one corner of Tseethe's mouth to the other. "Look, pal, I don't know who—"

Rollie pushed the button on his holowatch, off once, then on again. As a result, his real self was just a flicker of an image, more hallucination than actual form.

Tseethe erupted with a hearty laugh that rattled from his helmet's speaker system. "Ah yes. Dax Q. Phlyjollee."

"None other," Rollie agreed. Apparently Mr. Phlyjollee got around.

Tsteethe gestured at the three-eyed old woman before him. "And then I suppose this is...?"

"'And Guest,'" supplied Bertram.

"He's a *Tryfling*," piped up Wilbree, with the same sort of awed delight from the first time they'd met on Podunk.

"Nicetameetya," Tseethe said, shaking Bertram's hand heartily. "And what brings ya to the GCU, Tryfeman?

"Mostly an ICV and a stun-gun," Bertram quipped, earning an appreciative murmur from the group.

"He's going to save his planet," Wilbree input with a nod.

"Save Tryfe? What from?" asked Tseethe. "Meteors? Invasion? Bad haircuts? What?"

Bertram felt his face redden a moment. He wished this topic wouldn't keep coming up. It only poured salt on the wound.

Then something occurred to him. "Maybe you can help." Bertram lifted the Yellow Thing up over his head, and handed it to Tseethe. Given his holowatch disguise, it must have looked strange to them, to see this soap-on-a-rope-looking item appear out of nowhere. "Have any idea what this is?"

Tseethe drew it to the dome of his helmet and squinted. "Strange. Where'd ya get it?"

"Seers of Rhobux."

"And I didn't think the Seers of Rhobux gave anybody anything but confinement time."

"Does it look familiar to you?"

"Yeah, like something they'd serve at one of those all-you-can-digest buffets." Tseethe laughed.

"Really?" Bertram asked hopefully. At least it would have been something to go on.

But Tseethe just shrugged it off. "Nah. Sorta," he told Bertram. "But not so much." Tseethe passed the item to Wilbree, who turned it over in his hands, poked it a few times, shrugged, and passed it to Xylith.

She squeezed its spongy exterior and wrinkled both her noses. "It feels...squishy."

"We'd determined it's alive," Bertram said, and at this, Xylith handed it off quickly to Fess. "It's made of living cells."

Fess held it close to his faceted bottle lenses then passed it back to Bertram with one of his many digits. "O'wun might know."

"O'wun?" Bertram asked.

Tseethe's helmet bobbed in agreement. "Sure, sure, yeah. O'wun'd know. He's got a whole database of stuff like that rattling around in his brainpan."

"O'wun is a Non-Organic Simulant," Rollie explained.

"A what?"

"A humanoid replicant. What's the word you use on Tryfe?" Rollie cracked his knuckles as he tried to recall. "An android."

"And where is O'wun?" Bertram asked the group.

Tseethe snickered. "He's living large on Ludd, right now."

"Ludd!" This was Rollie. Bertram guessed being in confinement had really left him out of the loop with a few things. "Bleedin' Karnax, that's the most willfully backward planet in the GCU. And he's a sentient machine! The Luddites hate technology. They'd bash him to fraggin' bits if they knew what he was."

"Don't I know it," said Tseethe. "And he loves it. Got himself a real setup. Fezziwig Towers, it's called, I think. Posh home-unit, real member of the social scene. Guess he's got 'em all convinced he's a natural life-form."

"Thrill issues," confided Wilbree to Bertram.

"Speaking of absent parties…" Rollie leaned on the back of a chair. "Anyone seen that old prib, Backs? Y'know, after he *hid*, leaving me and Ludlow to deal with the Podunk Peace Guards? I'd like to have a word or two with him about solidarity between mates."

Bertram never heard the response because a voice piped over an announcement system while the ceiling lights flashed. "The Opening Remarks for the Intergalactic Underworld Annual Society Meeting will commence shortly. Please take your seats."

"Here's where we get to vote out that big-headed brooquat, Zenith Skytreg," said Tseethe, rubbing his hands together.

"He's very popular, though, isn't he?" piped up Wilbree.

Tseethe rolled his eyes behind the smoke. "Just sit down, man."

The group filed into a row, Bertram taking a seat between Xylith and Fess, and soon the crowd settled to silence. Any lasered bodies were carted out of the pathways for later safe-exiting. The lights dimmed. And suddenly, a glowing lavender fog began to pour in. Enterprising music played. Lights flashed onto the stage like lightning bolts.

The crystals on the stage reacted to the overhead lighting, refracting a variety of colors. And soon, a chorus of showgirls came kicking out in a line from one side of the stage.

Well, *show life-forms*, anyway. An assortment of unnaturally exotic females and males, all of one species Bertram hadn't yet encountered, with silvery hair, pearlescent skin that shimmered in the light, and costumes that weren't so much on, as hovered strategically.

They sang with an inconceivable chime-like beauty. Their chorus of voices had no sooner reached Bertram's ears when he began to think, *This is what Jason and the Argonauts had faced with the siren's song.* Amazing sound to drive sane men mad.

Bertram figured he was already half a stack of Pringles short of a full can, anyway, so he might as well just enjoy it. But he wasn't sure he actually *did* enjoy it. Tears had sprung to his eyes, completely beyond his control.

He looked around the crowd and it seemed as if every being with tear ducts had liquid streaming down their cheeks. The strange part of it was how the words of the singers' song didn't compare with the ethereal output of their phenomenal voices. It seemed wrong to find hundreds of hardened criminals—life-forms who'd frag you soon as look at you, as Rollie would say—weeping over lyrics so cheesy:

> Welcome to Vos Laegos
> It's a special day
> The Underworld has gotten together
> Here, to vote our say
> Who will be our leader?
> Who will lead the show?
> Who's the bossest crime boss?
> We can't wait to know!
> So please don't make us wonder.
> Please don't make us beg
> Let's call the toff to start us off…
> He's criminally glorious!
> Genius!
> Uproarious!
> He's one of us!
> Zeeeeee-nith Skytreg!

Bertram heard Fess let out a groan next to him. Xylith muttered, "Typical." And Bertram noticed Rollie, on the other side of Xylith, shaking his head at the introduction and saying "self-important slaggard." They still wiped away tears of awe, but none of them seemed terribly impressed with the man of the hour's big build-up.

And here it came. Down from the rafters of the stage, a giant softly-illuminated planet glided, mystical wings sprouting from its sides and sweeping up to frame the figure standing atop it in proud silhouette. Suspenseful fanfare reverberated from every wall as this globe sank, sank, sank…

Then the lights hit him. POW!

And a voice rang out. "Hellooooooooooooo, Underworld! Are we ready to blast the vote tonight?" Zenith Skytreg looked left and right, beaming over his constituents, and he motioned for crowd response.

The crowd hooted and clapped, the enthusiasm rippling across the auditorium like electricity through a live wire. Laserguns blazed skyward, loosening a few stalactites, which rained rock and dust on those below. Fess grumbled. Rollie uttered a Deltan oath. Xylith said, "Typical." Here and there, small pockets of Society members remained unmoved through the room's enthusiasm.

Zenith Skytreg appeared to be of the same species as the members of the chorusline. Like them, his skin had a pearly sheen. His teeth had a pearly sheen. He wore a pearly white suit, with an impressive pearly white collar. On his head, was a very full mane of silvery hair, thoroughly pomped into some dramatic ski-jumplike sweep. He was not what Bertram imagined the ladies would consider handsome; his eyes were too close together, his lips a thin line, his jaw too strong for the rest of his face. And, not that Bertram was an expert on these things, but the guy still projected a handsomeness, somehow. Perhaps it was the reflective halo of light that bounced off of him. Bertram just knew he wouldn't want to be competing for the attention of girls at a bar with this dude.

"Friends," began Skytreg, motioning the group to quiet, "as Official Leader of the Intergalactic Underworld these past three Universal years, I felt I would be remiss if I did not speak to you today."

"And get in a little last-minute campaigning," said Xylith under her breath. Both of her faces seemed to be of a similar mind about Skytreg. Her mouths pursed like they'd tasted something bitter.

"I have held many positions in my life," Skytreg continued, his voice solemn. "Professional songster, melody-maker and well-known raconteur... Devil-may-care heist-master... High stakes dealer on the dazzling Emperor's G'napps tables... Confidential yoonie card lender—shhh! Don't tell anyone." Here the audience laughed. "...Biblucian orphan broker, bless their little parentless hearts... Freedom fighter on behalf of the innocent Klimfal people... and Underworld Ambassador representing my very own birth world— this great big beautiful planet of Vos Laegos." He beamed, adding quickly, "Yes, that's right; this Society meeting is like coming home for me!"

Many in the audience murmured with interest at the poetic nature of this.

Fess folded several sets of appendages, defiantly. "Maybe that's 'cause you've always lived here, ya *froob*."

The life-forms one row up turned and shooshed him.

"But never," continued Skytreg, "never in all of the amazing things I have done during my lifetime, never have I felt the joy I've experienced in leading the Intergalactic Underworld Society and all you good people who gave me your vote of confidence not one year, not two, but three prosperous Universal years in a row."

Here spontaneous applause broke out.

"Your drive to make the criminal element be its best... Your ideas for new Underworld opportunities that I've been able to grow and shape in my hands into something wonderful... our support of the fine sponsors who truly understand the importance of our mission and aren't afraid to step up and say, 'Hey, I get it: well-done crime is an artform!'" Here, Skytreg turned around to reveal a number of business sponsor logos rotating electronically on the back of his pearly suit. He then spun to face the crowd. "You have made me grateful every day that I'm the gaseous celestial body you orbit around in the darkness of space. You make me proud to be a part of the best fragging Society of thieves, scoundrels and reprobates the Greater Communicating Universe has to offer!"

The cheering was simply thunderous.

"Smooth," grumbled Fess.

"Typical," sighed Xylith.

"Now, I understand that Underworld Voting Organizer, Twerk Xanthwoggle, has a few things to say to you before we vote and find out who will officially guide the Underworld for the next glorious Universal year. So thank you, Underworld members! You've been a supernova crowd." Zenith Skytreg gave a bow of his head, beamed and jogged off the stage to a seat up front, waving all the way.

Unlike Zenith Skytreg, Twerk Xanthwoggle filed onto stage like a man being led to the witness stand. He was a compact being with almost no neck and a small-eyed, mole-like appearance. His presence was calm and unremarkable.

But as he walked, the music started up and the Vos Laegos showbeings poured from the wings behind him. They kicked and smiled as they churned towards him like some pearly, powerful locomotive, lilting out another tune to an exhilarating orchestral accompaniment.

Twerk Xanthwoggle jumped noticeably at their sudden on-stage appearance, something which apparently had not come up in dress rehearsal. His small eyes popped wide, and he picked up his pace to the center podium with a rapid, running stutter-step. He flinched again as a second chorusline came at him from the other side of the stage. He was stranded, the riser forming an island of safety in a sea of mayhem. He grasped the podium, white-knuckled, as they sang:

> Here's the thing we've longed for
> We're about to start
> The Underworld is just about ready
> Who will steal our hearts?
> Who's been nominated?
> Who will thieve the show?
> Who has stolen, pillaged and plundered?
> We can't wait to know!
> So let's get right down to it.
> Possibilities boggle
> Call the bloke who knows the vote!
> He's not invidious!
> But fastidious!
> No prejudice!
> Just so pretty, yes?
> Twerk Xanthhhhhwoggle!

The Vos Laegos showpeople each raised a dramatic arm toward Twerk Xanthwoggle with a wiggle of high-tech, alien jazz-hands that gave off shimmery sparks. The voting organizer twitched, hand to his chest, presumably where his palpitating heart was located. He watched them filter off the stage, less in fascination than concern they might come back. As he became convinced the last of the chorusline had truly danced out of range, he dabbed at his eyes and cheeks with a handkerchief and tucked it away. Then he opened his jacket, and a small levitating teleprompter fluttered out to bob before him. He cleared his throat.

"Members of the Intergalactic Underworld Society," he said in a flat tone, "this day we determine who will lead our prestigious organization for the next Universal year. The position of Official Leader of the Intergalactic Underworld is an important one. It represents not just the direction that outlawed business will take moving forward, but it puts a face to our organization for everyone across the GCU.

"For many life-forms out there, the Underworld represents that thrilling 'how'd-they-do-that?' creative crime on every Uninet transmission. It gives voice to the 'little life-forms' out there tangled in interstellar bureaucracy because they have no one to stand up for them. And it offers convenient solutions to GCU business when things simply can't get done any other way. We are entertainment, empowerment and answers. And with that, I give you the candidates for this U-year's Official Underworld Leader."

A holoscreen behind Twerk Xanthwoggle appeared, showing the Intergalactic Underworld Society logo in tiny twinkling lights. They exploded like popping, sizzling pyrotechnics into the crowd.

Then a rich booming voice that Bertram thought sounded an awful lot like a film preview announcer said, "And the candidates for the next Official Leader of the Intergalactic Underworld are…"

"Zenith Skytreg." A shot of Zenith Skytreg's well-coiffed head projected out over the audience. "Criminal mind extraordinaire… Rebel hero… and *Heavy Meddler* media hero, Zenith Skytreg is the first life-form in Society history to serve three sequential years as Official Leader of the Intergalactic Underworld. Skytreg has raised millions of yoonies for the organization through his clever sponsorship deals with GCU businesses, putting a fresh, dynamic face on Underworld dealings." This was supported with shots of Skytreg on strange alien chatshows, at public events cutting ribbons, and posing in military wear shaking hands with small furry creatures. "Skytreg has taken the Underworld to a whole new level of Under."

The audience clapped and hooted. A few Society members even stood and cheered.

"Rentar Proximetra." Here came the image of a female humanoid with a shining bald head, a broad smile and a pointy chin and nose.

"Captain Proximetra led the battle of Pachengo Klatts… Single-handedly smuggled 300,000 unlicensed XJ-420 hand-lasers through Belglastnast customs—all upon her person… And uncovered and decoded the lost Archunder Scrolls, then sold them back to the Archunderans 'just because she needed something to do before dinner.'" Captain Proximetra was shown in a variety of high-action shots, and modeling one suspiciously puffy coat outside a Belglastnast security area. "Today she heads the GCU's Quad Two Underworld operations, and it's said she can hijack a freighter, build highly-sensitive explosives, and host an Underworld staff luncheon, all at the same time."

The audience response was impressive. Even Rollie's group gave respectful applause.

"Jor-Jan Chatta-Chu-Bular Meep-Meep," intoned the announcer. The image of Rentar Proximetra was replaced by the headshot of an impossibly narrow life-form of a rich, golden complexion. Its face was angular and beaklike, but everything else about it was slim, long and rounded, like strings of smooth, soft dough, formed into golden breadsticks. It appeared to be entirely nude and without any recognizable genitalia.

The voiceover continued, "For Quad Four residents, Meep-Meep has become a household name. Engineering the designer fake levitational shoe scandal that rocked Gapoochi-3, Meep-Meep made even hard-core fans of Gapoochi couture have to look twice at their footwear. Add to that, Meep-Meep's unique talents in air duct and crawl space infiltration...Shining brilliance overseeing the Grot fleet takedown and Jarendi scores...And holding the Underworld record for most gratuitous heiress kidnappings in a Universal Year...Meep-Meep's elegant style has earned the respect and attention of colleagues and victims alike."

More electric applause erupted from the crowd.

Images of the three candidates now hovered overhead, with Skytreg winking, Proximetra arching an eyebrow, and Meep-Meep blinking innocently. Next to them, to one side, was a single bar graph that read, "Percentage of Votes Submitted." It was currently at zero.

From the podium platform, Twerk Xanthwoggle cleared his throat and said, "Now we move on to the vote." He glanced furtively at the wings of the stage, but the wings remained dark and quiet. Xanthwoggle sighed contentedly, like a man settling into a hot tub after a rough day.

Suddenly, Bertram felt his arm butted sharply from the armrest. At first, he thought it was Fess, needing more room for the umpteenth appendage. But he turned to discover it was a table-tray-like device popping out to position itself before him. Hundreds of table-trays clattered out around the room. And each one of them said, "Please scan your Intergalactic Underworld Society Conference Admission Badge... *now*."

Bertram blinked. He saw Xylith next to him waving her badge before her table-tray screen. "Thank you, Xylith Duonogganon. Please confirm your Intergalactic Underworld Society member number... *now*." And Xylith began entering that information.

Bertram thought that for a bunch of people who promoted shady dealings and chaos, they really were very well-organized.

Before him, Bertram's table-tray was wondering at his lack of response. "Please scan your Intergalactic Underworld Society Conference Admission Badge...*now*," it repeated.

Fess, Bertram noticed, was already selecting his candidate. "See ya, Skytreg," he smirked, clicking the box beside the image of Rentar Proximetra. At the checked box, Bertram saw Captain Proximetra smile and point a pleased finger at Fess.

Xylith, he observed, was biting both of her lower lips, her hand wavering between the two non-Skytreg candidates. Finally, in a decisive move, she pressed the box next to Jor-Jan Chatta-Chu-Bular Meep-Meep. The photo of Meep-Meep bobbed its head in recognition. Xylith settled back in her chair with a relieved exhale. "There now!"

By this time, Bertram's tray-table was getting irritable. "Hey you. Will you scan your Intergalactic Underworld Society Conference Admission Badge...*now*? I don't have all day."

Bertram glanced at Xylith, who was giggling into her hand. "Dear, maybe you should just do as it asks."

So Bertram fumbled in his shirt pocket and scanned the "And Guest" badge.

"I'm sorry," said the table-tray. "You are not a registered member of the Intergalactic Underworld Society. To get information on our Society, and how you can become a member, please visit our Uninet site by clicking the address below or by saying 'yes'...*now*."

"You could be our newest recruit," Xylith told Bertram, her teasing smiles causing all four eyes to twinkle merrily. They were deeply purple, like summer violets, or a Baltimore Ravens jersey. "Why, in fact, you know what I think? I bet a Tryfe-man perspective is just what the Underworld needs."

"Oh, absolutely," Bertram replied, forcing a serious face. "My familiarity with technologies you no longer use...My deep knowledge of sports stats for games you don't play...My ability to quote from films you won't see and explain great thinkers you won't know...It'd be a huge asset to the Underworld cause. That's not even counting my vast collection of music you won't be able to hear."

"Nooo," she waved it away in that fly-around-the-mint-julep manner, which was strange because Bertram was pretty sure Xylith had seen neither. Her laughter was light and warm. "That's called expanding our horizons." Another smile, a twinkle. "Some of us *enjoy* having our horizons expanded, you know. And as often as possible."

"Ah, well…um…" Bertram felt his neck redden. "Thanks for the support, Xylith," he said. He was starting to like the way her two faces sometimes held slight variations of the same expression. The right face wore a sweet, good-natured cheer, but the left face was watching him through lowered lashes, and held a flirty little smile. "I don't actually plan to stick around the GCU that long, though."

"Oh, now that's a shame," she drawled, looking genuinely downcast. There went those lowered lashes again.

"I'm *waiting*," said the tray-table. "It's just a simple word: yes. You can say it in any one of 47 billion intergalactic languages. I'll understand it: yes."

Bertram explained to Xylith, "Well, it's just I have my planet to save…Or my head to be shrunk. I don't know, anymore. Whichever comes first."

"Of course, it's good to have your priorities," Xylith responded. One face smiled more faintly now, the warmth receding like the sun behind a storm front. Face Two looked on the verge to say something but then decided not to. The violet eyes seemed to turn several shades darker. Bertram sensed he made a mistake somewhere along the way.

"Okay, fine!" announced the tray-table. "So don't take an interest in Underworld affairs! See if I care!" And with that, it folded itself up, and went flying back to the armrest, batting Bertram's arm away in its path.

"Ow!" Bertram rubbed his buzzing, half-numb elbow. He turned back to Xylith, "Well, hey, you never know, I mean maybe if—"

But Xylith was talking to Rollie now. Bertram could just hear the words, "hideous aeroponic farming t-shirt" and "pathetic attempt at surveillance" reach his ears.

He glanced up at the bar chart levitating before the crowd and saw the number of submitted votes creeping, creeping toward 100%.

Ninety-seven percent…98%…

"Ya wanna check out the Marketplace after this?" Fess asked Bertram. "You never know, you might be able to get a cheap pair of off-the-back-of-the-ICV fake Gapoochi levitating shoes." He motioned toward Bertram's holey-socked feet with a flipper.

Ninety-nine percent, said the bar chart above them.

"I don't know if we can take the time." Bertram wiggled his poor abused toes, as they peeped out between his few remaining sock molecules. Shoes sounded great, as his feet really were banged up and aching. But Bertram only had a couple of bucks of Tryfe money with him and… "We're supposed to meet with the Prophets of Nett."

"Ah, yes," Fess gave a nod and pushed up those thick spectacles with a few smaller appendages. "Saving your world. Well, here's hoping the Prophets haven't hightailed it out of there like those Seers. I'd heard lawyers for the prisoners still in Rhobux-7 are threatening lawsuit."

Bertram frowned. "Why's that?"

"For illegally relocating their clients. Only, no one knows where to send the subpoena." Fess stroked his chin with a flipper while scratching his head with a tentacle. "Funny them going poof like that right after the Seers sent you on your way. Whole thing kinda sounds like a frame-job to me."

Bertram didn't want to say it, but he thought so, too. He glanced up just as the bar chart filled to the top and the total read: "100% of Votes Submitted."

At this, triumphant music blasted, and the tally board erupted into another burst of virtual fireworks.

Twerk Xanthwoggle, who had been noodling around with his levitating teleprompter notes while the votes were being cast, came to life again at the podium, looking almost surprised to see all those life-forms out there in the seats before him. "The votes are in, folks," he said. "And now, I will announce the voting percentages for Official Leader of the Intergalactic Underworld."

The audience was on the edge of its seats. You could have heard a yoonie card drop.

Twerk Xanthwoggle looked at the results before him with a blink. "My, this was an unusually tight race," he said and cleared his throat again, as if in apology for his observation. "Zenith Skytreg has received… 36% of the votes."

The audience waited.

"Rentar Proximetra received… 35% of the votes," he continued. And the part of the crowd that had devoured infopills for math were already celebrating. He shouted over them to finish, "And Jor-Jan Chatta-Chu-Bular Meep-Meep received… 29% of the votes. That means, the Official Leader of the Intergalactic Underworld Society for the next Universal year is Zenith Skytreg!"

Lasers shot the ceiling again, and two Society members had to be carted out for knocking themselves unconscious with falling rock. The applause and cheers rocked the seating. Some angry bleats erupted from different corners of the room. Some futile cheers for "Prox-i-met-tra! Prox-i-met-tra!" rolled through the noise, as did a few desperate chants of "Meep-Meep! Meep-Meep!" that made parts of the room sound like they were filled with spring peepers.

Rollie's whole band of friends were rising and grumbling and heading to the exits, along with a number of other Society members also disgusted with the results. The Vos Laegos chorusline was back on stage doing a little tribute number while Zenith Skytreg made his way to the stage, through the crowd, for his acceptance speech.

> Now we know the answer
> Now we've seen who won
> The Underworld, it has its new leader
> Lasers set to stun …

"We're leaving?" Bertram shouted over the din.

The three black eyes of Rollie's holowatch disguise were narrowed to slits. "I'm not gonna fraggin' well sit through another one of Skytreg's 'I couldn't have done it without me' speeches."

Someone shooshed him. He told them to do something with their voting machine that sounded uncomfortable and like it violated physics. Then, even at half his normal height, he managed to stalk out fiercely.

Outside the auditorium, Bertram could almost see the fumes steaming off the figure in the cloak. "Unbe-fraggin'-lievable," Rollie growled. "Another blasted year of Zenith Skytreg. When Rentar Proximetra has real battle experience, doesn't just send someone else in to do her dirty work, and was actually *at* the Feegar Rebellion, not just paying Klimfals to pose in pretty pictures."

"It'srigged," muttered Tseethe, totally invisible in his smoke-filled helmet. "Itjustcan'tberight. Iswearithe'spayingpeopleofforsomethin'. He'sgotsomethin'onsomebodyorhackedthevote. Idunno. Somethin'." Bertram barely made this out. It came out like bursts of Morse code.

"But guys, you're in a *criminal* Society," Bertram reminded them. "I mean, wouldn't you expect it—*require* it, even—to be rigged?"

At this, the group let out such a protest.

"Nah, that's for them unions," Rollie snapped.

"Honestly!" exclaimed Xylith, violet eyes rolling in both of her faces. "To smear the good bad name of the Society like that. It's like a laser to the heart."

"Ah, Underworld newbies. Gotta love 'em," said Fess, trying to ruffle Bertram's holographic hair with an appendage. The result poked Bertram in the ear.

"Heyit'sSkytreg," Tseethe replied, "Wouldn'tputitpasthim."

"He's very popular, though, isn't he: Zenith Skytreg?" came a voice trailing behind them. This was Wilbree.

Everyone turned to stare at him. Wilbree's white ears became rimmed with pink. He tugged at his collar, and smoothed beard-hairs into place that weren't out of it.

Rollie scowled. "You keep saying that. You didn't by any chance *vote* for that slaggard this time, did you?"

"I, er, well." Wilbree decided now was a good time to polish his sunglasses. He became absorbed with the task.

"Cosmic," grunted Tseethe, spinning on one booted heel and leaving him behind. "Stellar. This is who keeps voting him back into office. Now we know."

Wilbree looked downcast and slung his sunglasses on again. Xylith patted him on the shoulder.

"So," Tseethe turned to Rollie. They were now at the elevator to return to the main level. "How ya gonna get outta here?"

Rollie gave him a puzzled look. "Same way we got in. There's only just the one way, isn't there?"

"Yeah, but you noticed the Deltan RegForce out there, right?"

"Sure, and they were looking for a Tryfling and a Deltan. While we're a simple trioptic Underworld peddler and his poor, aged, incontinent maternal archetype." Rollie beamed with the face that was not his. "I'll manage. I always do."

"Incontinent?" Bertram protested.

There was a white flash behind the smoke in Tseethe's helmet. It might have been a grin. "Okay, well, good luck on Nett, Captain. Don't do anything I wouldn't do."

"Thereby leaving my options flexible." Rollie pushed a button to release the pressure-sealed door. "*Paar too.*"

"*Vimn-tsargh tsoo,*" Tseethe said, which Bertram's Translachew turned roughly into some sort of wishes for health. And Bertram and Rollie stepped inside the back of the Crater Club's kitchen refrigerator.

"I do hope you save your planet, Tryfeman," Xylith called into it with Face One, her voice 80 degrees warmer than the fridge they stood in. Face Two added, "Maybe we'll meet again sometime."

Bertram felt his neck redden again. "You know, I'd really li—" The door closed tight behind them with a final puff of sound.

Rollie snickered. They were moving out of the chill of the refrigerator and into the bustling kitchen. Maybe it was the jubies talking, but Bertram was still feeling pretty upbeat about things. For a catatonic megalomaniac without a gameplan, he thought he wasn't doing half-bad. His mind drifted to two pairs of soft rose lips and four sparkling amethyst eyes.

Rollie's voice jarred him back. "That one is more trouble than a bag of Marglenian fighting fish, Ludlow. Trust me." The words contained no tone of malice, just a kind of light amusement. He stole two towels from a kitchen workstation and tossed one to Bertram, draping his own over his forearm in an official manner.

Bertram took the towel but found he didn't really want to discuss Xylith with Rollie. He had a feeling it would put a damper on his jubies high, and he was enjoying not over-thinking things for a change. He slung the towel over his own arm and tried to look crisp and efficient, like he belonged there. He was uncertain of the effect, since he was also a three-eyed old woman in a cloak.

They were almost to the elevators, when Rollie paused and snatched a tray of colorful alien desserts from a nearby dumbwaiter system. He leaned over and grinned. "You know what you get once you've turned-on a two-faced woman, don't you, Ludlow? Strife in stereo." He laughed like this was the greatest joke he'd heard in a long time. Then he disappeared with the tray into the elevator.

Bertram just shook his head.

He'd only set foot in the car when the doors slammed shut and the elevator lurched up, up, and up at a break-neck pace. They reached the proper floor and it stopped so abruptly, the elevator practically poured them out. It was either a testament to the forces of alien physics or Hyphiz Deltan balance that the dessert tray remained intact.

Bertram's equilibrium was still settling when they exited the Rim Room door to the main hallway. And there in that hallway, now camped out in front of the Quake Room, were the Deltan RegForce officers.

They'd mixed it up a little, Bertram noticed. Yes, both the Deltan from the Uninet and his partner were still trying to blend into the crowd. But now the scholarly-looking Deltan had traded his hors d'oeuvre plate for an electronic conference booklet from the

Association for the Fraternal Order of Fraternia-12. And the pop-eyed RegForcer was wearing a hat with a large, round blue sphere bobbing on it that read, "Ask Me About My Moon Polyps."

With them were other life-forms, conference-goers either pulled into the cause or innocently waiting for their next event. But most of the beings milling around were more interested in cocktails in the Comet Room, receptions in the Rupture Room and Q&A in the Quiver Room.

They never spied what Bertram saw as two attendees shuffled by.

With a push of a button on a gadget hidden under his e-brochure, the heavier Deltan cast a thin red beam on the legs of one passing attendee. The beam waved and bounced along the humanoid's form in a quiet, little light display, then vanished.

The same thing occurred with another group trouping through, laughing and chatting. One member was singled out. That member was scanned with the red beam, none the wiser. The RegForce was randomly testing attendees. Perhaps they'd been testing all along. And, jubies or no, the back of Bertram's neck broke out in a sweat.

There was no subtle way to tell Rollie what he'd seen. And even if there were, there was nowhere to hide, only to go forward, to pass the officers directly and hope the three-eyed figures would not be subject to random scanning themselves. Bertram had a very strong feeling that the scanner would go straight through a projected holowatch image. Straight through the cloak and three eyes and the hairy, hairy mole. Bertram really didn't want to find out what would happen after that.

Worse, Rollie gave no indication he'd spotted anything worrisome. He strode down the hall with that tray of desserts held in a confident, professional way, like he'd been carting dessert to and fro for decades and was likely to do so for decades more.

So they pressed on, closer, closer to the Deltan RegForce officers, until too-soon they were passing before them. Now, Bertram's knees felt like rubber, and he was beginning to wonder whether Rollie's earlier incontinence joke might not be about to have some unexpected, unfortunate truth to it.

Yet Bertram forced himself to move forward, forced himself to move beyond and...

"Excuse me. Stop there, would you?"

Bertram's heart did a somersault, his stomach a cartwheel, and his brain commanded the whole crew to turn and look casually.

The Deltan with the scanner was looking right at Rollie.

Rollie addressed him with a placid efficiency. "Yes, sir?" Bertram noticed he seemed to be trying to smooth out his clipped Deltan accent.

"Where are you going with those?" the RegForce rep asked. His expression was mild, interested, but otherwise a cipher.

"Just there." With a free hand, Rollie pointed into a large bustling reception room.

The RegForce officer nodded gravely. "As I thought."

Done for, Bertram thought. *We are done for.* There'd be no saving the Earth from inside a Hyphiz Deltan prison. He doubted he'd find much sanity there, either. Probably just some large angry, alien cellmate named Mxylplx, who liked to knit stylish gags and handcuffs for his roomies.

But if Rollie shared Bertram's concern, he didn't show it. His three holographic eyes met those of the RegForce officer in equally mild interest. He waited. Waited as if he had all of the time in the world to wait. Which, knowing Rollie, was impressive since Rollie did not wait well for anything.

Bertram waited, too, but he could feel his body poising itself to run…Grounded and prepped like he would for a tennis match, waiting for the serve, the one move that would spring him into action. Bertram looked at the faces of the other life-forms standing with the officer. The pop-eyed fellow in the moon polyp hat watched keenly with too-blue eyes. The others glanced from the lead lawman, to the tray, to the lawman again.

Finally, the Deltan with the scanner said, "I'll have the Hanzigrette pudding, if I might." He gave an embarrassed smile. "No sense you carting it all the way in there."

Rollie nodded and let him take the pudding. Bertram waited as Rollie then strode purposefully into the reception room, placed the tray of desserts on the nearest flat surface—which happened to be the head of a refuse robot—and swept out again. Bertram fell quickly into step, and the two headed down the hallway, out of the Conference Center and Exposition.

It was only as they stepped into the Crater Club main lobby that Bertram exhaled with relief. "Holy heart arrhythmia," Bertram said under his breath, "I think I sweat straight through my boxers. At least, I hope that's sweat."

"Shut it," Rollie warned.

"What?" Bertram whispered. "But we're cool. He just wanted dessert, he—"

Rollie cut him off with a curt, "Shpp."

Bertram looked at the main entrance, where life-forms were gliding gently to the floor, complimentary beverages and spelunker hats intact, and expressions glazed with wide-eyed wonder. "Can we get out that way?"

"Here." Rollie motioned Bertram to another short corridor where Vos Laegos daylight filtered onto the floor in a rough sphere. The exit!

They'd no sooner stepped into the light when Bertram felt his feet lift off the floor, felt himself being swept by some strange, manufactured up-draft.

"Thank you for visiting the Crater Club!" said one of the staff members, standing on a balcony and waving as they silently glided to the surface.

"The Crater Club thanks you, come again!" said another, flashing a bright smile.

"We hope you'll visit us here at the Crater Club again real soon!" said a third.

And with an invisible shove, Bertram and Rollie were tossed up and out, onto the Vos Laegos City street.

"Thank God," Bertram murmured, wiping his brow. He sighed again, bigger this time. There just didn't seem to be enough oxygen to expel the energy from his jangled up nerves. He wanted the jubies back. The jubies would make things seem happy, possible, right again. But apparently natural endorphins beat the jubies two to one. He was sorry to see 'em go. "Wow, we made it, I mean I never imagined—"

"Run," Rollie said in a low, firm voice.

"What?" Bertram looked around the bustling Vos Laegos strip, trying to spot their latest peril. Left, right, Bertram's eyes were still getting used to the change in light between the dim Crater Club and the shining, sun-spotty outdoors. He didn't even know what he was looking at.

"Run!" Rollie shouted. The calm firmness had drained from his voice and was replaced with an edge of panic. In a flash, the XJ-37 was in his hand, capping off shots over his shoulder. He took off like there were wings on his feet. Bertram sprung to follow him as laser shots twanged in response where he'd stood just seconds before.

Keeping up with the Deltan, as he wound back through the hodge-podge maze of the Vos Laegos layout, proved difficult. Not only did Rollie have a long stride, but he had good solid boots with heavy traction, where Bertram was working with worn socks and soft feet—feet that hadn't seen the outside of an athletic shoe in public for going on ten years now. Then there were the Vos Laegos obstacles: puddles of spilled drinks, expressions of bodily fluids, meandering life-forms with no agenda and the luxury of not having the Hyphiz Deltan RegForce on their tails. Bertram had to keep his eyes fixed to Rollie's back instead of where he stepped and who he'd stepped on, or he'd never find his way back to the ICV.

Every now and then, Bertram would hear a shriek or crash. So in his wake he jettisoned assorted apologies—"My bad!" or "Put ice on that!"—and simply pressed on.

Bertram caught up with Rollie only as the Deltan slowed, feeling around one-handed for something within his holographic robes. "Where is it? Where. *Is.* It?!" the alien spat. "Ah?"

He pulled out an item from seemingly nowhere, which looked to be some kind of memo recorder. He held it up before his face. "Bleedin', fraggin', blasted, zoggin' son of a Keeltsar!" he shouted, and flung the unwanted item. It bounced off the sidewalk, bits and pieces showering from it.

"What are you looking for?" Bertram asked breathlessly as they continued on. If he recalled the catalog of stuff Rollie carted around on his person, it could be pretty much anything.

"It won't matter, if I don't fragging-well find it soon," Rollie hissed.

Bertram could hear the heavy running footsteps behind them closing in. A laser blast went off through Bertram's holographic hood, actually singeing the side of Bertram's hair. It smelled warm and too organic. He shrieked, and patted the side of his head, which was crackling with sparks. Then he turned and spied the buggy-eyed Deltan RegForcer, well in the lead of his crew and coming up fast. The man had an effortless grace, and long, taut limbs propelled him forward. His smile was one of a man who enjoyed what he did and was confident he'd get whatever he set out to capture.

"Ah-ha!" Suddenly Rollie erupted into a mad shriek of joy as they fled, hoisting an electronic something-or-other in a triumphant grip. The captain raised his arm high over his head—like some three-eyed, druidic version of the Statue of Liberty doing the New York

Marathon—and he pressed a large black button on the device in his hand.

"Zzzt," said the button.

Bertram had expected great alarms to wail. Robot armies prepped to exterminate. Explosives to go boom.

Rollie seemed to have found just the thing to make a good "Zzzt" noise.

"Oh, great!" Bertram shouted. "I can't go to Deltan prison. I have delicate features, I've never fashioned a shiv, and I took two free Tae-Kwon Do classes and we didn't even get to the Do. I'm gonna die."

"Just shut it and run, Ludlow," Rollie ordered. He looked to his right and then jarred to a halt, motioning Bertram. "Here! In here!" At first, Bertram didn't know how they could go "in," anywhere. The place Rollie indicated looked like just another part of the busy sidewalk; there was grass and exotic plants. But as Bertram spied the life-forms standing around some gaming tables he realized: this was the building they'd seen earlier from the air. The one crafted entirely of clear materials. Inside looked like outside, and the outside in. Bertram followed Rollie under a sign, which read, "The Greenhouse" in brightly lit lettering, which sprouted and appeared to grow yoonie cards.

People who live in glass houses shouldn't consider them viable hideout material, Bertram thought. He spotted the familiar faces of the two towering RegForcers on the street, just as they spotted Bertram.

Only Rollie, apparently, wasn't trying to hide. He'd seized some large leafy orchid, which turned out to be a Greenhouse employee, and said in urgent tones, "The observatory. How do you get there?"

The orchid looked startled at being manhandled; she must have been a delicate flower. "Down the hall, make a left, and take that elevator straight to the top," she gasped.

"Thanks." And Rollie dashed off.

Or tried.

Just being in the building itself was confusing. You could see where you'd like to go, but not how many corridors and rooms away your destination actually was. After a near concussion making the left down the hall, Bertram and Rollie found themselves feeling their way toward the elevator like blind men, an excruciatingly slow process.

Bertram imagined the casino made most of its money selling antiseptic and icepacks.

By now, the RegForce had plunged through the Greenhouse entrance and were scanning the lobby for their three-eyed fugitives. It wasn't long before Bertram and Rollie were in their sights. The bulbous-eyed officer glared, pressed his nose to the glass, shielded his eyes, and then pointed the other RegForce officers in Bertram's and Rollie's direction.

But soon he discovered, as they had, that seeing the escapees was one thing. Getting to them was quite another. As the Deltan and Tryfeman stepped into the crystalline elevator and shot skyward, Rollie laughed and waved. The RegForce was still busy trying to find their way out of what Bertram thought was a poorly-conceived restroom concept.

"They'll stumble their way out of the bathroom sooner or later, you know," Bertram warned. "It's not exactly hard to track us down, and now we have nowhere to run." He looked to his right and saw his companion was no longer the dark, three-eyed being, but a tall, lean Deltan with a weird thumb and very yellow hair.

Rollie just grinned, a smile considerably more demonic than that of his holowatch disguise. He stepped out of the elevator onto the Greenhouse roof patio, brandishing the electronic device in his hand skyward once more. He pushed the button.

"Zzzt."

Bertram sighed. He didn't know why he was so worried about life in Hyphiz Deltan jail when he was probably already in some kind of mental home. He thought it might be because his temple burned and his feet hurt. A real hurt. The kind of hurt you don't have in dreams, not ever. Not even the unbalanced ones of a raving Ph.D. candidate. Not unless something very unpleasant was happening to you in real life, as well.

So as he exited the elevator, on a sudden impulse, Bertram whisked a clear chair over from a clear patio table and wedged it in the clear elevator door. The door banged helplessly. Bells rang and rattled down the elevator shaft.

Rollie glanced over his shoulder, nodded with satisfaction, and then scanned the sky as if he were still searching for those imaginary robot hoards. Or some kind of deity.

Bertram, on the other hand, couldn't rip his gaze from below, down through the many floors, to the cluster of RegForce officers crawling around on ground level. They were feeling their way down the halls. They were congregating around the base of the frozen lift.

They were talking to management. One gesticulated wildly. Another stroked his chin thoughtfully.

Bertram didn't like it. They were planning something. Then they found the door to a stairwell and began the trek to the roof. "Company's coming," Bertram cautioned.

The wind picked up.

"Ah," said Rollie, whether in response to Bertram's warning or the burst of weather, Bertram wasn't sure. Rollie grinned again, his orange eyes reflecting the color of the dipping Vos Laegos sun. "Ready, Ludlow?"

"Ready? For what?" The wind around his head was really strong now, swirling his hair, and making an unnatural amount of racket. Whirring, clanking, grinding. "What the hell is that noise?"

And from nothing unfolded a light metal ladder that dropped down in front of them. Rollie hopped onto it and scrambled into the void, vanishing completely.

"Ah," said Bertram. He seized the ladder without question and followed the Deltan's path. Yet unlike Rollie, he was unable to resist one fleeting backwards glance over his shoulder.

The stringy pop-eyed officer was but one floor away now, his eyes wider and poppier than ever at the sight of this ladder, these escapees, vanishing into the ozone. He was trying to do three stairs at a time now in some futile tactic to catch up. But even his long, wiry legs couldn't quite manage it. Tripping, glaring, and causing a pile-up of half the Hyphiz Deltan RegForce, he pointed to Bertram, his mouth moving in some unintelligible vow for, presumably, bitter revenge.

Bertram slipped inside the ICV, the ladder folding itself back up, and retracting into the ship. He could still see the lawman's lips twisting with dangerous promises.

The hatch closed. They were leaving Vos Laegos.

11

Biking home, Rozz Mercer caught a glimpse of herself in the side mirror of a parked car. Dark circles, red rimmed eyes, wan complexion, and an almost-visible fog hovering right between the eyebrows... *Yep: there she is*, she thought. *The postergirl for insomnia. The Bettie Page of lost REM.*

Well, she'd slept a *little* over the last few days, she reconsidered, directing her bike up through the park. She must have, right? Or else she'd be close to seeing things and hearing voiceover narration. But between student teaching, her part-time programming gig, her own studies, and now all this hubbub about Bertram Ludlow going AWOL...

Well, the brain found sleep sort of gratuitous. *Like movie bonus material*, she thought. *Nice if you have the time. But who does really?*

At least *before* she'd been able to grab a good four to six hours if she worked it right. A couple of power naps between classes... An upright doze at her desk... And the full-on snorefest face-down in the campus coffeehouse. Management didn't care as long as she bought something, *anything*, and wiped up the drool when she left.

But since Bertram had gone, it was all different. Sleep teased and eluded, taunted and tweaked. Now she just had too damned much on her mind.

Not that she was so exactly hung up on the guy, she told herself. Sure, she liked him okay and all... He had a decent sense of humor, a little bit of style and, unlike the last guy she went out with, didn't seem to think of pain as a pastime to be savored and shared. Plus, she found Bertram attractive, in a tallish-Hobbit way. He was curly-haired, boyish and genuine, if you were into that. She supposed she was. Or, at least, it was a nice change from tortured and posed and poetic. And that was good enough.

But she didn't keep coming back to thoughts of Bertram Ludlow because of some deep magnetic passion. He just didn't inspire that kind of raw emotion in her, and that was probably just as well. No, she kept thinking about him because he'd vanished. And she didn't care what the campus police, the real police, or even the university psychologist had concluded. Bertram Ludlow was not the kind of guy to crack and bail. He wasn't about drama and danger. He wasn't about attention and angst. Bertram Ludlow was about calm, firm responsibility. He wouldn't decide to be impulsive without packing a change of underwear first.

He certainly hadn't left, of his own will, without his shoes.

She told that to the campus police. The real police, too. But both just kept asking her how well she really knew him. How long they'd worked together. How many times they went out. Did she ever see him take drugs? Did he drink? When did she see him last? How would she describe his demeanor? They kept saying disappearances like this were usually the result of a mental breakdown, not some sort of kidnapping. That the right answer was usually the simplest. And the university psychologist, well, she seemed mainly interested in knowing how many stimulants Rozz had been taking and what kinds. Like they really knew anything about anybody.

Losers.

Rozz swerved to avoid a suddenly-opened car door and wobbled back to balance on the rutty road. "Losers!" she shouted at the driver, just for good measure. It wasn't productive, but it made her feel better.

Only no, it really didn't. Because it was a pretty shitty system when a grad student could just vanish and everybody shrugged it off as "psychological strain," prompting fewer questions than it did bloodhounds.

It was a pretty shitty system when no one was willing to see who you were.

Of course, Bertram's disappearance had been on the news. Still was, in fact. But in ever-reducing levels of importance. Yep: "No new leads at this time," was what it boiled down to now. Ten seconds of airtime after the 20 minutes on Steelers' pre-season. That was the weight of Bertram Ludlow's life.

And oh, those police dogs? Those stupid mutts had just U-turned in the doorway and tromped on each other in the hall, confused and yelping. One seemed to have sniffed out Bertram to a nearby field, but that, the cops said, might just as easily have been a false positive. The young academic was gone. The scent was lost.

Bertram had smelled like coffee and ramen. Soy sauce with caffeine and a hint of fabric softener. Rozz had kinda liked that. That was gone, too.

It was these thoughts that preoccupied her. These thoughts that kept her mind relentlessly at work, twisting and turning over every discussion, every police interview, every moment she and Bertram had spoken before he vanished. Trying to understand. To think of any information that might lead to answers.

It was these thoughts that kept her from noticing the giant pothole before her.

The front wheel of her bike dropped into it like waffle to toaster, sending Rozz flying over the handlebars in a surprising display of pastry-popped aerodynamics. She turned, trying to catch herself, but only caught air—helmet flying from her short, fuchsia hair in one direction, her backpack and books skidding off in another. She met asphalt, hard.

The world spun.

She lay there a moment and groaned, slowly peeling her face from the ground.

She wiped blood from her lip, only to realize she'd bitten her tongue. She dusted gravel from her hands and noticed road rash there, too. She brushed gravel from her knees and then quavered to stand.

The ankle complained with a jolt that shot up her leg.

Twisted.

Just one more thing twisted around here, she thought and dropped into a patch of soft grass on the side of the road. Did that bike wheel look bent? The wheel looked bent to her. Bent and twisted. Such was life these days.

Or was that just her vision rippling? Suddenly, it was hard to focus, and she felt very queasy.

She settled into the grass to peer at the sky, to feel the level stability of the wonderful, solid earth under her back. It felt strangely warm and comfortable there in the sun. It dried the blood on her cheek, her lips, her knee. It caressed away concerns and nausea with soothing late summer heat that made her sleepy. So sleepy.

She could call somebody, she thought suddenly. Call someone with a car. Did she know anyone with a car? Probably. Though it wouldn't spring to mind.

Or maybe she could just sleep here in the park, her brain suggested lazily. Sleep in the nice soft grass and not get up for days and days and days...

Or maybe she had a concussion, she considered further, jolting herself back to consciousness. And should you sleep with a concussion or try to stay awake? She couldn't remember that, either. Did she not remember because she was concussed or because she never really knew? She didn't recall.

Life was such a bitch.

She saw the spaceship that moment, dark and smooth, and flying in low over the field. She didn't have a good perspective on how big it was. Initially, it looked no bigger than one of the yellow jackets wavering around her view, pestering, hovering, landing and tasting the blood and sweat on her skin. But as it came in lower, she began to sense the magnitude of the craft. Many times the size of a car, and almost soundless.

Most people only saw stars when they hit their heads. But Rozz... Rozz was seeing *spaceships*. And it was funny, Rozz considered, because she never had liked sci-fi that much. The stuff on TV relied so often on stark good and evil, big boobs in catsuits, and alien invasion. Not that she wouldn't have minded flying around space with... Oh, who was that guy?... That doctor dude?... Who?

Nope, she knew she wasn't going to remember. Her head throbbed too much to draw it out.

She heard a whirring sound, a few moments of silence, and then the clang, clang, clang of shoes on a hard metallic surface. She heard voices talking, which part of her recognized she really shouldn't be able to understand. They were tinny, but sounded like English. Only they weren't really English, were they? They were thousands of different languages... hundreds of thousands of languages... millions of different languages, maybe... which could be understood only by the ears of those who recognized them. Millions of different alien tongues being projected at once, until they found the right listener. Including Earth English.

Or Rozz Mercer had a scary-big head injury.

"I think this might just be the investment property for you," a female voice was saying in chirpy tones. "The planet is located in a quiet neighborhood. It has its own sun. A breathable atmosphere for the oxygen-dependant life-forms of your choice. And I can recommend a good exterminator with tenting services to take care of any of the pre-existing humans, so they won't be in your way. That could be handled before you moved in, of course. So please don't let that impede your decision about the property. Remember, we're very flexible."

Tenting? Exterminator? Humans? Rozz felt a chill run down her spine, or maybe that was just the sun going behind the clouds. She lifted her head to see the speakers, but the world spun out of control. It whirled her back to the welcome security of the ground.

"Well, Mimsi my dear, I *will* let you in on a little something," a second female voice began, its tones smooth and mellow. It was soothing, magnetic, with a musky heat to it. Maternal, yet with firmness suggesting scalding magma bubbled just under the surface. "I am actually less interested in the planet, than its people," purred the voice. "But I understand that it's a package deal, is that correct? If I take the Tryfe-people, I must take the planet, as well?"

"I'm afraid so, Ms. Pollux," said the one named Mimsi.

"'Ms. Pollux'?" laughed the other. It rang out like bells. "Ah, we're friends here, Mimsi. 'Spectra,' please."

"Spectra," repeated Mimsi. "Well, Spectra, the seller really wants a streamlined sale. So the bids are for the property and all of its contents."

"I respect that."

"Can you share what your plans are for the Tryfe-people?"

"Let's just say it has to do with the LibLounges and my infopill-of-the-day club."

"Ohhhhh," the one named Mimsi exhaled. "What an honor! I absolutely love the CapClub. You know, I used to have *such* a difficult time deciding what information I wanted to ingest. I mean choosing entertainment was just so...so..."

"Burdensome?"

"Why, yes! Burdensome!" Delight filled Mimsi's voice.

"I get that a lot," the other agreed.

"But now that I've joined your *Featured CapClub Feature-of-the-Day* infopill distribution, I never have to worry about what to ingest anymore. It's such a relief. And knowing that we ingest the book capsules you ingest yourself, well…I always just know it's going to be a poignant infopill worth my time. Oh, but I'm probably embarrassing you."

"No, my dear, the truth should not be hard to hear," Spectra said gently.

"Well, I wish I'd asked you about your goals for Tryfe sooner. But, of course, I hate to pry."

"Of course you do, Mimsi."

"If I'd known you were particularly interested in the Tryfe-humans, I would have arranged for us to encounter one or two of them. In a controlled setting, of course. They're not members of the GCU yet. Some of them get a little high-strung when they see us coming."

They laughed merrily.

"We even prepped the ship with Tryfe translators," continued Mimsi. "Not the easiest thing to do for planets outside the GCU, but that just shows how dedicated we are to our clients."

"It's interesting you mention it, Mimsi," said Spectra, "because I was going to ask about the Tryfe-human I see there in the grass."

There was a gasp. "Why, I totally missed that!"

Naturally, thought Rozz fuzzily, *they want to see the human.*

"It's a female," Mimsi said. "She looks hurt."

"I think you're right," Spectra agreed.

"She seems to have fallen off that contraption there."

"I believe you're right again."

"Do you think another Tryfe-human will be along to help her?"

"Oh, fer the love of God," managed Rozz around her swollen tongue, "could you thtupid halluthinationth clear off tho I can get thome fucking retht?" Struggling weakly to sit, Rozz choked back the nausea that washed over her in a cold, pounding wave, grounded herself, and looked up. And there she spied the two strangest things she'd ever laid eyes upon—and that was saying something; she attended the on-campus art gallery regularly.

What's more, shattering all pre-conceived notions, these visions involved neither big boobs, nor catsuits. Which just goes to show, you can't trust Hollywood.

The one being resembled an aging blow-up doll with tight, synthetic hair. All plastic and stretched and injection-molded. She wore some shiny-looking business suit with a large shiny nametag.

The other was simply immense—not in fat, but sheer size and sturdy Amazonian thickness. Thick fingers, thick hands, thick arms and legs and feet. The woman's aqua-blue hair was like an entire ocean's rolling surf. Her aqua-blue eyelashes were like great forest fronds. Her creamy skin was a quartz coastline, washed smooth over time by the waves. She stood a good ten feet taller than anyone Rozz had ever seen, like a moving, living monument to herself.

This alien woman's clothing appeared to be made of nothing tangible. Just gas reflections and moonbeams and stardust and solar flares, which changed, flashed and covered strategically, depending on how she moved. It was a fascinating, dizzying, mesmerizing sort of glamour.

Rozz Mercer, who under normal circumstances had quite a lot to say on virtually any subject, found her bitten tongue with absolutely nothing to share. And her brain, which had really taken one for the team today, decided that it had had about enough of this whole consciousness thing after all. It determined what it really deserved was a nice recuperative holiday in the sub-level.

It only took a moment for it to pack.

"I told you," said Mimsi Grabbitz, shaking her head sadly at the figure out-cold on the ground. "High-strung."

"Open the ICV if you would, Mimsi?" Spectra Pollux asked, lifting the girl as easily as a sack of new potatoes.

"You're putting her in the ship?" asked Mimsi, wide eyes growing wider.

"To borrow her. Just for a little while." The sack of potatoes didn't know it, but she'd aroused the giant alien's equally giant sense of compassion. "I can help her, you see. Make sure she gets well again." Spectra Pollux said. Though that wasn't the whole truth. The Tryfe girl had also piqued the lady's even bigger business sense. "And I do believe she can help me with my bid for Tryfe."

Excerpt from:

How To Gain Pals and Sway Life-forms in Cosmic Commerce
Chapter Nineteen

With permission from the
Eddisun Center for Ideas, Interceptive Marketing and Cliché Prevention

A Dose of Healthy Pre-Made Decisionry:
Spectra Pollux and the CapClub

Overview

It's as much a part of the daily routine as the hum of the Food Preparation Unit and the buzz of the personal molecular cleanser. It's the arrival of the *Featured CapClub Feature-of-the-Day*, and life-forms just can't wait to devour its contents. In almost no time, they feel the flood of information course through their minds and bodies, they hasten to their local LibLounge for in-depth discussion, and they wait eagerly for their next hand-picked literary, inspirational or autobiographical fix.

Called everything from "the one real intergalactic unifier" (*Maternal Archetype Today*) to "a pill-popping, pop-culture mind-frag" (*Anti-Matter Vortex* unimag), **Spectra Pollux's** *Featured CapClub Feature-of-the-Day* program is vastly popular, often controversial and always leaves life-forms talking.

Yet how has Pollux encouraged sentient beings across the GCU to hand over their infopill self-determination so willingly? How has one former Didactics professor from Rumoolita transformed a universe of independent life-forms with diverse interests into eager LibLounge and CapClub fans, ravenous for her next fortifying capsule selection? And how is this "pre-made infopill decisionry," as Pollux calls it, part of her greater plan for mass education and enlightenment?

This chapter shares the techniques Spectra Pollux has used to change the infopill market from one of "overwhelming selection and burdensome personal choice" to a smooth, streamlined, pre-determined process that, coincidentally, also leaves a lot of time for sitting around in LibLounges drinking frothy beverages.

Giant Dreams, Super-Sized Success

Spectra Pollux was born on Rumoolita, the youngest and smallest of three sisters in a world where size is greatly prized. Said Pollux, "I always felt my parents really couldn't see me. And I mean that literally. I was only three kroms tall when I was a teenager. That's very undersized for a Rumoolitan girl, where my sisters were four kroms easily and my parents were in the five krom range. I was stepped on daily during most of my formative years. On many occasions, they would call me for dinner, not realizing I was already there. And I just kept thinking, if I couldn't truly be large, I must *think* large. Thinking large has gotten me to the heights I am today." (*Pollux on Pollux*. Spectra Pollux. RP: 15.)

Young Pollux's attention to both her Didactics lessons and a passion for Kachunkettball earned her a scholarship to the GCU's illustrious Quad Three College and Spa. Among her non-Rumoolitan Kachunkettball teammates, the towering Pollux was a one-woman powerhouse. "Spectra was the best Lower Lobber the college has ever seen," said team captain and Upper Chucker, Zang Watley. "When she racked the ball in her shoop—why, not a player on the field wasn't worried about that painful rebound parzak!" (*Kachunkettball Illustrated*. "Spectra Gets Her Goal." Jeen Marplezot. RP: 158.)

It was also at Quad Three College and Spa that Pollux discovered her passion for teaching. Explained Pollux, "I realized infopills were truly under-utilized in pre-Didactics learning. So many students came to my class having never devoured the prerequisite infopills they needed for the hands-on portion of the class. As a result, I spent more time locating and distributing infopills than carrying on with my lesson plans. Soon, students were actually stopping me on the way to class, asking whether I could get them a pill on this or that topic on the side. They didn't want their friends knowing there was so much they hadn't devoured yet." (*Pollux on Pollux*. Spectra Pollux. RP: 35.)

It wasn't long before Pollux traced the source of the problem to print. "Parents were encouraging their progeny to read the print their family already owned, instead of spending the yoonies on infopills. I think that's really what motivated me in the Print Liberation Lounge initiative. Infopills were clearly the future, but print was continuing to block our path to greater enlightenment. The LibLounges helped remove those stacks of print and got people together, talking." (*Pollux on Pollux*. Spectra Pollux. RP: 82.)

It was as Pollux began choosing new selections for the Quad Three LibLounges she managed, that she saw the potential for pre-approved infopill selections. "Go into any infopill distributor and you're surrounded by walls and walls of bottled capsules. To find out what's on them, you have to push a button on the dispenser and waste time listening to a cumbersome several-sentence summary. I thought, 'Who has time to listen to summary after summary to find a good infopill? No one will learn anything this way.' I realized what we needed was something that would just say, 'You'll like this. Here: eat it.' And that's basically when the *Featured CapClub Feature-of-the-Day* was born." (*Pollux on Pollux*. Spectra Pollux. RP: 103.)

Today, the CapClub has subscribers across all four quadrants of the GCU, infopills dominate early learning, and print has largely become a historic tale GCU elders relay to their second-level progeny at holidays.

"I run the CapClub because I believe everyone in the GCU deserves a Pollux level of good living. I want you all to have more knowledge and more time to enjoy it, which is why I shoulder the burden of hand-picking each and every infopill that becomes my *Featured CapClub Feature*. Do I learn about each infopill before I digest it? Of course; I listen to each and every pill summary, which sometimes takes almost a whole Universal hour out of my day. Do I always understand what each infopill I promote is about? That's not the point. The point is doing what you can to become 'Your Best You.' And by following my CapClub choices, life-forms all over the GCU are doing that, every day." (*GCU Now*. "Polluxian Method: How to Be Your Best You." Spectra Pollux. RP: 4125.)

Pills of Pollux Promotional Pithiness
What lessons-learned can young marketers suck up and digest from Spectra Pollux's CapClub program? Wash down these helpful hints!

- **Never underestimate life-forms' innate need to offload responsibility for even the simplest tasks.** Spectra Pollux understands that no responsibility is ever too small to pawn-off onto someone else. And, says Pollux, that opens up niche markets. "Telling people what they want to absorb is just the beginning. We're starting to see lines of pre-chewed foods; child-rearing pills, so parents never have to say "no"; and even music club capsules that decide what music you should like and play as in-ear ambiance day and night."" But, remember, this is only the beginning. There are plenty of responsibilities still out there, waiting for someone to develop clever new ways to avoid them. The next idea might just be yours!

- **There's nothing like fear of ostracism to bring people together!** Spectra Pollux knows the universe can be a very cold place for the life-form who hasn't digested the *Featured CapClub Feature-of-the-Day*. So think: how can *you* make those who don't buy your product feel like the one-faced cousin at a Dootett family reunion? Make the threat of not having your product greater than the joy of having it, and you're on your way to Pollux-sized success.

- **Know best and share that often.** Spectra Pollux is known for her exquisite good taste; we know, because she says so in every CapClub announcement. Market research shows that 75% of the time, sentient life-forms don't recognize quality unless it's accompanied by supporting references to how stellar it is. Pollux's example shows that building your intergalactic reputation for cosmicness begins with you.

12

Bertram woke to a siren's blare. In the ship's cabin, a yellow light in the ceiling whirled, and a computerized voice was chanting, "Warning! System set for manual landing. Landing controls unmanned. System set for manual landing. Landing controls unmanned."

Bertram gave a start and leapt up out of the chair he'd been sleeping in for the past few hours. Ignoring the kink in his neck and a spine doing a fair imitation of a spiral-bound notebook, he ran across the room and pressed the button that opened the cockpit doors, only to find the cockpit empty. Out the front window, Bertram spied a large cluster of little planets—30 to be precise, though he didn't waste time counting. And the computer was absolutely right: one teal-green planet was much, much closer than Bertram felt comfortable with. They were in their descent and getting ready to land.

They probably needed a pilot for that.

"Rollie?" Bertram dashed into the main cabin and went through door-by-door. It was a mad rush of button-pushing, doors shooshing and painfully empty rooms, all the while the sirens wailed.

At last—just about the time Bertram pondered escape pods, and whether his driver was currently enjoying one—Bertram came across a small, dim, sparse chamber. And in it, placid as the guest of honor in a wake, Bertram Ludlow found the missing captain. Eyes closed, the alien rested on what looked to be a solid marble slab. A small, thin cushion, about the size of a washcloth was under his head. His utility belt and holster were on the floor beside it, his coat in a puddle beside that.

"Oh, thank God! There you are," Bertram shouted over the sirens. "Don't you hear that? You gotta get up. It's Nett."

The captain lay motionless as a frat boy who discovered Jell-o shots.

Bertram sighed irritably. His patience was in short supply when it involved possibly splattering across a planet. "Rollie, you can sleep it off later. We need you in the cockpit now."

But Rollie didn't hear. He didn't stir.

Bertram drew nearer, his own chest pounding now, as he stared at the prone, unmoving figure. Yet for the Hyphiz Deltan, there was no rise and fall of breath. Bertram shook the man gently—then not gently—to the same disturbing indifference. Bertram touched the figure's pale, scarred forearm, which was so cold and clammy, fishermongers would have tossed it in the pile and slapped on a price tag. "Oh God…"

Bertram felt the sweat beading up on his own back, felt his knees turn to cold, clotted gravy. He leaned in to listen to Rollie's heart, but he wasn't entirely sure where that would be. He tried the general chest-ish region, strained to listen over the shrieking sirens, and found the task hopeless. He grabbed Rollie's wrist for pulse.

Pulseless.

He raced to the main cabin, snatched the metal stew pot, ran back and held it up to Rollie's nose and mouth.

No condensation. On impulse, Bertram reached for Rollie's toolbelt on the floor and withdrew one of the knives the Deltan had there. He took a deep breath and, carefully, made a long thin cut on Rollie's bare forearm.

No motion. No flinch of pain. An orange-brown fluid came to the surface, but barely.

Bertram's felt his own shoulders slump, and his hope seep somewhere down into his big toe.

"Way to go, Rollie," he chided the body on the slab. "Great timing, you big alien bastard. Thanks a lot."

Bertram's mind swam as he tried to reconcile himself with the situation. Had the Deltan been unable to endure another year of Zenith Skytreg's leadership? Was this his way of escaping Altair-5 and beating the RegForce forever? Or had too many years of alien booze, prison terms, two-faced ex-wives and Feegar battles finally caught up with him?

Bertram had no time to mull it over. He sprinted to the cockpit.

"Warning! System set for manual landing. Landing controls unmanned. Warning! System set for—"

"I'm here! I'm here!" Bertram told the machine, diving into the pilot's seat and scanning the area. The sirens and announcement system whirred to a stop, a relief to the ears, if not the nerves. "All right," he began, "let's just hope aliens believe in owner's manuals." He started searching under seats. He ruffled through compartments.

Then he realized: "Unless the manual came in capsule format." It sounded like Truth the moment he said it. Stupid Forwardists. Couldn't leave well enough alone. They had to go changing all the owner's manuals to pills while decent people needed to not crash and explode.

"Okay, think, Bertram, think!" He slid behind the ship's wheel and scanned the front panel for some clue what to do next. Here, gauge needles appeared to be heading leftward. There, bar graphs were going up and down. And something in the corner periodically said, "Bip!"

Struck with an idea, in a clear, authoritative voice Bertram announced, "Computer, go to autopilot landing!"

He paused, listened.

The planet grew closer, frighteningly closer. The bar graphs jounced. The needles continued leftward. And that thing in the corner gave a "bip," possibly just to brighten the mood a little.

"Computer: landing instructions," Bertram tried again, his voice cracking now slightly under the weight of the task ahead of him. But advice wasn't forthcoming. *Backs'* ship had voice controls, didn't it? But either they were another one of those options Rollie felt was gratuitous, they were turned off, or the ICV was too busy screaming through the planet's atmosphere right now to chat.

So Bertram seized the wheel and gave it a good backwards yank— then a series of frantic ones—but the thing was either jammed or locked into place. He stroked the stubble on his jaw with trembling fingers and scanned for a wheel release. None of the buttons on the console said anything remotely useful.

"Underpressure? GravFloor Mode Lock? Upper Lower Lomb Casing? Lower Upper Umb Cover? Kretch?!" He scanned desperately now. "Where's the one that says 'Autopilot'? Where's the one that says 'In case of emergency'? Where's the one that says 'About to Die in a Fiery Detonation'? Where's that, huh, pal?"

"Who on flaming Altair are you talking to?" Rollie asked, leaning, squinting puzzled from the doorway. He motioned at Bertram. "Anyway—out. You're in my seat."

Bertram gaped. Rollie had color again. His eyes were keen. His movements were smooth, snappy and controlled. All signs pointing to a significant lack of death about the guy.

"C'mon. Move, time's wastin'." He twiddled impatient fingers at Bertram.

Knees still weak, Bertram barely stood and almost tumbled into the copilot's chair.

"And I see I'm bleeding," the Deltan observed calmly. "Your handiwork, is it?" He held up his left forearm where a long, very bloody cut ran up it, standing out bright rust on pink, scarred skin. Dropping into his seat, he drew a pen-like object from his belt, flipped a switch on the gizmo, and ran it along the cut. Humming, the little tool fused the skin together nicely but left a raised white line where the cut had been. It matched the other white lines he already had.

Rollie tucked the tool back in its case, took the wheel, flipped a few levers, spun a few dials, and even Bertram could tell the ship was in a better position for landing. "That's serious trouble on Hyphiz Delta, that is."

"What is?" Bertram managed.

"Assault."

"You were *dead*," Bertram reminded him.

"Asleep," Rollie corrected, as they swept over the largest planet in the Nett system. He hooked a thumb at the harness on Bertram's chair. "Fasten."

Bertram looked for the harness and secured himself in. "You weren't breathing," he went on. "You were cold. You had no pulse. You didn't bleed out."

"Mm," agreed Rollie.

"In Pittsburgh, we call the next of kin over that sort of behavior."

At this, Rollie raised a keen eyebrow, as if the information was all just some fascinating biological difference to note for later. "Hyphizites pretty near shut down when we sleep. Total sensory deprivation, extremely slowed vitals. It's a complete recharge, you know. Forty-five Universal minutes a day does me right, typically.

Others, well… say, an hour, hour and a half. That's why we got the laws."

"Laws." Bertram leaned back in the copilot's chair and closed his eyes. He had a headache again. He massaged the area at the bridge of his nose.

"About touching a sleeping Hyphizite," Rollie said. "Very strict stuff. Otherwise, half of us would be murdered in our beds. I mean, I could tell you some stories."

"I'm sure you could," Bertram said with some certainty. "And that slab is…?"

"Slab?" He blinked, then understood. "Hyphizite bed. I'd like to get one custom built but can't manage it right now."

"It's a *slab*," Bertram reemphasized.

"Great for the posture," Rollie told him.

Silence fell as Bertram watched the craft swoop in close over a body of brilliantly blue-green water glistening under a sun, to land neatly on what appeared to be a small lush island in its center. Flowers bloomed the size of compact cars. And a brightly plumed bird-lizard crashed through the foliage to peer at its reflection in the ICV's front glass shield. It stared riveted now, cocking its head to the side, a sac under its throat bobbing in time to the throb at Bertram's temples. Rollie flipped levers, spun dials, attended to the device that went "bip," and the ship settled neatly into silence.

Finally Bertram couldn't take it any longer. He found himself saying something aloud that he'd been feeling, on and off, for quite a while. "None of this is in my mind, is it? None of this has ever been in my mind."

Rollie gave him a brief glance as he double-checked the controls. "What tipped it?"

"Oh, I don't know, the level of detail. How real the pain feels."

By now seven or eight of the bird-lizards were peering at themselves in the reflective windshield, cocking, bobbing and raising broad, webbed flaps off the tops of their heads like great plumed golf umbrellas. It looked like a Steelers' stadium crowd during a bad rainstorm. Or singles' night at a warehouse district bar, where things were getting desperate.

"Also, I am not this colorful."

"Ah." Rollie nodded knowingly, then turned a thoughtful look to the creatures outside. Two had started up an enthusiastic yodeling serenade to the saucy feathered lookers they saw shimmering before their eyes, a song which could be heard faintly through the hull. "I only hope they don't try to mate with the ship," he said, frowning. "I just had it waxed."

✧

The bird-lizards scattered with a scrambling clatter and a whoosh of wings, love life put on hold, as Rollie lowered the ship's ramp and the two travelers stepped down onto Nett-30. The air was heavy with blossom perfume and the savory aroma of alien spices. The thick grasses had a vague blue tinge to them, just "off" enough to make Bertram want to adjust the color values setting in his eyeballs.

There was little question where they were headed. A path of glistening quartz-like paving stones formed a winding path through the greenery—or bluery, as the case was—around a series of bright gardens, and up a hill to a white pillared dome.

"'Least the planet's still here," Rollie mused, leading the way. "After the Seers' Tower blanked, I hadn't much hope for our Nett prophets."

"How do we know they won't arrest us on sight?" Bertram asked his back. The fact that Bertram really *was* a fugitive from justice—*intergalactic* justice, no less—was sinking in. And it was funny because on Earth, as far as encounters with the law went, Bertram Ludlow had only gotten one ticket in his entire life, and it was for biking in a cars-only area. He knew he was guilty and didn't want the hassle of a court appearance, so he'd paid the thing the day he got it.

Here in the GCU, however, Bertram was wanted for helping a dangerous prisoner escape...For a jailbreak of his own...For an assault on law enforcement personnel...And for who knew how many other charges. Yet the concept of turning himself in seemed impossible to imagine, almost laughable. Maybe it was because he knew he couldn't do anything productive for his planet if he were tucked away in a Hyphiz Deltan prison, making license plates for ICVs. (Or whatever intergalactic prisoners did there between, say, shiv-carving and dinner.)

Maybe it was because he'd simply gone too far to turn back now.

Hard to say.

Up and up they climbed, ducking under arches and through areas of strange giant fruits and vegetables ripening in the sun; forward to tiered fields of warm waving grains; past herds of round, bouncing pink livestock that made a cheery "squonk" as they went by; on and on. With each arch, they seemed to enter a new world. Until finally, they reached a set of elaborately carved white stone steps, and behind it, the white domed structure raised by hundreds of stately pillars.

On each side of the steps was a guard. To the left side was a beefy humanoid with dark gray skin, a hard face, and great shining horns springing from the top of his head. To the right, an equally powerful-looking humanoid covered in thick fur, with large clawed hands, and sharp teeth. Both were draped in cobalt blue robes with fine needlework in gold around the edges.

Rollie strode up to this pair and said, "We're here to see the Prophets of Nett." Even at his height, he stood several inches shorter than these immense creatures.

The horned being peered down on both their guests and raised a thick, hairy eyebrow. "And your names?" The voice was a low, bored rumble.

"Rolliam Tsmorlood and Bertram Ludlow," said Rollie crisply.

The horned being gave a slow graceful nod. "Ah. We have been waiting for you." From his robe, the horned sentinel withdrew a large mallet. The furred guard did the same.

Bertram took a step back, poised to defend himself should this be the start of some unpleasant cosmic version of Whack-a-Mole. He knew he would lose, given the size of both opponent and mallet. But he'd faced other bizarre obstacles lately, and he was willing to take what came and die nobly.

Or shorter and flatter.

His gaze darted to Rollie who was watching the guards like some taloned bird of prey, hand readied on his holster.

In a smooth, synchronized movement, the Prophets' guards each brought a mallet over, around, and with a great twist of the waist, struck a wide metal structure sitting behind them, on either side of the staircase.

Bells! Their clang cracked and reverberated across the gardens, fields and lake like the sound of the Titanic hitting a large willful icecube.

"Rolliam Tsmorlood and Bertram Ludlow!" the sentinels chorused. Their voices came out in a roar that, like the bells, jarred the internal organs before bounding far off into the distance.

The guards then turned and bowed.

"You may enter," the horned humanoid said.

Rollie bowed in return. "Thanks."

Finally remembering to breathe, Bertram managed his own bow. "Er... have a good one."

Up the stairs they went, under a sign of carved runes which read:

Nett Prophet Center
Taking Stock of the Future,
One Prediction at a Time

It was from there, Bertram and Rollie stepped into the domed structure. A cool breeze blew gently between the white pillars. And far, far down at the very end of the airy pavilion sat two figures, propped among pillows upon a throne: one male and one female twin, conjoined by a shared leg and arm.

As they drew closer, Bertram saw everything around them was made of carefully-woven fibers. Both twins were dressed in deep purple robes, the trim on their garb an elaborate series of golden runic arrows, zig-zagging up and down. The pillows upon which they leaned were small tapestries, each depicting scenes from the landscape outside: fields of grains, livestock, fruits, and beans, all in delicate silken threads. Even the domed ceiling above them was spanned by colorful banners of rich fiberwork.

Next to this regal display was a giant wooden loom, weaving all on its own. In, out, up, down, red, blue, white, black, silver, gold, the machine busied itself.

"We are the Prophets of Nett. I am Buhl," said the female twin.

"And I am Bahr," said the male twin. Each of them wore a crowning circlet of gold, emblazoned with constellations, the shining dots connecting into shapes forming a small menagerie of alien fauna. The patterns, Bertram noticed, echoed those carved into their throne, a grand golden settee, its finish crackled with age. The beings' own skin was a deep bronze, unmarred by the signs of time. Their hair was a rich walnut brown and fell in long waves to their shoulders, like unwoven skeins of thread. "Welcome, dear friends. We expected you."

Rollie's face wore a cool, skeptical expression. "So you know, then, that the Seers of Rhobux sent us." It wasn't a question, and its flat tone was unmoved by pleasantry. "Or, rather, that the Seers' *sign* did, where their planet used to be. You know about that, too, I assume?"

The pair turned to each other, smiled sadly, and turned back to the travelers with a brief bow of the head. "We do."

"And do you also know your coworkers failed to blank my archive as they'd promised, so now we're up to our necks in it, with the Deltan RegForce?"

"We have seen," said Bahr with a benevolent smile. "We understand your frustration."

"But we have also foreseen that today," said Buhl grandly, "we will not be here to assign blame."

At this, Rollie erupted with a bitter laugh. "Well, I think you're off your loom a bit then, Prophet," the captain told them. "Because right now, I'd like nothing better than to take that blame and launch it clear on up your colleagues'—"

Bertram cleared his throat and pressed a hand to Rollie's shoulder. "Er, let's not make the nice intergalactic soothsayers angry, 'kay?" He stepped forward. "Excuse my friend. He gets a little... hasty... sometimes."

Rollie gave him a narrow orange glare.

"But what the captain says about the Seers' promise to him is true," Bertram continued. "He did them some favors, and they never kept their part of the bargain. I mean, we may not be here to assign blame—" he shot another warning glance to Rollie, "—but it has gotten a lot worse for both of us because of them. We were hoping you might be able to intervene with the RegForce on our behalf."

"Our job is to ensure time continues forward smoothly. To predict what will happen and verify that the image becomes reality," replied Buhl. She directed an arm to the great loom to her right.

Bertram saw what she meant. It seemed the loom could weave an image in just a moment. Like now, in its fabric, a team of exoskeletoned beings carried one player high on their armored shoulders, as a crowd celebrated wildly. A second later, the image eroded, its threads unraveling to weave a whole new scene. This one was of an impossibly beautiful alien man and woman in the middle of a press conference. In another second, this picture would be gone, and yet another would appear. And on and on.

"You see?" asked Bahr. "Our job is to envision, weave and watch. We are not permitted to meddle in the affairs of life-forms."

"Well, your pals, the Seers of Rhobux, didn't have any qualms about that, now did they?" snapped Rollie. "Can you at least blank my archive?"

At this Buhl dropped her gaze in a defeated way. "We have lost all contact with the Seers of Rhobux," she said, shaking her head dismally. "Most disturbing."

"We can no longer access their systems," said Bahr, with a weary sigh. "Very unfortunate."

"Yeah, I weep for you." Rollie rolled his eyes. "I mean, it's not like either of you will be turning to ash or eaten alive on Altair-5 because of this 'disturbing,' 'unfortunate' glitch in the existential filing system."

"It is most distressing to *us*," Bahr emphasized, "as we have not seen any of this in our threads."

"Much has been blocked from us," Buhl said.

"It is an anomaly of considerable concern," Bahr admitted.

"So the Seers are up to something they don't want you eyeballing, and we're still stuck runnin' from the law." Rollie gave an irritable rumble at the back of his throat. "Stellar."

"Meanwhile," added Bertram, "I'm still supposed to save my planet from some untold evil. Your colleagues aren't exactly long on the details, are they?"

"Oh!" exclaimed Buhl. It was like she'd just remembered she'd left the iron on back in the other pavilion. "With that, I can assist you!" Her smile was beatific, filled with pleasure at the task. Even intergalactic prophets, Bertram supposed, needed a certain amount of job satisfaction in their days. "Your planet is to be sold, Bertram Ludlow."

"Sold?!" cried Bertram, stumbling back a step. "How can it be sold? We're...we're..." he searched for the right words, "still using it."

"Can't expect to get much for it. It's not even on a main trade route," Rollie input.

"Nonetheless, soon it will be sold," said Bahr.

"Who's the owner?" Bertram asked, feeling anger overcome him the more he considered it. Earth didn't belong to the Earthlings? How could it be, that all this time his entire planet was under some kind of unsuspected rental situation?

No, no, wait! It was even worse than that! How could it be that the whole planet's populace were...

Squatters?

"Who's the space cadet I'm going to have to track down and give a piece of my mind?" Bertram Ludlow asked.

Buhl's lips set in a thin irritated line. "It is not known who the current owner is. That, interestingly, is among the information that has been blocked to us."

"Most distressing," Bahr said again, his mouth following the irritated line of his sister's. "We would report the Seers behavior to our superiors, but we have been at this job for so very many centuries, we can no longer remember who that would be, or how to reach them." He waved a hand. "If we ever knew."

"We lost contact with Corporate many U-years ago," Buhl admitted, a wistful tone to her voice.

"The sale, however, is being handled by Alternate Realty, headquartered on Ottofram," said Bahr.

"When?" Bertram asked. Determination had begun to fortify him from his sore feet on upward. At last, he had something to go on. "How much time do I have?"

"They are taking bids now," said Buhl.

"Let us just say, I would not spend much time sight-seeing," suggested Bahr.

Bertram somehow expected as much. "And you saw all of this in your tapestry." He stared up at the giant ever-changing textile before them.

Buhl shook her head in the negative, a vague blush creeping over her smooth, bronzed cheeks. "On the Uninet at breakfast," she told him. "It is all over the news."

"Spectra Pollux also has a new CapClub book pill recommendation, and Jet Antlia has broken bonds with Stella Cygnus again," Bahr informed them.

"Great." Bertram exhaled, the gravity of the situation tugging at his respiratory system. "Just great." He thanked them for their help and turned one socked foot out of the pavilion, when an idea popped front and center. He paused. He turned back. "One more thing."

"Yes?" Buhl and Bahr met his gaze with eyes kind and interested.

"Do you know what this might be?" Bertram asked, raising the Yellow Thing around his neck for them to see. "The Seers of Rhobux gave it to me and said I should make sure I kept it with me at all times. That I'd need it. Which would be terrific. If I knew what the hell it was."

The Prophets, comparers of present and future, eyed the item.

Bird-lizards yodeled in the distance, while blossom petals flew on the breeze and swept across the pavilion's marble floor like silken confetti. The tapestry murmured its *wzzzssh-clonk-wzzzssh-clonk* as it made and remade itself.

After this long moment, Bahr said, "It looks a little like something off an all-you-can-digest buffet."

"A little," agreed Buhl, giving it another long look. She wrinkled her nose. "But not entirely."

"No, not entirely," admitted Bahr, tilting his head to the side and wrinkling his nose too. He glanced back at Bertram and shrugged a robed shoulder. "I am sorry, Bertram Ludlow. I fear we have failed you."

"You did what you could." True, Bertram hadn't much hope for it, but he'd figured it was worth a shot. "Thanks for trying."

"Much fortune to you, Bertram Ludlow, in saving your planet," Buhl called as Bertram and Rollie turned to go.

Bertram gave her a little bow.

"May you speed safely and swiftly to clear your name, Rolliam Tsmorlood," said Bahr.

Rollie just made a noise that was either a laugh or a growl, Bertram wasn't sure.

And with that, Bertram and Rollie solemnly left the Prophet Center.

The walk back through the gardens to the ICV was a quiet one. Bertram had a lot on his mind.

All this time, the people of his planet had been operating as if they were the rulers of their fate, with nothing but a fickle Mother Nature, and maybe a favorite Deity or two to answer to.

And now there was a whole other layer of truth to wrap around it. Yep, all those conspiracy theorists out there, wearing their sandwich board signs proclaiming, "Aliens Are Coming! The End is Nigh!" were going to have a whole new fleet of fears to probe into. Oh, we'd suspected aliens walked among us. We just hadn't really planned on them owning the joint.

It was especially concerning because, having been a renter himself for the last ten years of his life, Bertram Ludlow knew a little something about landlords.

See, it was actually a testament to the current owner that the people of Earth had remained ignorant about it for so long. In most respects, that was the kind of landlord you really wanted. The kind that gave you your privacy, let you do your own thing. One that wasn't always popping by when you weren't home, hitting your fridge and helping himself to your beer. Or stopping over unannounced, then criticizing the socks balled up on the floor.

No, this was the type of landlord that gave you the keys and then forgot about you.

And okay, so *yes*, in this kind of landlord-tenant relationship, maintenance issues aren't always the easiest to resolve. Like, it might have been nice if the owner had gotten someone in to fix the ozone layer. And, yeah, Earth probably could have benefited from some water damage repairs after a couple of key natural disasters. That might have been handy.

But at least the good people of Earth had been able to count on the peace and quiet. A sense of autonomy. A decent night's sleep.

As the saying goes: "It's the evil alien overlord you know."

Like, what if your *laissez-faire* landlord sells to a zealous newbie with a DIY bug?

Soon she's in there tearing up your bathroom, ripping out the kitchen cabinets, a stream of handymen trooping in and out at all hours, and helping themselves to a few of your albums along the way.

She's making improvements. She's got a vision. And before you know it, she's looking at *you* and wondering how she can get you out of there, so she can put some really high-end tenants in instead. Someone willing to pay 400 bucks more a month, plus utilities.

Life will never be the same.

This was what Bertram felt the Earthlings might be up against. Some home improvement junkie likely to take out a couple of tectonic plates simply because she didn't like the pattern.

Well, Bertram would just have to do what he could to keep that from happening, even though he wasn't wholly convinced he was the right man for the job. A man who had grown complacent about toothpaste for wall spackle wasn't exactly king of Apartment B1.

Lost in thought as he was, Bertram hadn't realized that they'd already trekked the long road back down the hill to the ICV. Of course, the ship was also a little hard to spot at the moment, for the wide array of local fauna that had found it and made themselves welcome. In addition to 30 of the bird-lizards flirting with the windshield on the ship's nose, there now were a good 20 squeaky-jumpy lavender things bouncing on the roof, maybe 15 chirpy-burpy orange things clinging to the side, and one brown leathery thing that looked a lot like a comfy recliner, sniffing the landing gear in interest.

Rollie cursed under his breath. "Stellar. A fragging zoo." With a worlds-weary sigh, he rushed at the bird-lizards, squeaky-jumpies, chirpy-burpies and the comfy-wumfy, waving his arms wildly. "Yaw! Get outta there, ya stinking bunch! It's an ICV, not a blasted wildlife refuge. Launch yourselves, before I hit the power and roast you with the rockets!"

Feathers and fur flew in a mad scramble. And as the last squeaky-jumpy bounced off into the bluery, Rollie lowered the ramp and clomped into the ship.

Bertram trailed him into the craft and then the cockpit. Rollie attended to the controls while the Earthman plunked down in the copilot's chair and fastened his harness, as if prepping for launch these days were all a part of some normal, everyday routine.

"So," Bertram began, breaking the silence, "to Alternate Realty on Ottofram, then?"

Rollie glanced at Bertram, then started up the ship. "For you maybe. Not me," he said, tapping a meter.

A sinking feeling hit Bertram's stomach, swallowed by a wave of dread. He almost was afraid to ask, but as anger buoyed up through the fear, the words came rushing out, too. "Hold on, what's that supposed to mean?"

"Quite simple, Ludlow; it means I am out of this," Rolliam Tsmorlood said quietly. He fixed Bertram with a sharp amber stare. "I said from the beginning I was only the A to B to C man. But it's gotten bigger than that, hasn't it? And now we're both all over the Uninet, it's zonky dangerous, and I've got to lie low for a while. There's nothing else to it." He checked some gauges, flipped a lever and managed to get a good "bip" going.

Bertram just couldn't believe it. Rollie—the guy who'd championed Klimfals in a major rebellion they didn't even seem to win the naming rights for…the guy who still felt *print* merited a comeback, fer Pete's sake—was abandoning the cause? Just like that?

"Lie low!" Bertram exclaimed. "Now? You heard the Prophets. My planet's being sold out from under us. It's not just me this affects, Rollie. It's billions of innocent people!"

"Not to say I'm unsympathetic to your problem." Rollie considered this further. "Though I am a little. It's just I happen to like living *not on Altair-5* better. I have to figure out a way to get my archive blanked. And I can't do that if I'm chauffeuring you all over the blasted GCU while you play the hero, can I?"

"Well, I get that. But it leaves me in a very bad position," Bertram said. "I still have to save my world from Extreme Planet Makeover. It's kinda high-pressure." He watched as the ship lifted up off the lush land of Nett 30. He could see the shining white dome of the Prophet Center appear to grow smaller and smaller below them. "I'm not going to bag everything just because you're a repeat offender and you're finally scared it's catching up with you."

Rollie attended to a lever, muttering as if to himself, "Ah, that's Tryflings for you. Always making things so much more fragging difficult than need be." He frowned at Bertram and continued, "No one is asking you to put things in *bag*s, Ludlow."

"In bags?" Bertram would have laughed if he hadn't been so angry.

"It's a simple case of you go your way, me mine. It'll be safer for both of us in the long run. Believe me."

But Bertram just grimaced, pushing at the sides of his temples. "And just how do I do that, when I don't know how to fly a ship, I don't have a ship, and I have no idea where Ottofram is?"

Rollie offered him that broad, serrated smile again. For its repetition, the effect never ceased to be chilling. "Don't worry, Ludlow," he said brightly. "I have just the ticket."

13

"Welcome to the Farthest Reaches® Cosmos Corral, Entrance Level," said a friendly computerized voice over the PA system. In the long metallic channel that connected the ICV lots, dozens of moving walkways fed from multiple levels, transporting life-forms from every part of the galaxy to the Main Terminal—their first step to untold astronomical adventures. Above this, a sign arced across the great tube's expanse. In glowing, blinking letters, the banner cheerfully proclaimed:

Farthest Reaches®—You'll See Stars with Every Trip.

Bertram's feet moved with the flow of the crowd—familiar feet though, technically, loaners. To the observer's naked eye, a tiny, round old woman, with a kind face, three eyes and an ample, hairy mole had just entered the structure. Who would guess that behind this grandmotherly figure, intergalactic fugitive Bertram Ludlow was hidden and, for the moment, secure? What RegForce officer would ever expect the pair of Podunk's Most Wanted had split up, sending a Tryfling—backspace and unsavvy—to face the GCU alone?

After the narrow escape from Vos Laegos, soon the old lady's image would be flashed all over the Uninet. Maybe it already was. But Rollie had been right; in the Terminal, Bertram Ludlow appeared as just one solitary granny of many such life-forms. The GCU was self-aborbed. It had places to be. And so the aged female continued in her quest for public transit without attracting undue attention. For now, Bertram found peace of mind in that.

Only a little.

The planet itself was called Mig Verlig, Rollie had explained back at the ship. And it was one of the largest ports for interplanetary mass transit in the entire GCU.

"Why, the Cosmos Corral is the perfect solution!" the Hyphiz Deltan had exclaimed for the second time now since he'd proposed it. His smile was beatific. "It's cheap, it's efficient, the RegForce'd never expect it, and there aren't even that many violent deaths on it each year." The captain seemed to realize he'd oversold it with that last point and turned a pinker shade of pink. But he kept right on smiling.

"If it's so great, how come you have your own ship?" Bertram had countered.

"Ah, well, the ICV...it's more than a ship. It's a portable home unit. Anyway," he cleared his throat, "can't very well carry cases of stolen goods round from place to place on mass transit, now can I? Lacks subtlety." Looking relieved to have that settled, he moved on quickly, tossing the holowatch and a few yoonie cards Bertram's way.

"Here ya go, Ludlow. Use the holowatch. Can't say it's a perfect plan, as a few of them RegForcers saw you in it. But they're not looking for you by your lonesome yet. At least it'll get you where you're going."

Bertram turned the watch in his hands. "Won't your lady friend want it back?"

The Hyphizite shrugged. "She left with my PT-20 launcher. I call it even," he said. "As for the credits, it's all I can spare right now. But at least you got a few yoonies to help you on, yeah?"

Bertram nodded. Like Rollie'd said, it wasn't ideal, but it was more than he'd expected.

"Stellar. Then—" Through the hatch window, Rollie scanned the Cosmos Corral's ICV lot for potential law enforcement. To Bertram's eyes, the lot appeared to be filled with tourists of varying species going on trips, returning from trips and seeing each other off. Rollie confirmed the security of the scene, turning back to Bertram with a brisk nod. "Guess this is *paar too.*"

Bertram had tucked the cards into his shirt pocket, searched for errant possessions—he had none—and rose. He paused at the hatch door, snapping the holowatch to his wrist, and he decided to satiate his curiosity this one last time. "Hey, what's *'paar too'* mean exactly, anyway? It seems like good-bye, but it never translates."

The captain sniffed or snickered. "Deltan phrase. Came from the entertainment industry, I think. Literally means 'may we meet again in the sequel.'"

"Ah." Bertram thought that sounded about right. *"Paar too*, then. Take care. Thanks for—" Bertram considered the kidnapping, stunning, and nearly being sold as a show animal, "—well, not for *everything*. But I hope you aren't ripped to shreds on Altair."

"Yup, hope your planet isn't demolished or your people mass slaughtered or whatnot."

"Cool, thanks."

"All right."

And with that, Bertram Ludlow trudged down the ship's ramp to face the whole of space on his own.

Now, sliding forward on the moving walkway, the Farthest Reaches Cosmos Corral Main Terminal was just minutes ahead. He craned over the crowd before him and spied a sign down at the end of the concourse which read "Ticketing."

Soon, he told himself. *Soon*. His little planet deserved a decent fighting chance; maybe that chance would be found on Ottofram.

A voice over the PA system announced, "As a courtesy to fellow passengers, Farthest Reaches reminds our guests entering the Terminal: please refrain from igniting combustible objects for oral pleasure... Solicitation on behalf of religious or private institutions is strictly prohibited..."

Bertram let the crowded walkway drive him further down the concourse.

"...Do not leave progeny or unicellular companions unattended..."

A hefty mauvish life-form behind him snorted steamy breath on his neck.

"...And for your safety, please do not hoverboard over the moving walkways."

Bertram ducked as a smoking figure in a hooded, cowl-like tie-dyed robe passed overhead on a slim floating disk. Humming to himself, the guy was cramming slim digital brochures into the hands of everyone along the walkway. The electronic lettering read:

It's the end of Life As We Know It...

"Ain't it the truth," Bertram muttered. Then the brochure flashed:

...And the Rebirth of Better Snacking!

Introducing new **Jerky Divine®**, the only snack food created from the regenerated and cloned cells of deceased Popeelie prophet, Chawtu Champs. Brought to you by **MetamorfaSys Inc.**, the trusted Product Gurus who first lit the way with **Pocket Pulpit®** and **Cloak-in-a-Can®**, Jerky Divine is the Afterlife delicacy for after sports, between meals, or on-the-go!

Jerky Divine is the only snack that wards away both hunger and disbelievers!

With every bite, you'll feel the spirit of the Munificent Popeelhonoromous inside you. It's cosmically-delicious with our specially-blessed **Sanctified Seltzer**, too!

And now *you* can join the millions of Popeelies GCU-wide in the Popeelie **"Mass and Mass Marketing" Jamboree**. If you'd like information on how you can share in three weeks of Popeelie singing, prayer and product demonstrations, just send 19,995 yoonies to—

Bertram sent the brochure into a passing refuse containment robot. He imagined it would take more than divine dinner and sacred soda-water to help his planet.

An announcement from the PA system again interrupted the scene. "The shuttle to Marglenia will be leaving from Gate Stop 198 in approximately 30 Universal minutes...

"The shuttle to Ottofram will be leaving from Gate Stop 149 in approximately 20 Universal minutes...

"And to the passenger who left the head of their Non-Organic Simulant in the lavatory, would you please see the nearest blue courtesy vis-u for a message from your Simulant?... That's Marglenia in 30 minutes, Ottofram in 20 minutes and—"

Ottofram!

Bertram's heart leapt and he broke into a run. He slipped around alien families, leapt over robots and their piles of luggage, dodged elephant-like trunks and actual trunks, and wound through the Blumdec Blasters professional kachunkettball team. It was the sort of behavior you didn't often see in the elderly, Bertram knew. But he'd made it to Ticketing and moved fleetly toward a free service counter.

The attendant smiled at him. She was a tall, flawlessly-skinned female with black-silver hair that shone like hematite. Bertram noticed the square emblem embossed into the base of her slender throat. The font was hard to read, but he finally made it out: "Natelle." It seemed like one helluva way to wear a nametag.

He put on his best Grandma Ludlow voice, a raspy alto laced with a North Jersey accent, the mist of evening toddies and the musk of 50 years of Virginia Slims. "Why, hello there, Natelle. One ticket to Ottofram, darling, if you please."

"It is my pleasure to assist, ma'am," she responded. And as Natelle punched in the ticketing information, Bertram noticed a strange scent wafting from the girl. A scent like floral disinfectant spray and new shower curtain liners. He was just wondering if it were some kind of misguided designer space fragrance, when she paused in her typing and looked up with long-lashed, still-unblinking blue eyes. "Primary or Secondary Corral seating, ma'am?"

"Whatever ya got, sweetie," Grandma Ludlow told her. "So long as I'm on that shuttle."

"It is my pleasure to assist, ma'am," she said again, looking at the screen before her. She tossed back that long, metallic black-gray hair. "I'm afraid the Primary Corral is booked, ma'am. But there is plenty of room in the Secondary."

"Fine, fine," Grandma Ludlow said, who normally would have traveled first class, enjoyed two complementary screwdrivers and lifted some extra pretzels to squirrel away in her purse for later. Yes, Lavinia Ludlow would have waited for first class. But Lavinia Ludlow also never had to save her planet; she didn't know from deadlines. "As long as it's leaving soon," said the old woman.

"It will attach to the Primary Corral and embark in less than 17 minutes, ma'am," the ticket agent said, and a ticket popped out of her console. "And how will you be paying for this?"

The old woman dug into her cloak and handed Natelle the yoonie cards. Or, rather, Bertram Ludlow dug in his shirt pocket and hoped no one would notice money appear from nowhere.

Natelle didn't seem fazed; he imagined in GCU customer service you had to make a lot of allowances. She took the first card and scanned it. Then paused.

Bertram got the distinct feeling the girl would have scowled, but that sort of behavior was frowned upon at Farthest Reaches®.

Natelle grabbed up the second yoonie card and scanned it. Paused.

Yup. There was that invisible frown, again.

She took the third, scanned it, and… "I'm sorry, ma'am, these yoonie cards are invalid."

"Excuse me?" said Grandma Ludlow.

"Yes, ma'am. Our system says that the owner of this account—the one who originally registered these universal credits—has had all of his or her yoonie cards cancelled. And that would include these, I'm afraid." For being afraid, her expression showed nothing but the same unrelenting joy.

"Does it say why?" Grandma Ludlow asked, trying to peer around at the girl's screen.

But Natelle just smiled. "It's a 533."

"533?"

"Governmental request."

"Does it say which government?"

"It's a 533," she said again. "Governmental request. A 533."

Bertram didn't press it; he had a strong idea which government did the requesting. Soon, he imagined, the Hyphiz Deltan RegForce would hear about how a three-eyed old lady had tried to use Rollie Tsmorlood's money cards at the Farthest Reaches Cosmos Corral to buy a ticket to Ottofram. Bertram didn't have much time to waste.

But Natelle smiled patiently. "I suggest you report whoever gave those cards to you to your local authorities. This has become a popular scam targeting life-forms of advancing years, such as yourself. Do you have any other yoonie cards you'd like me to check, ma'am?"

It was tricky to do casually, but now the old woman pulled a wallet from the ether and leafed through it. She tossed the remains of Bertram Ludlow's cashed teaching assistant paycheck onto the counter. "This is what I have, sweetie. My, er, grandson: he's doing an exchange program on Tryfe and he sends his grandma money."

"He sounds like a very nice young man," Natelle said politely.

"Adorable." In reality, Grandma Ludlow openly favored his brother A.J., but sometimes liberties must be taken.

"Unfortunately," Natelle could brandish that white sweet smile like a shining sword, "the Farthest Reaches Cosmos Corral does not recognize Tryfe currency, ma'am."

"Naturally," sighed Grandma Ludlow.

"We do, however, accept paper and coin-based money from the following galactic monetary systems," began Natelle helpfully, "A'Tau, Alpuck, Ambigodia, Armani…"

Dread swept over Bertram as he considered the difference between Earthling independence and horrific Evil Overlandlordship might just depend on a ticket to Ottofram.

"…Calderia, Chronos-12, Corgi Beta…"

"Look," said Grandma Ludlow, "darling, sweetie, beautiful, there's gotta be something we can work out." Grandma Ludlow was not above slathering on the endearments when she wanted to get her way. It was how she got a serious discount on her condo.

But the ticket agent just folded her well-manicured hands and continued on with the list of worlds with acceptable galactic currencies. "…Hyphiz Beta, Hyphiz Delta, Hysgorgle-5—"

"Is there a currency exchange around here, Natelle?" the old woman pressed. "Or some kind of traveler assistance?"

Natelle stopped in mid-list. Bertram thought he heard a slowing whir. "There is a Galactic Monetary Exchange at the end of this concourse." She pointed.

"Would it convert this?" The old lady held up her bills.

Natelle paused. Bertram swore he heard that whir rev up again. "I cannot affirm it, ma'am, as that system is siloed and I am not tapped into it."

Bertram nodded. As he'd suspected. His first Non-Organic Simulant.

"I would not want to hazard a guess as to the probability," she continued.

"But is there a chance?"

"I couldn't tell you based on available data."

Bertram had to hand it to those Simulants; they were nothing if not specific. "Fair enough," called Grandma Ludlow, moving in the direction Natelle had pointed. "I'll be back, darling. Hold that ticket!"

Galactic Monetary Exchange, Galactic Monetary Exchange… Bertram dashed past travelers from all over the final frontier, past restaurants wafting foreign spice, past souvenir shops with wares bearing the Farthest Reaches logo, past an 80s ATM…

Bertram backed up. Eighties ATM?

Okay, well, maybe not *quite* an ATM. But if anything had the look of alien retro technology, this thing did. The sign above the smudgy box read, "Galactic Monetary Exchange." A smaller sign indicated a large red button and showed a stick figure with four stick arms pressing it with a stick finger.

At least, Bertram *hoped* that was a finger.

In fact, he hoped that was an *arm.*

Bertram's finger pressed the button. And as he did, a blue fog clouded around his face. He instinctively recoiled. Was he being poisoned? Was this some kind of clever trap the RegForce had set up to ensnare him?

He sneezed.

The machine said in a motherly tone, "Sneeze contents verified. Nasal output identifies customer as chewer of Translachew brand translational gum 52.7 or greater. Vocal interface adjusted accordingly. Press 1 on the keypad if this analysis is correct. Press 2, if you would like to repeat Sneeze Verification. Press 3, if you would like to quit. Look confused, if you suddenly cannot understand this message."

I have dialects in my nasal mucus now? Bertram wondered. He busied himself by pushing "1".

The not-quite-MAC machine said, "Welcome to the Galactic Monetary Exchange, Valued Customer. When the money conveyance panel slides open, please insert the currency you wish to convert."

The panel slid open. Bertram gave it his cash. The panel slid shut.

The panel slid open again so vigorously, it spit Bertram's money out onto the floor. "We're sorry. Currency unknown. We cannot process currency of indeterminate type. The Galactic Monetary Exchange does, however, welcome currency from all locations within the Greater Communicating Universe."

"Of *course* it does," Bertram snarled at the thing, "and I'd *give* you some, if I friggin' *had* any of it, you stupid machine!" He glanced around to see if anyone heard him, then took three cleansing breaths. So this was it then. Unless he could beg a few yoonies from a sympathetic fellow traveler, or con security into just letting him on the Corral—probabilities both slimmer than Tryfe money converting in a GME machine—the quest to save his planet was all washed up. *Finito. Sayonara. Kaput. Paar too,* even.

(Tink-a-tink-a-tink-a-tink-a...)

It was funny, he thought, how a person could spend an entire academic career studying how people approach problem-solving and still end up stuck in an alien space port with a planet to rescue, no cash, and completely out of valid ideas.

(Tink-a-tink-a-tink-a-tink-a...)

He stooped to scoop up his bills from the shiny Terminal tiles. Maybe there was an off-chance he could sell them to an obscure currency collector, he pondered—(Tink-a-tink-a-tink-a-tink-a...)— when he noticed that metal, rolling sound behind him was sweeping in close and growing closer. (Tink-a-tink-a-tink-a-tink-a...)

Frowning, Bertram turned, searching for its source. Travelers hurried past, alien pets sniffed suspiciously, Farthest Reaches Simulants headed off to work after a brief recharge ... It all looked like just another day in the GCU.

(Tinka-tinka-tinka-tinka-tinka...)

The sound persisted and grew. Until...

(Pa-tinka!)

Something bounced near Bertram's feet and struck him hard in the ankle. Bertram bent to see the offending object but it took only a quick glance to see the object did not offend.

In some respects, the thing even had a lot going for it. Because there, between Bertram Ludlow's sore, socked feet, lay a well-worn, 16-sided coin. He had no idea what planet it was from, but it sat there waiting like a weary traveler in the Terminal light. He scooped it up.

Now Bertram scanned the crowd for its owner. The lady with the larvae in the rocket carriage maybe? Those kachunkettball players sauntering by? The floppy-eared dude in the overcoat waiting by the restrooms? The purple kid stuffing a snack cake into his face?

Bertram studied them all and returned his gaze to the coin now in his sweating palm. Lifeforms across the GCU lost change all the time, the unerring result of butter-appendages and gravity, plus a highly inconsistent monetary structure. But the 16-sized coin that *pa-tinka*-ed its course straight to him hadn't quite sounded like a coin dropped and lost. It had sounded like a coin on a mission.

By now the GME machine had grown impatient. "Would you like to try to convert again? Press 1 for 'yes.' Or press 2 to conclude this trans—" Bertram hit "1," and slapped the tiny coin on the tray. It couldn't be much. It couldn't be anything. But it was hope. Maybe, just maybe, he could convert it into something he could be sure Farthest Reaches would accept.

The machine drew in the tray. The machine hummed. Bertram heard an encouraging clinking noise.

"Please select a currency to which you would like your money converted." A numbered list of planets ran down the computer terminal. Bertram chose the code for Hyphiz Delta.

"Incorrect input," said the machine. "This unit is unable to dispense currency in negative denominations. Please select the currency of a less thriving economy."

Bertram rested his forehead on the machine. It felt warm and a little sticky.

Over the PA system came, "The Corral to Ottofram will arrive at Gate Stop 149 in ten Universal minutes. The Corral to Marglenia will arrive at Gate Stop 198 in 20 Universal minutes. And for the passenger who has yet to claim the head of their Non-Organic Simulant, your item says it feels deeply betrayed. Please come pick up your Simulant at your soonest convenience. Thank you."

Ten minutes, Bertram thought. *Ten minutes.*

Meanwhile, the machine asked, "Do you wish to attempt conversion into a different form of currency? Press 1 for 'yes,' press 2 for 'no,' press 3 for—"

Bertram pressed "1".

"Please select a currency to which you would like your money converted." The numbered list ran by again. Bertram selected Ottofram.

"Incorrect input," the machine told him pleasantly. "This unit is unable to dispense currency in negative denominations."

Bertram kicked the machine.

"Incorrect input method," said the machine. "This unit is unwilling to dispense currency while under duress. Press 1 to reevaluate your attitude. Press 2 to attempt conversion into another form of—"

Bertram punched "2" and selected a planet at random. "One moment, please," said the machine.

"The Corral to Ottofram will arrive at Gate Stop 149 in five Universal minutes. The Corral to Marglenia will arrive at Gate Stop 198 in ten Universal minutes. And for the passenger missing the head of their Non-Organic Simulant, your item has gone to Lost and Found along with one of our Abandonment Counselors. Please pick it up there. Thank you."

Five minutes now. Bertram's hands quivered uncontrollably. He refused to miss this Corral.

Plink.

The sound was over the rumble and groan of the machine. Bertram looked down and saw a coin at his feet, a small silvery coin this time, bearing the two profiles of the Empress of the Dootett star system. She reminded him of Xylith.

Then plink. Plink. Plink, plink, plink. Coinage rained out of the GME machine like a jackpot on the nickel slots. Frantically, Bertram stripped off the flannel shirt under his holowatch disguise. He tied it into a makeshift bag to catch the coinage spilling from the spout, then scrambled under legs and across the Terminal floor in chase of his rolling, errant currency.

"The Corral to Ottofram has arrived at Gate Stop 149. Linkage with the Primary Corral will occur in one Universal minute."

Heart lurching in his chest, Bertram tossed the last of his gathered money into the bundled shirt and sprinted to the Ticket desk, dodging and weaving around passengers all the way. A family of four slug-looking people were just leaving Natelle's desk, when Bertram cut to the front of the line amid protest, and tossed the money-filled shirt before Natelle with a solid thwack. "Here," he huffed. "Here it is. I made it. I got Dootett currency. Now give me my ticket."

Natelle brushed back long synthetic hair and eyed the shirt.

"Don't tell me," Bertram gasped, leaning on the counter, "you don't accept Dootett currency now."

"We accept Dootett currency, ma'am," she said.

"Great!"

"I just need to count it."

"The Secondary Corral for Ottofram is prepared for linkage … Linkage successful. Prepare the Corrals to Ottofram for boarding."

"Oh my God," Bertram moaned over the bulging shirt of money, sinking against the counter and onto the floor. "Oh, sweet Jesus."

Bertram managed to get himself into a kneeling position and peered over the counter. And that's when he saw that counting, for Natelle, was really just the work of a second. The ability to count objects almost instantly is one of the things that made Non-Organic Simulants so effective as money-handlers.

It's what also automatically disqualified them from all "Guess How Many Candies There Are in the Jar" games at fundraisers.

"You're missing *feeg burfkins* here," Natelle said. At Bertram's blank look, she explained, "About 0.00752 of a yoonie. I'm so sorry." Smiling, she stretched gracefully to feed Bertram's unneeded ticket into a passing refuse robot. "Next, please."

It was as the refuse robot sensed Natelle's smooth synthetic hand approach, and it flipped its lid for her, that Grandma Ludlow and Bertram flipped their lids, too.

Yes, after cancelled yoonie cards and disrespect for the mighty dollar...After snippy MAC machines and a roller coaster of conversion...After raining coinage and running, running, running... Grandma Ludlow and her grandson reached the joint decision that they had come entirely too far to miss the Corral to Ottofram by the breadth of a friggin' *feeg burfkin*.

So with catlike reflexes rarely displayed by the average retirement home resident, Grandma Ludlow snatched the pass from Natelle's tapered polymer fingers before it ever hit the refuse robot, grabbed the flannel-shirt-sack of coins, and took off like greased lightning, jingling all the way.

From all eye-witness accounts, that large-boned old lady could really move when she put her mind to it.

"You there! Stop that! You know it's prohibited!"

The robe-clad, pamphlet-pushing Popeelie sung contentedly to himself and was just about to fire up his Official Light of Popeelhonoromous® pipe in Transcendental Mint, when a Farthest Reaches Safety Simulant caught him in the act.

The Simulant, a stern android, his hair designed to be lightly receding for a more natural look, pointed at one of 40 signs posted just within eyeshot:

> Igniting combustible objects for oral pleasure
> in the Main Terminal is strictly prohibited.
>
> Please use one of the Designated Smoking Bubbles
> for all personal conflagration and respiratory enjoyment.
>
> *—Farthest Reaches* **thanks you!**

Rolling his eyes, because these sorts of things just didn't happen back at the Popeelie compound, the young Popeelie slumped off into a designated Smoking Bubble outside Gate Stop 149 to Ottofram, pipe in hand and his hoverboard tucked under an arm.

At that moment, Bertram Ludlow dressed as, well, Bertram Ludlow stepped into the tiny private room right behind the young life-form and closed the door, tight.

"Hey!" The cult member turned a hooded head to the Earthman, tassels quivering nervously from his sleeves.

Bertram knew he probably cut a startling image. His normally organized hair now wild, he was flush-faced from running, unshaven, and wearing a very wrinkled flannel shirt. What was left of his white socks was dark gray. In his hand, he held a used and somewhat smelly fast-food bag filled with Dootett coins.

"This Bubble's occupied, friend," the Popeelie managed.

"I want you to know," Bertram's voice was urgent, "I'm not going to let it be the end of Life As We Know It."

"Oh." Concern washed from the Popeelie's face now and he pulled a book capsule out of his colorful hooded robes. "Well, in His best-seller, *How to Build a Blissful Afterlife While Making Big Dosh in This One*, the Munificent Popeelhonoromous reveals that—"

The time for revelations had passed. Bertram set down his bag of coins, grabbed the hoverboard from under the arm of the shocked Popeelie, swung it hard, and discovered he still had a pretty wicked backhand.

That was all he really needed.

In a few moments, a newly robed Popeelie emerged from the Designated Smoking Bubble. One a little shorter, carrying a bulging bag from Entropy Burger, the satchel of electronic Popeelie brochures, and a slightly bent hoverboard.

Sure, some might have said this Popeelie moved furtively, for a person of the devout religious persuasion. But most would have been focusing on his incredibly comfortable-looking Popeelie hand-made sandals. Due to a popular MetamorfaSys Inc. informercial campaign, those sandals were the hottest item in the GCU since Translachew came out in a limited-time-only Smorg flavor.

Now, this Popeelie marched those soft, functional sandals down the Gate Stop 149 ramp to the Secondary Corral entrance, just as the final call for passengers broadcast over the PA. He stepped past a tangle of Farthest Reaches Safety Simulants sweeping the area for a plus-sized, three-eyed old woman with a plaid bag, who'd just stolen a boarding pass for this very Corral.

Popeelies—unlike ticket thieves—were a *burfkin*-a-dozen on Farthest Reaches public transport. Heading from here to there, there to here, spreading the good word about the Munificient Popeelhonoromous... Yes, from A'tau to Zarquahr, you'd find Popeelies journeying, singing, and selling their wares.

This particular Popeelie had a date on Ottofram. And it looked like he was going to make it after all.

Excerpt from:

How To Gain Pals and Sway Life-forms in Cosmic Commerce
Chapter Thirteen

With permission from the
Eddisun Center for Ideas, Interceptive Marketing and Cliché Prevention

Sects, Plugs and Music:
In Tune with Popeelie Marketing

Overview

While Musca Mij and the creative team at MetamorfaSys Inc. turned the GCU's awareness up a few hundred decibels on Popeelie products, the **Popeelie** people themselves wrote the basic tune. It was a melody that would eventually help them transition from a local three-person quartet with a vision for [REMOVED DUE TO PENDING LAWSUIT: POPEELIES VERSUS EDDISUN CENTER], to a mega-manufacturer with chart-topping existential hits. Theirs is a song of fun in fundraising... Of merchandise with mass appeal beyond Popeelie Mass... Of the kind of persistence that doesn't just knock at the door, it kicks it in and chases you around the room holding e-brochures. It's that infotainment jingle you only get out of your head with a table knife through the ear. It's the haunting song that pours from your sound system with a cleverly-added backbeat that's just right for date night. It's the idea that welcomes you with one hand and relieves you of your yoonie cards with the other.

In this chapter, we will examine Popeelie marketing on the grassroots level, and discuss how individual Popeelies have become the minstrels of the GCU, spreading their unique blend of sects, plugs and music to the cosmos' darkest corners

Tuning Up the Three-Person Quartet

Popeelie history states the sect's legacy began when, one cold evening, a bored, all-powerful deity called "The Munificent Popeelhonoromous," imparted wisdom to a young mootaab rancher,

Chawtu Champs. *The Great Popeelie Book of Knowing Stuff* describes the scene as follows:

And thus, the divine prophet Chawtu Champs did sing to his mootaabs, in a fine clear voice of both high and low, that did resonate hither and yon, taking a bit of a right turn at yon, and then going north in a straight shot with a short rest stop at Calderia, until eventually it made it to the Red Star of Gajitania, where the Munificent Popeelhonoromous did rest, having had a late night.

And hearing this beautiful music way up in his Gajitanian palace, where his magic lyre did need restringing and his Uninet service did go spotty, the Munificent Popeelhonoromous came down to the field on the planet Shlemmar, and possessed one of Champs' prized mootaabs in order to share words of appreciation.

And the mighty god did say, "Hey there! I really dig your sound, rancher man."

And Champs, he did an eyebrow raise, for the mootaabs before this had not so vocal been. And said him to the livestock, "Thanks, mootaab. I didn't know you spoke the lingo."

"Ah," said the mootaab, "I'm actually your god, the Munificent Popeelhonoromous come to hang for a while in the guise of yon tasty, fiber-bearing creature. But rancher man, you look kinda cold. What gives?"

And lo, Popeelhonoromous' omniscience was proven, for the mootaab rancher did indeed shiver, having forgotten his cloak back at yonder pub.

And with pity for the shivering rancher, the Munificent Popeelhonoromous did say, "Wouldn't it be nice to have a cloak so well-packaged and compact, that you could take it with you wherever you go, without burden, and in its convenience, not leave it pub-ward? Yea," he proclaimed, "Let there be Cloak-in-a-Can®!"

That is the tale embraced by Popeelies GCU-wide. Interestingly, according to online promotional bills and e-news reviews, before the Popeelies ever became a religious organization, Chawtu Champs, his sister Metonee Champs, and friend Tenurbas Staf were actually [CONTENT REMOVED DUE TO PENDING LAWSUIT:

POPEELIES VERSUS EDDISUN CENTER. The Popeelies (heretofore known as the "Stellar Plaintiff") assert that this document has been created specifically to defame, besmirch, belittle, mock, tweak, take the piss out of and otherwise silence the true word of the Munificent Popeelhonoromous (heretofore known as "M.P.") by the Eddisun Center for Ideas, Interceptive Marketing and Cliché Prevention (heretofore known as the "Slaggard Defendant") through lies, muck-raking, unnecessary logic, and poking around in the back of filing cabinets. This content has therefore been removed until POPEELIES VS. EDDISUN CENTER completes trial, or Slaggard Defendant repeals statements and offers acceptable monetary compensation in accordance with the Takebacksies Supplications 1542/b.] [END OF REMOVED CONTENT]

Robed and Ready

Suddenly, Champs had an entire repertoire of Popeelhonoromous' wisdom penned into three-minute songs, each with a strong hook. Combined with Chawtu's distinctive Soprano-Bass voice, this formed the signature sound for the god's followers, which soon became known as "Popeelies." Open jamborees drew crowds, and sold merchandise at the events, along much the same principles that cause people on vacation to purchase statues of animals covered in shells, windchimes made of eating utensils, or large yard statuary that will not fit in their luggage. The eye-catching tie-dye tasseled robes the band wore caught on due to their comfort and skill at hiding a planetary ring or two around the middle. Soon Cloak-in-a-Can was sold at every event. (*Heeeeeerrrrre's Popeelhonoromous!* Chawtu Champs. RP: 59)

Building on the incredible success of Cloak-in-a-Can sales, *The Great Popeelie Book of Knowing Stuff* relays, Champs soon turned to Popeelhonoromous for other innovative merchandising ideas:

And the god did ponder on the young man's question, and chomp dry straw in thought. And after a long moment, he did smile, and the clouds did part and the sun thus shone. And he did say, "You know what would be cool? You know when a jamboree just breaks out and you don't have a pulpit with you, but you need to speak to the masses? Go forth and make a compact pulpit you can take with you everywhere. That'd be real neat."

And lo, the prophet Champs did go to the great men who understood the forces of nature, and materials science, and nifty product design, and he did say, "Make me a pulpit to fit within a space so tiny and portable, that it does go 'boing.'" And yea, the Pocket Pulpit gave Popeelhonoromous' word great dignity to all who popped one open in his worship, or who used it for business meetings, in his spiffiness.

Today, Popeelie concerts and merchandise draw new recruits and new funding to the religion. With their main base on Shlemmar, Popeelies travel via mass transit to every corner of the GCU, telling life-forms about the joys of Popeelhonoromous, and selling an ever-expanding product line. A deal with MetamorfaSys Inc. has led to the group's greater notoriety through infotainment. And additions to the gift and gadget line now include **Jerky Divine®**, a sacramental snack food, and **AirChamps®**, the supple mootaab-skin sandal worn by all Popeelies. Reports indicate that Stella Cygnus has already bought three pairs of AirChamps, and the shoes are becoming so popular, even the prince of Calderia was told his were on backorder.

While, sadly, Chawtu Champs died several years ago in a freak meteor shower accident, his grand legacy lives on in the songs, and the sales, of Popeelie goods.

The Popeelies' Greatest Marketing Hits
So what can you learn from studying the Popeelie business score? Consider these noteworthy measures:

- **"No" Only Means They Didn't Hear You the First Time.** Straight out of *The Great Popeelie Book of Knowing Stuff*, the Popeelies are trained to understand that just because someone says "no," barricades themselves in a small space, hand-lasers you in the leg, or threatens to call law enforcement, doesn't mean they really don't want your product. Remember, a life-form can only stockpile so much water and nourishment in there. They'll have to come out sometime.
- **If It's Catchy, They Won't Notice They're Being Converted.** Popeelie music has always been catchy, melodic and great to dance to. Even those wary of Popeelie sales tactics praise the purity of Popeelie vocal styling. The joy of

Popeelie music opens doors to new opportunities. Always remember, a sing-along might just be the first step to an outpouring of brotherhood. Also cash.

- **Fill a Need, Dress a Celeb.** Celebrity involvement has always been key to Popeelie success. "Like the mootaab," said Champs, "if the alpha mootaab drinks the water, the others soon will follow." For example, Cloak-in-a-Can went on to renewed popularity once alpha celeb, Spectra Pollux, ordered a custom-made robe to wear around the pool. And when Stella Cygnus was seen at the Coalition of Planets Peace Awards wearing a pair of AirChamps under her gown, the Popeelie Uninet site crashed with orders 15.3 Universal seconds later.

- **Will may be Free, but Smart Religion Accepts Credit.** Chawtu Champs once said, "The mind is free. The will is free. And that leaves plenty of cash on hand to buy our amazing products." In that spirit, leading Popeelies suggest Champs would appreciate the most recent version of their Uninet site, which has three million different payment options for buyers of Popeelie merchandise.

14

On the Secondary Corral, an infant the size of an industrial bag of mulch shrieked with fury, its reddened moon-face a gaping maw. The rolls on its dimpled arms jiggled as it strained to reach for the tassels on Bertram's Popeelie robe.

"Gurgie likes to play," said the mulch-bag's mother with a placid smile. She towered over Bertram like a monument to pro-wrestling, using a series of loving choke-holds and head butts to restrain the teething André the Giant in her arms. From her smooth technique, it was clear this was just one more cage match in her normal childcare routine. For the rest of the Corral's travelers, it added that extra special something to the comfort and tranquility that wasn't the Secondary Corral.

The Secondary Corral was small and circular and ten chairs lined the wall. Ten beings sat in those chairs and the other hundred and fifty stood in the room's center, glommed together like condensed soup. The recycled air was on, but the closeness and the rushed travel formed a musky humidity that enveloped the crowd. It was the smell of Terminal fast food and alien sweat, strange colognes and well-traveled luggage, ripe mystery fruits and sick, plastic people and organics, halitosis and that great "new ICV" smell everyone was always talking about.

Bertram's robe, he noticed, had a smell to it, too: an herby-minty scent of pipe tobacco. It wasn't unpleasant but was heavy and pervasive. Between it and the thick air, his stomach roiled.

They hadn't even launched the craft before knees were bumping thighs, innocent elbows met vital organs, feet trod toes, and tails caused some awkward moments.

But it wasn't just the togetherness. It was the noise. No matter where Bertram looked, there was a holovision. And on each of the screens, a chorus sang "Farthest Reaches" in a loop over an efficient-sounding musical theme.

Soon a female who looked exactly like Natelle, the Mig Verlig ticket salesgirl, came smiling into view. Over the music, she began, "Welcome to the Farthest Reaches Cosmos Corral, serving the Greater Communicating Universe. I'm a Neo-Natelle model MR-9 Non-Organic Simulant. But you can call me Steffie." She winked at the audience.

Light dawned for Bertram. "*Natelle...*" It wasn't a nametag, it was a manufacturer's mark. He would have slapped his forehead, if he could have moved his arms.

"I'll be your Corral Guide today as we journey from Mig Verlig to Ottofram," Steffie continued. "First, let me tell you a little bit about our spacecraft. Designated Smoking Bubbles and lavatories are available through those doors on your right (just push your way through, don't be shy), and—"

Bertram's attention was drawn from the monitor by a firm yank at his clothing. As the woman towering above him listened to Steffie's safety instructions, young Gurgie had chewed one of the Popeelie tassels off Bertram's robe. The baby, outweighing Bertram by a good 40 pounds, grinned. A few threads poked through what teeth there were.

"—So for those standing and bipedal, a good wide stance is your key to better balance and happier travels," Steffie was concluding. "While for our three and four-legged passengers, we recommend placing the legs at equidistant spacing for the greatest stability. In the case of a sudden change in cabin pressure, Farthest Reaches recommends holding your breath. Please hold your own breath first, before trying to assist other passengers who may need their breath held for them. And if the Corral has to make an unexpected touch down, please remain calm and collected while we at Farthest Reaches do everything we can to attend to the safety and comfort of people who paid for service in the Primary Corral. That concludes our safety regulations for today. Thanks so much for your attention! This is Steffie signing off and saying, brace yourself and enjoy your journey!

We now connect you to the Farthest Reaches in-Corral Uninet programming, already in progress."

Steffie's smiling face was swapped for those of the newscasters, a man and woman both with thick hair molded into wide spheres like NASA space helmets. The woman was saying, "—Farthest Reaches Secondary Corral from Mig Verlig to Ottofram is the scene of excitement today as part of a RegForce chase spanning five planets. It began at the Mig Verlig main terminal, when an elderly Triopticon woman tried to purchase a Secondary Corral ticket to Ottofram from this Sales Simulant."

Bertram winced. His fellow passengers gasped. The name across the screen read, "Sally Simmi, Farthest Reaches Guest Relations." Pictured was the Non-Organic Simulant once known as "Natelle."

Said Sally, "It was all so strange. The lady was missing *feeg burkins* and did not have enough to purchase the ticket. But before I knew it, she had ripped the ticket out of my hand and disappeared." Sally turned unblinking eyes to the camera. "I think that says something important about the plight of the GCU's fixed income elderly and—"

Shots of Bertram's holowatch granny looped on the screen— images of Grandma Ludlow grabbing the ticket, snatching the bundled coins, and running like hell, over and over again. "Hyphiz Deltan RegForce representative, W.I. Tsmarmak Mook, explains."

"That granny was no granny," W.I. Mook said firmly. "What you see in the footage is a holowatch disguise employed by an unidentified Tryfling fugitive. He's wanted in connection with a confinement break and the disassembly of three Podunk Peace Guards. The Tryfling had been traveling with Underworld member Rolliam Tsmorlood, also wanted for confinement break, disassembly, escape from Rhobux-7 (if we only knew where it had got to), and other infractions too unwieldy for a soundbyte. This is what the Tryfling looks like without his clever holowatch disguise." It was the now-famous shot of Bertram stun-sleeping in the Podunk jail cell. "If you see this individual, consider him armed, dangerous and possibly still an old woman."

"Just look at those puffy eyes and that slack jaw," boomed Gurgie's mother. "You can tell he's a heartless hoodlum!"

"Oh, definitely," Bertram agreed, drawing further under his Popeelie hood.

The camera cut to the male newscaster. "Farthest Reaches' records show the Secondary Corral to Ottofram is in transit now, and local authorities await its arrival. To passengers currently on the Corral: for your own safety, if you encounter the Tryfe human, *do not* put yourself at risk. Repeat: *do not* put yourself at risk. Instead, laser the fugitive down in cold blood immediately. Now, if you're not a cold-blooded being, or don't have blood of your own, the RegForce recommends—"

A rumble of commotion rolled across the room as passengers whipped out hand-lasers, daggers, digital blow-dart guns and polymer-based explosives and eyed each other suspiciously.

"He could be on this Corral!" cried one passenger.

"*I'm* from Podunk," screeched another. "What if he disassembles *me*? I don't have insurance."

"In other news," continued the female newscaster, "a naked, unconscious male life-form was discovered inside a Designated Smoking Bubble within the Mig Verlig Cosmos Corral terminal today. Farthest Reaches security spent a full U-hour breaking into the Bubble after travelers complained it had been occupied an unusually long time. The Automated Life-form Presence-Sensory Privacy System was removed to extract the individual. The life-form, who remains unidentified and unconscious, is at Mig Verlig Holistic Health Center and Salad Bar under close medical supervision. It is not yet known if this incident is related to the Tryfe fugitive sighting."

Cold sweat had burst up on Bertram's neck. It made his paranoia double and the pipe smell grow strong.

Space was impatient. Space was connected. Soon there'd be security footage of Bertram running through the terminal, forcing his way into that Popeelie's Bubble. Any time now, the Popeelie would wake up with a hoverboard hangover and a tale to tell. Or maybe Bertram would just lose his hood to Gurgie's next snacking endeavor, baring his identity for all to see.

Yes, something somewhere would give; and it was only a matter of time.

All Bertram wanted was a quiet moment to concentrate on a sensible backup plan, but the chatter in the Corral had reached head-pounding levels. Had anyone *seen* the GCU's Most Wanted Tryfling aboard? Not yet, but one being was sure she had spotted the miscreant pickpocketing an elderly Ottoframan back in the Terminal. Another said he'd seen the Tryfling kick a snoogle and steal some larvae's lollystopper down at baggage claim.

"*I* saw the Tryfling give a pregnant life-form his seat at Entropy Burger," Bertram piped up finally, hoping to spin the rumor mill more in his favor.

Nobody wanted to talk to him after that.

Now perspiration was running in rivers down Bertram's back into his boxers, and the more he thought about what would happen when the GCU fuzz searched that Corral—and oh, *they would search it*—the harder it was to breathe. He wiped his face with his tasseled sleeve and noticed a jowly, floppy-eared life-form across the room, hands in his overcoat pockets, and staring at Bertram with piercing red-rimmed eyes.

Bertram bowed his head and adjusted his hood, feeling like he was going to pass out. He had to get out of there, and get out of there *now*. Didn't Steffie say something about lavatories and Designated Smoking Bubbles? That would have to do. He had to go somewhere, away from the condensed soup of life-forms, away from that damned holovision noise, away from paranoid thoughts of staring bloodshot eyes. He drew the Popeelie pipe he'd lifted from his assault victim and made a show of it. *Look, I'm a real Popeelie, I have a pipe*, he felt it said.

He then elbowed and tramped his way through the crowd to the sliding door, per Corral protocol. The hallway proved to be ten degrees cooler and 80% less armpitly than the Corral from whence he came. But he was far from alone. Life-forms waited in slouching queues or milled between the Corrals for want of anything better. There were holovisions on the walls here, too, and Bertram paused, twiddling the pipe. He looked for emergency pods, crawlspaces or any other sign of hope, until…

"Whoa, it's *you*," breathed a voice. It was a willowy male life-form with long wispy hair, a trunklike nose, and wild rubbery clothes. The life-form had stopped short at the sight of him, a green cigar tumbling out of his hand and to the floor. The empty hand flew to the being's gaping lips.

Bertram scanned the doors and wondered where he could run that didn't involve free space. Travelers turned to look at the figure in the tie-dyed, hooded cloak.

"Why, we were just talking about you," the life-form went on, astonishment in his voice.

"Everyone is," replied Bertram vaguely. Now if he could just squeeze himself into that air vent…

"We totally love your work, man!"

Bertram found himself ripping his gaze from air vent possibilities to stare at this obvious madman. "Oh, yeah?"

In a second, the travelers around him were *all* leaping in with warm words: "Yes, absolutely. Wonderful work!" "So fun, so clever!" Bertram couldn't imagine he was hearing right, yet he knew he was. It was like the whole group had been waiting all along for this one big opportunity to tell him how awesome he was. A few of them broke into spontaneous applause. Two even patted him on his perspiration-drenched back.

A crazed laugh almost escaped from Bertram, but he caught it into a strangled hiccup. They loved him. They loved his work.

"Your music!" continued the being with the nose breathlessly. "It's so totally original. So catchy. I mean, I went to one of your guys' concerts once, and it was the most zonkin' stellar time!" The man's face was alight with positive energy. Also, possibly the effects of a few in-flight beverages. He pointed. "And I'm on the waiting list for some of your sandals."

Yes, agreed the passengers. *They loved the sandals. They* especially *loved the AirChamps sandals.* They all took a moment to admire his feet, some of them reaching in awe for the chance to touch the buttery hand-crafted materials.

Ah. It made sense now. Bertram fought that manic laugh again and searched for a convincingly GCU-savvy response. It took only a second. "Zonkin' stellar!" he exclaimed. Then he remembered the satchel he was carrying and dug out the electronic "Mass and Mass Marketing Jamboree" brochures, which he distributed with gusto.

"Do you have a minute?" the life-form asked him, confidentially.

"Um," Bertram glanced back at the Secondary Corral. "I might. Why?"

"Well, I've got someone who'd totally want to meet one of you guys. He's really into religious philosophies, for one thing. He's way spiritual. And then, y'know, musically, I'd say you guys have been a real influence on him and…" He pointed at the door to the Primary Corral. "Would you meet him?"

"Er," Bertram glanced over his shoulder from the Secondary Corral to the secure upper-class section next door. As an option, it didn't *quite* have miraculous beams of light radiating down on it from the Munificent Popeilhonoromous' Gagitanian sunlamp, or anything. But it was pretty close. "Er, sure! Lead on."

"Supernova!" exclaimed the guy with the nose buoyantly. "He's in the middle of an interview right now, so we'll just slip in and jaw with him after wrap-up, 'kay? I'm Gumpert, by the way," he said. And, using a shining, metallic security scan card at the door, Gumpert led the way into the Primary Corral.

Inside was a group of seven creatively-dressed beings, each with trunk-like nasal appendages. They had arranged themselves on the furniture in a way that took great care to show how laid-back they were. There were stacks of instruments and instrument cases. There were small boxes that might have been recording equipment. There were cushy chairs aplenty, and coffee-tables that rose from the wine-colored, lushly-carpeted floor. Some of the life-forms munched hors d'oeuvres and drank what looked like fruity lava lamps.

The room smelled like fresh flowers, sea air and possibly the scent of nubile, newly-powdered Vos Laegos showbeings.

Bertram wondered how many more *burfkins* per ticket the Primary Corral would have set him back.

In the center of the room, one life-form with a bandaged finger basked in a spotlight. A lensed sphere hung in the air before him, recording the action.

A tall, navy-blue haired man with a face for holovision sat facing him. He glanced at the little device in his hand and said, "Dumbbell Nebula's hit *Quasar Love* has been number one on the *GCU's Top Million* for a total of four Universal days now, breaking all other Duration Records. How do you rate this success?"

The musician shifted in his chair. "Well, Zaph, for four Universal days, beings all over the GCU have been singing our music, screaming our names, throwing used undergarments and chucking pudding... It's been very exciting."

"And your publicity engineer has calculated your Resilience Curve at what percentage?"

"A 73 with, of course, the normal downward slope for a pop band."

"That's very high. So your popularity is expected to run out at..."

"Four-thirty-seven tomorrow afternoon, Ottofram time."

"Congratulations, that's quite a run!" exclaimed Zaph. "And you're still recovering from that...challenge...of yours we heard about?" His eyes darted to the bandaged finger.

The music artist eyed the finger with disdain. "I'm surviving, Zaph. Must be brave for the people counting on me, supporting me through these dark times. Four-thirty-seven tomorrow comes too soon to succumb to concerns about personal discomfort."

"And the Foobaz Frabblagundger Hangnail Prevention Awareness Program. It's going well, is it?"

"Very well, thanks," Foobaz said warmly. "Not a single hangnail has been reported since the initiative started."

"Since two days ago."

"Two days ago, yes," he said. "It's a raging success."

Zaph addressed his screen again. "How did you start playing your nose? Classically trained, or self-taught?"

Foobaz Frabblagundger settled back in his chair, and tossed his nose casually over a shoulder. "Well, I'll tell you, Zaph. It was purely by accident. You see, there was this allergist and—"

It was through the spotlight's glare, a simple glance around the room led the musician's eyes to fall directly on Bertram Ludlow. For one fleeting moment, Bertram felt like a doe frozen before an oncoming freight train; yet in the next, Foobaz Frabblagundger's face broke into a bright, radiant smile. "Zaph, excuse me: is he with you?"

"He who?" asked the reporter. But the music sensation had already leapt up and was approaching their guest. The journalist's eyes trailed, puzzled. Still beaming, Frabblagundger said, "I didn't realize there would be such major talent on this flight!"

"Hey, that's us!" Bertram said, injecting enthusiasm straight into his voice. "Fun for the masses!" He dug in his bag. "Brochure?"

The reporter had joined them, arms folded, surveying the figure before him. The press pass that dangled around his neck read, "Zaph Chantseree. *Heavy Meddler* News." "Interesting," he said. "I didn't realize Popeelies ever flew Primary. Business must be stellar."

"One of those singing cult dudes?" a band member in the back asked, craning to see. "Supernova!"

Another musician stretched his trunk to pluck an hors d'oeuvre from a tray. "My sister has one of those Cloak-in-a-Cans. Said she felt strangely compelled to buy one after 37 sequential ads interrupted her soaps."

A small Calderian perched on a chair arm added, "I went to one of those jamborees once, man. It was a truly cosmic experience; and a great deal for only 19,999 yoonies."

Here, Gumpert stepped forward. "I totally hope you don't mind I invited him in, Foobaz. But I know how much you enjoyed that Popeelie festival we attended."

"I did," agreed Foobaz Frabblagundger with admiration. "I learned so much about harmony, melody and how to cram existential theory of the cosmos into three minutes with a catchy refrain."

"You wouldn't consider sharing one of your songs with our viewers now, would you?" Zaph Chantseree asked, indicating the levitating sphere above them. The sphere swiveled and the spotlight swung from Frabblagundger's empty chair to Bertram's seat, bathing him in light. "It would be such a treat to hear you sing."

Sing? Bertram choked on the beverage someone had given him. They wanted Bertram Ludlow *to sing?* For *people?* Ones with *ears?* "Uh…"

But the interview was already so off-orbit, the reporter seemed determined to salvage it any way he could. "It would be a stellar chance for you to give the people a taste of your next jamboree," Chantseree encouraged from somewhere beyond the spotlight's glare.

Here, Foobaz Frabblagundger sounded awed. "Would you? It would mean so much."

"Yeah," pressed another. "They say once you hear a true Popeelie sing live, you'll absolutely never forget it. Give us a tune."

"Yes, please," begged a last fellow.

Now, Bertram Ludlow excelled at a number of things. He had a wicked tennis serve. He had the patience to deal with tedious statistics. He was a fast study. And recently, he'd learned he had a talent for impersonations.

But as far as singing went, his brutally honest self-assessment was that he was fairly high up among the very worst singers on his planet. He didn't have hard data to back it up, but he felt pretty sure any formal analysis would support his theory.

The problem with Bertram's singing wasn't a lack of passion. Because Bertram Ludlow loved music as well as the most music-lovingest person who ever downloaded a one-hit wonder. Indeed, in the shower, as he biked, and even as he crunched his thesis data, Bertram's singing was *filled* with passion and joy.

But what Bertram Ludlow had in passion, he sloshed on the pavement each time he tried to carry that tune in a bucket. Love of music didn't equate with talent for it.

Add to that the fact he had absolutely no idea what Popeelie music sounded like, and Bertram Ludlow felt he might as well just drown himself in his own sweat.

Which he was doing a pretty good job of right now.

"Er, do you have any favorite tunes?" Bertram asked, hoping to stall for time.

They debated. "How about '*Gimme Some Yoonies*'? That's a classic," said one.

"I like '*Bloke with the Hooded Cloak*,' myself," recalled another.

"Or '*Flock Me, Popeelhonoromous*'? That one's such an earworm."

"Uh, yeah. How does that last one go again?" Bertram asked meditatively. Even in the glare of the spotlight, he could see them exchange glances. He waved it away with energy. "Kidding, kidding! "How about I do a brand new one you guys have never heard before?" *And I do mean* never *heard before*, he thought.

He wished the Hyphiz Deltan RegForce would storm in. After all, by comparison, how horrible could the punishment be for jailbreak, assault, resisting arrest, stealing, more assault, identity theft and...

Sing, Bertram. Just sing, he thought. And what came out was this:

> Spinnnnnn me to the heaaaaaaaaavens...
> Let me seeeeeeee you jive 'n' swing...
> Cooooover me in moooooondust...
> While we're swingin' on Saturn's ring...

Yes, it was the very last song he'd heard pre-abduction, as performed by 40s big band sensation, Jumpin' Jimmy Jive. Initially, the lines wobbled out, hesitant and blushing; Bertram wasn't used to belting it out for such a crowd, usually just the backscrubber and a few stoic shampoo bottles. But as the song progressed, he felt the notes fill his chest, then erupt from his spirit.

Jimmy wouldn't be daunted by an alien crowd. *Jimmy* wouldn't hold back just because his whole cover and freedom and preserving his planet depended on this performance.

Soon Bertram found himself almost energized by the blinding light of the spotlight, wailing it out and giving it all he had.

> So kitten noooow, set my vectors...
> So baby noooow, launch my space probe...

Heading into the second stanza, Bertram had become frighteningly aware the rest of the song wasn't so space-themed after all—just a lot of stuff about wedding rings and bells that ding—and so he'd improvised. Something he was sure Mr. Jive would have done under the same circumstances. It was funny how any appropriately space-related metaphor he could substitute, ended up sounding like some raunchy double entendre. Bertram figured it would be lost on his alien listeners, but didn't imagine Jimmy could have slipped it past the censors.

> Launnnnnch me to Vos Laeeeeegos…
> And we'll swing it on Ottoframmmmmmmm…
> Send me to Nett Thirrrrrrty…
> And we'll hear the great Prophets' plans…
> So baby now, fire my thrusters…
> So kitten now, system's gooooooooooo!

At this big finish, the spotlight powered down, zipping back to the reporter's outstretched hand like baseball to mitt.

Dazzled by the shift in lighting, Bertram blinked away the stars and any lingering musical moondust and examined the faces before him. Foobaz Frabblagundger was scratching his head. Zaph Chantseree was corpse white.

Bertram blanched, too. Tough crowd.

Finally, in a soft voice, Frabblagundger said, "Extremely hard on the ears, friend."

A few heads bobbed. "An almost offensive lack of pitch, key, and purity of tone," observed someone else. "It made me sort of resent not being deaf."

"Wow, dude," breathed Gumpert, "I've heard Gorpish mud-rattlers with more rhythm."

Bertram nodded, thinking he should probably just head back to the Secondary Corral and await the RegForce. On the plus side, no one's ears were bleeding. So that was exciting.

Then someone added, "But that's innovation for you! Your work is so musically-advanced, it's gone beyond what our current ears can handle."

"Like, that's the far-out truth, man," Gumpert agreed. "It was totally unique, dude, just like you'd said. Completely unlike any Popeelie stuff I've ever heard. It, like, wakes you up and makes you go 'aagh!'"

"No argument here," affirmed Foobaz Frabblagundger. "It's musically off-putting to the point it actually makes you question 'what even is music and why do we want to hear it?' I love work that makes you really *think* like that."

Yes, they agreed, it made them all reevaluate why anyone would ever want to listen to music.

"Does your Popeelie chorusmaster know your solo work?" asked the smallest musician, leaning in to hear the answer. "You could be the next great sensation. Maybe even have a top ten hit!"

"We should add him to our group," Gumpert suggested. "Reinvent ourselves with him, and we could prob'ly extend our popularity for another, like, half day, at least."

Zaph Chantseree honed in on this like aardvark to ant. "Oh, you mean follow in the footsteps of those fellows who were from, er..." He stroked his chiseled jaw thoughtfully, "What's their name? That star system with all the space junk?"

"I thought it was comets."

"Oh, yeah!" the percussionist exclaimed from the back corner. "*Those* guys."

Foobaz Frabblagundger folded his arms and nodded. "Say, if we're talking about the same band, those guys were in the news for a whole few hours extra after they added that...person...what's-his-name...to their group. It could really elongate our Resilience Curve. That's a stellar idea." He turned to Bertram. "What do you say?"

Bertram's head was spinning. One second, he murdered Jumpin' Jimmy Jive, measure by measure. The next? He was stretching out their Resilience Curve and entering a world of fame, used undergarments and, apparently, lobbed pudding.

He toyed with the tassels on his sleeve. "I'm really flattered," Bertram told them. "But my duty is to the Mighty Popeelhonoromous. I've got sandals to model, pamphlets to push, and, um, I'm teaching a class on...on..." Under the secure awning of his hood, he found inspiration. "...Getting the cloaks back into the can. Thanks for the offer, though."

Foobaz Frabblagundger blew a frustrated sigh. It came somewhere from the lower nasal appendage region. "Really? You'd turn down 2,880 minutes of complete adoration from the GCU for some street performances, consumer ed and grassroots marketing? I think the Munificent Popeelhonoromous himself would make an exception."

"Ya'd think," said Bertram affably, "but...um...little-known Popeelie trivia: Popeelhonoromous is a real stickler for a good schedule. Likes the planets to spin just a certain way, is picky about how things orbit and when." He shrugged. "What can ya do?"

Foobaz Frabblagundger's face darkened as he watched his Resilience Curve for fame thud onto the X-axis at the all-too-soon 4:38 P.M. the next day. "Fragging shame," he said. "I thought Popeelies never turned down a good offer."

And Zaph Chantseree looked hard at the Popeelie before him, his unearthly blue eyes trying, it seemed, to pierce the hood's darkness with their own electric glow. "Yes," he said slowly, "I thought so, too."

Through the back hatch, a Non-organic Simulant in a Farthest Reaches uniform glided in. "I'm so sorry to interrupt. But the Corral to Ottofram is preparing to land. For our fine guests here in the Primary Corral, please ensure you're seated comfortably and enjoy a last bit of Mig Verlig moon cheese and Ottoframan smorg wine— courtesy of DiversiDine Entertainment Systems and Aeroponics®— before we touch down. I'll harness you in. And when you leave, please remember to exit *away* from the Secondary Corral. There's been an…incident. Nothing to concern our Primary passengers, of course. Just exit quickly from the craft, please, and duck if you sense the sound of laser fire. Thank you."

It was a strained silence as the members of Dumbbell Nebula gathered their belongings and rolled out the equipment upon landing. Two of the musicians waved hesitant goodbyes, torn between good nature and the fact their careers were rapidly approaching a hard stop. Gumpert was one of them; Foobaz Frabblagundger was not. The latter shot off on eight-inch-thick rocket-booster heels, tossed his nose over his shoulder and didn't look back.

A crowd of roadie Simulants—who had been specifically engineered to look sweaty and who all wore Dumbbell Nebula tour shirts—poured in to get the rest of the gear, while a throng of fans outside rushed Frabblagundger for autographs and to chuck pudding at him.

Zaph Chantseree, meanwhile, grabbed his equipment and trailed Bertram to the exit. To the back of Bertram's head, he said, "It was quite an offer Mr. Frabblagundger made you in there."

Bertram turned, shifting his increasingly heavy fast food bag of Dootett currency to the other hand. He hoped it didn't jingle much. "And I'm honored," Bertram told him. From his hooded view, Bertram saw the Hyphiz Deltan RegForce, the Ottoframan fuzz, and law enforcement reps from a dozen other planets surrounding the Secondary Corral, lasers drawn, and holographic scanners at-the-ready. Uninet news crews were darting between Frabblagundger and the fugitive search, those with more fluid cellular structures actually dividing in two to cover both scenes at once.

Bertram Ludlow kept walking.

"Do you realize what you gave up?" Chantseree persisted. "An almost-guaranteed 2,880 minutes of Universal respect, adoration, and a stellar buffet after the concert."

"Ah," mused Bertram, "but as Popeelhonoromous says, 'Give a man a Cloak-in-a-Can and he's warm for a day. Teach a man to put his cloak *back in* the can, and he's warm whenever.'"

There was a pause. Chantseree replied, "Forgive me, but I don't get it."

"Buy a Cloak-in-a-Can and you'll see," Bertram said mysteriously, with a wink. He tossed a brochure at the reporter and hoofed it.

15

"Welcome to the LibLounge. How may I help you Be Your Best You?" said Rozz Mercer for the umpteenth time. Her eyes darted to the giant figure in the corner, who watched on with the proud, hungry grin of a mother T-Rex. Surrounded by her 37 personal assistants and her two celebrity best buds, Spectra Pollux whispered something to one of the people at her table—Stella Cygnus, a creamily blue-skinned redhead so beautiful it almost hurt to look at her—then motioned for Rozz to proceed, with a shooing flick of her hands.

Rozz affixed the bright "LibLounge Smile" Spectra Pollux had been teaching her. Rozz had never been a smiler. She wasn't one now, either. She was only biding her time until she could enact Plan Two.

"I'll have, um…" It was the man who'd come in with the famous blue-skinned dancer. Jet Antlia was the name, supposedly a big-name unconventional poet in the GCU—a real renegade with the verse, they said. He was as handsome as Stella Cygnus was stunning, with copper hair, copper skin, soft jade-green eyes and teeth so white they were almost luminescent. He squinted at the projected menu board behind her, withdrew a pen from his pocket, and dragged the virtual menu's selections onto a second page of virtual choices. "I'll have the fat-free Mathgar Kidney PowerPunch and, hmmm…"

The "hmmm" drew out so long, it sounded like a hive of honeybees at choir practice. Rozz sighed. *Fer Chrissakes, what's the big debate? Just grab one. Any one.* But Rozz had a feeling that she and Mr. Beautiful were going to be here a while.

She took the time to consider her next moves. Plan One, she had to admit, hadn't gone so well...

It was possibly too impromptu.

See, after plucking Rozz from her home planet and transferring her to her own spaceship, Spectra Pollux had fixed up Rozz's noggin with an alien revitalizing beverage and some brain-cell-soother-over gadget. That was all it had taken.

In and out of consciousness for who-knew-how-long, Rozz had had a lot of extra time to summon up a big batch of steaming hot resentment. Resentment for her situation, in general, and for her Titan abductor, in specific. Much as she'd always said she'd like to travel more, Roslyn Louise Mercer would not allow herself to be dragged around the universe like E.T.'s favorite stuffed toy. So the healing gadget had no sooner hit the table, when the recovered Rozz hit the floor and ran. She reached out for the first door she could find, frantic for an exit.

She found one, but not the kind she'd expected. Within nanoseconds, sirens blared, space's vacuum inhaled all the oxygen it could eat, and Rozz Mercer clung desperately to the hatch knob, her feet a yard-and-a-half off the floor. It was only the kidnapper's great strength and surprising speed that got the hatch closed and Rozz back to solid ground again. If you could call "solid ground" the ground floor of a huge luxury interplanetary cruise vessel heading back toward Spectra Pollux's huge luxury complex, on some even huger planet called Rumoolita.

Yes, Rozz had better hopes for Plan Two. She'd learned a lot in her short time in the GCU.

Too much, maybe, she considered. Because ever since ol' Ms. Bunyan got a hold of her, Rozz had been absolutely *stuffed* with information. She was fed capsules on this...Pills on that... Languages, etiquette, GCU history, and every single *Featured CapClub Feature-of-the-Day®*, it seemed, since Old Man Time had looked around the universe and decided this whole Life thing would be a hit.

There was a lot of digestion to do.

At every meal, Rozz was given a new bag of capsules to suck down. Her head pounded with information the way Zeus' did, right about the time Athena burst from his skull in that very messy grand entrance. Her stomach felt like a roiling, swirling Greek whirlpool.

She was catching up on a lifetime of knowledge in a few days. She started to see how things fit together in ways she'd never expected... time, space, even why we always leave a dribble in the milk carton. Spectra Pollux was prepping Rozz Mercer to be the best LibLounge Book Capsule Discussion Group Leader and Barista the GCU had ever seen.

And Rozz not only devoured every little bit of information the Pollux woman gave her, she started sneaking extras on the side. A pill on celestial navigation here. A capsule on interstellar travel there. Star charts and solar systems, astrophysics and ICV driver's tests... Underworld hand-to-hand combat tactics and the complex defensive arts of Sum-Gai-Wowee Yup.

She slipped them all into her knowledge bank and then went about making frothy alien beverages for Spectra Pollux's personal LibLounge branch, and learning how to smile. Yep: if this was the way it was gonna be? Fine. Big Momma might just find out the knowledge she offered became her very own undoing.

Mr. Beautiful was still standing there, tapping his beautiful teeth thoughtfully, with a beautifully strong, beautifully-manicured finger. "Mmmmm... I'll have... Er..."

"Ask him if he would like today's CapClub recommendation," rang out Spectra Pollux's bell-like voice from across the room.

"Would you like today's CapClub recommendation?" Rozz asked flatly. She had to reaffix her smile, which seemed to have dropped off somewhere on the counter top. A glance at Big Momma earned a nod of approval.

"A recommendation!" the handsome man twinkled with delight. "That'd be stellar!"

"Today's featured book capsule, featured by the Spectra Pollux *Featured CapClub Feature-of-the-Day*, is Zenith Skytreg's best-selling autobiography, *Underworld: New Heights of Under*," Rozz chanted. "Join Zenith Skytreg on his detailed examination of Skytreg's personal journey, from his simple roots growing up in a modest 120-room home unit on Vos Laegos to eventually becoming the most popular Official Leader the Intergalactic Underworld has ever seen. Share in his joys. His triumphs. And more of his joys and triumphs. Does everything Zenith Skytreg touch shine like the Vos Laegos sun? Find out in this exciting tribute to Skytreg's greatness."

Rozz had eaten Skytreg's book with breakfast this morning. It didn't contribute to her knowledge base, just her acid reflux.

"That sounds *cosmic,*" said Mr. Handsome. "I'll take it."

She whirled on the wall of capsule dispensers behind her and chose the one labeled *"Featured CapClub Feature-of-the-Day."* A single octagonal pill tumbled down the chute and plopped into her hand. She put that in a pretty, ruffled paper cup. She pushed a button on the Food Preparation Unit for the Mathgar Kidney PowerPunch. She hadn't made one of these before and when she opened the FPU's door, the thing smelled like protein and internal organs gone external. There was a green fuzzy foam on the top.

Grimacing and gagging, she tucked in a decorative straw and put the concoction on the tray next to the capsule. She slapped the smile back on again. "Here you go. That will be 147 yoonies. And your yoonie card please?" She held out her hand.

Spectra Pollux motioned negatively, her intangible garment flashing in a bright red solar flare, then shifting into cooler purples and blues. "For Mr. Antlia, my dear, it is on the house," she said.

Mr. Antlia winked and pointed a finger at Rozz, as he took his tray. "Thanks, babe. Catch you later."

Rozz pointed and winked back. *Hopefully no one will catch me later,* she thought. She wiped the counter of slopped mathgar kidney. She glanced at the exit. She glanced at the ICV lot outside. The unspent energy of anticipation zapped through her nerves like electricity through a powerstation. No, it wasn't time yet. She could wait.

She could hear Pollux and her friends at the table.

"So you said she's from where?" asked Stella Cygnus, taking a sip of Mr. Handsome's drink. Her perfectly symmetrical features lost their symmetry in a wince. She handed him the glass at warp speed.

"Tryfe," Spectra told her. "A small blue planet outside the GCU that I'm placing a bid on. If I win it, this young lady will be the first of her species in my LibLounge Leadership pilot program." Her broad head gave a beaming turn to her Tryfling protégé. Her dress swirled into a soft yellow white. "I'm very pleased at the progress."

Jet Antlia, meanwhile, was slurping his PowerPunch with vigor. He paused. "What I don't get, Spectra, is why you'd want to start with some backspace, intellectually-inferior life-form—" Here Jet Antlia waved at Rozz cheerfully. "No offense, babe!" He turned back to Spectra. "—Instead of a well-programmed Simulant." He returned his well-formed lips to the decorative straw.

"Jet," began Stella in a calm, patient tone Rozz got the impression she used a lot, "we heard about the Simulants unionizing on the way over here. Remember? How they wanted higher wages, shorter hours and free on-site fluids infusions?"

He frowned over the straw. "We did?"

"Yes," she said, with a strained smile. "And how it's forcing companies to rethink their staffing choices because it's getting more expensive to keep Simulants on the payroll than hiring organic life-forms?"

"Exactly," affirmed Spectra Pollux. "And what's ideal about backspace people, like our Tryfe friend Rozz here," she motioned to Exhibit A, "is that she was basically a completely blank storage drive for me to work with. I've taken Rozz out of her backspace surroundings, and I'm giving her the most practical education that infopills have to offer. She gets freed from the unevolved confines of her home planet, plus she gets new enlightenment and a broader perspective. In return, she works for me in one of the LibLounges and shares that knowledge in our discussion groups. Also, she serves drinks and cleans up a little. It's win-win."

"And how long will she do that? Work for you, I mean?" Stella asked with almond-eyed interest.

"Oh," Spectra Pollux considered it like some fresh meadow breeze that had blown in, "Y'know, forever."

"Forever?"

"-Ish," added Pollux lightly. "Forever-ish. The Tryfling lifespan is only 70 or 80 years, you know, my dear. And she already has frittered almost 30 of them away on her home planet. But an opportunity like this isn't cheap. And there's not much point for me to invest in her training, in our partnership, if it won't have longevity."

"And you want to do this with everyone on the planet?" asked Stella Cygnus.

"If this works out, yes, absolutely. You know how many LibLounges there are around the GCU, Stella. Plus, don't forget the pill manufacturing plants and other aspects of production. We have the Uninet show. We have the *Featured CapClub Feature-of-the-Day* announcement that goes out. Yes, as many of them who can make the trip, I'd be happy to give them this wonderful opportunity. Unless they're too old, or feeble, or unwilling to see the value of my offer. In which case, we'll just have to let nature take its course." She gave that hearty Bacchus-like laugh.

"Your compassion is simply limitless," Stella sighed, admiration shining in her luminescent eyes.

"Just helping more people Become their Best Thems," Spectra's grand voice projected. Her gown had gone a warm petal pink. "So what's this I hear about you two breaking up again?"

It was perfect. As the dancer and poet began to rehash a list of injustices ranging from laziness to hair-scorching laser fire, Rozz gasped with shock at a capsule dispenser she'd purposefully emptied before shift. "Well, look at that! We're almost out of *Eudicot T'murp: Leaf and Let Leaf*... Let me just pop in the storeroom and see if we have any more."

Spectra waved her off, only half-listening, her gown pulsing a rich, neutral grass green as her friends relayed their relationship challenges. And Rozz ducked into the back room.

The great thing about the back room was the back door. Which led to the back path. Which led to the side path. Which led to the front path. Which led to the ICV lot of the private LibLounge on Spectra Pollux's very own personal property.

This led to Stella Cygnus' and Jet Antlia's waiting ship.

Looking left and right, Rozz crept up the ramp and into the vehicle, her senses alert, electric determination zapping through her every nerve. Rozz Mercer hadn't gotten a Master's in computer science and a double minor in statistics and psychology in order to become a glorified bartender at the Café of the Damned. She hadn't scrimped and saved and made her own way in life to spend the rest of it in indentured servitude acting as camp counselor for Interplanet Janet.

It was just not happening.

Rozz surveyed the layout. The ship's interior was, not unexpectedly, the height of luxury, but given the sleek exterior, the taste in décor was a surprise. Rozz entered a room lined with rich fabrics and layered in exotic handicrafts from the very corners of the universe. It looked more like an alien Kasbah instead of the inside of a space-age machine, some foreign den of mystery and intrigue.

Also infants.

She hadn't noticed the children at first. But then again, why would she? They blended perfectly into every scrap of fabric, every tuffet, every inch of wallpaper, every patterned rug they sat on.

Funny that with all the *Heavy Meddler* infopills Rozz had devoured, not one of them mentioned that the Bibluciats' skin contained layers of chromatophores—letting them change their colors quicker than a politician doing damage control. Nope, in all the discussion of the plight of Bibluciat children, no one bothered to say they were born chameleons, a technique that had helped secure the continued existence of their race in an otherwise harsh environment involving war and blackmarket rocket-boot production.

What this meant was, Rozz had barely set foot into the ship before at least 100 Bibluciat children surged forth at her, aged from just able to walk, to ready to fly their own ICV. What had initially *seemed* like an empty room now felt like the floors…the walls…the very furniture were crawling to life, and a scream escaped her lips that would have earned her more than a walk-on part in any half-way decent slasher flick.

A hundred Bibluciat orphans screamed, too, the sound stopping just short of shattering glass. A Bibluciat nanny came out of the woodwork in a literal sort of way, too, shouting, "Children, children, it's all right!"

The chauffeur—not a Bibluciat, but dressed to the nines in fabric and pattern—raced in from the cockpit, weapon drawn. "Who's there? Who are you?"

Rozz winced. She'd had the whole thing planned somewhat differently in her head.

First, nix the orphans. No orphans in this scheme, in camo or otherwise.

Next, hose the nanny. This was a nanny-free operation, and no plans had been made for the Poppins.

Thirdly, chauffeurs in the cockpit, *stayed* in the cockpit. No running into the main room like the friggin' U.S. cavalry. Not cool.

Fourth, stealth. Rozz, getting up behind him and giving him the ol' Thrusterfist Laserfinger move she'd learned courtesy of the Sum-Gai-Wowee Yup infopill. That was going to disable him until she could drag him out of the way. Then she was going to pull up the ramp, fire up the ICV, cloak it, and take off for Area 51.

She'd place the ship right in Uncle Sam's lap and say, "Here's the dealio, Unc. We have an alien problem," and then let 'em know the score. She figured it was going to be pretty hard to call her a crackpot or a terrorist with an ICV steaming in front of their eyes. Then, before they'd get any ideas about dissection or debriefing, she was going to slip into the ship's smaller shuttle pod, launch it, cloak it, and head back out into the GCU. On *her* terms, this time. The computer programmer gig was likely to be kind of a drag when you knew your whole Earthly existence was really an illusion.

That had been the plan, anyway. But she realized now that pill smarts shouldn't have taken the place of proper reconnaissance. That was where she went wrong. Her plan had more holes than a Pittsburgh road in winter.

Holes like she was about to have soon, she realized, if she didn't answer the nice man with the hand-laser. "I said, who are you?" he repeated.

"Oh, hi! I'm Rozz!" Rozz said brightly to the group, a kind of cheer that she normally locked away in sub-basement of her soul. "I work at the LibLounge!" She hooked a thumb. "Out there." She punctuated it with an even bigger smile. It made one of the smaller orphans cry. "I'd just wanted to see if you all wanted anything from the bar. We have a wide selection of infopills: fiction and non-fiction. And *all sorts* of delicious and nutritionally-balanced beverages. How about a couple pitchers of Blumdec Seagrass Slushies? Mootaab Milkshakes? Or perhaps I can tempt you with a Mathgar Kidney PowerPunch? It's all the rage."

"The children just had lunch," said the nanny. "We don't want to spoil our suppers now, do we?"

"Milk-SHAKE, milk-SHAKE!" chanted a half dozen kids.

"I wouldn't mind one of those Seagrass Slushies," the chauffeur admitted, holstering his gun with an embarrassed smile.

"Coming right up," Rozz said spritely. And making a quick exit, she scampered down the ramp and through the front door of the LibLounge. A little electronic bell simulated a bell tinkling.

It was there she faced Spectra Pollux, scowling from Rozz to the backroom to the front door to Rozz again. She seemed bigger, thicker somehow, when she scowled. And her dress had become a raging wall of licking orange-yellow flames. "Where *were* you? Mr. Antlia has been waiting for a refill." She waved long shiny nails at Jet Antlia's empty glass, green scum clinging to the sides.

"I was getting drink orders." Rozz said simply, peering up at her with her most innocent face. She waggled a finger to the window. "I thought the chauffeur might want something." She slapped the big beaming LibLounge smile on again and turned to the celebrity couple. "By the way, you have a beautiful family." *If you like happen to like kids who look like Bibluciat throw rugs, anyway*, Rozz thought.

"You took an order from the chauffeur?" Spectra Pollux asked.

"Yes." Rozz felt her heart pick up its pace to a jog. She felt the gaze of Spectra Pollux and all her 37 personal assistants judging her.

"I figured they'd come all this way...er, that he might be thirsty, too." *Hold your ground, Rozz. Hold your ground...Don't freak...*

"Uh-huh," Pollux said. Then: "See?" Big Momma turned to Jet and Stella, her gown swirling into a warm Caribbean blue which matched her hair. Foamy waves seemed to crash upon her considerable heaving bodice. "This is the kind of thoughtful quality service my customers would never get from a Simulant. I'm right, right? Am I not right? Right?"

"Yes, Spectra, you're right," agreed Stella Cygnus, along with the 37 assistants.

"What?" said Jet Antlia, who'd been daydreaming out the window. "Oh, yeah...No question."

Spectra Pollux patted Rozz's shoulder with affection. "Then get to it, my dear!" she commanded playfully, and Rozz slipped back behind the counter.

"Don't forget my PowerPunch," Jet reminded her.

She nodded and powered up the Food Preparation Unit. Maybe this was what had happened to Bertram Ludlow, she considered. Maybe right now he was in some other LibLounge pushing book pills and making Mootaab milkshakes.

If he were, more's the pity for him. Rozz was already thinking Plan Three.

16

"Breathtaking 20-bedroom Home-unit
on the Rings of Ragul-Sferra!"

"Get the Moon You've Always Wanted,
But Didn't Think You Could Afford."

"Stellar Fixxer-Upper 4 Sale,
Just Needs HandySimulant & U!"

Bertram had been sitting in the waiting-room of Alternate Realty
for twenty minutes now, and he'd read the digitized property ads on
the walls a dozen times.

"Darling Planet with Oxygen-based Atmosphere.
Rent to Own!"

"For Sale: ICV Park with Scenic Views!
No History of Meteor Crashes!"

"Planet Available in Up-and-Coming Solar System:
Going Fast!"

Bertram rose from his seat and approached the receptionist, a
shimmering orange-scaled man with an aquatic dome over his head.

On his black wetsuit, which undulated with the fluid inside, was printed a faux necktie, lapels and buttons in luminescent green paint. It was an interesting executive touch.

"Excuse me," said Bertram, "but I've been waiting twenty minutes already. You'd said you'd put me in touch with the person who owned Tryfe."

The receptionist's blue spherical eyes rolled dramatically in their sockets. "I *said*," he emphasized, ears fanning the liquid in short petulant waves, "I would put you in touch with the person who was *selling* Tryfe. That's different."

"How?"

The receptionist gave an irritable glub. Bubbles floated along the wall of the dome like someone had just tapped a water cooler. "The person who's *selling* Tryfe is Mimsi Grabbitz." He pointed to one of the many headshots on the wall, that of a female life-form who resembled the Booboo the Clown punching bag Bertram had as a kid. Only this life-form also had red 3-D balloon lips and a wig. "She's a trillion-yoonie agent you know, and Employee of the Month 17 times," drawled the receptionist. "She represents Tryfe's current owner."

"And I prefer to *talk* to the owner," Bertram told him firmly, "not an intermediary."

"No-can-do, Sweetums," said the receptionist, or at least that's how it translated. "Our job is to protect our client's privacy. You talk to Ms. Grabbitz or you can just take your little Popeelie-robed posterior on out of here."

Bertram opened his mouth to protest, but the receptionist cut him off with an emphatic, "She will be with you shortly."

That's what he'd said twenty minutes ago. Grumbling, Bertram slumped back to his seat.

"Get More Meridian for Your Money
on Megamorgit-Beta"

"Black Hole Available:
Double Your Acreage in No Time!"

"Have You Seen This Planet?:
Rhobux-7. Last Observed: …"

Mimsi Grabbitz stepped in, clad in bright metallic blue. Her lips and eyelashes jutted from a head that seemed too egg-shaped to be true. The hair, Bertram decided, might be real after all, but it perched on top of the egg like a newly-thatched roof. He was so mesmerized by her appearance, he had to force himself to focus on what she was saying.

"So, I hear you have an interest in Tryfe!" she chirped, touching him gently on the arm with a cool hand. "Right this way, right this way!" And she led him back through the door from which she'd come, straight into a nearby cubicle. There weren't actual walls in this cube, Bertram noticed, just a hazy pale blue energy that formed panels, following a mechanism along the floor.

"It's perfectly secure," Mimsi assured him, noticing his hesitation. She pushed a button, closing a door that wasn't there, and Bertram realized that they were now encased in this energy box. "Soundproof, you know! So everything you say is completely confidential. Have a seat."

Bertram sat. On her desk, he saw a photo of the real estate agent next to a male life-form who had the same stretched, injection-molded physique. In the picture, both of them nuzzled some sort of pet. It looked like a furry balloon animal with eyes and a great, lolling tongue.

"There we are!" she said, taking a seat herself. Bertram had expected the move to sound squeaky, like taut plastic on vinyl. He was disappointed. "So the Popeelies have an interest in Tryfe, do they? The cult business must be booming."

"I really just need to speak with the person who owns Tryfe," Bertram told her. "I heard you could help me do that."

The agent gave him a smile. It made her look like a surprised hot air balloon. "I've been designated by the owner of Tryfe to assist with the sale," she explained, "so if it's authorization you're concerned about or—"

"No, nothing like that," Bertram said, trying to sound friendly. "I just need to speak with the owner about a few things. And I understood that if anyone in the GCU could put me in touch, Mimsi Grabbitz could do it."

She ignored the flattery the same way a great white shark might ignore a garden salad in a sea of oblivious teenagers. "So you're not interested in buying Tryfe?" She gave a perplexed flap of her eyelashes.

From under his hood, Bertram Ludlow thought fast. "Oh we're *interested…*"

"Ah," she said. Her eyes narrowed a few millimeters in what might have been keen scrutiny. "I know what this is about."

"You do?"

She nodded, her lips pursed critically. "Did you think I wouldn't see the truth?"

"Er…"

"Oh, I know all about Popeelie business tactics," she went on. "You're trying to get the planet to sell By Owner. Remove the middle-man costs. That's it, isn't it? You're trying to cut Alternate Realty out of the loop?"

"No, I—"

"Well, I'll have you know, Mr. Popeelie, this sale doesn't work the way we normally do business, so you'd only be hurting yourselves."

"No, really, I—"

"Once the bids are in, and the less serious buyers are weeded out, the remaining bidders present their redevelopment ideas to the owner. So even if the owner likes your price, it's not an automatic deal. I understand the owner is very concerned about how the property will be used."

Bertram stopped stammering. The owner, concerned? He pursued this hopeful glimmer like a kid after a lightning bug. "So the owner's worried about Tryfling welfare, huh?"

"Tryfling welfare?" She giggled. "*Zoning violations*, dear. They can do *such* messy things to a person's reputation in the GCU. You know how it is. You violate zoning once and you're forever branded as being anti-intergalactic environmentalism." She waved her hand as if she were trying to whisk away the mess. "Anyway, once the presentations are done, then the owner selects the winning bid. Not before."

"And when's that?" Bertram asked. He realized the question had come out entirely too urgent, too interested.

"Soon. Very soon," she intoned. She gave a flick of her eyes that she may have intended as mysterious. It looked like air leaked out of her balloon. "I wouldn't take much time to place a bid, if I were you, dear. This is a very hot property and it's going at light speed."

That's more or less what his landlord had said about Bertram's basement apartment, too. "And where do these final presentations take place?" Bertram asked.

"Place a serious bid through me," she said, "and I'll tell you."

Bertram nodded. He saw he'd get nothing out of the Grabbitz woman but hot air. "Okay then, I'll talk to my people, who'll talk to some other people, who'll...er...grab folks off the street and get back to me. Soon as they do, I'll give you the good word."

"Of course," she replied. "Just don't wait too long. Or Tryfe'll be gone. Forever."

Gone. Forever. This sort of high-pressure treatment was probably why the woman was a trillion-yoonie seller, Bertram thought. She pushed the button on the energy field and the non-door opened. She rose to go.

"So, uh," Bertram picked up on the unsubtle cue and rose, too. He turned in the non-doorway, frowning. "What about the Tryflings then?" he asked. "I understand billions of people already live on Tryfe. Don't they get a say in this?"

"Sure they do, if they raise the money and place a bid!" Mimsi said brightly. Mimsi Grabbitz acted like having Tryfling clients for once would be an exciting challenge, a novelty like growing that first batch of Sea Monkeys. "We'll consider all bids. Even from backspace life-forms. It's in the Employee Handbook." She held up a slim e-Book Server from her desk, then plopped it back on the tabletop. "A part of our Compulsory Open-Mindedness Policy."

"So they've been notified? The Tryfe people did get a..." Bertram searched for the word, "open house flier announcing it?" He had visions of alien real estate handouts being dropped on the desks of every major leader of every country on Earth—and all in a language that not one of them could read.

"Hardly! That's so Last Millennium," the real estate agent responded. "No, we post everything on the Uninet now."

"But if the Tryfe people aren't part of the GCU, then they can't connect to the—"

"Of course, where they'd lose the bid eventually," Mimsi went on meditatively, "would be in the conversion rates. Even if they pooled their money and made it a co-op, given the current value of most forms of Tryfe money, I think it would be a little rich for their blood."

"How rich?"

She shrugged. "What's in your pocket right now?"

Bertram reached into his right-hand robe pocket and pulled out the Popeelie pipe and a bit of lint. He held it out.

"Congratulations. You have more buying power than Tryfe currency."

Bertram tossed on his most winning grin. "Will it get me a bid?"

She guided him gently toward the door. "My!" she giggled again. "Unethical, persistent, greedy…" She handed him a slim electronic business card. "Come see me about being a realtor if the whole cult job doesn't pan out, 'kay?" She twiddled fingers at him. "Buh-bye."

And with that, Bertram found himself back in the Alternate Realty waiting room.

Bertram Ludlow had a lot to think about as he wandered the Ottoframan streets. He kept his head low, his hood up and his options open.

Maybe it still wasn't too late to hitch a ride on Dumbbell Nebula's jet-shoes; say, to spend 2,880 minutes (less now) on the *Swingin' on Saturn's Rings* GCU Remix Tour and cash-in enough yoonie cards to bid for his own planet from the interlopers. Imagine, Bertram Ludlow as the covert owner of planet Earth. It had a refreshing sort of irony.

Okay, yes, there was that annoying 98% probability that Foobaz Frabblagundger wouldn't even talk to him now…

And the fact that even if he did manage to make it on stage, some sharp-brained spaceman would inevitably recognize that even the most innovative performers didn't sing like a rhythmically-challenged yak in heat…

Plus, Popeelies would undoubtedly be there to protest their unwarranted musical makeover and copyright infringement…

And there was the distinct possibility the Deltan RegForce would line the first row of the concert hall—and not for autographs.

Otherwise, it was an awesome plan.

But Bertram wasn't out of ideas. What about starting a Tryfe Preservation Awareness campaign, using the Uninet and a few minutes of Zaph Chantseree's time? Surely a Tryfling risking life and limb to save his planet was a big story, wasn't it? And who didn't like a good rallying cause?

Of course, Bertram would also be snagged by the RegForce quicker than he could say "ZT-112G polymer-casing hydro-reactive collapsible hand-laser." And he was pretty sure he couldn't coordinate any PR efforts half-stunned from inside a confinement cell, drooling on a cot that smelled like old mathgar kidney.

A sense of gray hopelessness washed over him. Or maybe that was just the cloudy emissions from the hovercar that flew past.

Bertram coughed.

"Psst!"

Bertram coughed again.

"Psst! Psst!"

Frowning, Bertram scanned through the cloud of smoke.

"Psst! You in the cloak!" The voice had a gruff, gravelly sound and seemed to come from the outskirts of the cloud. Bertram squinted, the fog dissipating enough to reveal the jowly, red-eyed life-form who had been watching him so steadily in the Secondary Corral. Bertram inhaled sharply.

"Kid, c'mere," rumbled the voice. The trench-coated being motioned to an alley for this little tete-a-tete.

With a furtive glance, Bertram turned on his AirChamps sandal and darted the opposite direction, picking up his pace to match his rapidly increasing heart rate.

"Kid, c'mon. I just want to talk with you," the voice pleaded closer behind him.

"Sorry, all out of Cloak-in-a-Cans," Bertram called. "You'll have to order from our Uninet site. The Popeelies thank you for your patronage."

"Kid, wait!" the guy shouted. "It's about Tryfe!"

Bertram stopped short. He spun around. The furred creature stood right there behind him, but how he'd caught up so quickly, so silently, Bertram couldn't imagine. "I know you were asking about Tryfe," rasped the being. "I think I can help."

"Who are you?" Bertram asked, eyes narrowed. "Why are you tailing me?"

"Just a fellow traveler with a little interest in the market," said the life-form casually. "I like to keep my mitts in it, so to speak." He held up furred paws in fingerless gloves as if they might yield explanation. "I heard you at Alternate Realty. You want to talk to the current owner of Tryfe."

"That's my business," said Bertram coolly. He folded robed arms. "What's funny is I didn't see *you* at Alternate Realty."

"Oh?" The hairy fellow gnawed a thumbnail.

"No," pressed Bertram. "I saw you on the Secondary Corral."

The being gave a slow, languid shrug. "Is it true those Popeelie hoods are death when it comes to peripheral vision?"

Bertram scowled. They *were* actually kinda hard to see around, but that wasn't the point. There was something off about this guy, something that stunk like the Shop-o-Drome under a hot sun on half-price perishables day. He could smell it from here. "Okay. Let's say you did see me at Alternate Realty. And let's say you have information. Who owns Tryfe?"

"That I don't know," he said.

"Naturally."

"But I know who one of the bidders is, if that would be of value to you?" His voice had lost some of its calm, bored tone. It held a tinge of over-eagerness now.

"Sorry, pal," Bertram said. "If you're looking for a payoff, you've come to the wrong place. I'm tapped." He hoped his bag of Dootett coins wouldn't jingle away his fib, but he wasn't about to be blackmailed for iffy information. Besides, that Entropy Burger sack contained all the cash he had in the universe. This guy was just going to have to get his paws on some other sucker.

"T'murp," said the being suddenly.

"I don't have antacids, either. Good luck finding yourself a pharmacy." And Bertram started away. He'd wasted enough time.

But the being ran to catch up. "No. I said T'murp. Eudicot T'murp. He's the one bidding on Tryfe."

Bertram paused. "Oh. Eudicot T'murp." Surely, Tryfe's future owner wouldn't sound like an onomotopoetic version of indigestion.

The being pushed his hat back and blinked soulful brown eyes. "T'murp went into Alternate Realty a few days ago, and then out touring with that Grabbitz woman. When they came back, the word 'Tryfe' was dropped like spare kaniggles from a holey pocket."

"You overheard this yourself?"

"The ears don't lie," the life-form rasped, holding up one shoulder-length, furry sound-processor in emphasis.

"And where is Eudicot T'murp?" Bertram asked. He imagined his new furred friend might be some undercover RegForce officer, feeding him a line, but it didn't hurt to ask the questions.

"Over at DiversiDine Entertainment Systems and Aeroponics," the guy said. He pointed across the cityscape.

Bertram followed the gesture with some surprise. "Here on Ottofram?"

The being gave a slow, deliberate nod. "Here on Ottofram."

Now that it was pointed out to him, Bertram could see the building from where they stood. Not because it was so close, but because it was so large. It was a complex of turrets and spires, domes and dips, broadcast towers and crystalline elevators. All with the word "DiversiDine" blazing forth. In the center, a robotic-hand-and-snack-cake logo rose from the complex triumphantly. It had to have taken years to get it all into place. Bertram turned back from the skyline. "Why would Eudicot T'murp be interested in—?"

But Droopy had vanished, the Ottoframan street clear. A few shed hairs floated on the breeze.

Bertram sighed. Yep, that was the GCU all over. If only, he thought wistfully, he could return to those simple, blissfully-ignorant days not so long ago, where he just believed he'd gone completely bat-shit.

17

The conference room was abuzz. Execs from the most active and innovative departments in all of DiversiDine Entertainment Systems and Aeroponics were ovaled around the table. They would have circled, but the table was elliptical by nature and didn't stand for such uninspired conformity.

Yes, gathered together in one room were the opinion-makers and stakeholders from every critical area of the company. There were the fine minds from Making Things Up, the group that had led so much of the bid campaign already. There were two reps from Putting Things Out There, looping them in for the tasks ahead. Seated were a few of the whizzes from Developing Stuff and Actually Knowing How it Works, a group ordinarily consulted only at the very last possible moment in the process, mostly after everyone had already convinced themselves of a lot of inconvenient untruths about what they were selling. And, of course, there was the Getting Big Yoonies and Figuring Out Where It Goes department, who didn't know why they were there but were already worried how much it was going to cost them.

There were also three consultants to DiversiDine, seated at the very back. But they didn't have a catchy department name.

Excited murmurs filled the room, like a caucus of Blumdec waterfowl putting the next migration date to committee.

Standing before this group was the DiversiDine corporate holovision, a monitor so big it spanned the wall, and so 3-D that in the last Ottoframan year it had triggered seizures in no fewer than 12 stressed-out, sleep-deprived ad persons. Poised in front of this holovision, sitting in his favorite levitating wingback chair, sat DiversiDine president Eudicot T'murp.

"Folks: thanks a bunch for your time today," said T'murp to the crowd, and their migratory squawking stilled to a rustle. T'murp never ceased to enjoy the little things like this; how a single hand motion or congenial word from him could cause a whole group to come to attention. It showed just how far he'd come from his South Klorofil youth. It proved money and solid leadership could overcome many obstacles, including the uneasiness that seems to arise when the boss starts to sprout in public.

"Lights dim," he commanded. And the overhead illumination dropped to the twinkle of distant stars.

"Now," said T'murp, rising from the chair to stand beside the screen, "some of you have been involved in our project from the beginning, but let's take a moment to get the rest up to speed." He pressed a button and onto the screen projected a map of the Greater Communicating Universe broken up into its four participating Quadrants. "DiversiDine has found a backspace planet containing the perfect life-forms and atmosphere to support our marketing interests. These people would serve as a pilot project market before we launch into the greater GCU. The planet is called Tryfe. It is located here."

The map on the screen shifted out of the familiar GCU territory and then drilled down, down, down, to a small solar system with a handful of planets rotating around a single shiny little sun. It then zoomed in, overshot, backtracked, and screeched to a halt on a pretty blue-and-white orb. With its bright color and swirls of cloud, the planet looked like an oversized replica of a child's spherical plaything. The sort of small, hard projectile progeny enjoy pelting at each other's soft tissues in particular.

"This is the planet we're bidding on," explained T'murp, "And soon, we'll present our redevelopment plans. Based on those, the owner will select the winner. Thanks to some of you in this room, DiversiDine has developed a particularly competitive plan concept. I'd like to show you a draft of that now."

T'murp pushed the button again and on the screen, the words: "There Goes the Galaxy" in large adventurous letters swept in. They exploded in fiery fragments.

From this meteorific inferno sprang the tagline: "Real Time. Real Challenges. Real Backspace™."

Cue the credits: "A DiversiDine Entertainment Systems and Aeroponics® Production…"

"A DiversiDine Entertainment Systems and Aeroponics® Feature Presentation…"

"A DiversiDine Entertainment Systems and Aeroponics® Real Reality RealTime DocuDrama™."

The camera focused on the planet of Tryfe, and a narrator's voice intoned darkly: "In a world that knows no life beyond its own, one average Tryfe humanoid has been mysteriously thrust into the cold depths of space. His task? To save his planet from unknown terrors. Join him on this exhilarating and dangerous quest as this simple Tryfling stranger—lost and trapped in a complex and frightening alien existence—is put to the test, transforming from backspace disbeliever to unsung hero…intergalactic fugitive…and cunning master of disguise."

T'murp paused the film and scanned the faces around the oval table. They blinked with a cozy grogginess, as if just waking up from a Zlorgon Sub-Atomic Headbanger coma. "Now, understand, this Real Reality RealTime DocuDrama™ is just one way we're proposing to leverage Tryfe and its people. Tryflings are very susceptible to advertising and consumerism, so mainly we plan to use the planet's populace for more subtle product testing and beta launches. But we feel the DocuDrama offshoot was the big grabber for this bid. I see this as the first installment in a series, involving a different hand-picked Tryfling star per season."

Someone from Putting Things Out There spoke up: "Research predicts a huge Uninet market for this type of programming. There's nothing viewers like better than watching shows about life-forms who are even more confused than they are. Storylines in that genre get a 98.7% Approval Rating in independent testing. It lets them feel superior without actually teaching them anything."

They all admitted, the concept was a tantalizing one and likely to be very popular with viewers.

"Won't the audience want to learn more about Tryfe, though?" queried another expert from Putting Things Out There. "I'm seeing Tryfe-related merchandising like scenic Tryfe pictorial e-books, pre-packaged Tryfe cuisine, and Tryfling-inspired couture."

"Brilliant! Taste Tryfe! Smell Tryfe! Wrap yourself in Tryfe!" exclaimed a breathless Making Things Up team member.

The leader of Developing Stuff and Actually Knowing How It Works sniffed. "I don't suppose anybody knows what Tryfe people eat, drink and wear?"

At this, the Making Things Up execs burst into team levity. It was some moments before they could compose themselves enough to explain they'd just brainstorm marketable options and work up a creative brief.

"Stellar," T'murp told them approvingly. "Jot down those ideas and we'll discuss in a post-meeting meeting." This was the warm reception he had been hoping for. He couldn't have asked for better if he'd scripted it out himself and paid them to say it. Which he did sometimes for fun when he got bored. Just not today.

"Questions." An employee from the Putting Things Out There department flagged him for attention. "Have you started any filming of this Real Reality RealTime DocuDrama™ or is that upcoming? Will the lead Tryfling be compensated for his work? What are the legal ramifications of having a backspace life-form appear in GCU media?"

T'murp smiled. "I'm glad you asked that. The whole process is quite cutting-edge. Let's move on, and I think the next segment will help address most of your questions."

He pressed the play button once more. The credits faded, and now a phosphorescent white-blue glow flooded into the screen's center. As the camera panned back…back…this glow transformed into a frail glowing figure. Then the camera swiveled 180, piercing the blackness to light a brown-irised eyeball. It was a face very close-up. The face was curious, pale, nervous, and altogether Tryfe-human.

The face was Bertram Ludlow's.

"…Soap on a rope?" queried the young man's voice, a hesitant, too-close mouth working the question. The camera 180ed again, focusing on three luminescent figures seated before the Tryflng in the darkness.

"You will know what it issss when you neeeeed to knowwwww," responded one ethereal figure, voice echoing off the cavern walls.

The executives in the conference room chuckled appreciatively.

"It *is* elegantly vague," agreed T'murp to the group. "Great job, Seers of Rhobux, for getting that hand-held camera into the

Tryfling's possession without a lot of fuss. It's worked extremely well so far, guys."

From the back of the room came a voice, insubstantial as the wind. "We thaaaaaannkk you, Missssster T'muuurp, for thissssss fiiiiiiinnne opportuuuuunnittyyyy," lilted the eerie tones of Kravsmin, or was in Glyddon? Maybe it was Kaenmoor. Eudicot T'murp never could tell them apart.

Naturally, the acoustics of the conference room were nothing like the dark chamber in the Seers Tower on Rhobux-7. Yet somehow the speaker still managed to make the words sound like they were spoken from the bottom of a cold, deep well. Eudicot T'murp imagined they could do the same in a shopping mall dressing room or on a crowded dance floor.

That was talent.

"We doooooo hooooope that we have served faaaaithfullyyy, and that as promisssed, we will therebyy beeeeee entiiiitled to the DiiiverrrsssiDiiine sssstooooock optionnnnnnsssss and retiiiiiremenntttt benefiiitsss we haddddddddd dissss—"

"Of course, of course," T'murp interjected, waving them to silence. A new clip on the screen had caught his attention. The scene was in a shabby confinement center, where a tall, sinewy male figure with yellow hair brandished a weapon that looked more like the product of a child's building set than a tool of violence. At the flip of a switch, the toy had turned several Podunk Peace Guards to puddles.

It was a masterful shot of demolecularization.

It was followed by a torrent of Tryfling shrieking and curses, which rattled the audio, while the camera captured the yellow-haired man beaming at his work. His smile was a lot like a well-fed Marglenian fighting fish picking its teeth after a particularly tasty tourist group.

One of the Making Things Up execs observed, "It's a shame we lost the Hyphiz Deltan so soon into the piece. We've done some preliminary viewer-testing and he got approval ratings from 76% of the audience."

"We assumed incorrectly that he would be attracted to this sort of cause," a second Making Things Up exec said. "It was completely in-line with previous initiatives he'd championed. A 94% compatibility. We're still analyzing where the accuracy slippage occurred." She shook her head solemnly.

Now the footage jarred forward to the pilot's cabin on Rolliam Tsmorlood's Interplanetary Cruise Vessel. The lens swept to the empty space where Rhobux-7 had been, and the camera bounded in on a small levitating sign stating Rhobux-7 was currently unavailable.

"Another nice touch there," praised Eudicot T'murp, as the group chuckled to themselves at the sight. He called to the Seers down the table. "By the way, where is Rhobux-7 now?"

The Seer on the left waved a hand. Kaenmoor. Or possibly Kravsmin. "Fear not, good man. It has simply been reloooocated..."

"To a nice quiet soooooolar systemmm..." supplied Kravsmin. Or possibly Glyddon.

"In the countrrrrry..." finished Glyddon, or possibly Kaenmoor.

"But how?" asked someone from the Developing Stuff and Actually Knowing How It Works group. "To pull a planet completely out of orbit you'd need a black hole or an even bigger planet—a sun with more mass and a stronger gravitational pull than the sun it was already orbiting."

"Orrrr," interrupted the central Seer with a giggle, "a very, very, very, very, very large shipppp."

"Shippppp," agreed the other two Seers.

"A ship?" pressed the Developing Stuff executive. "Impossible! It would have to be the biggest, heaviest ship in existence and then it wouldn't just pull Rhobux-7. It would inevitably take other planets along with it. And—"

The Seer just gave another wheezy laugh. "Imposssssibilityyyy is only imposing abillllityyyy on the not thoroughlyyyy mucked-abouuuuuut-with," the Seer responded with a smug, sightless wink.

"Mootaab pucky!" snapped the Developing Stuff executive. Guys from Developing Stuff didn't have much patience for inter-departmental hedging. They certainly weren't going to embrace it from outside consultants. "What does that even mean?"

Eudicot T'murp could see one of his more valuable engineering minds was experiencing serious turbulence against his smooth rationale. T'murp decided to change direction, or they'd end up in a three hour lecture on astrophysics, and he had a packed schedule planned. "We'll talk about this in a post-meeting-meeting conference, if you don't mind."

Grumbling, the executive turned back to the monstrous holovision screen. The current scene was focused on a close-up of a Galactic Monetary Exchange machine. A light rolling sound tinkled across the room from one audio speaker to the other. In a moment, there was a thud, and the Tryfling on the screen let out an affronted yowl of pain. The picture wavered and bobbed as Bertram Ludlow crouched. His hand reached and came up with a small, sixteen-sided coin.

The metallic surface of the GME machine reflected the face of a very perplexed Tryfeman, and the room filled with another round of laughter. "Look how confused he is! Do you see his face?" observed someone from Putting Things Out There.

"I *knew* we were backing the right Tryfling," said the lead manager from Making Things Up.

"How was he selected?" the head of Putting Things Out There queried, poised to take notes for a future media release.

"Well," the exec began, "it was part of a highly-scientific process. First we tapped into a Tryfan university database and created a list using bell curve calculations. We basically drew on the most average, unexceptional, Tryfe-representative researchers. From them, we eliminated any who were life-merged, had progeny or any other dependents. We also eliminated those with relatives within a certain square distance on Tryfe. This left us with whole list of Tryfe humans of such few ties to Tryfe's social and economic structure they were unlikely to be missed. From there, we weeded out the elderly and infirm. And then..."

"Yes?"

The executive blushed and hooked a thumb to his colleague. "Gobo closed his eyes and pointed."

Gobo held up the famous pointing finger and gave a demonstration.

Spontaneous applause broke out.

"And where'd the coin come from?" someone from Getting Big Yoonies and Figuring Out Where It Goes asked. The exec pointed to the screen. He was likely making a mental note to deduct the cost from the production budget.

"Digger Dugblud," input T'murp. "I have him tailing our Tryfling friend, just in case he gets stuck somewhere and can't extract himself. We've got to keep the DocuDrama moving for our viewers. This seemed the most expedient way to ensure it."

The camera perspective rose once more and the viewers saw the Tryfeman's hand slip the coin into the GME machine with trembling fingers.

"Do you think he'll ever figure out what the 'Yellow Thing' is?" asked someone from Making Things Up.

An exec from the Developing Stuff and Actually Knowing How It Works department gave a laugh. "Hardly. That audio-video recording system's a prototype from the Zegamemalon exploration program. It uses living tissue that adapts itself to virtually any conditions. It can handle intensely high temperatures, submergence in almost any liquid, endure crushing pressure, high force impact, and a lack of oxygen-based atmosphere. No one's ever seen anything like thi—"

There was a rap at the conference room door, and T'murp saw the slim, rigid silhouette of his personal assistant, Ms. Codewell, through the glass. "Excuse me just a moment," he said and motioned her in.

The door shooshed open. "Mr. T'murp," said Ms. Codewell, listening carefully to the receiver built into her ear. "I have a Mr. Dugblud on the vis-u for you. He said it's urgent."

"Can you patch him into us here?"

She nodded and, speaking into the chip implanted next to her mouth, said, "Mr. Dugblud, Mr. T'murp is patching you into the conference room now."

Her eyes flicked to the screen, triggering the switch. Eudicot T'murp was so glad she wasn't one of the Simulants currently picketing outside. He couldn't imagine what he'd do without her.

In a moment, the presentation video was supplanted by the image of a jowly, furred, trench-coated life-form, blown up to five times actual size. Ms. Codewell discreetly shot away on whisper-quiet hover-heels, and the door shooshed closed behind her.

"Digger," began T'murp, "what's the scoop?"

"It's the Tryfling," rumbled Dugblud. "He's coming your way."

T'murp felt a couple petals drop onto the conference table. "You're joking."

"He was headed nowhere," Dugblud explained. "You'd said to give him a push."

"A push, yes, but why is he *here*?"

"I told him you were one of the bidders on Tryfe," the gravel voice said. "He should be banging down DiversiDine doors in just a few minutes." Digger Dugblud waited for his employer's reaction just as patiently as he'd wait in line at the DiversiDine cafeteria on Free Smorg Day.

After a moment, T'murp nodded. The more he thought about it, the more he felt a strange pleasure at the idea of the Tryfling's Real Reality RealTime DocuDrama™ leading Bertram Ludlow to DiversiDine. It had a beautiful sort of synchronicity to it. And talk about cross-pollination advertising! "Nice work."

Dugblud acknowledged it with a bow of his head and slapped his hat back on.

"Keep on him, but don't let him see you," warned T'murp.

"Affirmative," said Dugblud, and the image cut from the screen.

T'murp sat on the edge of the conference room table. He smiled, crossing his fronds confidently across his chest. "The Tryfling's coming here. This might just prove to be interesting."

And in under a second, everyone seated around the elliptical table, including Eudicot T'murp, leapt up and raced to the window, jockeying for a good view

Bertram peered up at the headquarters of DiversiDine Entertainment Systems and Aeroponics, graceful spires surrounding its central, sky-scraper-like robotic hand. The hand brandished a snack cake so big even King Kong would have had to bag half for later. Outside the building, a group of men and women in yellow, black-trimmed uniforms marched in a circle, shouting and holding digital signs with slogans reading things like:

Non-Organic and Proud!

and:

Artificial People Have Real Needs!

and:

These Simmis Say Gimmie!
On-the-Job Perfection MUST
= Higher Pay + Better Benefits

On closer inspection, Bertram noticed at least three of the women appeared to be Neo-Natelle models. Two men looked like the lost brothers of the Farthest Reaches security guards. And all of them had a pretty good rhythm going, alternating shouts and pro-Simulant cheers. There was a crowd of about thirty, and they showed no signs of letting-up.

That was the thing about Non-Organic Simulants, Bertram supposed. They had the endurance to make these initiatives really work. At least until their power supplies ran out.

He wondered how they fared in rain.

It was a clear day above, though, the skies taking on a bright optimistic hue. He turned his attention back to the corporate megaplex before him, and the challenge at hand. Eudicot T'murp was bidding on Bertram Ludlow's planet. So how could Bertram make the most of that information?

Clearly, no one was going to just let someone waltz right in off the street to grill the most powerful man in the company about his real estate ventures. And even if they did—which was to say, they wouldn't—what would it accomplish? The man wasn't going to respond, "Oh, gee, I didn't realize anybody was living on the planet. Let me talk to the owner and dissuade him from selling."

Or: "I can't help you with that myself. But would you like to know when and where the secret presentations will be made, so you can sweep in and interrupt the proceedings with perfect timing and swashbuckling heroics?"

Or: "Since you seem like such a cool guy, if I win the planet, I'll just abandon all of my confidential plans for mass anal probing, baby-making and crop circles, and give you Tryfe people the planet for keepsies. Copacetic?"

Nope, Bertram was a realist. If alien babies, branded corn fields and a Tryfe-wide probe-fest were on the guy's agenda—or anything else for that matter—there wasn't much a half-hour chat over a cup of Jarendi Java was going to do to change it, no matter how impassioned and persuasive Bertram was.

So what the hell was there to do?

Screams from the Non-Organic picketers interrupted his thoughts once more. "Show us the yoonies!" called one.

"We're Non-organics and We're Organized!" shouted another.

"Regular fluids changes should be a part of our corporate benefits!" projected a third. "And vacation time! We need to give our mechanisms a rest just like anybody else! Tell T'murp you believe in equality for all life-forms, born and manufactured!"

A couple of organic DiversiDine execs entered the corporate campus, the unlucky folks. On sight of them, the Simulants turned up their shouting volume and began to close in. The organics quickly powered up their rocket boots, their suits yellow-and-black blurs that streaked into the safety of the building. The Simulants taunted and jeered long after they'd vanished through the doorway.

By that time, Bertram had his idea.

"He's going? Why is he going?" asked Eudicot T'murp from his window view. Bertram Ludlow, future Tryfling Uninet sensation, had swept down the Ottoframan street in his Popeelie robes and vanished from view. It had been looking like DiversiDine would get an exciting cameo scene in the Real Reality RealTime DocuDrama™, and now all those branding opportunities were being sucked into a great black hole of Not Happening.

He called for Ms. Codewell and had her get Dugblud on the vis-u again. In seconds, the Alpuckite's eager face appeared.

"I can't see the Tryfling. Where's he headed?" T'murp queried of Dugblud. The surprise and strain he felt was emerging into his voice. This was all so unlike him.

But Dugblud said he was on top of it and would report back when he had something. The man's drooping jowls might have even raised in a slight smile, before his furred face disappeared from the monitor.

Dugblud loved his job.

T'murp turned to the Developing Stuff team. "Can we tap into the hand-held directly?" he asked. "Watch it live as it records?"

"Can we!" The lead programmer beamed. He loved his job, too. "Does the Quargon Accellerator have a turbo boost that makes you wet your astro-togs?" he queried.

T'murp blinked.

"It does," assured the programmer, flushing at the neck. "Embarrassing." And he rose to make the live feed happen.

T'murp appreciated the expertise and loved the enthusiasm. The humor, however, sometimes needed its own version of Translachew. He made a mental note to work on that.

✧

"Life for Tryfe! Life for Tryfe!" said one protestor.

"Tryfling Oppression No Small Matter!" screamed another.

"Help Back Our Backspace Brothers!" shouted a third.

Over folded arms, Bertram Ludlow watched his circle of ten picketers with some satisfaction and couldn't believe he didn't think of this sooner.

It was a motley group, he knew. And not as many as Bertram had originally hoped for. But then again, he hadn't had much time for promotion and mobilization.

He lifted the lightened bag of Dootett currency and considered what the small investment had bought him:

- One bribed yet impassioned vis-u announcement over the University of Ottofram student center system.
- Some low-end e-posters.
- And snack cakes. DiversiDine ones, no less.

Irony came in shiny, shiny wrappers.

Anyway, Bertram had learned one important Universal Truth this day. It was something he had suspected all along but hadn't been able to confirm until now. And that was: it didn't matter what planet you were on, or what your species. Step into a university setting and some people will do simply anything for free food.

So Bertram's picketers marched with their makeshift protest signs, munching their snack cakes and putting on a pretty good show. A couple of them were genuinely embracing the cause, too.

"First, it's backspace planets like Tryfe," shouted one student, a gender-neutral life-form who may or may not have had eyes under long springy hair. "Next it's our own home planets!"

"More importantly," argued a second student, spiky tail waving in emphasis, "backspace people like the Tryflings should be preserved. Their primitive culture. Their mythology. Their simple way of life. We should use our technology to protect them, not to persecute them! Who will stand up for them if we don't?"

Bertram grinned. Yes, this was more like it.

"Rights for Tryfe!"

"Preserve Tryfling culture and heritage!"

"I like food!" That was the protestor Bertram had found living in a mulch pile alongside the University park. The aging, limping creature raised a fist in solidarity and smiled a broad, snack-cake-smeared, broken-tusked smile.

"You tell 'em," urged Bertram.

"Life for Tryfe! Life for Tryfe!"

"Hey you," interrupted a Neo-Natelle model VR18, exiting the Simulant picket line to break Bertram's circle of Tryfers. She tossed a lock of silky, steely-silver hair over her shoulder. "This is *our* demonstration. Can't you go demonstrate somewhere else?"

"Life for Tryfe! Life for Tryfe!" the students continued, winding their circle in a new path around her.

"Look, we're not stopping you from your protest," Bertram told her. "You do your thing, we'll do ours."

"Oh really?" pressed the Simulant. She hooked a thumb at Bertram's band. "You're diffusing our messaging. And we were here first, so launch yourself!"

"Life for Tryfe! Life for Tryfe!" Bertram's attention was drawn with pride to his energetically protesting troops; almost eight of them were even managing to march in unison without tripping over each other much. It was far better than he'd expected.

"Well?" the Simulant pressed, tapping a perfect, impatient foot. "Are you going to move or not?"

Bertram answered her by matching her defiant gaze, picking up a digital picket sign and stepping into formation with the others. "Life for Tryfe! Life for Tryfe!"

Snarling electronically, the Neo-Natelle model stalked back to her union colleagues and fell into step, shooting Bertram a sizzling glare. She bumped up her volume controls to shout all the louder.

"Artificial People Have Real Needs! Artificial People Have Real Needs!"

"Life for Tryfe! Life for Tryfe!"

"Non-Organic and Proud! Non-Organic and Proud!"

"Tryfe Oppression No Trifling Matter!"

"Simmis Say Gimmie! Simmis Say Gimmie!"

"Yaaaay, food!"

Back and forth it went, Tryfers and the Simmis … Simmis and Tryfers… Until Bertram noticed that outside his group's well-trodden path, bystanding Ottoframans had started to collect, curious to learn what all the noise was about.

As more life-forms gathered, rubbernecking hovercrafts slowed down to look, snarling traffic in the area. Workers began to trickle from the DiversiDine building and other nearby office complexes to gaze on the dueling demonstrations.

"I never realized it before, but they're right," Bertram heard a Simulant exclaim. "I never *have* had a day off. And yet every single organic in my department—even Kromblatz, who's completely incompetent—gets time off every year. That's not fair! I work hard! I want time off, too!"

And suddenly, that Simulant stepped in to support the Non-Organics' cause.

"Just because I'm man-made, doesn't mean I don't have feelings, hopes and dreams. Stab us, do we not initiate user-error messaging? Prick us, do we not leak specially-engineered fluids?"

There was a lot of self-realization going on at DiversiDine today.

But even more surprising was the split in loyalties. While the majority of Simulants leapt into the fray with their manufactured brethren, some of them actually began crowding around Bertram asking about the Tryfling cause.

"This is the real problem," one of the Simulants announced in response. "It's not just about the inequity that we face as Non-Organics. It's the inequities faced by *all* life-forms perceived to be inferior. Whether it's because we're considered less natural than everyone else, or simply less evolved. This is so much bigger than Simulants not getting equal benefits. It's a question of rights for all life-forms! It's empowering all life to have control over its own destiny!"

And, before Bertram knew it, a dozen very jazzed Non-Organics had fallen into step with the Tryfers.

"Have you gotten us patched in yet?" Eudicot T'murp asked from the conference room window.

"Almost, sir," said the voice of the technician from Developing Stuff. He'd flattened himself into the one-inch crevasse behind the monitor, whizzing cables around like the tentacles of a Vernjoolsian Mollusk.

"I just wish I knew what was going on down there," muttered T'murp anxiously. "It looks like a second protest."

"It looks like *war*," said someone from Making Things Up, peering down on the scene below.

"If those are all Non-Organic Simulants down there," T'murp began, squinting, "they must be shipping them in straight from the factory."

The words had hardly passed his lips when a life-form with a long spiky tail marched into view. Then another being with four arms. And two Dootett men. And three fronded Cardoons. There was even someone covered in bits of rotting wood; T'murp wasn't sure what that was about.

"They look pretty diverse, sir," the manager of Putting Things Out There observed.

"I don't understand. What do they *want?*" T'murp adjusted the zoom mechanism on the window—a handy little feature he'd installed for security purposes when he and the Smorg growers were on the outs, and they'd brought in that catapult. In a second, Eudicot T'murp was able to focus in on the signs.

"I believe they want 'Life for Tryfe,' sir," echoed the voice of the technician from Developing Stuff and Actually Knowing How It Works. He slipped out from behind the monitor and began to unflatten himself. T'murp could hear bones cracking back into place as he re-expanded.

T'murp turned, and on the large holoscreen they could now see precisely what Bertram Ludlow was seeing, hear what he heard. Bertram Ludlow was in the center of a large ring of life-forms, all shouting with real zeal on behalf of the intergalactically downtrodden.

"Well, what do ya know?" T'murp marveled aloud. "The Tryfling's organizing."

"He issss determinnnned," said one of the Seers.

"He issss dedicatedddd," said another.

"He issss bribing people with snnnnnacksss," observed the third.

"Want us to call security?" asked someone from Getting Big Yoonies and Figuring Out Where It Goes, lips twitching her implanted mouth-comm in anticipation. "It's a lawsuit waiting to happen."

Eudicot T'murp peered down on the Tryfeman's growing band, as a wave of warmth—of, yes, even admiration—washed over him. It was always just so interesting to see what life-forms could accomplish, against the odds, when they set their minds to it. So many beings were so much stronger than any of us even knew. Than we even knew ourselves. "We'll let it play out a while longer and see where it goes," said T'murp.

✧

Bertram could see the figures pressed to the windows in the DiversiDine towers, and he had no doubt Eudicot T'murp was among them.

Remember this, T'murp. This is the day you screwed with the wrong guy's home planet. This is the start of the Tryfe Freedom, Ditch-the-Alien-Landlord, Non-Probing, Keep-Your-Damned-Dirty-Crop-Circles-to-Yourself Initiative.

And sure, maybe, one or two of the demonstrators were half-crazed and smelled like woodchips. And maybe another bunch wasn't quite sure why they were there, so they had started a conga line and were tapping a keg. And okay, some newbies did seem to be adding their own personal issues and demands into the mix. And sure, more people than Bertram had anticipated seemed to be just looking for an excuse to shackle themselves to something heavy, and beat public property with sticks. But sometimes concessions had to be made in the name of planetary self-preservation and awareness.

Besides, the group had really grown, and the stir had even drawn the attention of the *Heavy Meddler* Uninet channel.

The *Heavy Meddler* ICV flew low, panning across the surging crowd. As it swept overhead, Bertram ducked behind his new friend from the mulch pile, just in case his Popeelie victim had come-to and spilled the beans on Bertram's latest wardrobe selection. It was all very well to get the "Life for Tryfe" issue some attention and make T'murp squirm, but it was a whole other thing to end up seized and conducting a final interview on the topic from the Ottoframan pokey. Something he pretty much figured was destiny for a high-profile intergalactic fugitive such as himself. Especially one with a knack for mobilizing large, angry mobs.

And sure enough, at the sight of the news crews, those who'd joined the Tryfe FDAL-NP-KYDDCCY Initiative specifically for the chance of getting in some good old-fashioned unrestrained anarchy, chose this time to pick fights with a few of the shorter-fused Simulants and secure their 15 U-minutes in front of the cameras.

They'd be longer than 15 minutes at health services later; Simulants are a whole lot stronger than they look.

So it was mere moments before the Ottoframan Peace Guards shrieked onto the scene. And it took even less time than that for Bertram Ludlow to quietly slide away from the roiling mayhem he'd created. He shielded the bright Popeelie colors with a spiky tail here, a leathery wingspan there, until he made his way to the edge of the chaos and extracted himself. Walking first quickly, and then breaking into a full-out run, the "Life For Tryfe" movement leader knew it was time to let the movement move on without him.

Bertram kept his hood down and expanded the distance by lengths, looking over his shoulder now and then for reporters or the law. He walked this way awhile. He passed Ottoframan fast food joints, alien salons, skin greening palaces, and a store display containing the very latest in DiversiDine electronics.

It was here his Popeelie sandals paused. A wall of holovisions was tuned into the live *Heavy Meddler* broadcast and projected the scene at DiversiDine headquarters.

"One moment we were protesting lack of equal rights for Non-Organics," a Neo-Natelle model was saying, "and the next minute these 'Life for Tryfe' people had moved in."

The broadcast cut to reporter Zaph Chantseree, free from the Secondary Corral investigation and now trying to catch up with the erratically weaving aged protestor with the mulched-up hair. It was like chasing a butterfly drunk on pollen.

"Excuse me! Er, pardon please?—I understand a number of protestors were recruited specifically for the 'Life for Tryfe' rally. Do you remember anything about the person who recruited you?" Chantseree extended a microphone for comment.

"Smorgs are nice," said the tusked life-form enthusiastically, weaving out of frame. "I had three."

Chantseree and the camera weaved, too. The reporter spoke a little slower and louder now, as if addressing a very deaf, very confused child. "Can you describe the person who brought you here?"

"He had three, but he gave them to me."

"So the person who gave you Smorgs to start this protest was a male life-form then? Can you describe him?"

The life-form leaned in and replied in a low confidential voice, "I like food."

Zaph Chantseree looked directly into the camera, "Back to you, Qwerty."

In the studio, newscaster Qwerty Zaqwer chirped, "Thanks, Zaph! Meanwhile, Eudicot T'murp has kept his silence regarding both the Simulant Rights and the 'Life for Tryfe' protests. The word on the Uninet suggests MetamorfaSys Inc. mogul, Musca Mij, has also placed a bid on Tryfe. Does this mean Mij will be the next target of this mysterious new Tryfe rights group? Current sources indicate Blumdec, where Mij is currently filming, has been calm. But how long will the peace last?"

"One question I've been hearing a lot right now, Qwerty, is 'Why is Tryfe suddenly such hot property?" This was Goudy Futura from the chair next to her. "Isn't it outside the GCU?"

"Why, yes it is, Goudy. Which is one of the things that makes this all so curious. And—"

Bertram Ludlow forced himself to step from the window and continue on down the street. So Musca Mij was placing a bid on Tryfe, too. Musca Mij, head of MetamorfaSys Inc., who was currently working on Blumdec.

Blumdec.

Bertram knew he couldn't risk a second ride on the Cosmos Corral to get there. Not when his holowatch cover was blown, and his Popeelie disguise had a slow leak. No, Bertram needed transportation of a more private type. Something where there would be no questions asked and no one to ask them. But also with power, power enough to get Bertram to Blumdec fast and safe.

Bertram pondered this as he passed an ICV rental, a mass of gleaming signs and shining vehicles. He paused, but then shook his throbbing head and forced himself onward. He didn't just need an ICV. He needed a pilot, too. One who'd understand his circumstances. One he could trust. And the only pilot Bertram knew was the one who'd dragged him into this mess in the first place. At the moment that guy was only interested in his own continued life off Altair-5—not that Bertram really could blame him. And even if Bertram *could* somehow figure out how to reach Rollie, the man wasn't likely to come out of hiding for a bag of Dootett coins.

The coins.

Bertram ducked into a doorway and peered into the bag. He dug a hand into it and pulled out a handful of the currency. His finger traced over the Empress' clean profiles on one coin in his palm.

He had an idea who he just might be able to call.

18

"The *rye nespyne* tastes mainly of *d'plyne*," intoned Rozz.

"Again."

"The *rye nespyne* tastes mainly of *d'plyne*,"

"Again."

Spectra Pollux's 37 personal assistants tittered.

Prickly black loathing rose within Rozz. She prayed it did not burrow noticeably into her voice. "The *rye nespyne* tastes mainly of *d'plyne*," she announced.

Spectra Pollux leapt up. The floor, chairs and table rumbled with her movement. "That's it!" the woman thundered, her features alight with joy. "That's how we answer when someone asks about our new *rye nespyne* juice smoothie!"

The 37 personal assistants clapped on cue.

"And what is *rye nespyne*?" Spectra Pollux solicited.

"A new taste experience straight from the outposts of Kerskyne. It's a fermented herb with a flavor reminiscent of the *d'plyne* nut of Kerskyne's northern sector. Only without the gassy after-effects."

"Perfect!" said Spectra, her gown turning a pleased tulip pink. "Perfect!" More applause.

Rozz felt her face go hot.

Spectra Pollux sat back down with a rumble and swept up both of Rozz's hands in her own giant mitts. "You have great talent for this, Rozz. You must understand that. Do you? Do you understand it?"

"I'm a natural," Rozz said wearily.

It was the same phrase Spectra Pollux had said to her a million times these last days. Rozz wasn't sure which of them she was trying to convince more.

"You're a natural," Spectra Pollux agreed.

"She's a natural," the assistants echoed among themselves.

"But the problem is," continued Pollux, "you don't feel it. You don't feel it in here." She pointed.

"My upper GI tract?"

"Oh. Well, no." She lost her stride slightly with this miscalculation. "Your heart, Rozz. Wherever you Tryfe people keep your hearts." Spectra Pollux turned large, saddened eyes on her, like rain puddles forming in two great moon craters.

The assistants shook their heads sorrowfully.

"You still don't feel that this is what you were born to do," continued Pollux. "You don't see how important it is. If you did, you wouldn't have tried to run away twice now. And we wouldn't have been forced to fit you with…" She took in a hitching little breath. "…That."

She waved great log-like fingers at the stylish, implanted metal headband Rozz wore. A string of green lights twinkled from one end of it to the other prettily. That meant Rozz was staying within the sanctioned range.

It also meant she would not be receiving the paralyzing electric jolt to the cranium she experienced the one-and-only time she tested the range's boundaries.

Rozz understood the fashionable head-hobble could be surgically-removed from her skull by a certified security agent with a specialized tool. That's what Spectra Pollux said would happen if Rozz behaved. If she proved herself trustworthy. If she got with the program and worked harder to Be Her Best Her.

But the headband would never budge safely on its own. Rozz was convinced of that; a little experimentation with a makeshift pry-bar had left her one step from having some very serious ninth and tenth piercings. And unlike the others, these were holes she was pretty sure wouldn't just close up.

So when Plan Three—trying to stow away in a mootaab milk delivery hovercraft—had gone FUBAR, Rozz set her sights on Plan Four. This involved sucking down enough infopills so she could perform a do-it-yourself tiara-ectomy. Preferably without her brain leaking out the sides.

She just needed to be patient and bide her time.

"Oh, I *feel* it," Rozz responded, forcing a smile she hoped was winning. "I *do*."

More giggles and snickers from the assistants.

Pollux surveyed Rozz' face but looked unsure at what she saw there. "Well, I hope so, because we're running out of time for you to start feeling it, Rozz. We will present our plan for Tryfe in just three Universal days."

"The day after tomorrow, after tomorrow," Rozz murmured to herself. She had been wondering when it would be. Somewhere along the way, her time in the Pollux compound had lost all sense of duration. It shrugged off the past and turned away from the future. It was an infinite, relentless Now filled with queasy information supplements, a ceaseless flurry of hired helpers, celebrity visitors, and customer service limbo.

In the evenings, she'd go back to her comfortable but sparse guest room, entirely too tired to even cry about her fate. Not that Rozz had ever been much of a crier. But the widening disconnect between her current life and her true emotions, which she was apparently hiding somewhere in her upper GI tract, was starting to become a little disturbing.

"When people see the Pollux name, they expect big things, Rozz. Very big things," said Spectra in that smooth, monumental voice. It sounded like Hera giving a lecture to the Mount Olympus Women's Association.

"Big things," agreed one assistant.

"The biggest!" exclaimed another, pleased to get the last word in.

"So if we disappoint in three days…if we fail to wow them and secure this bid, well…" Spectra's gown had shifted from pink to purple, to eggplant to blue-black in a heartbeat. It had become storm clouds on a night sky. "I'm afraid it will be a black spot on the Pollux star. I'm afraid I'll have no further need for your services."

"And you'll send me home in shame," Rozz sighed, drenching her words in forlorn embarrassment. It captured the fear of that black spot blotting her own rising GCU career…The dread of returning to her home planet a failure…The guilt of dashing the hopes and dreams of a whole world of aspiring baristas.

But Spectra Pollux's response was unexpected. "Send you home?" she repeated meditatively, as if the words were in a strange, quaint tongue. A smile spread over the woman's broad visage, slow and dark like the storm clouds gathering on her dress. "Send you…home? Why, Rozz—where is the incentive for you if I did that?"

A chill ran up Rozz's arms, leaving a trail of goosebumps. It wasn't the words so much as the tone. A tone cold and distant as space itself. It said volumes and yet, it said nothing at all. And when Spectra Pollux then told her to, "Now just be a dear and pop onto the Uninet and see when that new shipment of *Leaf and Let Leaf* capsules would be arriving, there's my star," Rozz almost wasn't sure if she hadn't completely imagined it.

The voice was bubbly. The dress had gone a calm aqua blue.

Rozz nodded, rose and hit one of the LibLounge's Uninet terminals, her eyes once or twice returning to Spectra Pollux, docked there in that comfy armchair in her own personal café. She was decked in colors as warm and soothing as any Caribbean ocean and attending to bits of business with one of her select 37.

Rozz would ponder the exchange later in her room this evening, she promised herself. She would replay it and decide whether she had invested too much dark meaning in the fleeting look, the tone. Or whether for her own personal safety, Rozz Mercer needed to step up implementation on Plan Four.

"It'll be here this afternoon," Rozz told her, accessing the infopill system. "Along with Stella Cygnus' *Bibluciat Adoption Guide,* Jet Antlia's newest chapbook *One-Word Poems,* and Jor-Jan Chatta-Chu-Bular Meep-Meep's *Completely Unofficial, Unendorsed and Unintentional Autobiography: All About Meep-Meep.*"

"Stellar," the benefactress said, "Stellar! And how is my *Featured CapClub Feature-of-the-Day* being received by *Heavy Meddler* critics?" she asked. She asked this every day. Spectra Pollux had fleets of assistants circled around her, yet she always had Rozz check on the critics' warmth to each day's CapClub suggestion. She also had Rozz walk her pet zakari.

Rozz slung on her Inviz-i-lissin™ headset ("LibLounge Rule Number 15: Always respect LibLounge patrons' digestion and discussion by keeping your personal audio and video devices personal") and accessed the newsfeeds.

Box after video box popped up on the screen showcasing the events of the day. But where the thumbnail images were normally a diverse collection of hot topics from around the GCU—including the lady Pollux—now they appeared almost synchronized and cycled to different angles of one big event.

Or, rather, most of them were focused on a crowd of life-forms carrying picket signs. And highlighted in the center of that crowd, wearing a glaring, multi-colored hooded cloak, was a head-shot of the very familiar, very MIA, yet very much alive Bertram Ludlow.

"Ho—" erupted Rozz. She clamped a hand to her own mouth, before her full comment—dedicated to the sanctified spiritual properties of excrement—could violate LibLounge Rule Number 21: "The LibLounge is a family establishment. No vulgar language in any dialect is permitted, unless for artistic purposes or for edgy celebrity interviews."

Spectra and the 37 were staring. "Ho," Rozz said, putting on a smile. "Ho, ho. Very happy to see the positive buzz about today's CapClub recommendation."

She turned back to the screen and just caught the last half of the newscaster's report. "—Tryfling intergalactic fugitive, wearing the stolen clothes of his Popeelie victim, is believed to be a key player in the recent mass protests assembled in front of DiversiDine Entertainment Systems and Aeroponics on Ottofram."

The camera zoomed in closer on Bertram's face and split-screened it with some grainy, black-and-white security camera footage shot through metal jail bars.

Now this, thought Rozz, her fingers seizing tight on a nearby dish towel, *this was just too much.* Tryfling intergalactic fugitive Bertram Ludlow?! Was the universe completely unhinged?

"But while a fraction of the protest propaganda does bear a 'Life for Tryfe' theme, observers have noted the crowd's diverse and growing list of complaints with the Ottofram-based conglomerate. Various groups have stepped forward claiming responsibility for the 5,000-life-form-and-growing impromptu demonstration, from the Coalition for Non-Organic Rights and the United Smorg Growers Association, to the Wholly Disgruntled Labor Party and the Not-Quite-So-Disgruntled-But-Fairly-Annoyed Party of Workers. It seems the only group that actually hasn't taken credit for the chaos here on Ottofram today is the Intergalactic Underworld Society. Zenith Skytreg comments."

Here Zenith Skytreg, sitting in a Vos Laegos casino lounge with a heaped plate before him from the all-you-can-digest buffet, told the press, "It's not in the Underworld's best interests for DiversiDine production to be at a standstill. About 20% of our profits come from stolen DiversiDine goods. We have a team that specializes in it. We'd have to completely rethink our territorial piracy structure."

The broadcast cut to a life-form labeled, "Eudicot T'murp, CEO and Founder of DiversiDine Entertainment Systems and Aeroponics. "Today DiversiDine represents the same quality technology and freshly grown snack foods we have always been proud to offer. We are also aware of, and are currently in negotiations with, the Non-Organic Simulant leaders about their benefits concerns."

"What about Tryfe?" shouted a reporter in the press conference audience.

"I think GCU teenagers should stop buzzing it. It's unfair to the backspace life-forms. Thank you. No more questions, please."

Rozz disconnected from the Uninet and slipped off her Invis-i-lissin headset, hanging it back on the hook so she could find it again later, which was always an issue with these designed-to-be-transparent technologies.

She was lucky she could even think that far ahead, she considered; she felt like she was in a trance. Bertram Ludlow was not only alive and roaming the Greater Communicating Universe, he'd been in prison, somehow escaped and was now an intergalactic fugitive.

Back home, the guy thought a kooky evening out was pizza with extra cheese and two-for-one Happy Hour beer specials.

Of course, back on Earth, Rozz also could go where she pleased without electrocution to the head.

Travel changed you, she supposed.

But it all came down to this: Bertram Ludlow really was in outer space.

And he'd been hella busy.

19

"As I live and respire, I simply cannot believe you're here sitting in my copilot chair!" Xylith's right face gave a smiling sideways glance at Bertram as she directed the ship over Ottofram. From the cockpit window, Bertram could see the crowd growing and surging around DiversiDine headquarters. Media ICVs and law enforcement ships hovered like giant wasps over the executive hive. She twiddled fingers gracefully at him. "Harness up now. There might be a bump or two."

"Thank you for coming," Bertram said for the third time since he'd climbed up the collapsible ramp through the hatch. He slipped the chair's harness over his head and clicked it into place. "I didn't know what else to do."

"You surely have gotten yourself into one heap of trouble, haven't you?" she asked gently. Her tone said that it didn't bother her one bit.

"I had some help in that effort," Bertram told her. He held up the fast food bag he'd been lugging around since Mig Verlig. "I believe this is yours."

Her lavender eyes fell on it, and her right face gave a bemused eyebrow-raise. "Why, dear man, I'm afraid Entropy Burger and I have never quite seen eye-to-eye-to-stomach. But I thank you all the same."

He shook the bag, which gave a melodic, monetary jingle. "Even to feed your yoonie card? As I promised, when we spoke earlier."

"Ahh." The planet appeared to be shrinking under them. Bertram felt himself finally begin to untense at the growing distance. "About that," Zylith began, "how exactly did you find my vis-u connection?"

"Uninet directory assistance. A good old-fashioned name like 'Xylith Duonogganon' isn't as common on Dootett as it used to be," he said. Before hitting the right target, he'd made two erroneous connections to two very sweet elderly Xylith Duonogganons, one of which barely let him get off the vis-u and made him promise to comm again soon. The other was in the middle of a hot Emperor's G'napps game in the Upper Dootett Retirement Units.

This Xylith worked to hold back a smile. "Why, you were listening to my secret and very personal voting information back at the Underworld conference, weren't you? What a horrible invasion of privacy."

Bertram shrugged. "We both know I'm trouble."

"Oh, we do; indeed, we do." She adjusted one of the controls. "Speaking of which, just where has your help in the trouble department gotten to, anyway? Why isn't our Captain Tsmorlood taking you to... where'd you say you wanted to go again?"

"Blumdec."

She nodded and programmed something into the sleek console before her. "Why isn't our Captain Tsmorlood taking you to Blumdec, instead of me? Did that creaking container of metal he calls an ICV break down again? Why, once it left us high and dry on Vos Laegos and there weren't any replacement parts for it for simply *worlds* over. He claims it's 'rare.' Which, so far as I can tell, is code for 'discontinued for safety reasons.' But, of course, there's no telling *him* anything. Especially when it comes to things no one in their right mind would ever want, like dusty old print and creaky old ships and..." She paused for breath. "Did you say it broke down?" Her voice rippled with a gentile eagerness.

"I didn't say. But no." Something told Bertram he should tread lightly here. It was unstable ground, likely to shake out in almost any direction. "He, um, he wanted to lie low for a while. He's got some..." Bertram chose his words carefully, "...Altair-5 problems."

At this, both of Xylith's faces gave a huff. "Altair-5... Well, yes, he *would* have pushed the RegForce to send him to Altair-5, wouldn't he? I know *I* wanted to send him to Altair-5 a few times myself. Only *I* don't have the connections."

"Actually, there was a glitch in the system," Bertram told her. "He was supposed to have his archive blanked, but the Seers—"

She swiveled in the pilot's chair and faced him, doubly. Four-sets of eyes fell on him with interest. "And Rollie just dumped you off on Mig Verlig to take one of those germy Cosmos Corrals and navigate the ins-and-outs of the GCU all by yourself?" Bertram opened his mouth to speak, but she didn't give him the chance. "I don't know how he lives with himself. I know *I* couldn't." She sniffed derisively. "I don't suppose he said where he was going?"

"No. Just that he planned to lie low."

"Typical." She sniffed again, with both noses.

Bertram thought you've never really heard derision until you've heard it sniff with two noses.

On the tiny planet of Ejellan, the windows were dark at the Dax Q. Phlyjollee Traditional Public Library and Print Museum. Satchel slung over his shoulder, Rolliam Tsmorlood glanced at the sun, high in the sky above him, and frowned.

Midday, yet pitch black inside. Didn't bode well.

Rollie stepped onto the moving walkway leading to the library's door, but it didn't roll. It didn't budge. A sediment of mud, dust and weeds had caked itself into its crevasses. A family of hexabulons— an insect the size of a large Tryfan dog and with the multi-legged defense skills of Sum-Guy-Wowee Yup—had woven a canopy of silken threads spanning the streetlights lining the walk from the ICV park, all the way to the building's dome. The strands glistened with the sun behind them. The dome was further snaggled with a thick layer of enthusiastic vines.

Someone needed to take better care of this place, Rollie thought. That Phlyjollee wasn't getting his money's worth from his staff. Someone fragging-well needed to have a little chat with them about responsibility and maintenance and remind them just who was boss around here. Remind them whose planet this blasted-well was, why they were here, and who generously paid their salaries.

Of course, money was something of a sticking point right now, Rollie considered, as he strode manually toward the front door. He'd stopped to fuel his ship only to discover his yoonie cards—even the old ones he'd tucked away before his unfortunate confinement on

Rhobux-7—had all been sliced from the system. Invalidated. He'd cruised into Ejellan's atmosphere on fumes, and the fact he made it at all was pure, beautiful luck.

But it wasn't luck that Dax Q. Phlyjollee had some money stowed away. A few yoonie cards, a bit of good old-fashioned Deltan currency. That was planning. Enough tucked aside just for times like this.

Where Rolliam Tsmorlood had a criminal archive that could wrap around his home planet three times, Dax Q. Phlyjollee was a businessman and philanthropist with only hair-thin ties to the Intergalactic Underworld. Phlyjollee's only real crime was collecting, trading in, and housing the now-forsaken and, in some places banned and illegal, hard copy print. Hardly enough for the authorities to get their astro-togs in much of a bunch over. And as for those rabid Forwardist slaggards who wanted to incinerate anything that didn't come in capsule form, well, the planet of Ejellan only had the one thing on it: this library. No one else knew it was here, aside from his librarian and his handyman. And it was looking like they had forgotten all about it, too.

But someday, Rollie figured as he ascended the steps, someday print would become something life-forms would look back on more fondly. Not as something that held them back, but something they could hold. Right now they weren't ready. It was too close, too soon. But sometime, someday, he was convinced, print would have a comeback.

And Dax Q. Phlyjollee would be waiting.

But Rollie's alter ego was not the only one who waited this day. As he moved closer to the library, hexabulons descended from under the eaves of the entrance, graceful and sure. They made the eerily melodic *plunk-plonk-plank-plink*, like fingers dragging over the teeth of a Tryfan comb.

Rollie didn't know Hexabulese, but he had the gist.

He had woken them. They had woken cranky. And they were famished.

Rollie had read once that a single pinprick's worth of hexabulon poison, housed inside the sharp fine hairs on each of their legs, held enough toxins to fall a mathgar. They could extend those hairs upwards of four feet in order to reach and wrap around their prey.

Today, Rollie Tsmorlood wasn't in a touchy-feely mood. He drew his trusty XJ-37 hand-laser from its holster and fired.

One, two … splut, splut. The hexabulons dropped like leggy, furry rocks.

"Blasted shame," said Rollie to himself. "But there really is simply no getting on with some life-forms."

He stepped over their inert bodies and pushed open the library door. Another job he had to do by hand.

"Exterminator!" Rollie called down the library halls just for the sake of doing it. But the only answer he got was the echo of his own voice. Pausing, he manually clicked the light switch on and off. No change. The power was out.

"Miss Ungerblunger?" Rollie asked. He wondered if the hexabulons had gotten to Miss Ungerblunger; though, generally, they preferred already uninhabited places where they could really spread out. They did enjoy their privacy. In between meals, anyway.

He set the XJ-37 to flare mode and it broadcast a clean stream of golden light in the marble rooms.

No webs, Rollie noticed with some relief as he played the light around the ceiling. He'd half-expected a wave of hexabulons to surge at him like foot soldiers from the Feegar Rebellion.

"Miss Ungerblunger, I brought you some books to catalog," Rollie announced, swinging the satchel from his shoulder and onto the circulation desk. A cloud of dust stirred.

He coughed. He hadn't been in Rhobux-7 that long, had he? For the love of Karnax, couldn't a fellow spend a brief stint in confinement without everything back home going to muck?

"I'm docking your pay, Ungerblunger," Rollie said. "You and Mr. Shimnyplank. You're not pulling your own weight 'round here. And it's not as if I ask a lot. Acquire some books. Catalog some books. Be here for the mad rush when books go trendy again. Oh, and it *will* go trendy," he insisted to the darkness. "Once they wise up and see what's good for 'em. It will." It bothered him slightly that the lecture was all one-sided, but not enough to stop. He had spent a lot of time in solitary confinement over the years. "You could at least tidy up a bit. Hire someone when there's a hexabulon problem. That's fair."

He moved through the aisles of bookshelves. Every book had its own special tale of recovery, its own unique secrets to reveal in the reading. At the end of the row stood Dax Q. Phlyjollee's office. Dust coated the mouldings, cushioned the floor, and lined the glass door with his name on it, which was printed firmly in Hyphiz Deltan. He played the light around the room, to the Klimfal flag on the far wall.

The one he and his squad had won back from the Feegars right before they were overrun, and he was taken prisoner. It was a flag he managed to hold onto in spite of the days of torture...The gnashing Feegar teeth...The—

He approached the flag, lifted it and its accompanying blanket of dust, and dug into the hole in the wall behind it. There he found the yoonie cards, as predicted, and enough Deltan *shingee* for a comfortable cash backup.

"Gonna siphon some fuel from your ICV, Miss Ungerblunger," Rollie called into the blackness. "I'll return with enough to repla—"

Miss Ungerblunger was sitting in Dax Q. Phlyjollee's desk chair. Before her was a small, portable vis-u with Mr. Shimnyplank's contact information burnt forever into the now-dead screen. And from the looks of things, she'd been sitting there a very, very, *very* long time.

He groaned. "Frag it all, I am sorry, Miss Ungerblunger," Rollie told her sincerely. He played the light over her leathery skin, her dusty cloud of hair. This wasn't the way anyone looked who became a meal for the hexabulon. He was glad she hadn't gone that way, at least. "You were...getting on a bit...weren't ya?"

He hadn't considered it at the time, but Miss Ungerblunger had to have been pushing 300. And Mr. Shimnyplank wasn't exactly a prancing young mootaab, either.

"I'll make arrangements," Rollie promised, "soon." And considering the reality of it, of the invalid yoonie card as a dead giveaway to his general location, he added, "Else, I'll send you a souvenir from Altair." The RegForce had undoubtedly heard about his failed purchase. They would not waste any time. "So you'll wait here, Miss Ungerblunger?"

Miss Ungerblunger was good at waiting.

He nodded. "Right. Note to Mr. Dax Q. Phlyjollee: hire a younger librarian next time." He turned on a booted heel and pulled the door closed behind him. For some reason, the gesture seemed only proper.

"I really got to get my fragging archive blanked," he muttered, playing the laser light along his purposeful path to the exit. "All this running's getting cursed inconvenient. Now...who do I know that's keen with a hack?"

✧

"He tried to buy ICV fuel, eh?" said W.I. Tsmarmak Mook of the Hyphiz Deltan RegForce, eyeing the message on his pocket vis-u. "On Calderia-4, it appears."

"The Tryfling fugitive?" W.I. Tstyko asked. Curiosity animated his face. He stretched to glimpse his colleague's screen, which over-extended his grip on the wheel and wobbled their course. Even with the ship's sophisticated equalizers and pressure balancing capabilities, Tstyko's turn at the helm always made Mook feel just a tad space-sick. He wasn't sure how the man managed it with so much clever technology available to save him from himself. But there they were.

"No: Rolliam Tsmorlood," Mook responded. "Given the recent situation on Ottofram, it would seem that the Tryfling and Tsmorlood have parted ways."

"Calderia-4," Tstyko mused. "Population: 129 billion. Capital city: Blunk. Major export: a variety of very wholesome grains, many of which make tasty bread for the perfect mootaab cheese toastie. Also birthplace to Foobaz Frabblagundger and most of the members of Dumbbell Nebula." He flashed a grin, proudly. Tstyko's brain had categorized data on almost every planet in the GCU. Some people religiously memorized kachunkettball stats. Igglestik Tstyko absorbed general facts about the entire universe for fun. "What do you think Tsmorlood wants on Calderia?"

"Hard to say, but without the fuel, one would presume he didn't get very far." Mook tucked the vis-u into his uniform's breast pocket and smoothed his lapel. "Perhaps this will be his last stop before Altair-5."

"Altair-5," recited Tstyko thoughtfully. "Population… well, none at the mo', though that's subject to change certainly. Capital city…" Tstyko squinted, as if the consideration were part of a painful process. "Why, I don't believe I've ever heard it, have you, Mook? Everyone always just mentions the Tarpits. So Capital city: Tarpits. Major export?… Really, it's more of an import situation than export. In that, we send the unredeemable troublemakers there and, well, pretty much the Tarpits and the wildlife handle the rest. So, imports: prisoners. Exports: horrible, nightmarish fables I can use on the ol' progeny when they're in Naughtyland." He gave a self-satisfied nod. "Works like a dream at my home-unit, too, let me tell you! No toe out of line there."

"It's fortunate the RegForce has such comprehensive mental health coverage that extends to employees families," Mook responded.

Tstyko either didn't hear him, or the comment was unable to wedge its way through the extensive planetary trivia he carried in his brain. He went on, "To be honest, I've never dropped anyone off on Altair-5 before. You ever been there, Mook?"

"Once," Mook nodded solemnly, "many years ago. When I was new to the RegForce. And I've never forgotten it." Visions of the past swam before his mild gray eyes. "It was the day we dropped off Feg 'Tsarangees' Zastaran, the Madman of Hyphiz Beta."

"Oh, right. That fellow who tried to overthrow the system's Regimentation Schedule and hacked into the RegClocks."

The RegClocks kept the official Regimentation Schedule time for all the people of the Hyphiz-6 system, a reassuring, highly-honored expression of Hyphizite order, efficiency and everyone's tax dollars at work.

"Remember the mayhem in the streets?" Tstyko continued, licking his lips as he warmed to the subject. "For weeks no one knew whether it was time for mandatory recreation, scheduled productivity, or…" He waved vague, yet all-encompassing hand. "…Or, you know, what-not. I kept trying to sleep when I should have been out clubbing. My auntie went mad with unspent energy and knitted cozies for virtually everything in the home-unit. And my brother worked in the factory for five U-days straight, simply because the RegClock never told him it was time to return home. He nearly died of exhaustion. It was a very dark time to be a Hyphizite."

Mook nodded again. "With a black-hearted crime like that, Zastaran was destined for Altair-5. And so my superior and I were tasked to send him to his fate. The heat was so thick and oppressive we could barely push our way through it. Steam would shoot randomly from the ground, as if the planet itself were filled with rage. The Altairan sun beat with relentless, hateful fury. There were warm semi-acidic downpours. Carnivorous plants and dangerous beasts had evolved to thrive in these extreme conditions, and while we had only touched down on the planet's surface a moment, we could sense the creatures creeping forward. Waiting for the right moment. Determined to fight for any scrap of resources—namely us. Everywhere there was the stench of sulfur. On Altair-5, there is no shelter. No rest. And no peace."

"Not ideal for a Deltan complexion then." Tstyko held up a pasty pink hand.

"As always, my friend, you've come to the very crux of it," said Mook dryly.

"So how'd things go with Zastaran, then?"

"We left him. And as we flew away, we watched him—this Madman of Hyphiz Beta—as acidic rain misted down on him. After all that trouble he gave us, after remorseless interviews where he shouted he was glad of what he'd done and he'd do it again, I remember watching him stand there alone, weeping like a small child." Mook shrugged. "Until, of course, he was eaten by an Altairan daisy the size of a tree."

Tstyko gave a considering grunt and a shudder. "Grim stuff, that. A bit morally ambiguous in some ways, too, if you think about it. I mean, sending our baddies to Altair is economically-sound, but it's not exactly a testament for our own civilized society."

"Justice is a double-edged sword," Mook admitted.

"Or sometimes," said Tsyko, a sudden thought lighting his blue eyes, "a giant meat-eating daisy."

20

"Let's see... Take a generous dollop of disenfranchisement. Add a dash of common sense. Dump in a couple cups of inequity. Sift in some facts about Tryfe. Add a pinch of group psychology. Cut in some chilled moral outrage. Pour in lots of gooey empathy. And mix!" Bertram had carefully crafted his pro-Tryfe messaging, and now he hit the switch. The machine chugged and pumped and steamed with merry energy. It wasn't long before he could hear something rattle and roll within it. Then: plunk! At the bottom of the chute, one swirly blue-and-white capsule appeared.

"Your infopill is complete," announced the machine.

Bertram cheered. "Now let's make, oh, 1,000 more of these blue-and-white babies, and we're ready to rumble." He entered data, pushed a button and turned to Xylith. "This thing's amazing. Half of Blumdec will be on the 'Life for Tryfe' bandwagon in no time. Musca Mij isn't going to know what hit him. If we can get enough people across the GCU supporting Tryfe, it won't matter *who* owns the planet. No one will want to touch it within a hundred light years."

Both of Xylith's faces wore bemused smiles. "I must say, I've never seen such enthusiasm for the on-board infopiller before."

"Oh, come on, it must have changed the world of personal mass communications!" Bertram exclaimed.

One face looked like it wanted to agree, but the other was reluctant. "Well, they come standard. But mostly people just use them to infopill their annual holiday comms and share the kind of confused family histories relatives gift other relatives." She shrugged. "Pro-Tryfe propaganda's a real step up."

For a few moments, Bertram watched mesmerized as the infopill machine rolled out pill after pill into a sack.

"Now, have you thought about how you're going to make your grand appearance on Blumdec?" Xylith asked. "Given your face is famous, your holowatch granny has been busted, and your Popeelie robe is notorious?"

"No." Bertram eyed a garment bag in her hand with suspicion. "But I'm guessing you have."

Smiling, she unfastened the garment bag with a flourish, revealing what appeared to be a shimmery, armored rubber scarf. Her fluid wave of the hand meant to display it to its full effect. "What do you think?"

"It's cold on Blumdec?" Bertram asked.

"It's an invisibility suit," she explained.

"A suit?" Bertram gave it a second incredulous look. "That's a suit?"

"You simply turn it on, and then—see these small reflective plates? Each one moves with the intimate angles of your body to deflect your image and create the illusion you aren't even there." She fingered the plates to show him.

Bertram was more concerned about the object's noticeable lack of width. "You do know that your intimate angles are not the same as my intimate angles, right?"

"It takes some getting into, I admit," she said, handing him the garment. "But I've found it very reliable in a pinch."

Pinch would be the word. Bertram tugged at the springy armored fabric and winced along with his imagination. "Xylith, what is it you do in the Underworld, exactly?"

"Oh," she blushed, "the suit's from my Vos Laegos showbiz days. Part of an act I did long, long ago. But it still comes in handy now and again for other more…" she peered mischievously through dark lashes, "…interesting activities." As Bertram hung on her words, he reflected that Xylith Duonoggonon probably could make a ham sandwich sound mysterious and steamy if she wanted to.

She reached forward and, as if from his ear, produced three other shorter, somewhat knobbier tubes. "Don't forget the boots and mask now," she said. She tucked them in his hand and started to the cockpit.

He held up the three slim tubes. Which were the boots? Which was the mask? "Xylith," he called, "you don't really expect me to wear this, do you? I'll look ridiculous."

But she had vanished into the control room. "You'll look like nothing, Bertram. Just a ripple in the warm Blumdec air," came her voice. "Hurry now. We'll be landing soon. Blumdec's waiting."

✧

The jungle blossoms were bigger than Bertram's thoroughly-masked head, and fronds of ruffled vegetation swayed playfully over the winding path. Under the rustle of flora, and the tuneful whistle of fauna above, music and laughter flew free in the not-so-distant distance. From the brush came the irregular whirring and snipping of robot gardeners, carefully painted in camouflage and garnished with twigs. The occasional insect buzzed by but never bit or stung. The e-brochure explained that all insects had been genetically mutated in this manner, for visitor convenience.

This was the Blumdec Grand Mij Hotel and Resort: "The only place in the Universe destined to live up to your completely unrealistic expectations." Xylith had assured Bertram that if Musca Mij were somewhere on Blumdec, this—the jewel of his marketing empire—was where they would find him.

Bertram peered over Xylith's shoulder at the map. "You're sure we're on the right path?"

"Well, the concierge did say Mr. Mij was just headed beachside." She pursed two sets of lips thoughtfully. "Also said something about 'extras,' but I didn't quite catch the whole thing, did you?"

He gave a negative shake of his head as she trailed a finger over their route. "See, here's the back lobby. Then we passed the holoparlors, the hands-free massage hut, the upside-down singing fountains, the upper pool, lower pool, gene pool, and now the regulation-size kachunkettball courts." She pressed a button on the map's surface.

The Map said, "You are here," and highlighted their location. "You are approaching the Blumdec Grand Mij Hotel and Resort's critically-acclaimed beach, the Purple Pleasure Lagoon, renowned galaxy-wide for its beautiful violet sand substitute."

"See? We're almost there." She inhaled deeply. "And my, would you just *smell* those flowers? The aroma is simply intoxicating!"

"You are correct!" affirmed the Map happily. "The flowers located around our award-winning grounds have been genetically adjusted to give guests a perfectly safe, perfectly balanced buzz of contentment throughout their stay."

"How darling!" exclaimed Xylith with delight, clearly starting to feel the effects of the flora.

"How seriously inconvenient," Bertram corrected, shooting her a look. "Xylith, how the hell are we going to get anyone willing to take up the 'Life for Tryfe' 'cause if everyone's..." he searched for the right word, "...mellow?"

She blinked two sets of lavender eyes. "Beg pardon?"

"I'm talking about outrage, Xylith. Disenfranchised outrage. That's why the 'Life for Tryfe' picketing worked so well on Ottofram. Everyone felt alienated and unequal. Where's the inequity here, Xylith? Where's the outrage? We're surrounded by engineered non-stinging bees and opium air-fresheners, for God's sake! It's completely..." he grabbed the first word he found, "...enfranchised. We can't get a movement going if everybody's feeling enfranchised. And I don't think snack cake bribes are going to work on this crowd. They're swank. They eat regularly."

Xylith sank down on a nearby bench in sudden understanding. The Map piped up that the bench had been designed for ergonomic comfort and placed for its spectacular jungle view.

"Well, doesn't that just frag all?" she groaned drowsily. "And to think we spent time whipping up these 'Life for Tryfe' infopills for nothing." She nudged the bag of pills resentfully with a foot. "Not to mention all the time you spent getting into your stellar little suit."

Ah yes, thought Bertram, *the suit*. So far, the invisibility suit had done its duty for the intergalactic fugitive-on-the-go. But its sweating, chafing, numbing, oppressive encasement had proven to be all Bertram had anticipated, and more. The ski-mask hood was certainly interesting; to see where he was going, he chose from two sets of eyeholes. And the matching boots? They had to be abandoned altogether; the Dootett foot, female *and* male, apparently not only had arches, but flying buttresses and domes, too. He would have been crippled in under a mile. So Bertram's feet now walked forward sandaled and fancy-free.

So far, no one seemed to notice the free-range feet strolling the grounds. But that was probably more about the engineered mellow than any keen fugitive stealth. At least, Bertram considered, the mask did filter out The Grand Mij's heady pollens. Much as he would have enjoyed wasting away in Bouganvillaville, the Earth wasn't going to save itself. It took a clear brain to devise a new gameplan.

"Let's go," said Bertram after a moment.

"Where?" Xylith asked his feet.

"The beach," Bertram replied. "If I want to make any headway, I'm going to have to put some backbone into this. And though I can't currently *feel* my backbone... hey, I'm here, Mij is here. He and I need to talk."

Sea-salted wind blew gently against Bertram's invisibility mask, while waves rolled neatly against the glossy plum sands and polished pebbles of the shore. Lush alien trees swayed in motions precisely conducive to relaxation. The breeze was ideal. The waves were right for the watersports. The famous purple sand substitute empowered the progeny with imaginative alien housing complexes. The sun didn't even scorch. Local sunbathers were leaping up and scattering—not because of its harmful rays, as there were none—but because of three caterpillar-wheeled vehicles that were just now plodding toward them like giant migrating seaslugs.

In a moment, a Mathekite emerged from the first off-road machine. He was dressed in tropical clothing and a hat that let his antennae poke through jauntily. "That's our man of the hour," Xylith whispered.

Musca Mij spoke into a sound projection device strapped around his waist. "Hey everybody!" he greeted the beach dwellers. "Don't mind us. We'll be practically invisible. Just continue with whatever you're doing." He motioned to the beings in the cruisers. "All right, guys! Haul in the cables!"

In mere moments, huge lenses had been assembled, artificial lighting was moved in, and extension cords criss-crossed the sand. "Now, I need a few volunteers," said Mij to the crowd. "Sex! Let's start with sex." He pointed at a sunbathing greenish being who blinked with surprise. "You. I need you to hold this phallic bottle of tanning oil and say, 'I never tanned this well on my home planet.' Go ahead; say it."

"I'm not here to tan," explained the being in a somewhat injured tone. "I'm photophyllic."

"You want to be immortalized in my next time-share ad or not?"

"I never tanned this well on my home planet," the being said, with a toss of the head and a caress of the bottle of tanning oil.

"Cut! Very nice," said Mij. "Next! Progeny, we need some progeny in this thing. Close up on that kid over there." The director knelt by an Ottoframan child. "All right, kid. What I want you to say is, 'I could play in this sand substitute all day,' and then Mom—" He pointed to a nearby Ottoframan woman. "You Mom?"

The young woman looked startled. "Sister."

"*I'm* the boy's maternal archetype." An older Ottoframan woman in a silvery mu-mu stepped forward.

"Yeah, sorry, not right for the part." Mij turned back to young lady. "Okay, Big Sis, you're going to pretend to be this boy's maternal archetype."

"But, I—"

"Look, I know, I know. Awkward for you; smart casting for me. Work with it... Okay, so when the kid says his line, you laugh. And you say, 'And sand substitute doesn't stick to your feet and towels like non-engineered sand.' Okay? Go."

She said her line like a professional.

"Great. Cosmic. Moving on." Here the Mathekite buzzed back to the vehicle. He withdrew a slim, aerodynamic-looking board and then buzzed over to Xylith and Bertram.

"You, Doll-faces, you look like you work-out." This was addressed to Xylith. "You're going to hold this Blumdecian WaveMaster 5000 SuperSport Ultra-turbo Mega Skimmer, and do you know what your line is? Your line is, 'And when the public beaches get too crowded, I always have room to skim the waves here.'"

Before Xylith could respond, Mij had snatched the Map and bag out of Xylith's hands, and thrust them at a roadie. Then he tucked the wave skimmer into her arms and fluttered back to the camera. "Okay... action!"

"Er... 'And when the pub—'"

"Hold it, hold it!" shouted the director, dashing into view. "Cut! Cut! What are these... *things*..." he waved several hands emphatically, "doing in my shot? These... these..."

"Feet?" Xylith supplied, peering down on the unattached pair of peds waiting at her side.

"Right. Is this a place for feet? Is this a time for disembodied body parts? This is about buying a timeshare on Blumdec that makes all of your biggest, most lavish vacationing dreams come true for one low, low price. And standalone feet don't say lavish dreams to me."

"It might if you were a foot fetishist," Xylith suggested, hopefully.
"True, but I gave up that kind of film-making long ago," he replied, shaking it off. "So let's get 'em outta here, people! They're cluttering up my paradise."

It was just as the Mathekite's roadies moved to declutter paradise that Bertram Ludlow found himself quickly calling out, "Musca Mij, are you trying to buy the planet Tryfe?"

The roadies paused. They looked around, exchanged glances, and scratched their heads.

"Aw, geez," sighed Mij, turning to address the voice. He, too, searched, puzzled, for the source of the sound. Finding none at eyelevel, his large multi-facted eyes went immediately to the beach clutter. "Look, I don't know who or what you are, but we're burning daylight here, kiddos. So take a hike."

"I'm with the *Heavy Meddler*," Bertram announced. "And I think the public deserves answers about this 'Life for Tryfe' business."

"I happen to *run* the *Heavy Meddler*," Mij said leaning down. He directed his comments to Bertram's right big toe. "Meaning, *I* pay *you*. So why don't you hot-foot-it off my beach and go kick up a nice Stella Cygnus piece for me back at the station? Much obliged."

"Who owns Tryfe now?"

The Mathekite gave a huff that smelled like old vegetables and fish. "Do I know? Look, Alternate Realty said if I wanted the property, I needed to present my ideas. So I'll present. I don't know who I'm presenting to. And I don't give a flying fraxbat who it is. Either you embrace MetamorfaSys Inc.'s vision of 'more is never enough,' or you don't. It's no hair off my antennae. Is this," he pointed, "some kind of medical condition you got there or—"

"I'm undercover. *Way* undercover," said Bertram.

He nodded. "You missed a spot."

Bertram pressed on, "When is the presentation? What do you plan to do with Tryfe? What about the people living there already? Aren't you concerned about what happens to their culture? Their environment? Life As They Know It?"

Musca Mij's laugh buzzed with amused exasperation. "Look…I admire your mandibles, kid, I do. You got some big ones. But you're bordering on professional insubordination here. In fact, your big toe is on the far line of that border. So let me offer you some friendly advice; take a long walk, Big Toe. While you still have a job to run back to. Now shoo." He waved two sets of arms.

"Don't you care that billions of lives are in your hands?" Bertram continued. "That you could trigger the end of the whole Tryfling race? That you'll probably be branded a backspace slumlord?"

By now, the roadies were rolling up their sleeves and moving in to declutter, so Xylith tugged where she thought Bertram's own arm might be. "Come on," she pleaded with him. "Just leave it be. There's nothing more we can do here."

"I'd listen to the lady if I were you, Big Toe," Mij said. "Progress marches on. I suggest you march along with it."

Finally, with a scowl Mij couldn't see, Bertram gave in to Xylith's tugging grasp. They were a few paces down the path, when the Mathekite called, "And by the way, kid: nice AirChamps® sandals."

"Yeah, thanks," Bertram grumbled. "Thanks a lot."

"Okay," shouted the Mathekite to his people, "moving on. Bring in this year's Ms. Big Dippers pageant contestants! And animals! We need fuzzy animals! Let the Argonian snoogle out of its cage!"

Everyone on the beach cooed. Bertram realized Xylith had been right. It was good they got out of there when they did.

21

"So T'murp's hiding in his glass tower over labor issues, while our friend Mij has no idea who he's presenting to and isn't really bugged about it."

Back on Xylith's ICV, the brief image of Musca Mij, with his big iridescent eyes and his many arms and shiny wings, crossed Bertram's mind. He chuckled. "Bugged." A slip of the invisi-suit turned the laughter into, "Ow."

"Do you need help in there?" Xylith called, sounding concerned.

"I'mfinedon'tcomein." He'd been talking to Xylith through the ship's lavatory door, less from modesty than the lack of suavity found in birthing yourself from a giant rubber glove covered in sharp reflective plates. Every tug, every pull, had potential for strain, abrasion and laceration.

He cleared his throat. "So next steps: I was thinking we could send our infopills to every news station in the GCU and—"

"Which infopills are these?" asked Xylith lightly.

"What do you mean?" Bertram had managed to extract his arm from the suit. The sleeve left his hand with a sharp, cringe-worthy snap. "The ones we made for Blumdec. The ones we never used. A thousand of those blue-and-white beauties, ready and waiting to share Tryfe's plight with the disillusioned masses. A thousand should be enough, right?"

"A thousand of them sitting on the purple sand substitute of Blumdec in the perfectly-controlled sunshine, you mean," Xylith said.

Arm Two would have come free more easily, Bertram considered, if only he could have unscrewed it at the elbow. "We lost the infopills?" he asked. With Bertram invisible, they'd agreed it would be somewhat less-obvious if Xylith carried the bag.

"They took them from me, remember? Mij or his roadies or someone. I don't know, I was trying to concentrate on the lines Mij gave me for that timeshare infomercial. And then, well, it all happened so fast." Her voice sounded strained. "I think it was those horrible genetically-engineered flowers; I don't *want* to be in Uninet commercials, Bertram."

The suit was now past the main danger zones and heading kneeward. "We can always make more infopills," Bertram assured her.

"Yes, but there aren't enough supplies for another thousand."

Bertram looked up from the fabric bunched around his ankle. "How many?"

"Two hundred. Maybe less. I'd used up quite a few with my last Underworld PR announcement."

Bertram nodded and turned back to the suit. Slowly, painfully, he teased the fabric into descent, taking some leg hair and skin cell casualties along the way until SNAP! He flinched and examined his ankle.

The reflectors had left tiny red welts. Catching his breath, he asked her "Could we get supplies?"

"We could."

"Maybe we'd better plan on it, then." Satisfied by this simple solution, Bertram seized the fabric around the second ankle. His physical strength was waning, yes, but he was determined to give it his all. He summoned his energies in one last move toward total invisi-suit liberation and—SNAP!

Bertram cried out and fell backwards onto the floor.

"Bertram! Bertram!" shrieked Xylith at the door. "Are you all right? Should I fetch the on-board Simmi-Doc? What was that noise?"

"The sound of freedom, Xylith," he gasped, rising to his feet. The suit now lay like a shed snake-skin on the cold metal floor. He reached for his street clothes, which waited welcomingly in a nearby pile, but the movement dislodged something tucked into his duds like a waiting grenade.

Across the floor rolled the Yellow Thing.

"Freedom does tend to favor sacrifice," responded Xylith's voice. "Are you sure you don't want the Simmi-Doc? It's no problem. It's in the utility room all charged up. I'll dust it off."

Bertram paused and frowned at the door. "You keep a Simulant doctor locked up in your utility room? Is that even legal?" On the heels of the Life for Tryfe movement, Bertram was gaining a healthy new respect for the plight of the average GCU Simulant.

But Xylith just gave an impatient sigh. "Oh, it's not like it's a full Non-Organic with personality and empathy programs or anything, Bertram. Just a low-level gadget model with simple first aid capabilities and—"

The Yellow Thing... The Simmi-Doc... There was something about the combination that united in Bertram's mind and struck him harder than the snap of an Invisi-suit pantsleg. "Xylith," Bertram almost couldn't breathe with the idea, "where did you say your Simulant friend with the thrill issues lived?"

"Who, O'wun? He's living on Ludd. And I assure you, the Simmi-Doc is nowhere *near* as advanced as O'wun, I—"

Bertram was leaping into his jeans. "And do you know what building? And how to get there?"

"Sure, I've been there a couple of times. I—"

Through t-shirt fabric he said, "And you'd said he has access to information? That he's tapped into systems and might be able to tell us what the Yellow Thing is? Might be able to track down records on Tryfe's sales history, maybe?"

"Why, I don't know," she said honestly, "but I have seen him hack into complex systems that surely did seem impossible. He was always up on the very latest technology. Until he moved to Ludd, anyway."

Bertram exited the lavatory. He never thought he'd be so glad to wear jeans and a t-shirt again. They'd journeyed all over space, so they stank a bit; but they stank in an empowering way he hadn't appreciated before. He handed her the invisibility suit, which had gained a fragrance all its own.

Xylith wrinkled her nose. "I'll just have this sent out," she said, tucking it quickly into a chute in the wall.

"Nevermind that." Bertram was guiding the Dootett lady to the cockpit door. "We need to go to Ludd. Right away. The Seers told me I'd know what the Yellow Thing was when I needed to know; I've waited long enough. How fast can this thing fly?"

Surprise and delight marked the expressions on her faces, like they'd both been waiting for just this kind of opportunity. "Funny, but I've never really pushed this ship of mine much." She stroked the cockpit doorway affectionately. "So let's just see what this ICV can do, shall we?"

✧

"Life for Tryfe! Life for Tryfe!" The *Heavy Meddler* newscast cycled footage of the dueling protests on Ottofram, with a "Life for Tryfe" beach party bonfire sing-along that had just erupted on Blumdec.

Apparently, a bag of infopills from an unknown source fell into the hands of a film crew working on Musca Mij's new timeshare ad. It was sampled, passed around, and somehow made its way to the beach-going guests of the Blumdec Grand Mij Hotel and Resort.

The infopills contained messaging about how disrespect for Tryfe, its people and their quaint, backspace way of life revealed just a slice of the greater inequity in the GCU. The message said Tryflings stood as a living metaphor of the prejudices, struggles and disappointments life-forms faced across the universe daily.

"We're all Tryflings in our own way," the pill imparted.

This spirited and enlightening concept rolled around in the hearts and minds—or more specifically, in the bloodstreams—of the hotel patrons. Some found themselves touched by it during their hands-free massages. Some were transformed by the idea at their gene therapy appointments. And many digested its ramifications during their post-lunch, pre-dinner buffets.

So by the end of the day, at the Grand Mij Resort's evening barbecue, the resort's guests enjoyed grilled-to-perfection Blumdec cuisine, artfully-decorated drinks, and felt moved to share their own unbearable lives of neglect, inequity and dashed hopes. They told tales of hearts-wrenching disappointment in the quality of upholstery in their much-anticipated Quasar-57 Luxury ICVs...The unrelenting anguish of their progeny not getting into the proper Uninet academies without extra, costly infopill supplements...And the eternal woe of being unable to find adequate Non-Organic Simulant housemaids these days that didn't want outrageous benefits packages.

Just *everyone* had weighty personal torments they wanted to get off their chests.

And it was as the fourth round of Purple Pleasure Perfection Punch hit their systems, that a few brave sympathizers even began to improvise with pro-Tryfe protest tunes.

It wasn't long before the music grew enthusiastic, competitive, and the media was there to catch all the action.

From his Vos Laegos Underworld office, Zenith Skytreg watched this display for just about as long as he could bear. Then he withdrew the exquisitely designed hand-laser from the finely hand-tooled holster at his side and aimed it at his holovision.

"This—" ZAP! "—is not—" ZAP! "—the way—" ZAP! "—it's supposed—" ZAP! "—to go!" he shouted. He smiled with satisfaction as the holovision smoked in a flickering orange ruin.

Two former Vos Laegos showbeings, who now worked for Skytreg's Underworld branch, ran in with fire quellers to tame the blaze.

Skytreg took a sip of his smooth Feegar bourbon.

Yes, the sale of Tryfe was supposed to be a quiet little transaction. One that Zenith himself could then blow into a nice, controlled media frenzy when he was good and ready. He had planned to be the shining hero poised to bring the backspace planet into the GCU fold. To ease the planet forward with his hand-picked redevelopment plan. Also, to get the fast yoonies from the sale to pay off some unexpectedly sizeable personal debts he'd incurred. Debts brought about by unfortunate circumstance and what could *only* have been a crooked dealer on the gaming tables that night.

He'd already shifted some the Underworld sponsor money to cover it. But it wouldn't be long before someone caught on to that. Rentar Proximetra had been named Underworld Treasurer for this coming year, and that woman was a stickler for flawless book-keeping.

She wasn't known for her sense of humor, either.

But now this "Life for Tryfe" foolishness had been stirred up and seemed to be spreading like a Simmiparlor virus. There was a leak somewhere, and an unhappy, very vocal Tryfeman was adding undue complexity to the matter.

While the situation, thankfully, hadn't happened before his re-election, Zenith Skytreg now wouldn't have the chance to set the tone for the announcement about Tryfe's sale and redevelopment. Instead, he was put in the position of doing damage control. And that, like knockoff Gapoochi spaceboots, just wasn't his style.

The fire was almost out now. Just a thin flicker of flame gasped under the layers of quelling powder, soon to die out. Perhaps the same could happen with this ridiculous "Life for Tryfe" business. If he could get some of his people to track down the Tryfeman and toss enough of the right metaphorical quelling powder on him... Well, Zenith Skytreg imagined the GCU would soon forget about such Tryfling concerns.

If there were anything he'd learned since entering Underworld politics it was that the GCU had an advantageously short memory.

Eudicot T'murp entered the conference room to see a large crowd of Making Things Up folks gathered around the holovision in rapt attention. Some life-forms were cross-legged on the floor. Some had pulled up cushions from the brainstorming room's sofa. And others were perched on the conference tabletop. They passed around a bowl of Sleemy Snaps. A refreshments robot made rounds with cold beverages.

For a while, the shot on the holovision screen had been at a strange angle, focusing on what appeared to be the wall of a nicely-appointed ICV bathroom.

Now it displayed a control room console and a moving starscape.

"How's it going?" T'murp asked.

"The Tryfling's on his way to Ludd," the head of Making Things Up said, offering T'murp the snack bowl.

T'murp politely declined. "Ludd? What's on Ludd?"

"Bertram Ludlow has a line on someone who could tell him about the Yellow Thing," said the Making Things Up assistant-manager. "He wants to dig up Tryfe's sales history to find its owner."

T'murp smiled at the Tryfling's undaunted spirit. "Poor, confused Tryfe kid. If it were that easy to get Tryfe's details, we'd have had that information ourselves U-days ago." He took a seat. "But you have to admire his optimism. Is there any chance of his 'expert' giving him good information about the Yellow Thing? Our Tryfling friend finds out it's a camera, and our show's likely to get a very abrupt ending."

"That kind of technical expertise on Ludd? Very slim," said the Making Things Up head.

The refreshments robot was tugging T'murp's pantleg and brandishing an assortment of DiversiDine-bottled juice choices.

"No, thank you," T'murp told it and rising, he addressed the manager. "Looks good. Nice job so far. Just keep an eye on it for me," he said.

"For you, Mr. T'murp, I'll use all six."

22

From the air, it looked like a crazed Renaissance faire had attacked some major U.S. city, usurped power, and called in a decorator. But such was Ludd's capital of Mallitt. Every building and skyscraper stood resilient in tiered and chiseled stone blocks. The roofs were thatched. Hand-sewn streams of pennants spanned the streets. The roads were cobble. The world was strangely quiet.

Xylith set the ICV down in a nearby field where trusting locals had parked their wagons. The only life in view was a bridled, segmented animal with six great thick legs and a back-end that looked identical to its front. It reared and shrieked as they stepped from the spacecraft, but it calmed as Xylith spoke sweetly to it and patted its hard-shelled back. It nuzzled her, pincers clicking happily.

They moved down the stone walkways like sole survivors of apocalypse, yet a brief slam of a shutter, or eye through a knothole signaled life did exist within.

Soon they reached the door of the Fezziwig Towers, an ornate, elegant example of Mallitt's architecture, and at its threshold, Xylith came to a sharp halt.

"What's wrong?" Bertram Ludlow was poised for new danger.

But staring at the entrance, Xylith's laugh bubbled up with embarrassment. "Oh, I keep forgetting. This is one of those interesting old manual doors." She pressed on the entry, and nearly toppled into the room as the doorman, who'd just come off break, rushed to let her in.

The lobby of the Fezziwig Towers was a highly decorative room. It was covered in hand-painted murals of everyday Ludd life, rich hand-carved woodwork, and blown glass lanterns crafted in the shape of local fauna. These last items bobbed like crystalline piñatas overhead.

O'wun's apartment was one of two penthouse suites. They reached his floor by an elevator controlled by pulleys and counterweights. A cheerful hand-painted sign with delicate curly lettering translated to read, "Max weight: 433 toks. Mind the gap."

As they stepped onto O'wun's floor, Bertram could hear the chatter and the music from stringed instruments twanging down the hall. The door was open, and Luddites laughed and ran from one suite to the next, while the party overflow mingled in the hallway. The inhabitants' clothes were brightly colored, painted, and beaded. They sipped from pottery cups.

As Bertram and Xylith passed, judgmental eyes fell on the lady in her metallic, non-natural fibers. Xylith noticed it, too. "Let's just find O'wun and get out of here," she muttered. "I forgot there's an unofficial dress code."

Inside, guests sat around a large sunken fireplace, where the loin of a once-great alien beast turned slowly on a spit, juices dripping, sizzling and smoking in a salivation-worthy reverie. A group of musicians played local instruments, while a swaying, giggling audience sang. All enjoyed ladled drinks of some thick liquid from a large blue kettle settled on one side of the room. Some danced.

Xylith scanned the room for familiar faces, but settled for tapping a tall stranger on the shoulder. "Excuse me, have you seen O'wun?"

The man turned. He was a sturdy middle-aged man with sandy brown hair that waved confidently over his brow. His jaw was as chiseled as the Towers' stone walls. And there was something so ... familiar ... about his gestures and features, thought Bertram. Yet he couldn't quite place it.

"Well, hello there!" The man was certainly eyeing Xylith up and down appreciatively. "Lucky me. Here an out-of-this-world celestial body comes looking for O'wun, but she feels my own powerful gravitational pull first." He broke out in laughter.

Bertram thought Xylith seemed to be resisting the guy's applied physics just fine. Her expressions had the planetary weight of Deeply Unamused.

The man cleared his throat. "O'wun's gone to the greenhouse for polegrots," he finally explained. "You know what they say: 'a party's not a party without plenty of polegrots.'" The man let out another explosion of hearty, manic laughter. "He should be back soon."

Bertram was still struggling with who on earth this guy was and why he seemed so familiar. The guy turned to Bertram. "Hey," he greeted. "You're a Tryfling, too, aren't you?"

And then Bertram remembered: Earth! Sure the face was different, older, more careworn, perhaps. But a decade ago, that face had been on the nightly news for months. It was a face emblazoned in the minds of millions of Americans. Yet it couldn't be possible that same face was here, now. Could it? "Is that...*you*...Modean?" Bertram breathed.

At Bertram's words, the face lit like rocket fuel. "Well, if that isn't just a blast from backspace. Someone remembers!" he exclaimed and snapped to attention. He gave a little salute. "Major Thomas D. Modean. Pleased to meet you, fellow Tryfe Human. And you are...?"

"Ludlow, Bertram Ludlow." Modean's handshake was like still-warm steel.

"And who is this shining star at your side, Bert?"

"Bertram," Bertram corrected.

The astronaut had turned a beaming white smile on Xylith.

"This star is shooting. Out of this atmosphere. For less charted territories. Pardon me." She indicated the drinks kettle and extracted herself.

Major Modean paused to admire her as she left. "Hard to tractor beam; I *like* it. Sleemy Snaps?" He offered a bowl of crunchy-looking green spirals.

Bertram shook his head. "So what actually happened to you on that spacewalk? There was this weird flash of light and you were just...gone."

"Ah. Yes." The man's voice became suddenly heavy and his cheek gave a nervous tic. "I guess it all started when the equipment I was trying to repair exploded. The impact took out my tether and jammed the SAFER joystick." His eyes gained a faraway expression. "No matter what I tried, I could not get myself turned in the right direction. Then the SAFER's jets failed. Before I knew it, I was drifting...falling...floating weightless...farther and farther away from the capsule." Bertram knew all this from the NASA footage, but he didn't want to interrupt. "Years of intense training, and still there was nothing I could do," Modean continued. "It was my biggest nightmare, come-to-life. In fact, I still wake up in a cold sweat dreaming about it." The astronaut brought the pottery cup to his lips with a shaking hand and took a long, restorative drink.

"But the weird flash of light," Bertram pressed.

"Qwaybop teenagers on a joyride to Tryfe," answered Modean. "Pure luck they saw me and gave me a lift." He gulped down the rest of his punch and slung his cup onto a nearby table. "I've been knocking around the GCU ever since."

"We mourned you as a nation," Bertram informed him. "You're on a collector's stamp."

"Cosmic," Major Modean said, but that may have been about the four-breasted blue woman who passed by.

Bertram struggled not to stare himself. "So, um," he cleared his throat, "what brings you to Ludd?"

"Well, I've already done the GCU tourist thing. Experienced the... the wonders." Modean's eye twitched again, and he turned the full force of his gaze on Bertram. One pupil, Bertram noticed, was slightly bigger than the other. "But Ludd is simple. Ludd is pure. On Ludd, I don't have to touch anything that will jettison or explode. On Ludd, Barry..." He latched a hand painfully onto Bertram's shoulder, "on Ludd, I feel at home."

"Bertram," Bertram mumbled, taking a step back. "But what about Earth? Earth is simple, and you'd get a hero's welcome. We still have anniversary tribute specials for you that interrupt regularly-scheduled programming and stuff. People care."

"Go back? To Tryfe?" Tom Modean mused. "Oh, I've thought about it, Bernard. I've thought long and hard. But for me, Tryfe is a lot like a high school reunion. Sure, part of you might want to try to rekindle those old flames and stir up those old memories. But *should* you?"

The blue woman was eying him with interest from across the room. Modean gave her a salute. "Oh yes, I've known the GCU. I could return and share my knowledge with the people of Tryfe. But why disrupt their blissfully ignorant lives? No, I'll stay here where things so rarely explode or jettison. I'll keep my wisdom to myself. I consider that my final gift to them."

"Well, you do realize that bliss may not last much longer," Bertram pointed out. "It's all over the Uninet; Tryfe's being sold for redevelopment any time now."

"I don't have the Uninet. Or a holovision. Or a vis-u. Or anything mass-produced that could potentially jettison or—"

"Explode?" suggested Bertram, but Major Modean was now giving the blue woman his best "come hither" glance.

"All that's not really not a part of Ludd's…orbit…you know?" concluded Modean. He took an appetizer off a tray someone offered. "No: here, it's about calm, connecting and creativity. We paint, we sculpt, we build, we blacksmith, we farm. In fact, I've got myself a great crop of whizzly leaf growing this year and, come harvest, you won't *believe* the party we're going to have. As the kids say: 'supernova!'" He nudged Bertram with an elbow. "Consider yourself invited, Bart."

"Bertram. Look, Major Modean—"

"Tom. Or Tommy. Or Toe-MAHS, if you get launched by the exotic. I get launched by the exotic."

"—You could be a big asset to Tryfe right now," Bertram persisted. "You know people in the GCU. You could make them listen. By joining me in speaking up for our home planet, you could help me preserve it."

But the astronaut was now holding up and admiring a hand-crafted fruit bowl from a nearby end table. "You ever weave a Luddite basket, Barton? You just haven't relaxed until you've woven a basket in the traditional Luddite style of weaving. I never felt such peace and focus until the day I wove a traditional Luddite basket. It's like having the threads of the cosmos right in your hands."

There was a gentle touch at Bertram's elbow, and he saw Xylith had returned to his side.

"Major Modean isn't operating on all rockets these days," Bertram told her in a low voice.

But Xylith just pointed to the penthouse doorway. "O'wun."

And Bertram noticed a tanned, middle-aged man with a receding hairline enter. He carried a basketful of something that looked like budding prickly-pear cactus without the spines. At the sight of him, the party-goers cheered.

O'wun smiled at the crowd and nodded his appreciation—a smile that transformed into delighted recognition as Xylith came to view. "Xylith! I didn't know you were coming to the party. I'll put these in the Food Preparation Room and be out in just a—"

"O'wun, we need a favor," she said and ushered him into the kitchen, Bertram at her heels.

"We?" He set down the veg with a thump. Turning, his eyes fell on the Earthman.

"O'wun, this is my new friend, Bertram," Xylith said.

Bertram gave a friendly nod.

The Simulant's first response was an abrupt laugh. "Ah, so does the Captain know about your 'new friend'?" O'wun rolled the polegrots into a sink and pumped water over them. "And if not, " he looked up, grinning all too organically, "can *I* tell him?"

"Why, you really do have thrill issues, don't you?" Xylith said, shaking her head. "Yes, Captain Tsmorlood knows Bertram. In fact, I wouldn't even be here if our mutual friend, the Captain, had done the decent thing in the first place, and even remotely bothered to—" She stopped herself, closed two sets of eyes in self-reminder and held up her palm. "No. Nevermind. This is not the time." She looked at O'wun. "So about this favor."

"Anything. You name it. Hand me that knife, please?"

She did. "Bertram is from Tryfe. And I imagine you've heard all about how poor little Tryfe is being sold and redeveloped with innocent backspace people still living on it."

"Actually, I haven't." He sliced the succulent thin, each slice the same perfect thickness as the other slices. "I don't have the Uninet. Or a holovision. Or a vis-u. Or anything mass-produced."

"Oh, but O'wun, my *star*..." Her tone had suddenly become smooth as caramel syrup. "...I know very well *you* don't need any of those silly things. You've got this great big beautiful machine right up here." She tapped his temple with a gentle hand. "You can't tell me you don't connect from time-to-time. Get a bit of that ol' juice running through your system and—"

"Shhh." His eyes darted to the small window off the counter that opened into the lounge. "Will you please respect where you are?" he hissed.

"Well, we were wondering if you might not be able to use that great, big, gorgeous mind of yours and tell us something about this."

At her cue, Bertram held up the Yellow Thing.

O'wun barely glanced at it and went back to chopping. "No. Absolutely not. I don't recognize it, and that means it would require research." Chop, chop, chop, chop. "My researching days are over."

"But you could do it if you wanted to," pressed Xylith.

"This is Ludd. And when in Ludd, we do like the Luddites do. No research." Chop, chop, chop.

Bertram stepped forward. "It was given to me by the Seers of Rhobux," he explained. "And right now it's the only clue I have to saving my planet. Anything you could tell us would be invaluable. Xylith says you're a whiz at this sort of thing. Better than any other Non-Organ—"

A knife flashed through the air and pressed Bertram's throat. "Any other what?" O'wun's face was right in his. You could have counted the pores of his skin, if he'd had any. "Any other *what*?!"

"Any other...any other..." Bertram's mind ran quickly, "...completely retired programmers?" he suggested. He braced himself to be stuck like a pig, so it was little wonder he jumped like a greased one when the swinging door burst open.

It was as if Death had just heard the hot scoop on a potential murder-in-progress and didn't want to be tardy for his cue. The tall, black-clad figure swept into the Food Preparation Room, purposeful and right at home, overcoat tails flapping behind with a cool self-confidence Bertram found just a little annoying.

"Ah. O'wun. There you are. Need a favor," said Rolliam Tsmorlood. He looked from O'wun, to Bertram, to Xylith, and for a split-second, surprise widened his amber eyes. He burst out laughing. "Well, frag me senseless. If it isn't Tryfe's Most Wanted and Light-fingers Lady Duonogganon. What brings you here?"

"He's going to tell me about the Yellow Thing," said Bertram, indicating O'wun.

"He needed a lift," explained Xylith, indicating Bertram.

"First, I need him to blank my crimes archive," said Rollie, taking a seat on the counter.

"Does no one care I'm holding a knife here?" O'wun asked the cosmos. He gave a final, resigned snarl and tossed the blade into the sink. "I am not researching your Yellow Thing, and I am not blanking your archive. You've come to the wrong place. Now you are welcome to go right around back into the lounge," here he motioned a circle in the air, "and enjoy some refreshments. But otherwise, I'm sorry, you'll have to leave."

Rollie sniffed. "You were more fun when you were openly Non-Organic."

O'wun's eyes darted to the small window again. "Shhh. Please. Now I'm not going to ask you again." He took Xylith's arm with one hand and pushed Bertram's back with the other, both in the direction of the kitchen door.

Rollie leapt from the counter. "You mean, we're not allowed to discuss technology at all here?" he asked, raising his voice. He wore a carnivorous smile Bertram recognized. "Even with you being who you are?"

"Don't do this to me, Rollie," warned O'wun in a low voice. "Don't you dare do this to me."

"What do you mean, mate?" asked Rollie loudly. "I just want to make sure I know the rules. I'd hate to violate any of the rules and customs here. I am, as you know, such a stickler for rules. Are we not allowed to discuss things like...oh...the differences between organic-born and Non-Organics in terms of risk-taking and logic?" He stepped nimbly past O'wun, Bertram and Xylith and paused at the swinging door.

"Rollie, I'm serious. Shut up," O'wun hissed. "I'll be bashed to pieces."

"Are we allowed to have technology here ourselves?" Rollie's grin widened and he opened the door. "And if so, how much technology is permitted? Can it be bigger than an XJ-37 hand-laser, do you think? How big a violation is a pocket vis-u? And what happens if the technology is really big. Like, I dunno," he sized up O'wun, "...Round two kroms, 160 toks? What of it then? Is that too much technology or does that get a pass?"

"Fine. Fine. Get in here," O'wun said through gritted teeth. He seized Rollie's forearm and yanked him into the kitchen. O'wun then poked his head out once more just to tell his guests he was almost done with the polegrots, but they'd need a little more time.

Ducking back inside the Food Preparation Room, O'wun's broad forehead went from that of clear-browed charming host to scowling blackmail victim. "You slaggard."

"So they tell me." Beaming, Rollie resettled onto the counter. At O'wun's folded arms and dark stare, he added, "Am in a bit of a rush."

"Just for that," O'wun turned to Bertram. "I'll look up your Yellow Thing first."

"Oh, um," Bertram pointed, "also anything you can uncover on who owns Tryfe. I did a Uninet search but nothing remotely helpful came up, so I thought you might be able to, er..."

Rolling his eyes, the Simulant withdrew a spindled, wooden chair from a hand-crafted table and sat down with a huff. "Fine. Also recover information on Tryfe." Soon a soft whir emanated from him, and his eyes went to screensaver.

Bertram watched the interesting fractal patterns swirl and change colors, while Xylith guarded the door and Rollie finished prepping the polegrots.

Bertram jumped slightly when O'wun's irises returned. "Well?"

"Not in there."

"What?!"

"The Yellow Thing's not in there. I scanned it against images from all over the Uninet, all linked databases, all networked systems. But no pattern match."

Bertram let out a frustrated groan and grabbed up the Yellow Thing. "What *are* you?" he asked it. He hadn't tried that before, and a part of him hoped it actually might speak up and share.

It held its silence.

"And Tryfe's owner?" Xylith asked.

O'wun's answer began with an awestruck laugh. "I know you said you didn't find much, so I hit a few places that might not get pulled up by a standard Uninet search. And talk about *blanked!* Intergalactic Office of Planetary Deeds and Dry Details? Blanked. Alternate Realty property listings and internal databanks? Blanked. Backspace Geographic Assessment archives? So very, very blanked. And when I say blanked, I mean *blanked.* Blanked like *I'd* do 'em. Sure, there were entries for Tryfe, but they'd been scoured so clean you could eat off them. The only thing I could even recover was a vague residue imprint of one word in the Universal Property Transfer Directory. I'm not even sure it's right." He regarded his clasped hands before him. "G'napps."

"G'napps?" asked Bertram. "Like Emperor G'napps, the guy with the Vos Laegos table game?"

"It's Emperor*'s* G'napps, Bertram," Xylith corrected gently.

"I only know what I saw," O'wun told him, "and it looked like 'G'napps.'"

"The Emperor isn't *named* G'napps," Xylith went on. "G'napps were a type of ancient clothes fastener certain royalty used back in the Eedythead System's Golden Age of Dressing Nice. See, the playing pieces look like—"

"Stellar," interrupted Rollie, "now you know, Ludlow. The good ol' Emperor bought your planet. So, O'wun," he turned to the Simulant, "on to blanking my archive, then?"

"He thinks he's funny, Bertram," Xylith explained. "There isn't any 'Emperor G'napps.'"

"Will you all please *shut up* for a minute?" O'wun shouted, and Bertram was worried he'd grab that knife again. "Okay, Rollie, where am I looking for this crimes archive of yours?"

"Seers of Rhobux have it. Should be in their data system."

O'wun nodded. "That may take some time. Take those polegrots out to the guests and have a cocktail. I'll be with you as soon as I can. And by the way, thank you *so much* for dragging down my party. Next time, bring a bottle of Smorg wine like everyone else."

With that, O'wun went to screensaver.

Tomorrow morning, the old kachunketball stadium, on the planet Skorbig. That was where Rozz Mercer would present with Spectra Pollux, and the fate of Earth would be decided by whoever rocked the hottest alien Powerpoint.

That's how Rozz saw it, anyway. And while she was still at the mercy of her electric tiara, she also knew there was someone else out there in the GCU who cared about her planet just as much as she did. And *he* was still free to do something about it.

Rozz had spent the last two days trying to figure out how to get a message to Bertram Ludlow. She'd thought there might be a way through Spectra Pollux's *Featured CapClub Feature-of-the-Day*. It had some benefits, after all. It reached GCU-wide, it was regular talk on the *Heavy Meddler*, and between holovisions, vis-us and the Uninet, it was almost a total lock that it would reach Bertram Ludlow's ears wherever he was—short of dead or dungeoned.

Each *Featured CapClub Feature-of-the-Day* was pre-determined by Spectra Pollux herself and was selected weeks prior to release. It was stored in an announcement database that would automatically notify her infopill subscribers what awaited them. This was picked up by the GCU media.

If they were back on Earth, Rozz could have simply used Spectra's computer when she wasn't around to send a new message. Or, with no direct access, she might have hacked into Spectra's computer from another networked terminal.

But a little poking around, and Rozz learned Spectra Pollux connected directly to her network with a chip implanted in that giant head of hers. She could just think and dictate the information straight in. What she needed the 37 assistants for, other than as salaried desk toys, was anybody's guess.

As for where the data was stored, and how it networked with the subscriber messaging system, Rozz hadn't been able to track it down. Someday, having consumed enough of the right infopills, Rozz thought she could probably handle the task. But right now, she was running out of time and ideas and—

"Can I get another?" One of two reporters, who'd been in the corner interviewing Spectra Pollux for her umpteenth time this week, waved an empty glass at her. Rozz liked the look of this guy. He had an interesting exoskeleton, and a tasteful business suit.

"Altairan Sun Slush, right?" The beverage gave off so much heat, one whiff could singe your nose hair.

"Right."

"Brave man," she said.

He leaned on the counter and gave a pleasant, clicking sort of sound. "I'm a Halypaynean." He tapped a fist to his abdomen. It made a solid thud, in spite of the suit. "We can stomach anything."

"You're the media; occupational benefit." Rozz slipped on her protective hood and gloves and started on the order.

She couldn't hear the interview over the purr of the drinks machine and the thickness of the hood. But by now she knew the sort of questions they'd ask. "How many infopills do you ingest yourself before you find one you'd recommend for your CapClub?" "What's your favorite infopill of all time?" "Do you prefer them in time-released capsule or tablet form?"

It was always the same. And as always, Spectra handled it with dignity and efficient grace. But oh, how Rozz would love for the GCU to see the woman, just once, become the storm-clouded fury that Rozz witnessed that time. Oh, how satisfying it would be to give the GCU a glimpse of Spectra when she wasn't Being Her Best Her.

And—like the jolt of an Altairan Sun Slush hitting an unsuspecting gullet—Rozz had a sizzling idea.

All along, Rozz Mercer had been making her problems too complex. Yet there was an easy way to accomplish what she needed to get done. One so simple, she couldn't believe she hadn't thought of it before.

Rozz was just pouring the Altairan Sun Slush into a clean, lidded cup, as the reporters were getting ready to leave.

"Looks like I'll be having that drink to-go after all," the Halypaynean told her, waving his antennae in his species' equivalent of a dashing smile.

"Enjoy it before the container melts," she warned. "The LibLounge isn't responsible for eroded beverage containers and any injuries associated thereby." Her eyes darted to her employer, still sitting in her favorite spot, having a tete-a-tete-a-tete-a-whatever with the 37. Her gown was a light, buttery yellow. The timing seemed right.

So Rozz tucked the cup into a tray. "In fact, it's probably safer if I just bring it to your ICV for you. Are you ready?"

Hal looked impressed. "Such service!" He motioned to his colleague, and the trio emerged from the LibLounge into the bright Rumoolitan daylight.

It was before they got to the ship that Rozz paused, positioning herself so Spectra had a clear view of her through the window. *No, I'm not running away. I'm not doing anything suspicious, Spectra. I'm all about transparency.* She put on a CapClub Customer Service smile so big you could probably see it from space.

"Before you both go, there was a *little* something I was hoping to share with you," Rozz said cheerfully. "I know your story's about Spectra's work with the LibLounges, but I also know there are just so many wonderful things Spectra wouldn't tell you herself because she's entirely too modest." A snicker caught in Rozz's throat but she swallowed it back down and readjusted her radiant grin.

It gave the journalists time to exchange intrigued glances. "Really…"

"Oh, you wouldn't believe the number of shipments of infopills that authors send Spectra to sample, hoping she'll choose their work." This was true.

Rozz went on: "Because she's generously willing to give even complete unknowns a chance, she washes down everything from skilled vanity publications to well-meaning but rough first attempts, to weighty scholarly works and possible best-sellers." Also true.

"She makes notes about each and every infopill she ingests— good and bad—and adds it to her database." Totally true.

"In fact, she cares so deeply about her *Featured CapClub Feature-of-the-Day*, just yesterday she pulled the recommendation for tomorrow, because she'd decided it didn't meet her exacting standards." Big, fat, unadulterated lie.

Interest played over their exoskeletoned faces. "Really..." they said again. It was the sound of a lie being sucked down, smooth and easy like a creamy mootaab milkshake.

"Absolutely. Spectra was all jazzed about the infopill one minute and then yanked it the next. Gone. Right out of the database. It made such an impression on me, because she'd never done that before. I thought it said a lot about her thoroughness that she could endorse something whole-heartedly and then completely dump the thing flat like that."

Rozz thought she smelled a nice whiff of scandal. Or perhaps that was the Sun Slush.

Ol' Hal smelled it, too. He leaned in and lowered his voice. "What infopill was it?"

"*Breakfast with Bertram at Skorbig Stadium for Independence Day.*" She thought a moment and added, "By Eartha Shatter." Rozz wondered why she didn't ask for "Prince Albert in the Can" while she was at it, but with her luck, Prince Alber Tinthakan would be some big-time planetary muckety-muck with copyright paranoia.

Hal was making notes. "And what made her change her mind so strongly about this particular infopill?"

His partner clicked with amusement. "Sounds like it needed a good editor."

"I don't really know," said Rozz lightly. "I haven't digested this one myself. We didn't get shipments of the infopills here. Just the one Spectra digested and, of course, the infopill summary." Rozz cast the invisible line and...

Hooked. "So what's it about?"

Shrugging, Rozz smoothed short pink locks from her electric headband. "Like I said, it was deleted pretty quickly from the database. I barely glanced at it. I'm sure there'll be a summary somewhere on the Uninet, though."

Lies, lies, and more colorful lies.

"And how was she acting when she said it had to be pulled?"

"Oh, y'know," Rozz had been working on her casually indifferent gestures lately, "kind of excited or, well, agitated or..."

"Would you say 'panicked'?" suggested Hal.

"Me? Why, no, I don't say *anything*," Rozz told him sweetly. "This is completely off-the-record. Aside from your drink order, you and I have never spoken. I just thought it was really important you understood that Spectra cares so much about her CapClub choices, she completely freaked out and changed her mind at the last minute over one of her recommendations."

Ah, the giant, gaping black hole of a lie. Rozz almost smiled of her own accord on this one.

"*Breakfast with Bertram at Skorbig Stadium*," Hal said.

"*For Independence Day*," Rozz added. "But, remember, you didn't hear it from me."

Nope. They didn't hear it from her. "An anonymous source," it would say. "A close friend of Pollux who preferred to remain nameless." As they sauntered back into their ICV, Sun Slush in hand, and she waved a friendly CapClub Customer Service goodbye, Rozz Mercer knew one of those *Heavy Meddler* boys would be hitting the Uninet way before lift-off. Yes, he would scour the system, looking for any information on tomorrow's missing *Featured CapClub Feature-of-the-Day*, and author Eartha Shatter.

And he would find nothing. A nothing that would quickly become a curious nothing. A suspicious nothing. A guilty nothing. Sweet, sweet nothing.

And with so much nothing before them, one thing was certain. Pretty soon it would be the nothing everyone was talking about.

Everyone, and possibly even Bertram Ludlow.

Welcome to Plan 4, Part A. Rozz wasn't sure how Part B would hash out. But she could wait.

She walked back into the café with a spring in her step and a tray under her arm.

The tray of polegrots had taken a serious hit, and the bucket of thick Luddite punch was half-empty. With supplies dwindling and their popular host AWOL, it was becoming increasingly difficult to divert curious, social, and unhelpfully-helpful guests from the Food Preparation Room.

O'wun was still on screensaver, and there was no telling how long it would be. Bertram had tried analyzing the low whirring around the man, looking for insight into his estimated return to the alert and Organic world, but it offered no clues. They could but watch and wait.

Shame the guy didn't come with a graphical Progress Bar or something, thought Bertram. *Maybe that came in later models.*

At least the party seemed to be a success. With guests taking up instruments, traditional Luddite dancing had broken out. This involved a mix of hopping, clapping and slow fluid stretches. From a Tryfe perspective it landed somewhere between yoga, a 19th century minuet, and a mosh. Xylith had dragged Bertram onto the makeshift dance floor for one such song—an exhausting, prolonged exhibition, Bertram felt, since he was more of a minimal stand-and-sway guy when it came to high-pressure dancing. Meanwhile Rollie positioned himself as a long-legged barrier to the kitchen.

By the third chorus, as Bertram traded footwork for a leg cramp, he was saved by a loud, chirpy and persistent pair of notes which echoed from somewhere in the penthouse. "Bing-bong!"

A curious hush fell over the room. The music stopped, the dancing stilled. The crowd waited to have their greatest fears affirmed.

"Bing-bong!" announced the synthesized notes again, and now in a frantic search, the guests worked to find the keeper of this non-natural sound, this violation of all that was Ludd, this "bing-bong."

It was only a moment before the sound was traced, someone was seized and all eyes ("bing-bong!") fell on a single guilty face amongst them. This face flushed more deeply orange than it started, a life-form that looked like she ("bing-bong!") wanted to evaporate on the spot, into a fine, bright, terrified fizz.

Hands trembling, she withdrew a pocket vis-u, glanced at it, her face now a deeper rust and ("bing-!") turned the gadget off.

"Um."

Someone gasped. Someone else let out an astonished cry. And then…someone started to laugh.

"A 290-BX?" This guest queried, indicating the device in her hand. He withdrew a small flat silver box from the pocket of his own beaded vest. "290-BT," he said, with a snicker. He addressed the wan, blank faces before him. "What? I love Ludd, too, but I need the kachunkettball scores."

A murmur of nervous giggles rippled through the crowd, and one woman lifted up her pantleg. A mini-holovision was holstered to the life-form's calf. "I only use it to see *As the Worlds Revolve*. Margor is just about to learn she's been accidentally life-merged to Luto's evil genetic clone and—"

An aged being held up a beautiful beaded necklace with a large central polished stone and turned the stone over. On its opposite side was a big red high-tech button. "Just in case I've gone physically prone due to medical emergency and I cannot self-elevate," she admitted.

Now laughing and hugging, three other partygoers felt free to show their favorite long-hidden small technologies and soon, in an atmosphere of unity, convivial brotherhood, elation, and personal electronics, the music resumed and the party sprung to life once more.

With this relieving flurry, the Lady of Bing-bong had returned to her normal shade of peach and took a moment to see what the urgent message had been.

"Big news?" Tom Modean asked over her shoulder.

"Oh, it's my *Featured CapClub Feature-of-the-Day* subscription," said the guest, reading the message. "Spectra Pollux says there have been some rumors suggesting that tomorrow we'd receive the infopill *Breakfast with Bertram at Skorbig Stadium for Independence Day*, by Eartha Shatter—"

Bertram Ludlow's breath tripped on its way to his lungs.

"—But that it was pulled at the last minute due to some unnamed scandal. Spectra says not only was that title never on the recommended list, but she's never heard of the work before and certainly never digested it. She indicates we will get, as planned, a very special copy of Jet Antilia's *One-Word Poems*, with discussion questions created by Spectra Pollux herself and—"

"Excuse me," Bertram forced his way into the tight group, "what was that title again?"

"*One-Word Poems?* You know, Jet Antilia is *such* a renegade how he comes up with these ideas and—"

"No, no, before that," said Bertram, grabbing her arm to see the handheld device. "*Breakfast with* who?"

She yanked away, flashed him a dirty look, and squinted at the message again. "*Breakfast with Bertram at Skorbig Stadium for Independence Day*. By Eartha Shatter." She shrugged. "Never heard of it."

Bertram turned to Xylith, urgency surging through his veins. "Is there a Skorbig Stadium?"

"Why, I don't know." Her voice was all nervous embarrassment. "I've never really followed sports. There is a planet called Skorbig."

Rollie answered from above and behind them. "Skorbig Stadium, yeah. Defunct kachunkettball venue, been empty for some time. Used to be where their local boys, the Ergowohms, played. Named for some kind of flying creature, I think. But then, I followed the Blumdec Blasters."

Bertram looked up at the Deltan. "Would it take us long to get there? Would we be in time for, say, breakfast tomorrow?"

"Be cutting it close. Depends on your craft, I s'pose." Rollie ran a meditative hand over bristly yellow hair. "But Ludlow, what's the big deal? We're talking about a fragging infopill title, and definitely under the category of Fiction."

"Or a message. A message for me," Bertram said.

As Rollie opened his mouth to protest, Bertram raised a hand. "Look. You're a GCU-savvy guy. Have you ever met a 'Bertram' before? Are there 60 kinds of bertram in your Translachew translator? Do flocks of bertram cut through the universe in elegant migratory formation?"

Rollie considered it. "Type of aquaduct on Ny-El-5 called a bertram," he mumbled. "And I think Bertram might've been one o' them popular progeny names 'bout ten U-years back on Quaydar." He frowned. "No, that was Berglat." Reluctantly, logic and probability won out over his desire to be contradictory. And that seemed to annoy him. "Okay, it's odd. I'll give you that. But who would send you a message?"

"How do I know?" Bertram whispered. "The Prophets of Nett maybe?"

"Oh, because they've been so fragging-well helpful so far, right?" Rollie rolled his eyes. "Ludlow, they can't even find the colleagues in their own blasted branch office."

Xylith jumped in. "How do we know this isn't a set-up from the Podunk PeaceGuards? Or—or the RegForce?"

Rollie nodded. "Tsmarmak Mook isn't stupid, you know. It could be to lure you into the open."

"It could," Bertram agreed, "but do any of them know my name?"

Rollie opened his mouth and closed it a few times. He looked like a codfish short on ideas. Then a blood-curdling scream reverberated from the Food Preparation Room, transforming his unsaid retort into an energetic curse. The Hyphizite was halfway to the kitchen before Bertram had taken a step.

Bertram arrived a moment later to find the orange woman standing before O'wun, wan and shaking. O'wun was just coming out of his screensaver coma.

"H-he—he's a machine!" she stammered. "Here. On our beautiful Ludd. He's a machine! Ludd save us, a machine!"

"Oh, here we go," sighed Rollie.

"A Non-Organic Simulant? Here?" someone wailed.

"O'wun? A Non-Organic? All along?" queried Major Modean, muscles tense and eyes wide, like O'wun might explode or jettison at any moment.

Bertram scanned the terrified faces of the group. "Geez, what is *wrong* with you people? Lady," he addressed the orange woman, "you have a *pocket vis-u*, fer crying out loud! And you," he indicated another party-goer, "you're addicted to 3-D soaps."

"Oh, *everyone* cheats a little now and then," snapped the orange woman.

"Yeah," interjected someone else. "It's not as if it's our *whole lifestyle*."

O'wun meanwhile had loaded enough data to put recent events together. "Uh…machine? Where? Who's a machine? I think you misunderstand the situation. I just have an…an…unfortunate vision problem. I really should get it checked. Come to think of it, I'd better take care of that, post haste." He got to his feet, nodded a greeting to each guest and grinned uncertainly at his neighbors who were beginning to pick up pots, pans and the spare poker for the rotisserie. He walked past them calmly, slowly, then burst through the swinging door at a full run.

Rollie groaned. "Aw, frag it; I don't even know if he blanked my archive," and dashed after O'wun.

"Ladies first," motioned Bertram to Xylith, and they followed suit as the mob surged forward.

Bertram and Xylith raced down the hall and dove into the elevator just as O'wun was cranking the doors shut. "No!" shouted O'wun, "no, don't come on here, we'll—"

"Lies!" screamed a party guest.

"Betrayer!" shrieked another.

"Sham!"

"Property devaluer!"

"Stellar party, O'wun!"

These voices reached into the elevator as Bertram and Xylith clattered into the box despite O'wun's protests. The moment their weight hit the floor, the metal can shimmied and dropped at breakneck speed.

"What's happening?" Bertram screamed.

"I was trying to tell you, not enough counterbalance!" shouted O'wun. "Why don't you people listen?"

Bertram and Xylith were pitched hard into the wall, while Rollie and O'wun both leapt for the thick rope attached to the elevator's pulley system in hopes of slowing it down. But the elevator had gone too far unfettered. It picked up enough speed so the rope skimmed virtually gripless through their hands.

Down, down, the elevator careened, screeched and clattered against the shaft, until finally it landed with a groaning, ear-splitting crack that bent the metal frame and tossed everyone off their feet. Everyone but O'wun, who either had built-in, cat-like Simulant equilibrium, or magnet shoes. "Anyone hurt?" he asked. The Non-Organic materials from his hands smoked slightly.

If Bertram had a headache before, it absolutely pounded now. He thought he could almost hear it as it banged, pulsed and throbbed— as if it lived and breathed outside his very own skull.

Dusting herself off, Xylith paused, and looked ceiling-ward. "Thunder?"

Bertram realized now the rumbling *was* coming from above, in the very walls of the structure, deep thumping and bumping that made O'wun frown. "The stairwell!" O'wun yanked on the elevator gate, which fought him until he finally bent it free. It was true; Simulants really were stronger than they looked. "Time to go."

Bursting into the lobby, they blew past the murals and the carvings, their rumble sending the glass animal chandeliers jouncing. The doorman, in fear of the oncoming stampede, flung the front door wide as Bertram's group fled through the threshold and into the Luddite street.

"My ship's over here," called Xylith, motioning toward the field of wagons.

"And mine," echoed Rollie.

But what they saw there now in the makeshift ICV lot was not two shining ICVs to safety. It was one great metal ICV skeleton with flattened landing gear, a pile of bent bits, and a crowd of life-forms banging away at what was left of it with large rusted gardening tools.

"My ship!" Xylith shrieked. "Have you no sense of personal property?! I just got this! And it's lease-to-own!"

"It's art supplies now, lady," said one of the Luddites, cackling as he tucked a couple of dented solar shields under his arm.

The roar of the Fezziwig Towers mob was growing in the distance. Some keen eyes had spotted the struggles at the ICVs, and now O'wun's neighbors were rushing forward once more, leading a feverish charge toward them down the Luddite cobble street.

Xylith was still focused on the inspired local artisans, as they hauled off her rescue vehicle part-by-part. "You put that back! That's not yours, you...you scab!" spat Xylith, both of her faces pink with rage. "This is willful destruction of private property! This is a lawsuit just waiting to happen! This is...really bad press for the Ludd tourism board, and you better believe they'll be hearing about it, mister!"

Rollie withdrew the remote from his coat pocket, pushed a button, and a ramp began to descend from an empty space in the field next to Xylith's craft.

"Rollie, hurry!" shouted Bertram. O'wun's neighbors were coming up close, and somewhere along the way, they'd pulled together a selection of atmospheric flaming torches. It wasn't quite dusk, so some of the dramatic effect was lost, but Bertram was impressed they'd taken the time to try.

They still didn't blaze as hot as Xylith's fury. "This is non-Underworld-Society-sanctioned theft and—and—"

The ramp from nowhere hit the soft grass with a gentle "whump."

"—And bad art, too, is what it is," continued Xylith, really going for the jugular. "Cliché and trite and...and...derivative! Nobody does space salvage pieces anymore! Nobody! Hear me? And—"

Rollie grabbed her around the waist, hauling her up the ramp with one arm, while holding the XJ-37 hand-laser on the Luddite artists with the other.

Bertram and O'wun made quick work of climbing into the ICV themselves, the ramp already retracting under their frantically pounding feet.

The hatch sealed. Rollie dumped Xylith, who was still expressing her strong views on the unconventional techniques of the Ludd welcome wagon, into a chair. He turned to peer out the hatch window as the group closed in on the ship that wasn't there.

"Ah," the Deltan confirmed with interest, "they've finally figured it. Little slow on the uptake, them Luddites." He moved swiftly to the cockpit and settled down before the controls. "Harnesses, people, harnesses."

CLANG!

Xylith busied herself with the take-off harness. "Rollie, er, how rare is this ship again?" she asked.

GONG!

"Only a few operational cross-galaxy," he called back, over the engine. "Why?"

BLANG!

"Might be one less soon," she told him. "Hurry."

But it was in two swings of a Luddite's bat that the ship lifted off, and Rollie was chuckling to himself as he peered out the cockpit window. "Ah, lookit 'em scurry there. Scurry, little Luddites, scurry. Back to your techno-dullness and derivative art."

He pushed a few more buttons, hit a few levers, and even from the other room, Bertram heard that familiar "bip" that said things were probably going to be all right.

Through the hatch window, Ludd appeared increasingly small and trivial below them. It wasn't soon enough.

O'wun gave a whirring exhale and released his harness. He stretched and shook his head solemnly. "My penthouse, my friends, my traditional basket weaving, my role as the building Social Director...Two Universal years of work to fit in and earn their trust, gone in the blink of an eye. All thanks to you."

He directed this last comment to the pilot who clomped into the room to join them.

"I want to know how I'm ever going to recoup my investment in that beautiful ship," Xylith addressed the Hyphizite, crossing her legs, a sour look on both her faces. "It was just loaded with options. And the Underworld insurance isn't likely to cover damage by pedestrians with bludgeons."

"We are headed to Skorbig next, aren't we?" Bertram asked the captain. "Remember, we have to get there by breakfast."

One by one, Rollie surveyed each of them over folded arms and a narrow amber glare. He turned to O'wun. "You: a Simmi living in a renowned anti-technology world, and this is *my* blasted fault? Your logic boards have fried.

"You," he touched Xylith under a chin. "Should've cloaked it. You been to Ludd before. You know better. But you got sloppy. It's space junk now. So shut it and move on.

"And you." He turned on Bertram. "Yes, we are headed to Skorbig. And we'll talk more about that in a bit. But first things first."

He leaned on the back of O'wun's seat and sized him up. "Did you blank my archive?"

O'wun met his gaze by turning his head at angle that wasn't quite normal. "This is what you're worried about? These are your priorities? After ruining my life and barely escaping the raging mob with torches?"

Rollie smiled in response.

"No," O'wun said flatly. "Rhobux-7 has no Uninet connections anymore. All gone. Completely offline. So whatever trouble you're in, you're still in it." He settled into his seat. "Serves you right, too, if you ask me; I am never going to get my rental deposit back."

Rollie grumbled something even Translachew wouldn't translate, though Bertram guessed it touched heavily on the theme of rental deposits and personal orifice logistics. He flexed his hands. Bertram noticed a thick rust-colored rope burn trailed down the center of each of the man's palms. He rubbed his crooked thumb over one of the wounds thoughtfully.

At his long silence, Xylith made an injured, sympathetic sound. "Oh, don't you worry yourself, Rollie. You won't end up on Altair-5. We'll figure out a way. We always do, don't we?"

O'wun's brow creased in surprise. "Altair-5? Nobody said anything about Altair-5."

But Rollie just made a non-committal noise that might have been concession. A second later he looked up, eyes seeming to blaze from some inner inspiration. "Bleedin' Karnax," he breathed, "you were right, Ludlow!"

You were right, Ludlow. These words were so rare to hear, Bertram almost didn't believe them himself. "I was? When?"

"The RegForce *doesn't* know your name," he said. His voice was low and filled with strained gravity. A smile expanded slowly across his face, like dawn might break over the Altair-5 horizon. "The Seers of Rhobux *do*."

Bertram remembered how those voices like wuthering winds said his name over and over again. "Bertrammmm Ludlowwwwww…" Shuddering, he glanced out the hatch window. There was nothing to see right now but the same old shiny white star systems. He wondered when exactly the great fabric of space had become as dull and unremarkable to him as midway on the Pennsylvania Turnpike. "You think the Seers are leading me to Skorbig Stadium?"

"Said it yourself; who else knows your name?"

Bertram shrugged. It was hard to say. Word in the GCU traveled fast. "Thing is, Rollie, the infopill title seemed really...Tryfan...to me. You think it's a trap?"

"He always thinks it's a trap," said Xylith. O'wun let out a bitter laugh.

Rollie ignored them. "Decent chance we'll be fragged the moment we set foot in that Stadium," he said. "But I'd risk it for a little chat with the Seers of Rhobux. Anyway, there's still a tiny, infinitesimal, microscopic sliver of hope we might not be ambushed and blasted into a hundred billion particles." He smiled. "So that's always nice."

23

It was a wonder the tips of Rozz's fingers, her nose, and her smallest toes hadn't broken off. Such were the frigid temperatures blasting through from Spectra Pollux the rest of the day.

In truth, Pollux had been taciturn and icy to everyone, even her select 37, the entire afternoon. And it didn't take a swirling, twirling mood dress to tell Rozz the issue was CapClub-related. Spectra Pollux was used to admiration, innovation, placation, and prostration. Questions about her decision-making abilities, and a quick grind through the rumor mill, had never really entered into it until now.

Image is such a capricious wench, Rozz considered philosophically. She guided her second crate of presentation paraphernalia into the Pollux ICV and secured it to the floor.

Not that Pollux's current image issues were of her own making, Rozz reminded herself. Rozz alone was the one to blame for that. But somehow she just couldn't cuddle up to the guilt.

Maybe space had hardened her. Maybe it was too many hours supervising the GCU's CapClub groupies and telling them what intellectual goodies they were supposed to draw from their latest infopill. Maybe it was the fumes from those Altairan Sun Slushes she made day after day; that was bound to have an effect. Or maybe that stylish taser headband had shorted out the part of her brain responsible for conscience and empathy.

She tested the crate's security and returned in the dimming evening light for the last of the equipment. She'd decided she would keep that banded head of hers down until Skorbig. She would wait and see if Bertram received her message. And if he showed up on Skorbig with assembled troops, picket signs, and a fleet of media to apply some well-placed pressure? Well, Rozz would take what opportunities presented themselves. But if somehow her broadcasted cry for help eluded Bertram in his travels, or it was just too damned vague, Rozz supposed the bid would help decide her fate. And she'd work it out from there.

What a shame, she thought. *Space could be such a blast if not for all the pushy, control freak E.T.s.*

Rozz was locking down the last of the presentation goodies when the shadow of Spectra Pollux fell over her.

The woman's face looked so clear it was almost dewy. Her lips were turned in a small stiff smile, like the rosebud on a tuxedo lapel. Her dress was an unreadable mix of fog and sand.

"Oh!" Rozz jumped in spite of herself, and she compensated by indicating the travel-safe containers. "I think we're all set, Spectra. Everything for the presentation is ready to go."

Spectra made no move as if she heard her. The rosebud smile blossomed slightly. "Rozz, sit down."

Rozz looked around the ship's hold and took a seat on one of the larger cases. She waited. From Rozz's seated position, Spectra Pollux seemed to loom 100 feet tall. She imagined that was the idea.

"We'll be leaving soon, Rozz, leaving for Skorbig," Spectra said. "And I think you should know, I'm disappointed."

Rozz widened her eyes in a way she'd been working on lately. It made her look extremely innocent, if slightly dim. "Oh? Won't the ship get good fuel mileage?"

"I am disappointed," Spectra began again, her tone a firm demonstration that now was not the time for innocent or dim, "because you have failed to appreciate what I've been trying to do for you. For everyone on your planet."

"I know what you're trying to do for us, Spectra," Rozz told her.

"I had thought I could transform you into the best CapClub leader there ever was. That I could mold you into someone informed, efficient, friendly, and quick with a mootaab milkshake."

"I do all those things, Spectra," Rozz reminded her gently.

"And do you also tell *Heavy Meddler* reporters lies about my organization? Do you also start rumors that make it look as if I have something to hide, that imply that my business is corrupt? Do you hint I'm covering over some sort of scandal? Do you undermine me? Is that how you repay me for wanting nothing more than for you to Be Your Best You?"

"Mostly I wipe the counters and gather up the print ashes from the LibLounge incinerators," Rozz said.

"I suppose," Pollux sighed as if to herself, "that there is simply no empowering some life-forms. That certain beings are not equipped to appreciate the wonders, the beauty, that's presented to them."

"You're disappointed," Rozz added helpfully.

"I'm afraid our work together has lost some of its twinkle for me, yes, my dear. With your repeated attempts at running away from what's good for you and by spreading these vile rumors, you've become a burden I have only chosen to bear because I believe so strongly in second chances." She motioned as if all the weight of the GCU had been placed across her impressive Rumoolitan shoulders. "But tomorrow morning's presentation is your final chance to make it up to me. To yourself. To all of Tryflingkind."

Rozz wondered how long Pollux had been rehearsing this speech.

"I am still willing to offer your people this opportunity, Rozz. I believe that it is possible that I can lift your species up out of backspace degradation and into the exciting world of fast-serve health beverages and infopills. But the question is, Rozz: do *you* believe it?"

"I didn't start those rumors, Spectra," Rozz lied sincerely. She was a little scared how easily it came.

Spectra's gown had become a flat, gray swirl, like a cyclone in motion. "I saw you talking to those reporters," she said.

Rozz paused and bit her lower lip. She dug the floor coyly with the toe of her uniform's boot. She found herself giving it a long, appropriately awkward moment. Finally, she said, "You know what I told those reporters?" A giggle started to form, and Rozz quelled it by clearing her throat. "I told those reporters how much you balance every day, without so much as a complaint. I told them how devoted you are to your CapClub subscribers. I explained how thorough and caring and altruistic you are with every choice you make for us. I told them all of those things because I owe you so much and I know you'd never, ever tell them yourself." She gave the wide-eyed expression her Best Her. "I told them what I did because *I believe*, Spectra! I *really, really do!*"

The "do" hung in the air like chimed bells, pure and hopeful. Spectra Pollux let it hang there, while she sized Rozz up for what seemed like years. All the while, the shades of the woman's gown wavered from stone gray to pebble brown and back again. It was pebbles buffeted by surf and whirling with sand. It was shifting and unreadable.

Finally Spectra Pollux said, "We'll take off in a few minutes."

And since lightning didn't shoot from Spectra' dress in wild electric abandon and strike her where she stood, Rozz guessed she must have made a pretty convincing show of it. At least for now.

The smell was overpowering. It had taken a team of experts and a number of days to crack open the false wall to the hidden room inside Oogon Bungee's impounded ICV. And now, with the seals blown, 29 booby-traps unboobied, two anagram security codes puzzled out using a primitive form of Hyphizite speech, 12 separate locks undone, and much time wasted setting explosives on what was, remarkably enough, explosion-resistant materials, they were in. The panels were finally all removed, and W.I. Mook was almost certain what lurked inside had to be dead.

He based this on what he described in his official report to the Podunk Peace Guards as "the fragrance of decomposition and excrement emanating forthwith."

The RegForce had become involved because the Peace Guards had desperately required technical assistance and requested Mook's help specifically. At this stage in their fledgling membership with the GCU, they simply weren't equipped to deal with this sort of advanced lock system, and with half their patrol on temporary disability, Mook hadn't minded stepping in.

He made sure to take meticulous notes for their records. It was an amusing novelty to write by hand with instrument and paper. He hadn't done that since one of his childhood Didactics classes, a course that taught things students would rarely use but which reflected a lengthy Honored Tradition. Like diagramming the action words in a Hyphiz Deltan sentence. (Most Deltan sentences were 85% action words.) Or making pottery ashtrays for your parental archetypes, though the planet had been publicly conflagration-free for 200 U-years.

Truth be told, Mook was curious himself what Rolliam Tsmorlood and the mysterious Tryfe man had been doing in the ship belonging to Oogon Bungee. Tstyko had bet Mook a wheel of mootaab cheese—the finely-aged variety, too, none of that flash-processed flavorless muck—that Tsmorlood had stolen the craft for himself.

Mook, however, was of a different mind. Tsmorlood's own ICV had been there, cloaked, on the Podunk grounds. Mook found the look of Tsmorlood's transport, like most Protostar models, to be ponderous and cumbersome, as if some tumorous growth had spawned other tumorous growths in a quest for full-body domination. Yet the rumor that wafted along Underworld channels suggested Tsmorlood was irrationally fond of that vehicle and unlikely to ever seek an upgrade.

So *why was* Tsmorlood there?

Upon cracking the seal to the hidden room, the RegForce team backed off and gave it a few minutes to air out. "If I'd known," began W.I. Igglestik Tstyko meditatively, "I would have brought along my protective outerwear and breathing apparatus. My wife gave me a very smart set for our last Hy Holidays. I've been looking for a chance to break it in."

The Hy Holidays in the Hyphiz system were a multi-day celebration involving get-togethers, letting off steam and—in the Tstyko household, at least—gifts of new hazardous materials protective gear.

At Mook's questioning glance, Tstyko added, "Oh, I *know* the RegForce provides them to us, Mook. But it never is the same as owning your own." He peered into the darkness of the ICV. "I'd say that's had enough time to blow the stink off, wouldn't you?"

"Highly doubtful," mused Mook, "but as the philosopher Nangara once said, 'It is better to be the head and forepaws of the raging rorrdrasher than the tail-end, as both the view and the air is always clearer.'"

"Nangara said that, eh, Mook?" Tstyko queried cheerfully. He was always upbeat on these sorts of RegForce outings. "Why, she really was a bit of bright beam, wasn't she?"

"I suggest we focus on the task at hand, Ig." Laser drawn, Mook stepped silently into the hull and approached the once-hidden room.

It was pitch black and still smelled like the backend of that rorrdrasher. Mook withdrew a handkerchief from his jacket pocket and held it to his nose. He said, "Lights." And the overhead lights flickered on, revealing the compartment's contents.

Food wrappers and empty beverage containers littered the floor, all of them bearing the name of DiversiDine Entertainment Systems and Aeroponics. Star charts and slim digital travel guides sat in ragged piles, sporting ads for locales across the GCU's four corners, as well as some outerland expeditions. A few were blank now, their power sources having drained with time.

On one wall was a to-do list, detailing elaborate PR plans for sweeping some future Intergalactic Underworld Society election. Items had been crossed out and added in an increasingly hard-to-read hand.

One emptied storage container in a far corner of the room had become a creative toilet.

And there in the back—crouched behind several crates of some DiversiDine product Mook did not recognize called "DrinkThis"— was the laser-wielding inhabitant of this uninhabitable space, Oogon "Backspace" Bungee.

Bungee's plan may have been to leap at them, lasers flaring, and make his exit over their motionless forms. But with days of crouching among the cargo, it was his numbed knees and not his will that failed him. The daring plan was unexpectedly downsized to a forward-flailing tumble, a wild shot into a crate, and a blast of beverage that drenched the scene. It ended as Tstyko's quick aim left the prisoner stunned in a puddle of DrinkThis and disappointed dreams.

"How *interesting*," observed Mook in this aftermath, dabbing at his misted face with the handkerchief. He tucked it in his pocket and then grabbed the prisoner's left arm. "It seems Tsmorlood wasn't trying to steal the craft after all; he was simply visiting an old friend."

Tstyko took the right arm and shot Mook a glare. "I see what you're doing, you know."

"One, two, three: LIFT." They lifted.

"This is your tricky way of pointing out I lost our bet, isn't it?" Tstyko said.

Mook permitted himself a small, if slightly gloaty, smile over the prisoner's lolling head. "Remember, I prefer golden mootaab, Ig— not white, not chartreuse." They dragged the prisoner down the ICV ramp into the bright Podunk light. "And Extra Nippy, please. I do so love that tang."

✧

"Now how in Altair's blazes would *I* know where Tsmorlood and the Tryfe boy are? I been in storage, haven't I?" protested "Backspace" Bungee, squinting into the spotlight that beamed into his grooved and leathery face.

The RegForce had heard rumors that the law enforcement on less-civilized planets still used these bright light torture techniques to intimidate suspects and gain confessions. So when they discovered one such machine in the Podunk station, Tstyko was simply over the moon to try it out.

"You mean to say," began Tstyko, hand on the device, "you met Tsmorlood and the Tryfling fugitive at the Podunk canteen, and you all just sat round in silence, reading the, er, the advertising thingies the drinks sit on?"

"Coasters," supplied Mook.

"Right. You only sat round reading the coasters?" Tstyko bumped the light up a notch. He'd been delighted to see it had 11 different intensity settings, from Sunny, Arid, and Scorcher all the way to Second Degree, Third Degree, and Extra Crispy.

"I never said we didn't speak," corrected the prisoner. "I said I dunno where they are." His tone was firm and unruffled, like RegForce interrogation was just a part of his daily schedule.

CLICK! Setting Three. Suddenly the room was like high noons on the place formerly known as Rhobux-7.

"What did you discuss?" asked Mook, hands folded neatly before him.

"Did some catching-up, is all. Current events, politics, the fragging-pathetic state of the Deltan RegForce these days. Like that." Bungee looked up at the blazing white light through his slitlike eyes and turned to Tstyko. "If you're trying to give me a tan, son, might as well conserve the resources. It's too blasted late." His chuckle was like fine sandpaper.

CLICK! Setting Four. A hot smell came over the room.

"How did Tsmorlood meet the Tryfling?" asked Mook.

Under the blinding light, Oogon Bungee shrugged. "Never heard, never asked," he said. "Ask too many questions in my line of work, some fellahs get nervous. Others think you know things. Word spreads, and suddenly, the RegForce gets wind and hauls you in for questioning." He indicated the room as an ironic case-and-point.

CLICK! Setting Five. Mook's beverage gave off a fine evaporative mist. Tstyko put on sunglasses. Bungee wiped absently at the perspiration coating his face and neck.

"Where do you perceive they were going?" asked Mook.

"I regret I did not request a copy of their itineraries," Bungee said, in a fair imitation of Mook's own refined tone.

Tstyko skipped Six and went straight to Seven—CLICK! CLICK! The non-organic upholstery of Bungee's chair made a sizzling sound.

"You RegForce got no sense of humor," Bungee grumbled.

"So Tsmorlood didn't mention plans to meet anyone? Or something he wanted to do, now that he was out of confinement?" Mook continued.

"Look, I just caught him up on Simmi labor problems and the latest Underworld news. No time for much else."

"What of the Tryfling? Did he say anything?" pressed Mook.

The prisoner folded his arms and leaned back in the chair, the surface of which had cracked in several places like parched earth. Its filling was popping out in bursting poofs. "What's it worth to you?"

"No-no," Tstyko warned gently and cranked up the machine. CLICK!—Eight! CLICK!—Nine! CLICK!—Ten! "What is it worth to *you*?" he yelled.

By now Bungee was sautéeing in his own juices, and the topcoat on the table was bubbling. Mook glanced at the settings.

Tstyko was giving him the Third Degree.

"All right, all right!" croaked the prisoner. "The Tryfling said he had to 'Save Life As He Knew It.' And no, I got no idea what that means. Didn't say much else, but he sure was a nervous little fellah. Followed Tsmorlood around like a lost Argonian snoogle. Surprised Tsmorlood put up with it; kid's not really the patient sort." Bungee squinted into the darkness. "Bergerom, I think his name was."

"The Tryfling's name is Bergerom?" Mook clarified, raising an eyebrow and lowering pen to paper.

"No, wait," said Bungee. Mook paused mid-word. "Ber-trom! That's what he'd said. Ber-trom!" Bungee winked and drummed a finger on his now-blistering temple. "Memory's still as sharp as a Feegar incisor."

"Could it be...Bertram?" Mook suggested, forcing himself to be calm, though a gleeful flutter of recognition filled his chest.

"That's what I said, didn't I?" insisted the prisoner. "Ber-tram. That mean something to you? Enough to, say, cut a de—"

"Turn it off, W.I.," Mook told his partner.

Tstyko looked startled at the controls before him. "What? But Mook—"

"Turn it off, I said."

"Aw, why? It goes one hotter."

But Mook was buzzing for one of the Peace Guards to return Bungee to his cell. In a moment they had left the interrogation room.

"Mook, I don't get it," Tstyko told his partner's back as they swept through the narrow halls of the station. "What's so important about this fellow's name being Bertram? Isn't that some kind of...giant water-container-bridge-hickey...out in the Ny-El system somewhere? What's the big blasted deal about some Tryfe person named for a water-container-bridge-hickey?"

"Because of the recent controversy regarding the *Featured CapClub Feature-of-the-Day*," explained Mook. At Tstyko's blank expression, he went on, "That very strange title of the missing infopill everyone's been talking about? The one that seemed so intentionally awkward?" Tstyko's metaphorical screen remained blank. Shaking his head, Mook persisted, *"Breakfast with Bertram at Skorbig Stadium for Independence Day,* by Miss Eartha Shatter?"

"Oh," said Tstyko and wrinkled his nose. They stepped outside into the fresh Podunk air. "You know I don't really hold with all that Uninet *Heavy Meddler* CapClub fiddle-faddle in my off-hours. Waste of time, really. No," he continued proudly, "I've been learning the zeelaylay. Ancient 18-stringed instrument from Hyphiz Beta you play with two hands and a foot because...well... the Betas had some interesting evolutionary attributes digit-wise a while back and—Mook?"

They were standing in the ICV park now, and Mook was lowering their ship's ramp. Tstyko glanced at his Universal watch. "A bit early for off-duty, isn't it? You know as well as I do: 'Regimental Hours four to 15, pre-determined productivity' and—"

"We're going to Skorbig," Mook told him. "Skorbig Stadium."

"Ah, but the Ergowohms haven't played there in many, many U-years. I doubt you can even buy signed merchandise there anymore these days."

"I realize that, Ig." Mook started up the ramp.

"Oh. Well, about that CapClub thingie: you do know the stuff they say in infopills isn't always real, don't you?" He was jogging up the ramp himself. "Some of them are about real things. But some of them are completely made up." Igglestik Tstyko looked so pleased to impart this information.

"Let's play a new roadtrip game, you and I. Just for today, shall we, Ig? It's called 'Thought Projection.' You think of things you want to say, and you try to send them to me using only the power of your mind."

24

"Flinky Rolls! Sleemy Snaps! And delicious luke-warm Frallip Squash! Get your Flinky Rolls, Sleemy Snaps and Frallip Squash here!" cried the vendor.

The smell wafting through Skorbig Stadium was one of anticipation, activity and energy.

Also Flinky Rolls.

Alternate Realty "For Sale or Lease" signs lined the property's perimeters, while dense overgrowth clogged the cracks in the back ICV lots and around the fences. Once-glossy color peeled along the stadium's metal panels, and seating had faded under the Skorbig sun. Old team advertisements for the Ergowohms—Skorbig's famed kachunkettball gladiators, now lost to history and trading deadlines—rotated in inconsistent pixilation. But these ruins of sporting past had been scrubbed and polished until they found new dignity. Lights beckoned in the early morning mist. On the roof, flags had been raised, bearing the logos of DiversiDine Entertainment Systems and Aeroponics, MetamorfaSys Inc., and Spectra Pollux's beloved CapClub brand. Skorbig Stadium was once again alive and alert.

Someone, thought Rozz, was making a very big show of this. She searched the morning skies and wondered if it were the high stakes today or the Frallip Squash that made her stomach roil with acid.

The crowd—and there was a bigger group than Rozz had expected—was a mixed one. Half the stadium seats faced a broad, curtained stage, which settled in a third of the stadium's former field.

In the tiered seating Stage Right, under the shadow of a flapping MetamorfaSys flag, was Musca Mij and his entourage. Rozz recognized him from the many *Heavy Meddler* pieces and the biographical infopills she'd digested.

He looked both shorter and more iridescent in person.

Then a few minutes ago, Eudicot T'murp and his team had entered, taking their places in a section flying DiversiDine colors.

He was not quite what Rozz had pictured, either. Sure, she'd absorbed his infopill for *Leaf and Let Leaf.* She'd gone over it in endless detail with various LibLounge discussion groups as a part of her leadership training. But she imagined no amount of capsule learning could prepare a GCU newbie to gracefully meet-and-greet a guy who buds and drops leaves in between how-do-you-do's and friendly frondshakes.

Rozz found she had to drag her attention away from one such moment of fascinating defoliation—maybe the guy had pre-presentation jitters—and instead, she settled her focus on the executives with him, all professionally-dressed and buzzing with activity.

Center stage housed a group Rozz didn't recognize but, male and female, were very animated and unnaturally beautiful, their complexions a rich pearly sheen. A dozen of them wore bright matching uniforms.

There was also some lady with an Alternate Realty nametag pinned to her well-tailored suit. She bobbed from group to group introducing herself and making nice with the presenters.

Rozz, meanwhile, sat in Spectra Pollux's CapClub section, far Stage Left with her 37 assistants, some tech support, and a few experts on backspace behavioral development just for good measure.

No one anywhere was Bertram Ludlow.

Spectra Pollux had been surveying the crowd, too, and now she assessed the Universal clock on the scoreboard and let out a huff of air. "This is ridiculous. It's almost time, and no one has told us anything."

She had been irritable the whole trip—sniping at the 37, grumbling at Rozz, and turning down at least three vis-u interviews on the Eartha Shatter infopill mystery. Now she rumbled to a standing position like a formidable geological eruption from the planet's crust and motioned to the woman with the Alternate Realty badge. "Excuse me, in what order will we present?"

"Hi there, Ms. Pollux," chirped the realtor, peering up at her, "Cosmic to see you again." She extended her hand. "If you just bear with our host a teeny-tiny bit longer, you'll get all your questions answered. I promise." The woman's head bobbed fluidly, like a plastic bag caught on a breeze.

Spectra rumbled again and sat.

Rozz shielded her eyes from the rising sun and scanned the skies once more. *Bertram Ludlow*, she thought, *where the hell are*—

A terrified scream caught in her throat. Swooping toward them from the east was a taloned red-and-purple bird the size of a jumbo jet, immense wings spanning the Skorbig skies.

Rozz remembered from *The Biggish Infopill of Illustrated Intergalactic Avianoids* that this was the long-necked ergowohm, native to the planet. The wings were layered in jutting quills, formed of clustered and hardened feathers all along its sides and back. Its beak was like a giant scythe. This particular example of the species did not appear to flap so much as glide, slowly, methodically, drawing menacingly nearer to the crowd—many of whom had fled their seats and started down the aisles in shrieking panic.

Rozz, however, remained seated and frowning. *The Biggish Infopill* claimed ergowohms typically reached no longer than two kroms in length; while between razor beak to feathered tail quills, this alien avian spanned ten times that, easy. Where the ergowohm of infopill study flapped, this one knifed downward into the stadium like a mad hang glider, and it came to settle on the greens with a bump.

It rested front-and-center before the empty stage.

There was a grinding sound from the creature's bowels and, momentarily, a door opened in the side of the bird. It gave birth to a single emerging figure, a miniature version of itself, but alive and in anthropomorphic form. The creature looked so much like a big league sports team mascot, Rozz expected it to start catapulting t-shirts into the crowd.

Those who had run from the bird-shaped aircraft now were frozen in place, waiting to see what came next.

A voice reverberated through the stadium sound system: "Ladies, Gentleman and Non-Gender-Specific Life-Forms…Welcome to the 'New Life for Tryfe' Bidding Competition!

"And here's your host for this morning's exciting event. You might know him as the newly re-elected leader of the Intergalactic Underworld Society, three times running. You might recognize him from his Uninet musical specials, live from Vos Laegos. You may know him as the warrior who risked his life to liberate the Klimfal people and go on to write, produce, direct and star in 12 different documentaries about these monumental achievements. But now, you'll also know him as the current owner of the planet Tryfe...Here he is, let's give a Skorbig round of applause for...Zenithhhhhhh Skytreeeeggggggggggg!"

At a touch of its wing, the purple-and-red bird mascot before them vanished, and a man in a pearly white suit with purple-and-red trim was in its place. He raised his arms high and waved to the cheering crowd.

Rozz wondered vaguely who was hooting and applauding so wildly and not still recovering from a coronary like everybody else. But she traced the raucous enthusiasm to the beautiful pearly beings now in the front center row. Rozz realized they were wearing kachunkettball cheerleading outfits.

"Welcome everyone!" said Skytreg warmly, the rising sun sparkling on his silvery hair like he'd planned it that way. "Great to see you! We have an exciting morning of Tryfe bid presentations ahead of us, so let's get started!"

"WOOOOOOO!" screeched the cheerleaders with a joy so high-pitched, dogs on Earth may have howled. Rozz found tears running down her face, though she couldn't for the life of her understand why. Then she noticed everyone, even Spectra Pollux, was sniffing and wiping their eyes. The cheerleaders shot some kind of guns, which sprayed bursts of colored electricity like mini, personal fireworks into the air.

Wreathed in a blinding smile, Zenith Skytreg motioned them to quiet. "Now, I know what you're thinking. You're thinking, 'Zenith: it's just a property sale. Why all the secrecy? Why all this extra orbiting?' Well, folks: if you'll recall, not that long ago, I was running for a little position called...Official Leader of the Intergalactic Underworld." He paused to allow knowing chuckles from the crowd. "I recognized that the Society still desperately clamored for my knowledge and guidance. But I had already enjoyed three sequential U-years in this illustrious position myself. I said to myself, I said, 'Zenith, doesn't someone else deserve a chance to live up to this leadership precedent?' 'Yes,' I told me wisely, 'the answer is obvious. For a win to have true meaning, the race against my opponents must be at least marginally fair.'"

He stepped closer to the stadium seats. "But what we do today, you and I, is the first step in helping Tryfe carve a bright new future. And the first step we've taken has already been brave. As brave as the day some of us single-handedly took on the Feegar cannibals in the fight for the peace-loving Klimfal race. As brave as betting that last yoonie on the roll of the Emperor's G'napps table, even as bouncers have their lasers set to Castration. We place our bets and take our chances because we believe there can and will be something better with the next flick of the G'napps."

"And once the GCU and the Uninet media understands, as we do, what Tryfe really needs? It will be cosmically big. As big as the brands you represent and the reputations you've built." He eyed the faces in the crowd like he was speaking to each one personally. "Under these circumstances, could I be *absolutely certain* our landmark work on Tryfe wouldn't unduly influence Underworld voters in my favor?" He shook his head no. "I knew I had to withhold my name until after the elections. I just couldn't let the shining possibility of my own overwhelming success get in the way of an honest race."

The cheerleaders cheered and "Awwwwwed." Rozz just sat back in her chair shaking her head. Bertram's "Life For Tryfe" protests had clearly forced the guy into some very fancy footwork today. She glanced at the sky again, the sun now well over the horizon, and wondered whether Bertram might not have even more in store for Zenith Skytreg, before the morning was through.

"But now," Skytreg clapped his hands together, "we move on, to the second thrilling part of our journey—the presentations! And in the spirit of Skorbig Stadium—a location our friends at Alternate Reality kindly arranged for our use today—I thought we'd begin our festivities like the illustrious home team, the Skorbig Ergowohms, once did. The presentation order today will be decided by..." he beamed, "a quadroff."

Under the delighted "Wooo!" of the cheerleaders, a murmur of excitement and surprise rippled through the audience.

"Mr. T'murp, Ms. Pollux, Mr. Mij, would you come here for your safety gear and join me for the quadroff please?"

There was a rustle of commotion in the DiversiDine section. From the MetamorfaSys Inc. area, Musca Mij flew onto the field in an instant. And Spectra Pollux rose with confidence to join him.

"Spectra, *no*," Rozz found herself pleading in a low voice. "A quadroff?! Geez, have you ever watched kachunkettball?" Rozz had taken in at least three different infopill issues of *Kachunkettball Hourly* during her time at the LibLounge. She would never forget the piece on how Mergle Farcrumple, who played Upper Chucker for the Blumdec Blasters had lost his head, literally, in an overzealous kachunkettball quadroff between his and three rival teams. Rozz didn't necessarily *like* her alien "mentor" that much, but she wasn't quite sure she wanted to see the woman permanently separated from that Brobdingnagian noggin of hers.

Yet Spectra only paused and offered Rozz another one of her little rosebud smiles. "My dear," she said, "there was a time I found glory and personal balance as a kachunkettball Lower Lobber for the Quad Three College team. I believe I have it covered."

As she turned away, Rozz wondered whether they wouldn't be covering that massive skull of hers in an extra-large resealable baggie. It would solve a lot of Rozz's problems, but still…

The 37 cheered her on with energy.

The kachunkettball field was set up as a center circle inside a larger area shaped like a plus sign. Along each arm of the plus sign, various mechanisms swung into play, designed to catch and rebound the ball. And at the end of each arm of the plus was a goal—a tube that had one input and two branching chutes outward. One outgoing branch led to a net, preventing the ball from going further and thus, securing the point for the scoring team. The other led to an open chute, which shot the ball back out into play. Typically, four teams competed simultaneously, but with just three companies bidding on Tryfe, one of Skytreg's cheerleaders had been brought in as a fourth warm body in the quadroff.

The presenters each had helpers, assisting them with their safety gear like eunuch slaves to a gladiator reenactment society.

"At the sound of the buzzer, the ball will be put into play," announced Skytreg. "The first player to command control of the ball will go first. The remaining order will be judged by my charming support staff—" the charming support staff "woo-ed" helpfully, "— for quality of competitive play."

Strapped and wrapped, Spectra Pollux and Musca Mij stepped eagerly onto their hoverboards in anticipation, and each took up one of the giant ergonomic gravy ladles folks called the "shoop." Eudicot T'murp, however, had called in a substitute player. This was due to his advancing age and also the fact his Getting Big Yoonies and Figuring Out Where It Goes reps said it was a financial liability to have their leader in a position where large metal objects were flying at his limbs. His spot went to an ambitious DiversiDine exec.

In a moment, the buzzer rang and a ratcheting sound began. This mechanical cracking grew in intensity, echoing across the field until—PA-TONNNGGG! From a round hole in the ground sprang a large, silver sphere. It shot into the air like water from Old Faithful, and the hoverboarding players each raced to catch it and sling it goalward with their shoops.

Spectra made a smooth, well-balanced dive, but it was Musca Mij who tossed the shoop from one set of hands to the other—KONNNGGGGG!—just in time to scoop the ball from the right angle and fling it toward his goal. Along the way it clipped the unprotected ear of T'murp's player, the poor sod, who toppled off his already-lurching hoverboard. The guy dropped to the ground as the hoverboard whizzed off unmanned.

"Time!" shouted Skytreg, beaming beneficently at the group before him. The buzzer sounded again. "Cosmic! Absolutely stellar! Congratulations to Musca Mij, who will present first today!"

Applause of both the enthused and milquetoast variety rustled through the arena. Musca Mij's name erupted into a shower of color and lights on the scoreboard.

"And, judges, who will follow Mr. Mij?"

The Charming Support Staff in the front row each pressed a button. The scoreboard flashed a new name on its face in a spray of light.

"Spectra Pollux!" cheered Zenith Skytreg. "So this means, Eudicot T'murp will deliver our third and final presentation of the day. Thank you for playing along!"

The bleeding but still capitated DiversiDine exec was accompanied by six Vos Laegon medics and led woozily off the field into his company's section.

Spectra returned to her seat winded but with an exhilarated sort of glow. Meanwhile, Musca Mij took the stage, carrying a small, simple case. He pushed a button and a presentation table unfolded. In a moment it projected a pretty 3-D planet into the stadium sky.

"Tryfe," began Mij, "A world of natural resources, naïve charm and an insulated and unique world culture virtually untouched by the GCU..." He grinned. "Hoo-boy, does somebody need a face-lift!"

✧

"What we really need is a camera," Bertram mused, pacing the lounge of Rollie's ship. "Not just any camera. One with a live feed straight to the Uninet, to broadcast everything as it happens. That way no matter what goes down today, the whole GCU would see everything we see. And the truth would come out."

Bertram had been increasingly worried about just what would happen to him after there was nothing more he could do for his planet. He envisioned himself missing his one golden chance to help Tryfe and billions of humans dying under some alien-inflicted plague or military invasion. He pictured himself drowning in guilt, unable to disconnect the cognitive patterns associated with being solely responsible for the greatest failure in his planet's history—failure even beyond past ethnic cleansings, religious wars, and canceling cleverly-written TV series' after just one season. He pictured himself unable to move forward but unable to ever go back home.

Or perhaps he'd wind up crazed with fear and regret like Major Tom Modean, alternating cheesy come-on lines with half-mad lectures about the merits of Luddite basketry to every four-bosomed woman that crossed his path.

But lately, he'd been envisioning himself nabbed and spending the rest of his days in a GCU prison. Or dumped on Altair-5 along with Rollie, only to be finished off by the living nightmares that lurked at the Tarpits. "If we got it on camera," Bertram said, "at least our efforts would have meaning."

"Meaning, yes…" Xylith watched him pace past her for the twentieth time and Bertram could hear a big "but" coming on. "But… don't forget, with leverage and enough public pressure, we might just be able to get you and your people out of this altogether."

Bertram gave a bitter laugh. "And that would be great, Xylith, but this is space. If I've learned anything, it's that in space it's always wiser to plan for everything to get screwed up beyond imagination," Bertram said.

"Wiser? Well, it would also be wiser to go as far away from Skorbig as possible, get yourself a new holowatch disguise, change your name to Berglat Smiggett and open a booth selling polegrots in the Shop-o-Drome on Golgi Beta," said Xylith. "But where's the fun?"

"Where's the sense of duty?" Bertram corrected.

"Where's the adventure?" Xylith gave him that flirty gaze again.

"And where's the—" Bertram paused and frowned. "Berglat Smiggett, seriously?"

She shrugged.

"Much as I hate to interrupt," Rollie called from the pilot's chair in the adjacent room, "we're heading for touch-down. All those interested in getting personal with the ceiling, by all means, *don't* fasten your harness."

"It's just a shame we don't have a camera with a live feed," continued Bertram.

"Who says we don't?" Rollie glanced in the ICV equivalent of the rear-view mirror and scowled at what he saw. "Harnesses! Fragging harnesses. Bleeding Karnax, you people are such low-functioning life-forms sometimes."

By now, Bertram was wobbling his way into the cockpit and stumbled into the copilot's chair. "We have a camera?" he asked hopefully. "And it actually works?" At Rollie's dagger glare he harnessed himself into the seat.

"O' course it works." Rollie hooked his crooked thumb into the room behind them. "You've met."

"What, you mean…" He peered over the harness into the other room. He didn't see anything there except for the seats, the smudgy paneled walls, the smudgy paneled ceiling, the built-in Uninet terminal, Xylith and… "O'wun?"

"*Oh no,*" responded O'wun promptly. "No. You are not dragging me into this. Isn't it enough you wrecked my life back home? Now you want to get me on the bad side of GCU law? What, is this some kind of elaborate campaign to see me dismantled into my smallest, most intimate nanotechnologies?"

"O'wun was the best video correspondent the Feegar Rebellion ever saw," Rollie told Bertram proudly. "Most of the war footage archived on the Uninet was his doing."

Impressed, Bertram struggled to peer into the room behind. "Hey, that's pretty cool, O'wun," he called. "So do you think you could—?"

"No."

"But don't you want to—?"

"No."

"Okay, but just why can't you—?"

"No."

✧

"And that's why Tryfe is the ideal place for thrill-seekers looking for that vacation spot off the beaten path." Musca Mij clasped two sets of hands together in front of him and didn't bother to control the pleased little buzz of his wings. "In summary, topographically, Tryfe has it all. Deserts, oceans, mountains, jungles, and rivers, all with an oxygen-based atmosphere.

"But what it needs is a serious Do-Over. Clean up the Tryfling infestation using our patented three-step Fumigation, Sanitation and Rejuvenation process. Then, using the talents of MetamorfaSys Inc.'s Planetary Transformation Consultants, we will renovate the property into an edgy, thrill-a-minute, mind-blowing exploration planet that appeals to the modern GCU adventurer who thought, until now, he'd done it all." Here were 3-D renderings of GCU tourists hoverboarding over the Grand Canyon…Hypersailing the Sahara…ICV-bungeeing over the Alps…and dining in weather-proofed ice hotels on the Arctic tundras. "Our plan offers the kind of High Intensity, Supervised Adrenaline-Based Vacation Experience and Completely Orchestrated Fun you expect from a MetamorfaSys planet." A montage of these newly-crafted wonders swirled in the globe above him. "Thank you."

Musca Mij exited the stage as Zenith Skytreg stepped back onto it. "I can barely talk, my breath is so taken away," exclaimed Skytreg, all evidence to the contrary. "Thank you, Musca Mij, for that high intensity presentation of yours. Extreme enjoyment on my part! And next up, we have Spectra Pollux, the creative mind behind the CapClub, ready to tell us all about her plans for Tryfe. Spectra?"

Rozz was already sweating, and it was soaking her temples and trickled under that stupid tracking headband. She tugged at the collar of her sticky-hot LibLounge barista shirt for relief. Throughout Mij's presentation, nausea had washed across her in waves. And the more she heard about Mij's plan for her people, the more she found it almost impossible to sit still in her chair. It was panic, pure and fierce, and it caused a fearful energy to rise up within her. Her trembling legs wanted only to run, run from Skorbig Stadium and just keep running.

Yes, Mij was planning to wipe out everybody on Tryfe, just so some asshat E.T.s could sip Martian Mai Tais from the skulls of the human race and hover-surf over the blood of millions of Earth people.

Not, literally, of course. That would be gross. But to Rozz's mind, it solidified the decision she made now.

She gave one last glance to the skies for signs of her fellow Tryfling, but cloud formations smothered her hopes. Bertram Ludlow, his "Life for Tryfe" team and the media were not coming, and she chided herself for wasting so much valuable time working to trigger a plan that wasn't entirely self-determined.

Yes, Plan 4B was all up to her, and it always had been. But now in an ironic twist that brought the nausea again, it also involved helping Spectra Pollux win this stupid bid simply so Musca Mij wouldn't. After the planet was awarded, well, Rozz would figure out how to extract her people from a lifetime of minimum wage milkshake work. But at least they'd live like minimum wage men and not die like mootaabs.

For this moment, she would give it her Best Her.

Rozz followed Spectra to the stage, the way they'd rehearsed it, calm and efficient.

"Thank you, Mr. Skytreg," said Spectra, her strong motherly voice projecting to the farthest seat in the stadium. "So far today we've heard much about the planet Tryfe. But now, you're going to hear something a little different. Ours is a tale of life-forms. Of heart. Of life-forms *with* hearts, in different parts of the body than we might expect, but which beat equally to ours in their desire to succeed. I'm talking about the people of Tryfe," she said.

In support, the scoreboard displayed images of all the Tryflings her creative staff had grabbed from satellite TV transmissions.

Rozz snickered when clips of Mussolini giving a speech popped up, sandwiched between universally-beloved children's TV host, Grampa Cardigan, and an early Shirley Temple talkie.

"I'm talking about people like my Tryfling friend Rozz here," Spectra went on, her voice warm and authoritative. She motioned to Rozz as Exhibit A. "People who have too long been disconnected from the GCU and who deserve a chance to make their way in the competitive cosmic landscape around them. I believe that with the right infopill education and rigorous training, these primitive Tryfe people can be nurtured into ideal, reliable employees, eager to assist in LibLounges across the CGU. As Rozz will demonstrate now...Rozz," she commanded, "make our audience some mini-mootaab milkshakes and tell us all about the latest CapClub recommendations, won't you, dear?"

Rozz put on her best CapClub Leader smile and fired up the portable milkshake machine she'd packed. "Today's *Featured CapClub Feature-of-the-Day* is *One Word Poems*, by Jet Antlia. In this eye-opening chapbook of insightful one-word verse, Antlia chooses select terms from the Universal vocabulary to stand alone on each page, thereby transforming simple, little-thought-about ordinary language into the breathtaking poetry of the new GCU. With no context, additional support text, illustration or even, in some cases, proper spelling— what do you think the author might be trying to say through his work's sparsity and seemingly sloppy randomness?... Anyone?"

25

"There it is!" shouted Bertram, pointing at the red-and-purple peeling construct ahead on the horizon. "There!"

"I see it, Ludlow. I see," Rollie grumbled. "I have flown before."

"Then how come we taxied halfway over the planet to get here?" Xylith teased from the other room.

"Aw, that's not me. It's *this* thing, innit?" Rollie flicked one of the gauges. "It's fragged. Outputting bad data. Got no precision."

"What's with the flags?" Bertram observed the bright flapping fabrics among the stadium's nose-bleed seats as they swept in from the south. They seemed to bear writing but were too far to read.

"Flags?" Xylith asked, craning to see.

Rollie squinted, turned a few dials, and the front window zoomed in on them, magnifying the logos into view.

"DiversiDine," Bertram affirmed aloud, "MetamorfaSys Inc., too... I don't recognize the third one."

Rollie gave a bitter laugh. "LibLounge CapClub. Looks like someone wants you and CapClub management to meet pretty blasted badly, Ludlow."

Bertram frowned at him around his harness. "Why do you say that?"

"*Breakfast with Bertram at Skorbig Stadium for Independence Day* as the *Featured CapClub Feature-of-the-Day*?" Rollie prompted. "Either you got one big fan in Spectra Pollux and this is a blasted funny way of getting an intro, or someone's desperate to set her up as your next target."

"If she's planning to buy my planet, then she is my next target," Bertram responded. "Anyway, what would she do with Earth? Tempt us with 12 free infopills for a yoonie and then hook us all into lifetime CapClub subscriptions with outrageous shipping and handling fees?" He watched as their ship descended, now hovering over the ICV lot. "Hey, don't land so close; they'll see you come in."

"Already cloaked," said Rollie. "And I'll park where I fragging like. I have flown before."

"Yeah, yeah."

The pre-recorded music composed by Dumbbell Nebula reached even the cheap seats, while the video scoreboard treated the audience to a spell-binding 3-D celebrity chorus projected out over the stadium tiers. Holding hands, flippers, and other publicly-acceptable appendages, the slick promotion video sang of hope and Tryfling advancement through gainful GCU employment in the LibLounges. Spectra Pollux had arranged for famed friends of every species to ring out her grand finale message:

> GCU for Me
> GCU for You
> GCU for Everyone,
> 'Cause the CapClub makes it true
> GCU for Him
> GCU for Her
> GCU for Tryflings,
> In a LibLounge anywhere

Rozz had heard this a million times now, and the lyrics never got any better. Contrived sentimentality, easy rhyme, predictable plotline… She figured it would be a lock to break Number One on the GCU music charts.

The singers had poured syrup over two stanzas of lyrics before Stella Cygnus took over, doing dramatic interpretive dance moves and warbling her sincere solo. She was surrounded by Bibluciat orphans trying desperately to blend in with the production stage and avoid all the attention.

> If you'll only step
> From that empty Tryfling world
> I'll be here and gladly reach out
> For that frothy-fresh beverage
> You made with your own two hands...

> GROUP: (Two hands!)

Well-known faces from all four quadrants of the Greater Communicating Universe swayed and sang in unity.

> GCU for Me
> GCU for You
> GCU for all of Tryfe,
> 'Cause Spectra Pollux tells us to

Foobaz Frabblagundger—who had managed to extend his Resilience Curve by an unheard-of 29.1 hours through his rumored involvement in a Spectra Pollux initiative—played a rousing stanza of instrumentation upon his nose. It culminated in a round-style singing extravaganza, interspersed with samples of Jet Antlia's cutting edge one-word poetry.

> GCU for You ("tandem")
> CGU for Me ("expatiate")
> CGU cures Tryfling strife
> Just the way it ought to be ("globule")

The musical promo ended on the digitally-altered images of the Tryfling footage they'd shown earlier. Thanks to the wonders of GCU graphics manipulation technology, these individuals now smiled under a Spectra Pollux logo banner, shining tears of joy in their eyes. They were wearing LibLounge barista uniforms.

Rozz felt that while the jaunty LibLounge visor looked pretty dashing on ol' Grampa Cardigan, tangerine really wasn't Mussolini's color.

When the music faded, and the lights went up, a pause of several silent seconds stilled the room, before the place exploded in applause. Much of it showered from Spectra's own staff, true, but Skytreg's people "woo-ed" shrilly and with real enthusiasm. Even Musca Mij clapped with several sets of hands, showing his professional respect.

Rozz exhaled. Spectra took a bow and then motioned Rozz to collect everyone's empty milkshake glasses. When she returned to her seat, Rozz noticed Spectra Pollux's suit was all blushing optimism.

Pollux apparently hadn't spied what Rozz had seen when they were on stage. Or if she did, she didn't note its significance. Not far away, Rozz had caught a strange stir of wind behind the stadium, in the ICV lot. Roosting ergowohms had exploded from the surrounding brush. Leaves had whirled upward in a sudden rush. A hum, even and persistent, underlay Spectra's own presentation soundtrack. It was as if something unseen and mechanical had arrived and planted itself firmly on their doorstep.

It had made Rozz give an honest, for-real, human smile. She had a sneaking suspicion it had been no natural anomaly that sent the leaves twisting, the air humming, and the ergowohms heading for safer ground.

No, she was sure it was Bertram Ludlow's sweet ride, cloaked and ready-for-business. It just had to be.

Things, she thought, were about to get hot.

"We have this saying on Tryfe that the eyes are the window to the soul," Bertram said, peering around at the open panel in the back of O'wun's head. It was encrusted with a startling number of tiny technologies. So many that it looked like a miniature Manhattan cityscape had been tucked inside the guy's cranium and Bertram had an aerial view.

With a little pointed tool, Rollie was carefully triggering a yellow inset button located somewhere around Central Park South. O'wun's eyes gave three horizontal rolls and stabilized. His view appeared on the pocket vis-u Bertram held before him. The footage was sharp and appeared to be uploading properly to the Uninet site they'd set-up earlier. "I guess O'wun's soul gets the GCU equivalent of high-def picture quality and surround sound."

Rollie closed the back of O'wun's skull, leaving the flap of hair that had been kicked up in the process. It was like a shag area rug in dire need of carpet tape. "All right, O'wun?"

O'wun smoothed it down and Bertram thought he heard it click into place. "Clear," O'wun said.

Rollie gave a crisp nod. "Stellar." He pulled a laser from an inner coat pocket and handed it to O'wun. "Here. In case."

"An XQ-40," said O'wun holding it up admiringly. "Very nice."

Rollie had pulled a second hand-laser from his coat and handed that to O'wun, too. "In case, in case."

"Um, Rollie," Bertram frowned, "I was thinking we'd go with more words than weaponry."

But the Hyphiz Deltan had withdrawn a third and fourth hand-laser, as if GCU outerwear had clown car capabilities, and he held them out for Xylith. "Careful with these now. They've got—"

"No need to trouble yourself, my star." And Xylith lifted a pantleg to withdraw a slim metallic lavender rectangle from her silvery boot. At the press of a button, the rectangle unfolded—click! click! click!—into an impressive example of stylish fragmentation and stun power. "A girl flying solo should always have a little something on hand, don't you think?" she told him with a double-wink.

Mumbling and trying to look unimpressed, Rollie regifted one of the weapons to Bertram.

Bertram had seen this coming. And while the idea of wielding unfathomable alien firepower was enticing on some basic male evolutionary level—a deep-rooted childhood holdover from long summer nights playing *Slikk Slaughter: RoboTrooper* on the PC—the cognitive psychologist in him still wished he had more time to think through their moves. "Look, Rollie, I don't know, I—"

"It's very easy." The Hyphizite held up a hand. "Press this, it's on. Grip that, it fires."

"And what seals up the holes in me when the bidders' bodyguards think I'm on an assassination mission and try to take me out?" Bertram asked.

"Different gadget," explained Rollie, pulling one from his coat and handing it to him.

"Oh." It was the hole-mending-thingie he'd used to seal the cut Bertram had given him back when he was dead. It also sort of wiped away 75% of Bertram's objections. Rollie reached to retrieve it, but Bertram stuffed it quickly into his own pocket. "I'm just concerned this path we're on is going to end with everyone demolecularized and no one growing back."

"Ah," said Rollie, bright with interest. "Well, to that I'll share with you the advice my own Paternal Archetype imparted the day he passed that hand-laser on to me."

Bertram waited.

"Plant. Your. Feet," Rollie told him. "Plant your feet." Clapping Bertram on a shoulder, Tsmorlood returned the second pistol to his jacket, opened the hatch, turned, and stalked down the ramp to Skorbig.

"My dad told me 'always remember to floss'," Bertram said to Xylith as they walked down the ramp. "We're gonna die, aren't we?"

The Skorbig concession stand held the residue of years, and its menu-board was long-blank. Dried leaves from local vegetation stuck to the counter, nestled in empty shelves, and crunched underfoot. From here, they had a clear view into the stadium. A figure paced the stage before a broad video screen, and his voice bounced through the stands.

"DiversiDine Entertainment Systems and Aeroponics is the GCU's total amusement experience, from the programming we produce and the vis-us we develop, to the beloved snacks that become tasty habits with every can't-miss moment…" The presenter was Eudicot T'murp, Bertram realized. CEO and president of DiversiDine, in the flesh.

Or, well, the foliage.

Bertram checked the pocket vis-u connected to O'wun and verified what he already knew; systems were go. O'wun was pumping this to the Uninet. The GCU was tapped-in.

Rollie and Xylith rejoined them now after a quick recon of the stadium. The Hyphizite was flushed with delight, his laugh low and amazed. "Did you see?" he queried incredulously. "Front center. It's *Zenith fragging Skytreg* out there! *Zenith Skytreg.* How in Altair's tarpits is that brooquat wrapped up in this?"

Out in the stadium, fanfare and an on-screen explosion signaled the start of T'murp's video promo.

"Maybe he's in the market for new Underworld office space," suggested Xylith.

"On Tryfe? Not flashy enough," Rollie sniffed. "Unless he could convince the Tryflings to worship him as their god, wouldn't be worth his effort."

"It's a sizable crowd," Xylith observed, "but none of them scream 'RegForce' to me."

"Can't rule out holowatches," Rollie reminded her, "but yeah. RegForce you can almost smell. No Seers of Rhobux, either. Just keep an eye on Mij's bodyguards and Skytreg's little Vos Laegon beauties. They can pack some trouble. O'wun, you pan the audience so our Uninet viewers get to see all the pretty faces of today's attendees. You give each of 'em a nice, clear close-up. Make sure you get Skytreg, too. Then you keep your eyes on the stage. You follow Ludlow no matter what happens, you understand?"

O'wun understood.

"Ludlow," Rollie began, "Xylith and me, we're going to cover you best we can. Which, by Underworld standards, is pretty fragging stellar. You just do what you got to do out there. Things go zonky, you get yourself out. Hear me? You get out first and head toward the ship. You remember where the ship is?"

"I do." After their narrow Ludd escape, Bertram had learned how important it was to pay real attention where you parked a cloaked ship. He imagined a lot of elderly members of the Underworld eventually got nabbed because they were wandering around ICV parks looking for their see-through transportation.

Now Rollie turned to his Underworld colleagues, his expression grave. "Xylith, O'wun, if I'm caught or too fragged up, I want you to take the ship. Keep it cloaked. Go to Tseethe's. I'll catch up if I'm able."

"And if you're not able?" Xylith's lavender eyes wore concern in duplicate.

"Then picture me building a nice summer home on Altair-5, and expect a Uninet postcard." He gave a flash of a smile he didn't entirely seem to mean. "Right. Now, the RegForce and every other law unit across the GCU is likely seeing this live and heading here now. Meaning, there's not much time for fancy stuff. So Ludlow, good luck saving Life As You Know It and whatnot. Always liked Tryfe. Try not to get lasered. And don't forget—"

"Plant my feet?" Bertram suggested.

"Ah, they grow up so fast," Rollie said to Xylith, with a wink, and darted through the threshold into the arena's nosebleed seats.

"Make Tryfe proud, Bertram," Xylith told him. "It's been a real pleasure subverting the iron-fist of intergalactic authority with you." And with a quick one-faced kiss as light as the antennae of a ratuk flappameria, she darted into the arena, laser drawn, taking a path that mirrored Rollie's.

That left him with O'wun. "Ready?" the Non-Organic asked.

"Just need to get my battle-cry on," said Bertram. It sounded a lot braver than he felt. But sometimes that was good enough.

O'wun nodded. "After you."

"It's my first populist rebellion, you know," Bertram told him, hoping to stall a moment longer. And drawing a deep breath he hoped wouldn't be his last, Bertram Ludlow ran into the stadium shouting, "Life for Tryfe! Life for Tryfe!"

Heads turned as he raced forward, down the stands. "Life for Tryfe! Life for Tryfe!"

Surging ahead, Bertram surveyed the crowd. He caught the eyes of Mimsi Grabbitz, the Alternate Realty agent he'd met with back on Ottofram. In the far aisle he spied Musca Mij, who buzzed with interest at this new change in events.

But in the nearest section, Bertram's eyes were drawn to a bright shock of hot pink hair, on a head that just now was swiveling toward him. It revealed a familiar face wearing an angelically exhilarated smile. The figure also seemed to be wearing a fast food service uniform. Bertram blinked rapidly to process the information. "Rozz?"

At the sight of him, Rozz leapt up from her seat, clapping and fist-pumping. "Yeah, you rock 'em, Bertram! Life for Tryfe! Life for Tryfe!"

The giantess of a woman next to her scowled. The lady's suit went from pink to black so swiftly, Bertram wasn't quite sure he hadn't imagined it. "Rozz, what are you doing? Sit down!" the giantess hissed.

All Bertram's logic neurons had gone off at once. They whooped "Contextual Impossibility! Overload! Overload!" Rozz Mercer was *here*. Not in the Psych Department computer lab. Not enjoying two-for-one beers with Bertram at the Murray Avenue Tavern. Not even face down snoring in the University coffeehouse, chocolate croissant for her pillow. Rozz Mercer was in *space*. At *Skorbig Stadium*.

Bertram had to wrench his gaze away from the pink haired programmer, before he lost all momentum to save the planet.

Instead, he turned to address Eudicot T'murp. T'murp stood tall at the podium, and behind the man towered the most enormous holoscreen.

On that screen was playing—oddly enough—Eudicot T'murp, live, at the podium. And behind Movie T'murp was the movie holoscreen. And on and on. Limitless T'murps and unending screens marched dizzyingly into the distance, like performance art honoring M.C. Escher.

Bertram would have latched onto his old madness theory, but he knew the GCU better than that these days.

Then he remembered: O'wun. He turned around, expecting to see the Simulant-turned-independent filmmaker right behind him. He'd been told to focus on the crowd, but these Underworld people were a notoriously self-determined bunch and—

The space was empty, and a scan of the seats found O'wun crouched four rows up, ducked behind a Sleemy Snaps cart, and busy panning the crowd like he'd been told.

Bertram grabbed the little vis-u from his shirt pocket and frowned at it. The footage was of the crowd. As it should be. He shook it. Only the crowd. From the front left. Four rows up.

Now the screen on the stage showed Tryfling hands holding a portable vis-u displaying footage of the crowd.

Bertram waggled the portable vis-u in his hands.

The vis-u on the mega-screen waggled, too.

Bertram waved a hand over his mid-section.

A two-story hand waved over the whole of the screen on the stage.

Bertram grabbed up the Yellow Thing, as it dangled on its string around his neck, and the whole view on the screen rotated to nauseating effect. Heads in the audience tilted. One life-form fell out of his chair. And then the whole image adjusted and righted itself.

Bertram winced. "I'll 'know when I need to know,' huh?" he muttered as the implications of the Seers cryptic words sunk in. He'd had this stupid thing with him all over the GCU and back. He'd had it the confinement center on Podunk. He'd had it in the Underworld meeting at Vos Laegos. He'd had it on the Cosmos Corral. He'd had it while he slept, and while he ate, and while he— "Holy crap!" He wrested the Yellow Thing from around his neck and flung it to the ground like he was making the last touchdown in the final quarter of the Superbowl.

The screen image rolled and joggled.

The audience joined the presenter on stage in merry laughter. "And *that's* how we've been doing the single-camera hand-held live feed. Yep, viewers won't miss a single eye-popping moment of all the *Real Reality RealTime DocuDramatic*™ Tryfling action!"

Eudicot T'murp pushed a button and the screen shifted from the perspective of the Yellow Thing on the ground, to an action montage featuring the highlights—or low points, depending on how you looked at it—of Bertram's recent days. The words "There Goes the Galaxy" blazoned forth front-and-center.

"So, in summary," T'murp continued, "with DiversiDine as Tryfe's winning bidder, we won't just offer Tryflings the thrilling chance to user-test DiversiDine products before they go to market. We'll leverage their quaint lifestyle as part of a ground-breaking new entertainment concept. One, I might add, that's already become a real fan favorite for our test groups."

On the screen, one interviewed User Tester said, "I'm simply hooked on *There Goes the Galaxy*. I can't wait to see what that zonky Tryfeman will be up to next!"

Another wondered, "How will Tryfling Bertram Ludlow get himself out of this latest jam? My familial unit and I are dying to know."

And a third: "I'd be interested in learning more about Tryfe. Can you imagine never seeing a piece of Translachew gum before? Having never touched a vis-u or piloted an ICV? *There Goes the Galaxy* made me look at the GCU from a whole new perspective!"

"Our plan," continued Eudicot T'murp, "is for each season of *There Goes The Galaxy* to feature a new Tryfe person in a new challenge, making it both educational and compelling. So let's give a big round of applause for our very first *There Goes the Galaxy* Tryfling Uninet star…Let's hear it for Bertram Ludlow!"

In an odd 180 of those childhood nightmares where Bertram went to school naked and with nowhere to stick a hall pass, now at the sound of his very name, life-forms in the stadium went wild. Some rose in a standing ovation. Even a few of DiversiDine's biggest competitors clapped him on the shoulder or reached to shake his hand.

"Nice job, kid," someone said.

"Good luck out there," said someone else.

"Very brave for an unevolved life-form."

It took a moment of this unexpected and uncanny behavior, before Bertram was able to find his motor skills and break free of the startling adulation. "No!" he shouted, recoiling from his newest, biggest fans. "What is *wrong* with you people? The people of my planet don't want to spend their lives testing your crappy products!"

"Aw, you'll never even know you're doing it," Eudicot T'murp explained kindly. "It's fun. You'll get into it."

"We don't want to be the unwitting stars of your crummy Uninet series, either!" Here, Bertram ran the rest of the way through the stadium seats and leapt up on the stage. "What you all seem to forget is, we are people—like you."

He glanced at the leafy appearance of Eudicot T'murp, into the iridescent eyes of Musca Mij, and at the mountain-hewn physique of the woman in the CapClub section, who Bertram realized had to be Spectra Pollux.

"Well, not *like* you exactly," he hedged. "But we have lives and hopes and dreams, like you do. We have our own world that we love, like you. And if and when we figure out long-distance space travel, and join the GCU, it will be *our* decision to make. Not yours." In his most passionate tones he announced, "We will not be the playthings of some self-proclaimed 'superior intelligence.' We didn't spring up in this universe to have our fate in the hands of some money-grubbing alien corporation. Or some sneaking, sell-out Seers. Or some…some…Underworld politician thinking about reelection." Here he gave a pointed look to Zenith Skytreg.

Now Bertram noticed Rozz jumping from her chair and scrambling to join him on the stage. "And believe it or not," shouted Rozz, "we don't exactly dream of spending our lives providing deep explanations for shallow poetry. We rarely get up in the morning and wish some big-boned alien chick would snatch us from everything we love and offer us a life of indentured servitude behind a glorified beverage cart! (We can be slaves to corporate bureaucracy on our own planet, thank you very much!) And very few humans want to become Our Best Us if it's by someone else's martyred, manipulative, big-headed, big-mouthed, celebrity-blinded, bigoted, bouffant, mood-dress-wearing standards!"

Rozz exhaled, like a Rumoolitan-sized weight had been lifted from her. She exchanged a surprised grin with her fellow Tryfling, as if just coming-to and realizing he was there. "Hey, Bertram. Great to see ya," she said warmly. "How goes?"

"Not bad. I'm an Intergalactic Fugitive these days. You?"

"Hanging in. Could do with a few less bossy aliens."

"Ditto that." He nodded knowingly and turned back to the crowd and announced, "Tryfe is not now and has never been for sale. This goes beyond GCU real estate paperwork. Tryfe belongs to the people born on its soil. Who dwell under its sun and its moon. Who call it home. And who—by the way—call it Earth, not Tryfe. I mean, geez! You've got all this advanced technology and know-how, but you can't even get the planet's name right? That drives me *nuts!* And—"

He was just starting to enjoy the topic and was about to tell the GCU a few other enlightening things about itself, when the words died somewhere in the back of his throat, around the central uvula region.

Across the Stadium, an ICV had swept in. Bertram recognized its sleek features and the aforementioned advanced technology. It belonged to the Hyphiz Deltan RegForce and it came here prepped to buck tradition—and maintenance crew regulations—by landing smack-dab on the kachunketball playing field.

Bertram closed his gaping mouth. An effective public speaker knew when to wind things up. "Er, okay! Thanks everybody! Great crowd! Gotta go."

He grabbed Rozz's wrist and started out across the stage. "Bertram, I don't think I can—"

But Bertram was too busy listening to the voice that boomed from the descending ICV: "BERTRAM LUDLOW AND ROLLIAM TSMORLOOD; THIS IS THE HYPHIZ DELTAN REGFORCE. WE NEED TO TALK."

Bertram and Rozz had scrambled off the stage and down through the stadium seats. All the while Rozz was unhelpfully trying to wrench her arm from his grasp. "Bertram, listen to me." She touched her silvery headband absently. Decorative red lights blipped along it. It wasn't her style, but Bertram knew how space changed a person. "Dude, I can't go with you. I'd love to, but Pollux set the radius on this damned thing, and if I go out of range—"

"Ludlow!" This was Rollie, still covering the audience. One-handed, he dug into a pocket of his coat. "Take this."

He pulled out a print copy of *Guide to Karnaxic Meditation: the Uptight Stressed-Out Non-believer's Edition*, glanced at it and cursed. "Sorry." He stuffed it back into his jacket. He withdrew something else. "This."

It was the remote for the ship. "Here. Let yourself in. I'll be along shortly."

"Rollie, we could all make it if we leave now," said Bertram.

"*I* can't," interjected Rozz. "Spectra has me hooked up with this totally messed-up—"

"BERTRAM LUDLOW AND ROLLIAM TSMORLOOD!" The RegForce ship rattled, as the landing gear unfolded from its undercarriage. "PUT DOWN YOUR WEAPONS AND AWAIT FURTHER INSTRUCTION."

"Rollie, it's time to go," Bertram insisted.

The Hyphiz Deltan's focus was riveted to the ship. "No."

"What?"

"Not for me. I got something I need to try first." He glanced only cursorily at Xylith and O'wun who'd just joined their small knot of insurgents. "All of you. Move. Now."

"What do you mean 'something you need to try'?" queried Xylith's face on the right.

The left face added, "Are you *that anxious* to tour Altair-5, Rollie Tsmorlood? Only someone who thrives irrationally on risk to the point of being dangerously self-destructive would even consider staying to 'try' something under these circumstances."

"Actually, Xylith, I could use your help."

"Oh," she said, brightening. "Sure. No problem."

"IF YOU NEGLECT TO PUT DOWN ALL WEAPONS IMMEDIATELY," continued Mook's voice from the RegForce ICV, "WE SHALL BE FORCED TO FIRE, AND I DON'T IMAGINE YOU'LL LIKE THAT AT ALL. CONSIDER THIS YOUR FINAL WARNING."

"More running," Rollie advised the rest of the group. "It starts with the feet. Go."

He didn't need to tell Bertram Ludlow twice. Well, he did; technically. But Bertram was too busy tugging Rozz toward the exit to count.

✧

"Bertram, will ya let go?" Somewhere between the empty Flinky Rolls dispenser and the long-abandoned souvenir stand, Rozz wrested her arm free and scowled. "I go much further, the next thing you'll be smelling is deep-fried frontal lobe."

Bertram stopped. "What are you talking about?"

"This!" she pointed to the headband. "This. This is what I've been trying to tell you. It's an electric head hobble. Spectra Pollux had me haberdashed with it the last time I tried to escape. She's got it set for a range. I go out of the range, I get zapped." She grabbed him by the collar of his flannel overshirt. "And I've *been* zapped, Bertram. Oh, there has been zappage. And I do not recommend it."

Bertram couldn't imagine anything that looked so much like designer couture could have that much kick. "It's that bad?" The words escaped his lips almost on reflex.

But Rozz Mercer flushed with outrage. "Bad?! You tell me. Last time, I wet myself, threw up, and completely forgot my own favorite color."

He glanced at her shocking pink hair. "Er."

"I still don't remember the name of my cat."

He hated to break it to her. "No pets, Rozz."

She blinked tired, dark brown eyes. "Shit. Wonder what that was then."

"Look," began Bertram, surveying the exits for unwanted company. "You can't just stay here. And after your little speech, I think you've pretty much blown any chances for upward mobility with your employer. Did you have a plan?"

"Plan? Yes, I had a plan. 4B," she snapped. "If you didn't show, I was going to lay low until I could get my hands on an infopill on DIY tiara extraction. Then work the system from within. But you came and went all Rosa Parks on their asses, and I got caught up in the moment. So I guess that's out now."

"Then *Breakfast with Bertram at Skorbig Stadium for Independence Day* was yours."

"Of *course* it was mine. Do you think these GCU wackos have attention spans long enough to write a title that clunky? I was thinking on the fly, pal."

O'wun cleared his throat. "It's a Klinko Cranial Boundary Determinator, isn't it?"

She tossed him a suspicious gaze. "Yeah, why?"

"Those are red lights flashing along its decorative outer casing," he observed.

"I'll take your word for it." She tried to catch her reflection in the dusty metal of the display case. "So?"

"It's not armed," he said.

"What?" Bertram and Rozz made it a chorus.

"It's listed as part of the errata in the latest edition of all their technical manuals. A product-wide miscommunication in the instructions." He sighed, adding, "A common problem with using non-native Klinkon translators who aren't always able to apply cultural context. In the Klinko star system, red is the color of freedom and joy. Now if it were lit green—"

Bertram gave a strained laugh.

But Rozz's face was almost as pink as her hair. "Are you shitting me? This thing works, I assure you. It's shot so many volts through me I microwaved my own tongue."

"Perhaps it *was* armed," said O'wun patiently, "But it's not now. I imagine when they adjusted the programming for you to be able to come here—"

This was all Rozz needed to hear. She'd latched on to Bertram's wrist and yanked him to the exit.

"You're welcome," O'wun called, moving to catch up. Bertram hadn't realized Non-Organic Simulants had a sarcasm app.

✧

"So this is *your* doing," Rolliam Tsmorlood told Eudicot T'murp over the barrel of his XJ-37. "*You* hired the Seers of Rhobux to arrange the kidnapping on Tryfe. *You're* the reason those sightless slaggards went offline and off-orbit without blanking my archive. And *you're* the reason the RegForce is ready to send me to Altair-5."

An explosion rocked the field, not of his making, and Rollie glanced over his shoulder to see its cause. Three sections over, the lady from Dootett had cheerfully zapped out the RegForce ICV ramp, just as they were about to deboard. The ramp retracted and jammed the exit hatch with a *whizzz* and a metallic groan that echoed throughout Skorbig Stadium.

It was a nice effort and Rollie was glad for the extra time. Especially when he tended to get so wrapped up in his own work. Any card-carrying member of the Underworld would tell you: you rush a delicate armed coercion opportunity, you get scab results.

With a nod of thanks, Rollie returned his full attention to DiversiDine's CEO. "So because you set me up," he continued, "you're going to make it up. You, T'murp, are going to give me something I want."

"And what's that?" asked T'murp warily. Half of DiversiDine had abandoned their stadium seats for less volatile views of the action. The other half was frozen with trepidation. That seemed to include T'murp.

"Power," Rollie said simply. "Power *you* leverage to blank *me*— with *them*." Here he pointed to the RegForce ICV. The exit hatch and attached ramp were wildly lurching open and shut, open and shut, like hungry jaws. "That done, you're going to tell me where the Seers are. Me and them need a meeting of the minds."

Rollie wasn't sure what reaction he expected from the man— possibly pathetic begging or blatant denial—but it wasn't the one he got. "Gosh, Rollie," mused T'murp quietly, "you seem to be taking this awfully personally." He sounded surprised, and he addressed this primarily to the Deltan's hand-laser.

The businessman's mild tone and the offensive lack of perspective lit a small new fury in Rollie's mind. "Personally?! How in Altair's tarpits is this not—"

"I didn't choose you for this job, you know, Rollie. The Seers did. And I didn't decide who picked up Bertram Ludlow and got things launched, either. That was the Seers, too. Of course, now that I've seen your work," T'murp smiled warmly, one of the buds at his right temple flowering out into something purple, perfumed and pretty, "I agree, you were a stellar choice. I mean, the test groups love you. All that…" he paused, considering his words carefully, "…energy. Do you realize you're on your way to being a household name?"

"I am on my way to fragging Altair-5," Rollie corrected, low and firm, "or an unfulfilled lifetime of uncharacteristic skulking and relentless paranoia. Both of which make me, in effect, dead. So you start filming your statement to the Uninet demanding that I'm blanked of all recent events—" Rollie snatched a pocket vis-u from one of T'murp's less fleet-footed assistants who was trying to contact help. He plugged in the number of Bertram Ludlow's "Life for Tryfe" Uninet site and tossed the device to the DiversiDine president. It wasn't the quality video production they'd get through O'wun, but it would do. "—And you tell me where the Seers are. Now."

T'murp looked hesitantly at the vis-u in his hand. It seemed that telling the whole GCU your plans through a *Real Reality RealTime DocuDrama* came a lot more naturally than pulling a few strings and setting things right for the fugitives you created.

And the more he thought about it, the more Rollie saw what he hated about mainstream business; there was no sense of honor, no higher understanding. He swallowed his increasing anger and peered at T'murp through the sight on his favorite weapon.

Even to himself, his voice came out too unnaturally calm, too unnervingly distant. "You realize," he pondered, "one pull of the trigger at the right spot, on the right setting, and we're, any of us, just so many particles in the atmosphere...Vapor on the breeze...Dust sifting back into the cosmic void."

His finger flirted lightly with the trigger. The design was so smooth, so easy on the hand. It was elegance in advanced weaponry. It was beauty and brutality unified. It was temptation and terror in one cool metal package. "The philosopher Karnax called life-forms' pitiful need to believe in our own enduring legacy as 'untraceable whisperings in the Universal cavern.'" He considered T'murp carefully. "What'll your whispers say, I wonder?"

Not that Rollie had ever given the launch to an unarmed sentient being before—at least not so he remembered. His more final laserings had been of the frag-or-be-fragged variety. But given the inconvenience he'd endured at the hands of T'murp's pet project and the growing unharnessed outrage coursing through him, the idea was starting to have a certain hungry allure.

He toyed with the concept for a brief, entrancing moment longer before some more stabilizing Hyphiz Deltan brain chemicals stepped forward and reminded him that sizzling the fellow in front of everybody and Karnax probably wouldn't do much to promote Rollie as your average, basically-decent fellow who got a raw deal. It suggested instead he sweeten the situation from a different angle first: diplomacy. He'd heard it worked for some people.

Likely people who didn't own XJ-37s.

"Besides—" began Rollie slowly, trying to clear out the last mental images of fragmented cells dancing on the breeze. He offered a smile he intended to be winning, but judging from the way T'murp stared, it probably wasn't. "—Altair-5's a polite way of saying 'death sentence.' You don't want one of your leading men thoroughly killed before your show even premieres, do you? How would that look to viewers?"

To Rollie's surprise, this did seem to be more T'murp's language. His leaves seemed to perk up, and now he was nodding. "I see your point."

"Good." Across the kachunkettball field, the RegForce's hatch had come to a halt and was stuck half-open. The officers were now combining any and all lengths of on-hand cords, belts and blankets to create a rope long enough to descend. Rollie said, "Looks like you'll be able to tell your tale to 'em directly soon enough."

"On the other hand," T'murp considered, greening further, "it's not as if you really had a lot of screen time in *There Goes the Galaxy.*"

Rollie didn't like this particular shift in tone.

"Yes, and think what a poignant DocuDrama finale it could be," input Zenith Skytreg coolly, now emerging from the crowd, "if you end it with a member of your own cast being sent to Altair-5." Skytreg directed his hand-laser to the Hyphiz Deltan. "Sure, Tsmorlood wouldn't live to cameo in any reunion specials. But I tell you, Eudicot, it would make GCU entertainment history." Skytreg's hand-laser had an overly-elaborate casing——the kind only idiots with more yoonies than sense would choose—but at this range, it could still frag a guy's skull into whisperings.

Surprised by this change in odds, Xylith directed her aim from the RegForce and the crowd in general to Skytreg in specific. It would have been a Mexican standoff, if this hadn't been the GCU and the participants weren't Vos Laegon, Hyphiz Deltan, Cardoon and Dootett respectively.

In the GCU they called it a "Jeff."

Skytreg tossed Xylith a glance but instead focused his bright, too-close-together eyes on the Hyphiz Deltan. "I'm sorry to interrupt the morning's intimidation meeting. As Official Leader of the Intergalactic Underworld Society, I do appreciate your efforts. It's so rare I get to see really well-done duress in action these days." He took a step forward. "I'd also like to add that the Society does have an excellent opt-in mental health plan; I know: I negotiated the package personally. So if you do get out of here alive and physically well, perhaps you'll consider taking advantage of it. Regardless, I can't let you kill my winning bidder."

At the words "winning bidder," a murmur rose from the crowd. Instantly, business plans shifted, budgets opened up, dreams were squashed, and T'murp looked like he expected this win all along. "Everyone loves a good DocuDrama," he said modestly.

Skytreg smiled, holding aloft his own pocket vis-u in the hand not brandishing the laser. "Precisely! According to my sources here, our little Tryfe friend's film is getting Uninet attention off the charts.

Everyone's entranced with the idea of *There Goes the Galaxy*. They love the Tryfling's spirit. They love his determination. They even love his Tryfe accent. I wouldn't *dream* of standing in the way of this entertainment phenomenon."

Skytreg returned the vis-u to the pocket of his pearly suit. "But might I suggest two things, Eudicot? One: buy the rights, quickly, to the footage Ludlow released. People already seem to think it's a teaser for the series. And two: what would you say to a full Underworld ad sponsorship to run during the show's premiere?"

For Rollie, this was just too much. The Underworld of old would have focused on strengthening its blackmarket shipping network, upholding piracy with finesse, and crafting kidnappings done with a certain graceful mystery. Now the Society was sponsoring mindless mass-market programming? Rollie swung his weapon from T'murp to Skytreg. "That's right. Wear down the Underworld's nobility even further," he growled. "Where are your fragging standards, Skytreg? You realize we wouldn't even be in this spot if you hadn't decided buying and selling inhabited backspace planets made for a nice side income."

Skytreg laughed and folded his arms. "It seems your information is as skewed as your outlook, Tsmorlood. What makes you think I ever bought Tryfe?" He gave the same kind of smile he'd have given someone's temperamental progeny, condescension wrapped in thin tolerance. "A desperate Farquotichian tossed it into the pot on the Emperor's G'napps tables last U-year. It so happens, I won that round." He moved his own laser to center on Rollie's forehead. "Doesn't serendipity just blow your mind?"

Now Rollie noticed the Vos Laegos showbeings, in their purple and red cheerleader uniforms, had clustered to form a tight wall around Skytreg.

Vos Laegons, he knew, were one of the few creatures in the Universe with the ability to change their shape into a stable, secondary form at will. Rollie had read once it had something to do with their evolution and the species' natural ability to survive under harsh desert conditions, without a consistent food source. Millions of years ago, it was by luring in unsuspecting predators, only to turn them into quick all-you-could-digest buffets. These days it largely involved tourists, dark alleys and drained yoonie cards. But it was the part about the transformation and informal dining that tended to stick foremost in the brain.

So Rollie was not terribly surprised when they morphed into pearly-skinned horrors prepped for business.

"I see. Your fine ladies and gentlemen are going to do your dirty work for you," Rollie commented to Skytreg. He kept his voice steady and his gaze on Skytreg because, frankly, the overall group effect was terrifying. "It's just like the Feegar Rebellion, innit? Why bother to fight in a war when you can just say you did and stage the heroic photos later? So much tidier."

Rollie waited.

Skytreg's face grew grave with interest. "And how would you know I wasn't in the Feegar Rebellion?"

"Because *I* was." Rollie watched his expression. "I led one Klimfal defense group, Rentar Proximetra the other. I made it my business to know the troops. Mine and hers." Rollie's amber gaze was unflinching. "You weren't among them."

One of Skytreg's silvery eyebrows raised, just a fraction. Rollie wasn't sure, but he felt the man's complexion lost some of its luster.

"Interesting." Skytreg leaned in closer now, his fellow Vos Laegons making way for him. In a quiet, confidential tone, Skytreg said, "I wondered why your name sounded so familiar. I bet it was *your* war record I drew on. Only," he considered, "in my version, I wasn't left behind to fend for myself against the Feegars because my team scattered like scared snoogles. I didn't get myself captured and tortured for…how many Universal weeks was it? And I didn't sit around in irons waiting until my second-in-command eventually realized I was missing and came back to rescue me." Skytreg smiled. "But it's nice to finally put the name with a face." He whirled around and gestured, shouting, "Here he is, Officers! I stopped Tsmorlood for you."

As if following the Hyphiz System RegClock, the RegForce arrived on cue. Tstyko, with his driven scowl, dashed onto the scene like a man afire, and Mook brought up the rear, still winded from scaling down the side of his own ICV.

But the thing about Hyphizite Regimentation, Rollie thought, was its beautiful, boring predictability. It was easy to plan for this sort of entrance, in times everything else had gone south. And what Rollie liked in particular about his plan of combat today was its efficient, elegant simplicity…

Though some would also call it "blowing a whacking great hole in the risers below his feet."

The blast rocked the seats. The showbeings fell over willy-nilly like the pins on an Emperor's G'napps table. Rollie noticed Skytreg, the simpering, cowardly slaggard, ducked for cover like the slippery sludge he was. Xylith made a swift break for the exit. And the Hyphiz Deltan himself plummeted down into the floors under the seating with a thump and a clatter, bruised and battered on the chunks of rubble below.

26

Rollie glanced at the empty circle of sky above, righted himself despite some interesting new pains, and dashed into the darkness. Funny, he thought, how his choices for ending this regrettably-detoured scene of restitution came down to vertical logistics: up or down? Down or up?

Things went south, and so did he, because Up was considerably more problematic. He'd never gotten around to investing in a good pair of jet boots; seemed frivolous somehow when his plain old boots still had some life left in them. And while he imagined he *did* have a grappling hook-and-line tucked in a pocket somewhere, laying hands on it quickly was the tricky part.

In truth, that was one of his greatest faults, he admitted now, as he ducked through Skorbig Stadium's winding behind-the-scenes halls; he lacked organization. Having the right tools was one thing. Finding them in a pinch was something else entirely.

He could hear the thud as others made their way into the stadium inner-sanctum through his make-shift door. Running footsteps echoed, and he picked up the pace. Tstyko, he knew, could run—really run. Every few U-months, it seemed, Hyphizite news reported Tstyko winning this inter-solar system marathon and sweeping that Quadrant competition. Why, W.I. Igglestik Tstyko was *born* running. Likely made for an exceedingly confusing delivery for the Hyphiz Delta Progeny Farm nursing staff, Rollie imagined. But on the plus side, it was over fast.

Rollie took a quick left, hoping twists and turns would buy him time. This path opened into a narrow hall, filled with benches and lined with rows of purple-and-red storage containers: the Skorbig Ergowohms' locker room.

Even though it had been years since this room had seen sporting action, it still smelled of old shed armor, determination and discarded dreams. Or perhaps you had to have played kachunkettball yourself to catch the scent. Rollie had never been on a major team. But he had enjoyed the kind of roughhewn, back-alley, makeshift stuff unregulated progeny tended to embrace, particularly when it involved honing hand-to-eye coordination, strengthening important balance skills, learning leadership and teamwork...

Oh, and knocking other progeny hard with great metal implements when they weren't looking.

Too bad this wasn't the time for fond reminiscence, thought Rollie. He sprinted past the last of the lockers, took two long strides into the next room, and met with something that slid out from under his feet like a fruit peel in a Hyperbolea-3 pratfall competition. Around him items rattled and rolled, crashed and clattered. He struggled to stand, only to find himself toppling backwards once more in startled self-preservation...

He was face-to-beak with an ergowohm, razor-maw wide in a silent shriek.

He leapt in reverse now, and with safe distance came understanding. Its stillness. The glossy paint. The large crack running down its form. With spread wings, the creature was almost as tall as Rollie and had bumpers built around his haunches. One bumper sagged sadly off the side. It was a statue, a kachunkettball field obstacle, broken and forgotten, nothing more, and it was one of several.

Rollie caught his breath among the architectural salvage and returned it to its proper spot lungward.

What he'd crashed through, he saw now, included an array of kachunkettballs, hearty metal spheres rusting where they stood. And next to them, Rollie grabbed up and swung one of the ladle-shaped shoops. It was bent beyond proper use but retained a good grip.

Enough. Time was wasting. He searched for the door, then turned, then turned again. There was no outlet but the way he'd come in. Yet he could hear Tstyko and the others with agendas, clamoring down the narrow maze of halls his way.

He paused one Deltan second—long enough for anyone from the Hyphiz System to make a passable decision—and moved to the objects he'd spied in the corner.

They were official championship-sized hoverboards, used by the team's most dexterous and diversely talented players, the Upper Chuckers. The hoverboard offered this position a whole extra level of play. The team not only counted on the Upper Chuckers to keep the balls in motion for above field activity but also tasked them to prevent these foot-and-a-half wide metal spheres from raining suddenly on their teammates below.

A kachunkettball to brainpan meant quite a bit more than a GCU-sized headache. And in mani-ball mode, you'd better hope your Upper Chuckers had sharp eyes, deft hands, and a ready steel umbrella.

Rollie turned on one of the hoverboards and it whirred weakly. One of its jets was set at an odd angle, and the power pack was low. He turned it off and tried another. That casing was good, the jets were a go, but the power pack was dead as an Altairan exile. He tried a third. Better power, but a cracked casing and some strange whir.

Keeping an ear on the approaching onslaught, he pried open parts and pieces of seven such hoverboards with swift, nimble fingers, clapping together the best of the best like the world's most frantic, unleisurely puzzle. He doubted the compilation board had enough juice to get him back to the ship. But, like life to-date, Rolliam Tsmorlood was willing to take it as far as it would go.

Igglestik Tstyko was not remotely out of breath and could easily have run the length of a dozen more subterranean sporting labyrinths, with lungpower to spare. The key was pacing, he considered. You start out at Windsprint, proceed to Blindingly Fast and then give it that extra push toward Sonic Boom right at the end.

Physics, however, dictates that the faster you go, the harder it is to dodge large, unexpected flying objects coming at your head from the other direction.

At first Tstyko wasn't exactly sure what launched toward him. It seemed to be some blurred assemblage of black elbows and knees and what might have been flapping leathery black wings. But whatever it was had matched Tstyko's speed if not his direction, and it skimmed the ol' brainbox so closely, it nipped off Tstyko's RegForce helmet and a few yellow curls, to boot.

The force and surprise of it found him relocated lengths away and half-inside a locker. Based on the shouts and clattering down the hall, it sounded like Mook and the assortment of completely unnecessary interlopers had encountered the living projectile, too.

Good on the interlopers, Tstyko thought, exiting unsteadily from Locker 12 and revving himself up from Surly Sulk to Stellar Speed in seconds. *Impeding an official investigation is bound to result in bystander injury,* he lectured internally. *An important lesson for them.*

But if justice were to be served, every moment counted. And these people would have to learn, RegForce time couldn't be wasted on frivolous things like peeling yourself from the pavement or un-jamming your ankle from your ear.

The ICV was quiet. Bertram Ludlow perched on the edge of the copilot's chair, glued to the view of the stadium outside. What was taking so long? Where was Xylith? Where was Rollie? Why weren't they back yet?

And why wasn't Bertram in there helping them?

He stood up. "I can't stand it any more. I can't sit here and let them take on the RegForce themselves. A lot of this is my fault. I should be there."

"Your fault?" In the other room, O'wun snickered from behind an old hardback book he'd found wedged between some seat cushions. He brought it with him absently, as he leaned in the cockpit threshold. "Bertram, it's *the Captain.* If it weren't this, it would be something else. Rollie Tsmorlood's only happy if he's active in the Underworld. The only reason he's never run for Skytreg's job is he hates titles and feels the Underworld should be more individually-driven."

Bertram said, "O'wun, I think it's gone beyond politics this time."

But O'wun laughed. "Friend, it's *tripping* in politics. Rollie's got this idea there's not as much value in undermining GCU authority if the Underworld has a hierarchy, too—and right now, Zenith Skytreg is the highest arc in that hierarchy. Rollie wants to reform the whole Society. I'm surprised you never got a lecture on it."

Bertram did recall Rollie saying something about it in the Podunk bar, but Bertram had been concentrating on his own mental illness at the time. "Okay, well…Xylith, then," Bertram persisted.

"She's another one," O'wun continued. "Xylith's perfectly willing to get involved in anything that gets her out of her Citadel for a while."

"Look, just because—" He blinked. "She has a Citadel?"

"Well, not hers. The Empress'." At Bertram's blank expression, the Simulant gave a well-programmed sigh. "Xylith's the only female progeny of the Dootett Empress' over-brother's under-cousin. She has a title and everything. 'Her Mostly Elevated Demi-Scintillation,' I think they call her."

Bertram recalled the image on the Dootett coin. "I *thought* there was a resemblance."

"She gets bored," explained O'wun. "That's how she fell into the whole illusionism and sleight-of-hand niche. A little hobby so she could slip out for some non-Imperial me-time."

Bertram was seeing the invisi-suit with all new visibility. "She did say she played Vos Laegos."

"Now she leverages her skills for the Underworld. A huge embarrassment to some of the Imperial family, of course. But the Empress likes her, so she gets a free pass."

From the pilot's chair, Rozz snickered. "Geez, Bertram, sounds like your new friends really know how to party." The words had barely left her lips when movement outside caught her attention. "And it looks like the party is on the move!"

Out of a far corner of the stadium, banging up through a maintenance cellar door, Rolliam Tsmorlood emerged in dramatic but not-so-grand style. He was crouched on a thin flying disk. It wobbled erratically and in bursts, soaring, sinking, blasting out smoke, and lurching upward again. The Hyphiz Deltan clung and balanced feverishly, like a gymnast-turned-rodeo rider determined to make jet-powered mechanical bulls the next big thing in public transportation.

"Lower the ramp, lower the ramp!" Bertram shouted at no one in particular. He scanned the buttons, levers and the thing that went "bip," his hands wavering to take action. Yet when confronted with the control panel, from button to "bip" he realized he was no closer to figuring it out than the last time. "Where the hell's that remote gone?"

Sizing up the system, Rozz's voice held a note of surprise. "Hey, isn't this a Protosta—"

But O'wun reached over her to address the issue. There was a hydraulic shoosh and the ramp began its descent.

Bertram leapt from the copilot's chair and ran to the ship's hatch, to see an unending stream of life-forms bubbling up from the underground in pursuit. W.I. Tstyko, swift stride and lasers drawn, was unable to target Rollie's hoverboard in its erratic flight. W.I. Mook followed Tstyko closely, weapon in one hand and voice projection device in the other calling orders. MetamorfaSys Inc. bodyguards, too broad and weighty to keep up effectively, were still trying hard to earn their pay. Stadium security guards, who hadn't seen this much action since the final game of the last at-home kachunkettball series, moved along with the throng. And two life-forms with their realtor, in the market for a piece of sporting history, had arrived at what was fast-becoming a really bad time.

Meanwhile, from the gates poured a flood of graceful Vos Laegons in kachunkettball cheerleading uniforms, two of whom held tight to a struggling Xylith. Behind them wandered the gaggle of bewildered marketing executives, who seemed to be wondering where any of this was detailed in the *How to Gain Pals in Cosmic Commerce* handbooks. And just beyond the stadium, the media and law enforcement from a dozen neighboring worlds were trying to find a decent place to park.

Bertram drew the hand-laser Rollie had given him, uncertain where to shoot.

By this time, Rollie and the hoverboard had jolted, lurched, soared and sunk several hundred yards, up and around the weather-worn In Memorium statue of Mergle Farcrumple of the Blumdec Blasters, and had almost made it to Ticketing.

The Vos Laegons, meanwhile, had begun to sing a haunting native lullaby. The music moved slowly across the Skorbig Stadium grounds, enveloping it like a heavy fog. The chorus of voices were painfully beautiful, enchantingly strange, and a whole lot more impressive now that they weren't singing out hastily-written lyrics about Underworld politics.

Bertram felt the familiar tears begin to stream down his face, but there was more to it this time—so much more. His heart began to thump a frantic thrash metal beat. His knees went weak with cold terror. His entire body broke out in icy sweat. Soon gravity pressed down hard, while his breath was being squeezed out of him. In a moment, Bertram Ludlow had lost his footing and was sliding down the ICV's ramp to the weed-strewn parking lot surface.

On the hoverboard, Rollie held tight another fifty feet, grappling desperately to the machine before the effects of the Vos Laegons were too much for him, and he lost grip.

Down, down, he dropped hard onto the rusting wire frame of a long-dead topiary in the shape of a flying ergowohm. Dust, rust and pollen kicked up in a cloud around the fallen figure. The hoverboard splash-landed in a nearby decorative pond, small fizzles of electricity fingering the surface.

The Vos Laegons surged forward with fluid confidence, no longer in any particular hurry. Their song rang out with inconceivable purity, layer over layer of harmonies and movement.

Teams of law enforcement from the other planets were arriving in formation and promptly dropping like rocks, incapacitated in an instant by the Vos Laegons' song.

Bertram saw it all from his spot, slumped on his side at the base of the ship's ramp. He had no strength but to stare.

And listen: footsteps! And feel it: movement! Yes, O'wun was there now, efficient and unmoved by the drowning waves of music— the advantage of being Non-Organic and also preferring the Luddite folk scene.

Bertram felt the man's Simulated hands grab his own non-simulated arms easily. He felt the world dip as O'wun slung him over a shoulder, crouched again for Bertram's dropped weaponry, and marched back to the ship. As he was stepping over Rozz's prone form in the threshold, a slight switch of the wind carried the music new directions, dispersing the sound. It wasn't much, but it was reprieve enough for Bertram to manage, "Free. Xylith. Get. Rollie." Even yet, it was hard to think clearly, but Bertram knew he had to try. "Let's do. The Underworld. Proud."

O'wun smiled, dumping Bertram in the doorway with the sprawling Rozz. He then disappeared to do as asked.

❖

Rolliam Tsmorlood didn't know the phrase "give up."

Actually, that wasn't quite true. He knew it in Dootettish, Alpuckese, Mathekite, Calderian, every language in the Hyphiz

System—even Tryfan Chinese, Spanish and English. All learned the backspace way, gum-free.

Just not Vos Laegon.

Translachew did devote gum to the language. But it tasted horrible and why bother, when Rollie was already *reasonably* fluent, and all he really needed were phrases like, "One Carsoolian Vodka, please." Or: "Where are the Simmiparlors? I'm looking for a date."

It worked just fine until now.

Now he was regaining his breath from a considerable fall and preparing to say something flip and memorable to Skytreg and his flock of showbeings. Skytreg was even expecting it; it was written right into the Underworld Society Membership Agreement:

Members of the Underworld agree to confront adversaries in potential life-threatening situations with commentary that is both flip and witty, optionally containing catch-phrase potential to be trademarked at a future date.

But language failed. Those Vos Laegons packed a walloping *a cappella.*

Hyphiz Deltans, spry as they were, held up better than some species against it. But it was still like slogging through muck to try to sit up, a struggle to make even well-trained muscles obey the will, and almost impossible to see through his watering eyes.

Slowly, he managed to swing one leaden leg over this wire creature he'd landed on. Slowly, he realized O'wun was running to help. And too soon, he realized O'wun had stopped, and the "zot!" noise that had flared at them wasn't just another Feegar Rebellion post-traumatic stress flashback coming on. It belonged to a real-life weapons discharge hitting something.

"O'wun?" Rollie managed. His Simulant friend was frozen in place, with surprise creasing his brow. There was the smell of charred nanotechnologies and steaming polymers. Gray fluids dripped down his neck from a hole that went clear through his cheekbones. Sparks flew. Bits sizzled.

Rollie winced. *Sorry, old friend.* O'wun needed far more technical help than Rollie could give. Yet there was no time to dwell.

The Deltan struggled to slide from the back of the wire frame creature but paused, looking down. He recalled this particular odd physical sensation from past battles, getaways, and one very spirited life-merger ceremony. But he was hoping to deny it as part of the Here-and-Now.

There was no denying the hole in his coat, though. Or the amber liquid sticking to its lining, rapidly slicking his shirt and trickling down his waist. It clung to his skin as his chest burned like fire. Wet fire.

Looks like Tstyko bagged himself a two-for-one.

Breathing hurt more than Rollie remembered from past laserings. And the world was quickly becoming wrapped in a thick soft fiber before his eyes. He wondered which heart, which set of lungs, had taken the hit. Some vital organ was clearly going down.

Why hadn't Tstyko just full-on fragged him? Set lasers to Demolecularize and been done with it?

Ah, but that wasn't *regulation*, was it? Killing him now would be on the RegForce's heads. But send him to Altair-5 and they could blame it on the daisies.

He numbly patted at a pocket and remembered, through the growing fog, that Bertram Ludlow still had his tissue reparation device.

He felt his knees buckle under him. He hit the ground hard, took a moment for the waves of pain to subside, and then began his struggle for the ICV ramp.

A loud voice projected over the singing: "Rolliam Tsmorlood, this is the Hyphiz Deltan RegForce." Rollie worked to raise his head, which felt liked it weighed more than a whole ICV. There was a figure before him.

Boots.

Gray trousers, yellow piping.

A broad jacket with bright, shiny buttons in honor of years of exemplary service.

And a face that looked like a very disappointed Didactics professor, peering down on the worst student in his career.

In other words: W.I. Mook, with soundproof headgear.

Mook motioned to Tstyko who busied himself quite happily by clapping Klinko brand Wrist and Ankle Boundary Determinators onto Rollie's unwilling limbs. All four of the devices glowed a bright effective green. Then he motioned to the Vos Laegons to cut the musical interlude.

Tstyko grinned down at Rollie, tugging on the hobbles and shouting, "I bet you know where you're headed, don't you? Well, I'll give you a clue: it's most certainly not the purple sand substitute of Blumdec!"

"Tstyko, the earplugs?" Mook gave an indulgent smile. "Take them off."

Tstyko must have lip-read. "Oh! Yes! Righty!" Still beaming, he slung off the headset and said, "Now I know what you're thinking, Tsmorlood. You're thinking you're rather badly wounded and likely won't make it through the next hour, let alone all the way to Altair-5. But don't you worry." He patted Rollie's shoulder. "Our ICV has all the medical equipment we need to have you healed up and feeling sunny for a really cosmic exile." He stroked his chin. "You know, for the few minutes it lasts, anyway."

With this, Tstyko rose, removed a little device from his pocket, and marked off, "Taunted prisoner in a sadistic yet light-hearted way" from his Apprehension To-Do Checklist.

Mook began: "Rolliam Tsmorlood, you are under official Hyphiz Deltan Regimental Enforcement Squad apprehension for offenses proven to span GCU planetary and quadrant-associated borders. Thereby, as the legal enforcement from your planet of origin, we take you into custody on behalf of those systems.

"You are charged with unapproved premature liberation from a GCU penal colony, premature liberation from a Podunk Confinement Center, assault on Podunk law enforcement, destruction of a Golgi Beta moon polyp stand, impersonation of Crater Club personnel, holding reputable members of the intergalactic business community hostage, destruction to a historical sporting landmark, theft of a private property hoverboard, and resisting apprehension. This is in addition, of course, to the charges associated with a 300 U-year sentence to be served for—" He looked flushed and winded. "Oh, nevermind, we simply haven't got this kind of time."

He offered an apologetic smile to Zenith Skytreg, Eudicot T'murp, Spectra Pollux, and all his brethren in the various local law enforcement agencies, many of whom were just now peeling themselves from the ground. "Thanks very much for all your help. Er, I am sorry if it put you out at all."

Considering they all looked like mootaab toasties that had been landed on by an ICV in the middle of a picnic lunch, Rollie thought weakly that it probably had.

Good.

Mook dragged Rollie to his feet, as new pain shot through the Deltan. Mook turned to his partner. "I'm just going to tuck Captain Tsmorlood into the ship before he completely drains out on the pavement. In the meantime, W.I. Tstyko, if you would be so kind as to ask Mr. Ludlow to come down here a moment?"

"No!" shouted Bertram Ludlow from the hatchway, waving his borrowed laser. He'd seen it all and he'd seen enough. After everything they'd accomplished, it couldn't end like this; he wouldn't let it. His people as test market subjects against their knowledge? O'wun powered down and punctured? Rollie half-dead and on his way to the wild Altairan world of carnivorous herbology? And Xylith—

Wait, where *was* Xylith, anyway? Hadn't Bertram seen her being held, just moments ago, by two of Skytreg's pearly people?

He scanned their numbers, searching for a glimpse of shining dark hair among the silver. The showbeings were still there in formation, as if prepared for an impromptu encore show. But if Xylith Duonogganon had ever been in their strange and shiny hands, she wasn't now. Her Mostly Elevated Demi-Scintillation had vanished.

Paar too, Xylith. And thanks, Bertram thought.

Unfortunately, W.I. Tstyko was still very much there, moving swiftly toward the ramp and scowling at Bertram's lack of instant cooperation.

This is it, Bertram thought. *There's nothing more to lose.*

With a strong, certain hand, he picked up the weapon Rollie had given him and tried to remember what the Deltan had said about working it.

"'Press this button, it's on…'"

He pressed the button.

"'Grip that, it fires.'"

He gripped.

Then he remembered:

Ack! Plant your feet, plant your feet, plant your—

✧

Bertram Ludlow's head felt like had it met a flying kachunkettball, his skull an unwilling shoop. He tried to sit up, but his body clanged with pains. They bumped and rebounded their way down along every joint, nerve, muscle and bone.

He moved to look around and found himself lying on a slab in a dark room. There was a stiff, smelly tarp tucked over him. An apron with the LibLounge logo had been folded neatly under his head. The door was open and light poured in.

He remembered what had happened.

He just didn't know what happened from there.

He took his time getting into a standing position and considered throwing up on the tarp. But that would take so much energy. He shuffled out into the main room, making a mental note to vomit later when he was feeling more up to it.

On the far wall, the panels—once smooth and even—were dented so it looked like a toss-up between modern art or a general Bertramesque shape. Underfoot, a burnt streak cut across the flooring.

Yeah. *That part* he remembered…

Plant your feet.

He peered out the hatch window. Stars danced before it. He was no longer on Skorbig. He had made it to free space. He wasn't bound by a Klinko system. Tstyko wasn't waiting to interrogate. Eudicot T'murp wasn't handing him bottles of fizzy drinks and asking him to rate the flavors.

Like a zombie, Bertram moved toward the cockpit. He frowned. "Rollie?"

There was someone in the pilot's chair, but judging by the shapely legs and lack of black, it wasn't Rollie. "Xylith?" He peered around the corner.

Relief washed over Rozz's face at the sight of him. Her smile was happy and alight. "Dude! Welcome back to the land of the living."

"We're—" He stared at her seated there before the controls, and then he looked out the front window, trying to process the sight. "We're flying."

"Yes," she said, indulgently. She offered pity in her warm brown eyes, like she'd assessed the situation and decided she should speak slower and louder to him from here on out. "This. Is. Space," she told him and pointed.

"No, I mean *you. You're* flying." He moved to sit in the co-pilot's seat; his muscles shrieked at the movement and the contact of it. He was hating touch. Touch was excruciating.

"*I'm* flying," she agreed. Forced patience was still in her voice. "That's right."

"You don't know how to fly a spacecraft," he pointed out. "You don't even own a car."

"Oh!" There was that relief again. "No, see, this is a Protostar model 340-K. I ate an infopill on that."

Bertram blinked.

"Well, why not? They're very rare. There are only a few cross-galaxy."

"The infopills?"

"Protostars," she said.

Bertram stared.

"There was a rundown on the way they worked in *Rockethead* magazine," she explained. "Supposed to be a miracle of misguided engineering."

Bertram sighed. The gentle exhale of air made him wince. "Where's Xylith? What happened to Rollie?"

Here, Rozz's expression darkened. "I'm sorry, Bertram, I don't know about the woman. But cops still had the blond guy when I launched. I got the impression they were kind of in a hurry to take him somewhere."

"Altair-5."

She nodded. "Altair-5."

He considered letting out a groan but thought it would hurt too much. "And why aren't we in custody?"

"You really don't remember." Sympathetically, she reached to touch what Bertram learned was a sizeable bump on the back left of his head. It rattled that kachunkettball of pain down his body again. He twitched with raw nerves. "Sorry." She put her hands back on the steering wheel where they couldn't do so much damage.

"I remember Tstyko was coming up to get me, I fired, and…"

"I closed the hatch and floored it," she said simply and then rolled her eyes. "I mean, not that you can *floor* this thing, per se. It's so *not* the way a Protostar works. You have to kinda jiggle it around a little and—"

"Rozz, you're saying you launched, left the planet, and now, if I look back there, I'm not going to see a whole fleet of GCU law enforcement still on our tail?"

Rozz's expression did not exactly exude confidence.

So against all pain, all nausea, and all desire to believe she was right—Bertram scrambled across the ship to peer out the back hatch.

He'd even planted his feet in preparation.

But when he looked out that portal to blackness, there was nothing to see but the stars they left behind them.

Rozz's voice bounced back through the ship. "We're clear, right?"

"Clear," Bertram told her, returning. "Maybe." He still didn't like it. Dread joined the physical pain in a close tete-a-tete. "Why would they let us go? They all know I'm trouble."

"Uh-huh." The tone was non-committal.

"Come on," Bertram pressed, "you saw me; I'm a dark horse. A rabble rouser. A revolutionary for Tryfling rights. An Intergalactic Fugitive."

Rozz coughed politely into a hand and then grew quiet. Finally she said, "You're the star of an up-and-coming reality show. And they're already losing one major cast member. I'd say celebrity has its perks."

"Hm." It was an interesting theory, and it did explain some things. He let the idea rattle around like a kachunkettball in his mind. Bertram leaned back in the copilot's chair.

For a long moment, they sat silently watching the stars. The thing that went "bip," did.

"You know what we should do?" Bertram said finally. "We should go to Tryfe—er, Earth—and warn everyone." The very idea filled him with hope. Maybe he could still make a difference. He looked eagerly to Rozz for response.

"Oh." She frowned. "Yeah, about that. Um, Bertram, originally I was hoping for a better time to mention this..." She bit her lower lip. "Aw, what the hell." She turned to meet his gaze. "Warning people on Earth is probably going to be harder than you think."

"Because if we start yammering about space aliens and extra-terrestrial test market takeovers, people will think we're several squares short of a full candybar. Yeah, I'd expect some of that," Bertram told her with a reassuring smile.

"No," she corrected, "because there's something wrong with this meter over here that controls the coordinates." She tapped a gauge.

Now it was coming back to him. Rollie had said something about some gadget being "fragged." "Ah."

"Annnnnnnd…" Rozz continued, "also because of landing."

"You mean where to land, because we can't be specific."

"Er, no. I mean how to land. Like, at all. Because of me not being really, you know, so much educated on that part."

It was like the kickback from a hand-laser all over again. "You know how to take-off and fly but you don't know how to land? What about the infopill? The rundown in *Rocketleg* magazine?" he protested.

"*Rockethead*. It was a two-parter," she said.

"And the second part?"

"Out next U-week."

Bertram gave her a hard stare.

"Look, I don't control the publishing schedule," she said.

Finally, he nodded, wondering why he was even surprised. Such were the wily, wily ways of space. He rose. "Okay. That's fine. It's all good. No freaking out necessary." He was saying this more to convince himself than Rozz. "I'll just check the Uninet for landing instructions. No problem." But in the cockpit doorway, a second thought stopped him. "Your infopill didn't happen to mention how to, um, start the Uninet computer, did it?"

"The Uninet system wasn't standard to this model," said Rozz. "If it's got the Uninet, it's custom. I mean, the Protostar was all about handling and performance, so any system like that would weigh it down and—"

"No." Bertram winced and put up a hand. "Just silence." He pushed at his temples as the great kachunkettball game in his head went mani-ball. "Just silence."

ABOUT THE AUTHOR

Jenn Thorson is an author, marketing writer, and a compulsive weaver of fictions in the car, shower and other places she normally can't find a pen. She lives in Bertram Ludlow's hometown of Pittsburgh, PA, but is definitely mostly sure she's never met extra-terrestrials there. Her stories have been published in the *Humor Press*, the journal for the *Lewis Carroll Society of North America*, *The Timber Creek Review* and *Romantic Homes* magazine.

IF YOU ENJOYED THIS BOOK...

There Goes the Galaxy is a self-published novel. So if you enjoyed this book, the author would be mightily grateful if you'd tell a friend or three about it.

One way to help is by reviewing the book on **Amazon.com**. Amazon ranks its books, in part, by the number of customer reviews a book receives. So you can help *There Goes the Galaxy* reach *even more* eyeballs by going to Amazon.com, searching for "There Goes the Galaxy," and clicking the **Create Your Own Review** button. (You'll need to login to an Amazon.com account to post a review.)

Other fun ways to help share Bertram's adventures with fellow Earthlings are:

- "Like" *There Goes the Galaxy* on **Facebook**, for news and spacey fun, at: **Facebook.com/ThereGoestheGalaxy**

- Visit **ThereGoesTheGalaxy.com** and snag one of our FREE book badges for your blog or website!

- Follow the author, Jenn Thorson, on **Twitter** at **Twitter.com/Jenn_Thorson**

(Jenn promises she won't spend the whole time referring to herself in third person or talking about her lunch.)

41393628R00215

Made in the USA
Charleston, SC
27 April 2015